Back to the Bonnet

ഗ❈ഗ

THE SECRET LIFE AND
EXTRAORDINARY ADVENTURES OF

MISS MARY BENNET

WHO FIRST MADE THE READER'S
ACQUAINTANCE IN PRIDE AND PREJUDICE
BY JANE AUSTEN

ഗ❈ഗ

JENNIFER DUKE

For my family

When Cassandra had attained her 16th year, she was lovely
& amiable, & chancing to fall in love with an elegant Bonnet
her Mother had just completed, bespoke by the Countess
of ----, she placed it on her gentle Head & walked from her
Mother's shop to make her Fortune.

Jane Austen, *The Beautifull Cassandra*, from her juvenilia

. . . next week [I] shall begin my operations on my hat,
on which You know my principal hopes of happiness depend.

Jane Austen, letter to Cassandra Austen, 27th – 28th October 1798

People assume that time is a strict progression of cause
to effect but actually – from a non-linear, non-subjective
viewpoint – it's more like a big ball of wibbly wobbly,
timey wimey... stuff.

The Doctor, from *Doctor Who*, episode: Blink

PROLOGUE

My dear Harriet,

Upon receiving this letter, you will also have acquired my bequest to you. Keep it safe and out of the hands of others, excepting your mother who will confirm that is it of greater value than you might imagine.

I am fortunate for the good health enjoyed in my latter years but I regret to inform you that it is now declining. I assure you I suffer very little but for the fatigue that overtakes from time to time. However, although I have my home, my books, my music and my nephews and nieces about me, I miss you, my clever god-daughter, exceedingly.

Fearing that your return from the continent might come too late for me to explain your inheritance to you in person, I decided to take up my pen. Yet, before doing so, I faced a dilemma. Describing to you the events I wish to relate might lay me open to accusations of insanity – or even criminal charges – should my letter fall into the wrong hands. Therefore, I settled upon presenting my story to you as if it were a fiction, merely the manuscript of a three-volume novel, even though the chapters you are in receipt of contain an honest account of my life and adventures, occurring between the years 1811 and 1812.

I have rarely spared any time for novels before. I have not been inclined to ponder ridiculous tales of unlikely passions or horrors far from credible. For swooning females, I have no sympathy, and for noble souls wrestling with something monstrous within them, I have even less. I know you would leap to the defence of these Dickenses and Brontës but leave me to my Darwin and J. S. Mill. However, in recalling and depicting reality with attention and precision, and in dressing it in the form of a fictional narrative, I have surprised myself by taking much pleasure.

Pray burn this letter, dear one, so that any who might happen to read the manuscript or find the object to which it alludes, do not suspect the truth. I will end by thanking you with all my heart for *your constant friendship and by telling you how proud I am of you. I cannot express how glad I am to have lived to see you thrive so well in the world, marrying not once but twice, chusing your husbands so well – God rest their souls – that you shall never suffer want.*

I hardly think that you will have need of this inheritance but I am sure you will find your uses for it, as I have done. I can still remember the day I inherited it from your namesake. It is strange to think back to that time, sixty-six years ago when I, a girl of nineteen, had no awareness of how my family's fortunes would turn and turn again, all due to something so seemingly ordinary.

As I say to your mother frequently, you and she have been the gilders of my days. I wish you both every possible happiness in the years to come.

Your affectionate godmother,
Mary

VOLUME I

VOLUME I, CHAPTER I

The Inheritance

Thursday 8th August 1811

The piece was marked *fortissimo* and so, despite Lydia stamping from her bedroom above, I played as loudly as I could. In this, I served my own purpose as well as fulfilling the wishes of the composer. I had been on time for breakfast, set the tea to brew and locked away the tea jar, all the while breathing in the tantalising fragrances of toast, bacon, oatmeal and pound cake. Shaking my head at my family's tardiness, I had resorted to the use of the pianoforte. My stomach growled as I played a piece which marched along in military regularity with the ticking clock in the vestibule. It was technically a duet, though the part I played sounded well enough by itself.

As usual, my playing worked, the footsteps on the stairs indicating my successful reminder of the correct hour for breakfast.

The conversation at the morning meal contained nothing I had not heard before. It was dominated in equal parts by Mama's moans of despair that she and Papa had never had a son, by her bewailing that there were no promising suitors in the neighbourhood for any of her five daughters and by her shrill fits of giggles at Lydia's descriptions of how well the officers she had seen yesterday looked in their regimentals.

"And the other gentleman was taller and broader-shouldered than any officer I've ever seen," said Lydia, "though his face was not half as handsome as that of the one who winked at me."

"That wasn't a wink," said Kitty, "he was sneezing."

"You're only saying that because neither of them noticed you."

"That's not true. Mama! Tell Lydia not to tell such tales."

"He winked at you, my dear?" said Mama to Lydia, smiling.

"Indeed! Then I pretended to be affronted. You should have seen it. Oh, I cannot wait for the Autumn balls. Just imagine, dancing all night with a fresh officer for every dance!"

I deduced that the uniformed gentlemen Lydia and Kitty had seen on Meryton high street were likely there to make enquiries about a prospective site for the soldiers' camp or the standards of available accommodation for officers. I sighed at the thought of how I must expect a total absence of intellectual mealtime conversation once the militia based themselves in the town two months hence. How excitement over a redcoat could escalate to such a pitch, I would never understand. Predictably, Papa retired to his library as soon as he had finished his breakfast.

Mama went out to speak to the housekeeper, Mrs Hill. She would be directing her regarding what fish might be got for dinner, it being a Friday. My older sisters, Jane and Lizzy, stole into the front parlour, speaking in low tones as they passed the servants, Sarah and Sally, who hovered in the vestibule waiting for the rest of us to vacate the table.

"Which one of them is in love, do you suppose?" said Kitty, looking up from her book.

"Lord, I don't know," said Lydia. "You won't mind if I take the last piece of pound cake," she said, cake in her mouth before either of us had time to respond. I narrowed my eyes at her; she had already eaten her share. "When do they ever talk to me of interesting things like that?" she added, sending crumbs flying from her mouth.

"Perhaps neither of them is in love," I said. "Personally, I have no interest in prying into other people's secrets and you would be much more content if you refrained from doing so."

"Oh do stop reading, Kitty." Lydia took out the box of spillikins. "Let's have a game."

Kitty put aside her book. I tutted, eyeing the title *The Castle of Otranto*.

She blinked at me. *"What, Mary?"*

"Reading such melodramatic novels will do little to develop your mind. Murder? Revenge? Ghosts? You'd be much better off reading Hannah More."

Kitty snorted. "Don't we get enough sermonising on a Sunday?"

"Some would benefit from more," I muttered under my breath, turning my attention to my last bit of bacon.

"Spillikins," insisted Lydia.

I dabbed my mouth with my napkin and left them to their game, taking with me the two books and a pamphlet I had borrowed from the circulating library.

Upstairs, I made myself comfortable upon the window seat in the oriel. I liked this spot. Not only was it a comfortable place to read, it also afforded a prime view of the roads. Here, I could note the comings and goings of the villagers of Longbourn, the carriages on the London road and possible visitors along the road which intersected it, either townsfolk from Meryton or our friends from nearby Lucas Lodge.

It was pleasant to take in the view on such a fine day as this was. The brightness and clarity of the air was all the more satisfying for coming in the wake of stormy weather earlier in the week, which had left its mark on Longbourn by bringing down a roof tile which still lay on the drive. The same gusts, I now noticed, must have been to blame for compromising the stability of the pig sty fence belonging to our tenants in the farmhouse along the road. At this moment several pigs were eating their way across a vegetable patch at their leisure. I laughed as a red-faced Mrs Camfield rushed out and, one by one, ushered them back into their sty, all the while calling out in vain for Mr Camfield's assistance. A true advertisement of the attentiveness of husbands!

The commotion finally over, I returned my attention to my reading. Flicking through Mary Wollstonecraft's *A Vindication of the Rights of Woman*, it became apparent to me that it was much too full of revolutionary talk. The forms and traditions of society might not be perfect but they served a purpose. To cast them aside would lead to chaos with no one knowing their place or what was expected of them in the maintaining of a peaceful, prosperous country. I shuddered and moved on to works with greater solidity of fact, namely, a volume of *Flora Europaea* and Lamarck's *Zoological Philosophy*. I tried to ignore Lydia and Kitty clattering their way up the stairs, laughing and chatting much louder than necessary as they went to their room to ready themselves for a walk to Meryton.

Whilst deep in my study of botany, a smudge of blue caught my eye – a walker on the Meryton road. At first I thought that it might be Charlotte Lucas come to visit – she had a muslin gown of that very forget-me-not hue – but, as the figure drew closer, I saw that it was only Aunt Philips. I rolled my eyes and resumed my reading.

As I expected, Aunt Philips and Mama did not make it into the parlour before their gossiping began. Their voices carried from the vestibule with all the dramatic pauses, crescendos and diminuendos of an Italian opera. I was forced to abandon the passage on the properties of aconitum and put the botanical volume down.

"Mr Bennet, my dear," cried Mama, rushing into his library, "such news!"

"Oh?"

"Netherfield Park . . . is *let*." The floorboards creaked as Mama bounced up and down on the balls of her feet.

Silence from Papa. On the infrequent occasions that I had gone into the library whilst he occupied it, he would continue to read, the lines in his brow deepening, and he would make me wait a long while before answering any question I had and, even then, he did not look up. I could not imagine his attitude differing when Mama invaded his sanctuary.

"Mr Bennet?"

"I do hear you, Madam."

"Well then, it is let to a Mr Thorpe, a *single* gentleman—"

"Who has been seen in both a barouche and a phaeton—" interjected Aunt Philips.

"And who knows what other fancy carriages besides," continued Mama. "Imagine what his fortune may be. Wouldn't it be a fine thing if..."

Her speech became muffled as the library door closed. *If he might marry one of our girls*, she would be saying. Mama's exuberance was most premature; we had not yet even met the man. However, it did no harm to be aware of this potential opportunity for our family. It had been years since an eligible newcomer had settled in the neighbourhood and subsequently married a local young woman. She had not even been that young. Six and twenty, I believe.

I recognised the black and green of Uncle Gardiner's carriage, as well as his chestnut horses, one with its distinctive white sock, and wondered which of the Gardiner family we were to expect. The children, though not as noisy as Lydia, nevertheless had the ability to agitate my nerves and distract me from my studies. With relief, I noted that it was only my uncle and his manservant who descended from the carriage.

"Fancy! A Gardiner family gathering," laughed Aunt Philips when Mr Brook, the butler, opened the front door. She gave the poor servant no time to say a single word to my uncle.

Mrs Hill's light step came and went as Uncle Gardiner handed her his hat.

"Heavens! What brings you here, brother?" said Mama, emerging from the library.

He must have set off first thing in the morning to make the twenty-four mile journey from London. Such urgency piqued my curiosity and drew me to the banister.

"Good day sisters," said my uncle, "as you know, I am the executer of our aunt's will and—"

"Oh yes indeed," cried Mama. "Poor Aunt Harriet. Do you bring what she left us?"

"I do."

Kitty and Lydia joined me, leaning over the banister much further than was quite necessary.

"And you have only one servant with you?" Mama continued. My uncle's manservant stood behind him carrying a box under one arm. "What if your business were talked of in criminal circles? What if you had been set upon by robbers? Our inheritance would be lost." She paused for a moment before adding, "As might you be, to be sure."

My uncle either coughed or laughed, perhaps the one masked the other. "I did not consider myself to be in any danger," he said. "Besides, if the highwaymen of Hertfordshire were picking out bearers of bequests, they might have selected a more lucrative target than myself."

"She left us no precious jewels?" asked Mama.

"Would you consider turquoise or amber to be—"

"No. Not really."

"Well, I believe she left you such things as she hoped you might remember her by."

"Ah," said Mama, clearly trying not to sound disappointed. "But to be sure, we shall treasure whatever it is she wished for us to have," she added.

"What's in the box do you suppose?" giggled Lydia. "I want first pick."

I gave my sister a hard look. "That is disrespectful to the memory of our great aunt."

"Oh, don't be such a bishop. Come on, Kitty. Let's see what the old lady was so keen to send us." She hurried down the stairs, Kitty following after.

Lydia had to wait, though, as Uncle Gardiner's journey had given him an appetite. However, once he had suitably fortified himself, Mama herded us all into the front parlour. Lydia lifted the lid of the box, which sat in the middle of the room, and peeked inside.

"Wait, Lydia," said Lizzy.

Lydia sighed, dropping the lid, and slumped on the floor.

Papa came in and shook Uncle Gardiner's hand. "So all went off well with the funeral?" he said. "Poor Miss Gardiner. I always took pleasure in her company. She was an eccentric woman, certainly, but at times she spoke more sense than half the gentlemen I know put together."

"Thank you, brother. Indeed, she always—"

"Let's see what she sent us." Mama flung off the lid of the box and she and Lydia bent over it. "You know, despite the ridiculousness of Aunt Harriet's talk of having been given treasures from some African prince or other – evidence of senility though that clearly was – I had nurtured a hope that she was referring to some forgotten family heirlooms or something. Hmm." She took out a pair of gloves. "Still, there are some attractive things. Look at that lace, Mr Bennet, I daresay it's finer than any I've seen Lady Lucas wear, wouldn't you agree?"

"I do not profess to be an expert in lace, Mrs Bennet," he replied.

"In fact, I believe I recall Aunt Harriet saying that she wanted me to have these gloves."

"I do not recall that, sister," said Aunt Philips.

"I think you were not there at the time. Jane, you simply must have this shawl," she said, turning her back on my aunt, "it particularly suits your colouring."

The warm, earthy hues of the shawl were a good match for Jane's golden hair and green eyes. She was always considered the most handsome of us Bennet girls. If any of us might make a prudent marriage, it was bound to be her.

"If it emphasises your beauty in the eyes of any potential suitors, be they eligible ones of course, so much the better," I said.

Jane's expression as she stared at me was difficult for me to decipher. She held out the shawl and looked around at the rest of us. "Perhaps someone else might want—"

"And you ought to have this parasol, Lizzy," continued Mama, thrusting the object into Lizzy's hands. "You get far too tanned in the summer months."

"You do," I agreed.

Kitty had joined Lydia and Mama by the box and together they rifled through its depleting contents. I hung back, uncertain whether this vulturish behaviour was quite seemly.

"I always thought that inheritance was meant to be a more formal business than this," I said.

Aunt Philips took a silver brooch which she recalled admiring once.

"Here, Kitty," said Lydia, "you will have the amber pendant and I the turquoise ring."

"That just leaves this ugly bonnet," said Kitty, pinching the brim between her forefinger and thumb and letting it hang as far as her arm would stretch, as though it were a dead rat.

"That will do well enough for Mary," laughed Lydia. Her meaning did not escape me. I knew I was the plainest, for all I was the most accomplished female in the room. However, my superior talents and intellect did not save me from colouring at Lydia's words. "Here you are!"

Lydia snatched the bonnet from Kitty and tossed it over to me but I was not prepared to catch it. It flew past me, knocking a Wedgwood vase from the side table. I stared, watching it fall, quite unable to move. The fine china smashed. Mama shrieked.

"Have a care, Lydia!" reprimanded Lizzy.

"It's not my fault. Mary should have caught the blessed thing."

"You can hardly blame Mary," said Jane. "She had not even agreed that the bonnet would be hers."

I retrieved the bonnet from the corner of the room, shaking off ceramic shards whilst Mama told Kitty to fetch the smelling salts for her agitated nerves and to ring the bell for Hill to clear the mess.

"Mary, you can take the shawl," offered Jane. "Really, I don't mind."

As I looked from the shawl to the bonnet, recognition washed over me. I had not spent much time in Great Aunt Harriet's company but I was certain that I had never seen her without this bonnet. She would put it on before we set out to walk anywhere, tying the ribbons right up to her chin. She would clutch it one hand as we sat playing cards of an evening. She even kept it on her lap when we dined out at the house of my aunt and uncle's friends, the ribbons tied about one of her wrists. I would not have been surprised if she had worn it instead of a night cap.

Why had such an unsightly item of millinery been so important to her? Kitty was quite correct in describing it as ugly. The shape was decades out of fashion, being the sort that would sit high upon the head, rather than framing the face as all bonnets did now. It was not unlike an overly large dinner plate, slightly raised at the crown and angled up at the back. I wondered if such hats from the earlier part of the mad king's reign, long before his son became regent, may have been a factor in inspiring the monarch's insanity. At any rate, their absurdity could not have helped. But the antiquated shape and size were not the only objectionable aspects of the bonnet. It was covered in a fabric of coarse, grey wool, the plainness of which failed to be ameliorated by clusters of yellow embroidered flowers, and from its sides hung silken ribbons of reddish brown, a colour which did nothing to enliven the grey. Why had my great aunt kept such an item when her family had run a milliner's shop in Cheapside for generations? With a whole warehouse of bonnets to chuse from, why keep this old one?

Once, about three years ago, she had visited us at Longbourn. She had found me at my window seat, where I was crying, teeth clenched in anger. I still carried Lydia's words in my mind as well as the image of her mocking smile. "At least I will not be a confirmed spinster at the age of sixteen, as you are!" she had said. What hurt more was not the comment itself but that Papa had stifled a laugh at it. I was an object of his ridicule. Great Aunt Harriet had sat beside me and said, "One day, Mary, this bonnet shall be yours." If by that, she had meant to offer me comfort, she had failed. I remember fixing my eyes on the bonnet and all I saw was a confirmation of my own plainness. Now the bonnet had come to me, just as she had said. The bonnet of a spinster.

Inspecting it more closely, my gaze fell upon a patch of pale silk, half hidden under a fold of the inner lining. Upon it, in tiny white letters, were sewn the words: A STITCH LOST. I frowned, curiosity clawing at me as I puzzled over what it could mean.

"You can keep the shawl, Jane," I said, clutching the bonnet that no one else wanted. "This will be mine."

VOLUME I, CHAPTER II

A Stitch Lost

I took myself off to my room, placed the bonnet on my dressing table and sat before the mirror in an attitude I rarely held for more than ten seconds together. I twisted and pinned my hair, attempting a similar style to Jane's. Upon assessing the result, I laughed, removed the pins and smoothed my hair back into its usual, simple style.

"You and I are better suited to plainness," I said to the bonnet. "Perhaps, like your previous wearer, I'll end up a spinster." Another might have thought my words sounded pessimistic but, in fact, they held within them a flicker of hope. If my other sisters married well enough, I might have no need to marry at all. "Well," I laughed, "perhaps I should have it put about that I talk to items of millinery; that ought to eliminate the possibility of a suitor."

I ran a finger over the bonnet's embroidery. How silly, I thought. Why bother trying to decorate something that can never be made beautiful? The flowers were yellow, Great Aunt Harriet's favourite colour. I noticed that a petal on one of the flowers was either half finished or unravelling. Taking out my sewing box, I unpicked two loose stitches, intending to tie off the thread to stop the design from spoiling any more. For a moment, I considered unpicking the whole thing then and there but I hesitated, inspecting the strange message stitched into the inside of the lining: A STITCH LOST. Glancing at my reflection as I held the bonnet, I felt a sudden urge to see what it looked like on me.

It fitted perfectly. It was actually most comfortable to wear but, as I expected, it straddled the border between the ugly and the ridiculous.

Then, all at once, my stomach lurched and my perceptions tumbled into the unbelievable. My reflection blurred, as though I were looking at myself through a misted window. The clock face on my mantel became an empty side plate. I tried to focus on the hair brush before me but it sank into a vapour, solidifying a few inches from where it should be before sliding back to where it was and vanishing again. My head was a spinning top as the whole room rebelled against the laws of science. Objects shifted, faded and danced about, tormenting me for my insistence that they were behaving impossibly. All of this happened very fast and I wondered if I was about to lose consciousness, though I did not feel faint. Dizziness swirled through my head for an instant, followed by a churning of nausea, and then I was upon the window seat at the front of the house, a book in my hands, open on the page enumerating the qualities of aconitum.

How I had managed to walk from my room to the oriel with no memory of doing so, I could not say. Neither did I recall deciding to return to my studies. I knew I had not fainted nor hit my head as I felt no pain. Staring at the page before me until the letters swam, I feared the loss of my highest faculty, so much more developed than in most female minds – or male ones for that matter – namely, my *reason*.

I no longer had the bonnet with me, so I returned to my room, searching through my drawers and closet, as well as under the bed, but it was not to be seen. I could hear Lydia and Kitty laughing in the bedroom next to mine when they ought to have been downstairs. I spent some time in perplexed thought but logic failed to illuminate what had occurred. Eventually, afraid of what I might discover, I left my room. Looking out of the window, I watched a patch of blue draw nearer. Again, a woman was making her way to the house. Again, it was not Charlotte.

A weak trembling in my limbs persuaded me to sit down when I heard Aunt Philips' voice. Surely she was already here, talking with Mama and Uncle Gardiner in the front parlour? But no, she was arriving and telling Mama about Netherfield Park and Mr Thorpe.

And then Mama, thrilled with excitement once again, was sharing this information with Papa.

"Mr Bennet?" said Mama.

"I do hear you, madam," he replied.

The clock began to chime and I counted, gripping my stomach to suppress the queasy feeling which surged within me when the clock failed to stop after tolling two, a sensation which continued long after the mocking silence which ended the twelfth note.

The crunch of gravel drew my gaze to the drive. There was the black and green carriage with the chestnut horses. Uncle Gardiner descended and strode to the front door, his manservant behind him, carrying the box which, reason dictated, ought now to be sitting empty in the front parlour.

I listened to the repeated conversation of Mama and her siblings, leaning against the banister once more. Again, Lydia and Kitty joined me.

"What's in the box do you suppose?" giggled Lydia. "I want first pick." She looked at me and rolled her eyes. "Don't stare at me so, Mary. It may be mercenary of me but I daresay we're all thinking it."

"My thoughts were . . . elsewhere," I managed.

Kitty tilted her head as she regarded me. "They usually are."

"How droll, Kitty," laughed Lydia. "Come on, let's see what the old lady was so keen to send us." They hurried downstairs.

For a good while, I remained motionless. I could not deny that whatever was happening was, indeed, *happening*. What ought to be impossible was, in fact, *fact* and I was determined to understand it. Descending the staircase, with a trembling hand on the banister, I rejoined my family.

After Uncle Gardiner had eaten, Mama gathered us together, just as before. She and Lydia hovered over the box, a pair of crows picking at bones, organising our inheritance.

Finally, Kitty drew out the bonnet.

"That will do well enough for Mary," said Lydia. My heart began to race. "Here you are!"

Prepared this time, I reached out and caught it. The Wedgwood vase stood on the side table but I kept my eyes on it for some moments just to make sure it remained in one piece.

"Mary," said Lizzy, "Jane asked you a question."

"Oh," I said. Jane was holding out the shawl. "Oh, yes." I recollected myself. "I mean no. No thank you, Jane. This is mine. Please excuse me, I have a headache." This was no lie and I attributed it to the strangeness of all this nonsense.

I leant against my bedroom door to close it behind me and looked once more at the patch of silk inside the bonnet. Using my nail, I pushed down the fold of fabric which overlapped the piece of pale silk. Beneath A STITCH LOST were the words: AN HOUR GAINED. I had unpicked two stitches. I had put on the bonnet. Then, rather than it being two o'clock, it was midday again. I stood motionless, as though I had been fashioned out of ice, and I stared at the bonnet in my hands listening to the steady tick-tick-tick of the clock downstairs.

Once I had found the use of my limbs again, I threw the bonnet inside my closet and slammed the door shut.

"What is this all about, Great Aunt Harriet?"

I shivered at the thought that my great aunt's eccentricity must have extended far beyond that which anyone was aware of, transforming perhaps into something far worse.

Over the next few weeks, the bonnet remained out of sight in a band box in my closet and life continued much as it had done before.

Papa lost little time in calling on Mr Thorpe after his arrival in the neighbourhood and reported to us, much to our disappointment, that he was a gouty man, exceedingly advanced in years. The following weeks saw him unable to return the visit because he had business in Town. You could imagine our surprise when we finally met him at the October ball at Meryton assembly rooms and found him to be a man in his mid-twenties with not a grey hair to be seen, let alone a gouty foot.

"My sister will be glad that I'll be able to introduce her to such a charming family when she joins me at Netherfield," said Mr Thorpe, with a bow to Mama and a wink directed at Kitty who went decidedly pink. "Well," he said, casting his gaze around the bustling room, "this is remarkably merry. D— fine way to spend an evening! Much better than the way I'd planned to do so before Denny and Chamberlayne told me of the ball. I always find officers are reliable sources of information when it comes to seeking a pleasurable evening."

"I should say," said Lydia.

"And how were you planning to spend your evening, sir, before you heard of the ball?" asked Kitty.

"Oh, you know, likely with a glass or three of wine and nothing to entertain me but a book. So the elder Miss Bennets are dancing at present, are they?" he said, peering at the throng of dancers.

"And what is it you're reading at present, Mr Thorpe?" I asked.

"Oh, only a novel."

"Oh," I said, having hoped for better.

"Harris Walpole's or someone or other."

"Horace." No one appeared to note my correction.

"*The Castle of Otranto?*" said Kitty.

"Why yes."

"I'm reading that too!"

This drew Mr Thorpe's attention back from the dancers. "Fancy that, Miss Kitty. I first read it last Christmas. And how do you like it? Of course, it's just a novel but I do find the part with the ghost rather exciting. You know, with the skeleton head."

"Skull," I said.

"How dreadful," remarked Mama.

"Indeed," agreed Mr Thorpe. "Better than reading a sermon though, is it not?"

"That depends on the sermon I suppose," I said, while Mama and Kitty laughed.

"I say, Miss Kitty, are you engaged for the next dance?"

I spent some time wandering about the ballroom, listening and watching. I had no expectation of being asked to dance but there was often something entertaining to be overheard, particularly by the time the punch bowls required refilling.

"—and there she was, taking snuff with the gentlemen!—"

"—that friend I mentioned – Crawford – well, I'd recommended Netherfield to him, only Thorpe got there first. Can't say I know which I'd rather—"

"—she accounts for it by the application to her hair of a rum and egg white concoction—"

"Lord, no! I'd sooner dance with *Napoleon*—"

"I heard he's thinking of *buying* Netherfield if his family approve of the situation," whispered Maria Lucas to Lydia.

"Lord, he must be rich," my sister replied.

"I don't know a man with three carriages who isn't," giggled Maria. "He seems to like your sister." Maria inclined her head towards Mr Thorpe as he bowed to Kitty at the end of their dance.

"Well, he has not yet danced with me, has he?"

Maria laughed.

Kitty blushed at Mr Thorpe's attentions, though I suspected he was the sort of man whose gallantries had little by way of real intention behind them. He danced the next with Jane and again with Kitty when Jane was claimed by Captain Carter. After their second dance together, he brought Kitty some punch and I found myself a quiet corner to sit at, close enough to hear part of their conversation.

"Five seconds flat, by Jove," Mr Thorpe exclaimed. "I told him he'd be sick if he ate a pork pie so fast but he did it all the same. Ha! But I digress. He did indeed sell me a d— fine animal, you just have to look at her loins. It's all in the breeding. Shapelier loins you'll be hard pressed to find – horses loins of course. So, you live at Longbourn you said? The village west of here?"

"Yes, indeed," said Kitty. "But Longbourn is the name of our house as well as the village."

"I see. Big place is it?"

"Quite large, I suppose. Though nothing to Netherfield."

"Few houses are. I'm d— pleased with the place. Do you have tenants?"

She nodded. "Some."

"Excellent. The place must provide quite a living. Did you say you had any brothers?"

"None at all."

"Indeed?"

As many wealthy young men do, Mr Thorpe had taken the time to form a fashionable knot for his cravat and no doubt had even perfumed his handkerchief. However, despite his smartness of appearance, there was something vulgar in this line of questioning which my younger sister appeared not to notice. I was reminded of the previous occupant of Netherfield, Colonel Harpenden, who had a taste for ale but always drank it in a champagne glass. He had not remained long at Netherfield after our last visit there some years ago. He died rather suddenly, it is said, after his housekeeper served him soup that contained celery root, a vegetable he severely disliked.

"You know, I'm dashed pleased to have settled myself in this neighbourhood," continued Mr Thorpe.

"You are?" Kitty's cheeks reddened but not in a way that became her.

"By Jove, yes. And to think of the brief amount of time I have been here. I was making my way from Cambridge to Town on the day that storm blew up, you remember it? I was travelling alone and my gig got caught in the mud. It was growing dark and I couldn't find help to get free. So I took myself and my horse to the nearest house I could find."

"Netherfield?"

"Indeed. The place was empty but I found a way in and took shelter for the night. And – now this is rather deep for me – but I think my gig was meant to get stuck there."

"Really?" Kitty smiled. "I've never heard anything so . . . well, as though it came out of a novel."

"Don't tell anyone, mind." He winked again. He seemed to do that a lot, making me wonder if, in fact, he had something wrong with his eye. I continued my perambulation, listening to the conversations of others. I paused when I neared Mama and Aunt Philips.

"Does not this appear promising, sister?" asked Mama.

"Well, should he not favour Jane, perhaps Kitty will take his fancy," Aunt Philips said.

"Indeed – who would have thought it? Kitty marrying before any of the others."

"The only thing more surprising would be Mary doing so."

"Hmm." Mama nodded.

The Camfields were busy at work the next morning, fetching pales of water and feeding their livestock. One of their sows looked about to farrow, her underside bulging with its great burden. There was more traffic on the roads than I expected, a post-chaise on its way to London as well as a gig and a coach making for Meryton. The usual hour for breakfast had passed but, owing to overindulgence at the Meryton ball, none of my family had emerged from their rooms. Personally, I prefer a clear head. I returned to my room with the intention of selecting books for my daily study.

The bedclothes diverted me from my task, one side of the quilt hanging lower than the other. As I adjusted it, I winced at the shrill laughter coming from Kitty and Lydia's room. Their chatter was indistinct. However, I surmised that they were discussing the new occupant of Netherfield Park. My tidying task done and books on botany, anatomy and philosophy chosen, I set my mind to reflect upon my observations of the previous evening. Mr Thorpe clearly found novels of the supernatural enjoyable, though he attempted, several times, to persuade us that he did not think much of novels at all. He spent much time with Kitty but persistently looked about for Jane. He gave the impression of someone rich but asked pointed questions in an effort to establish what our level of wealth was, something a gentleman of means would be unlikely to do.

"If only I could know Mr Thorpe's mind," I said to myself.

At that moment, the door of my closet creaked open several inches. I had felt no draught; the window was shut and the unmoving trees outside testified to the stillness of the air. The closet door opened further and this time the grating of the hinges was accompanied by a sound I could not account for. It was as if two fat birds were warbling to one another in a far off tree – only the sound came from a pile of blankets and linen. I shifted the folded bedclothes out of the way.

The sounds were coming from the band box.

I recoiled, staring at the lid. "Impossible," I said, whilst acknowledging that the evidence of my own ears suggested otherwise.

Eventually, I drew closer, noticing how my heart galloped as I took out the box from the closet, placed it on the bed and removed the lid. The muffled sound was more akin to human speech now, though still quiet. Taking the bonnet in my hands, I hesitated before placing it on my head. As soon as it was in place, the twittering voices became as clear as if the bodies they came from were in the room with me.

"But do you not agree that it would be a d— fine thing?" It was Mr Thorpe's voice.

"But after you were married – assuming you succeed – what do you imagine your wife would think then?" I recognised this voice too, it was Mr Denny, one of Lydia's favourite officers.

"Well, I only intend to get a *rich* wife. As long as she brings money to the marriage, she need not care about my lack of it."

"Risky way of going about it though, Thorpe. My friend Crawford would have had no trouble with the rent. He was deuced annoyed with me when he got to Hertfordshire, upon my own suggestion, only to discover that Netherfield was no longer available."

"Well I'm mightily glad I got there first!"

"I don't envy you the rent though."

"It need only be for a few months, I've more than enough inheritance for that. In any case, it's an investment. Families with rich girls don't seem to favour my sort."

"The *aspiring* sort?"

"Indeed. So you see it's d— logical to pretend to be another sort altogether."

"The landed gentry sort."

"But of course you won't mention any of this to anyone? Word spreads fast in a small town."

"It's usually you who spreads it, if memory serves."

Mr Thorpe laughed.

"You know me, though. A gentleman's business is his own, I say."

"I knew I could rely on you, Denny."

I could hear other sounds now, a 'there you are, sir', followed by a clink of china and the laughter of gentlemen in the background. Mr Thorpe was likely at The Bull, the lodgings used by Mr Denny and several other officers in Meryton. He began talking of carriages and horses, subjects I did not have the patience to pay attention to. I had barely formed this thought when his voice grew muffled, as though he were talking from behind a wall. Then all sound faded from the bonnet. Perhaps I had imagined it, but it appeared as though the bonnet ribbons twitched a few times before hanging limp and still. Whatever oddness the bonnet exhibited though, my priority was to process the truths it had illuminated for me.

I shook my head, my lips pursed. "You won't get away with this, Mr Thorpe," I growled before hurrying down the stairs.

"Where are you going, Miss Mary?" said Mrs Hill as she carried a tray of toast from the kitchen.

I'd left my usual bonnet in my room, hardly realising that I still had Great Aunt Gardiner's in my hands. It would have to do. I put it on, flung on my cloak and shoved my feet into my boots. "I'm going to Meryton."

"At this hour? What about your breakfast?"

I snatched a couple of slices of toast from the tray. "I need to see an officer," I said, not realising how much of a joke it sounded until Mrs Hill burst out laughing.

"I would have expected to hear such a thing from Miss Lydia but not you, Miss Mary. Why, only the other day she—" Hill's speech faded, failing to compete with the crunch of gravel beneath my feet.

VOLUME I, CHAPTER III

The Strange Incident with the Officer

Hands in fists, jaw clenched, I marched along the road to Meryton. I was not in the habit of allowing anger to take hold of me but, when it did, I felt as though my body did not know how to contain the emotion. Mr Thorpe *lied* to us. Hiding his circumstances, he would attract a flurry of mindless girls such as Kitty, only to break their hearts in favour of gaining that of an heiress. No doubt he'd be going after Miss King as soon as he discovered the fortune she was due to inherit. But no woman should be so deceived!

Lucas Lodge came into sight but as no one was in a position to observe me, I vented a little of my rage by spitting on the ground and stamping my foot. "He is no – true – gentleman," I proclaimed through gritted teeth.

"You're about early, Mary." Charlotte was collecting eggs from the henhouse. I coloured, hoping she had not noticed my unseemly behaviour. She frowned. "Is everything alright?"

"Men were deceivers ever, Charlotte," I said, shaking my head. "Be wary of them."

I continued on my way. From Lucas Lodge, I left the road, taking the shorter route into town via three quarters of a mile of dirt track through fields. My path took me past numerous relatives of mine in the church graveyard, then on to the high street.

I made my way to The Bull Inn where I hoped not only to find Mr

Denny but to find him more of a gentleman at heart than Mr Thorpe had proved to be but, before reaching the front door, I paused. What if Mr Denny denied the truth to defend his friend, pretending not to know what I was talking about? What if I was, in this endeavour, achieving nothing but making myself vulnerable to ridicule?

A flash of red down the alleyway alongside the inn caught my eye. I only saw the officer for a blink before he disappeared behind the building. However, his hair looked distinctly like that of Mr Denny. I followed him, hoping that I might discuss the situation in private without leaving myself open to general mockery.

"Excuse me?" I called in a whispered shout. The alleyway was narrow, its bare walls either side of me softened only by a patch of ivy which required little sun to thrive. As I neared the back of the building, I stopped. A chill crept over me and I had the strangest impression that I had been here before. However, I had no recollection of the place. My memory was usually faultless. I could not understand why it was behaving in so contrary a manner now.

"What?" The officer turned. It was not Mr Denny. Rather than presenting the warm expression I had expected, this man glared with steely eyes, his brows pressing down towards the bridge of his nose.

"I mistook you for someone," I said. "It was my mistake."

He cast his gaze about my person, discomforting me not a little, then turned away. "If only a handsome girl had made such a mistake."

Not for the last time, I was glad of my plain looks. My heart beating at an extraordinary rate, I dashed back to the sunlit street and decided to remove myself from the vicinity of The Bull in order to regain my composure. I reached Clarke's library at the same moment that an officer quitted it, colliding into me.

"Miss Mary Bennet!" cried Mr Chamberlayne. "Good Lord!" He stared at me with even more attention than the other officer had done, only there was no hint of threat in his manner. However, I was at the same time unnerved by his regard for he looked a little too long at my bonnet. "Thank you." He laughed and took my hand. "Thank you!" He

34

repeated, shaking his head and grinning at me.

I withdrew my hand and stepped back. "Have you been drinking, sir?"

"No 'sir' please. Call me Chamberlayne."

"I know who you are, though I am surprised that you know my name."

"I confess, I did not before today."

"Pray, explain yourself, Mr Chamberlayne. What might you possibly have to thank me for?"

"No, I suppose you wouldn't know," he said, laughing again. "Come, let us talk."

"But I am unaccompanied, I can hardly—"

"Oh really, Miss Mary!" He lowered his voice and leant closer. "Does convention hold you back? You who deny all conventions of time, twisting it from its proper course?" His gaze lifted to my great aunt's bonnet again and I instinctively put my hand to it. He nodded.

"How do you—?" I looked around. The street was too busy. "Come on," I said. "I know a place where we can speak alone."

"But what of my reputation, Miss Mary?" he said when he had caught up with me.

I ignored that remark as well as his childish smirk. This was serious. I had to know how much he knew about the bonnet and what it could do.

We had just walked into the alleyway which led to the graveyard when I froze. In front of me was Lydia, entwined in Mr Denny's arms, her lips secured to his.

"*Lydia!*"

Mr Denny started, breaking away from her.

Lydia looked at me in surprise, her gaze darting between me and Mr Chamberlayne.

"Oh, Mary!" she said. "You're not interested in the officers too now, are you?" She did not scruple to stifle her laugh at the ridiculousness of this idea.

"Lydia, you really cannot behave so—"

"Oh, don't make such a fuss, Mary," she said, frowning at me. "You really can be a miserable old bishop, do you know that?"

"I can't believe you just . . ."

Lydia walked off before I could finish my sentence. Mr Denny bowed, lowering his eyes sheepishly – though his lips twitched into a wolfish smile – before making himself scarce.

"I'll talk to Denny later," said Chamberlayne, frowning.

"He has no right to kiss a girl in public like that, let alone my sister!"

"Eyebrows would be raised even if he was seen kissing his fiancé."

"His hypothetical one, I hope?" I said.

"No. He's engaged to Miss Morris. That is, he's meant to be."

"Insufferable!" I repeated this word several times as I meditated on the ungentlemanliness of apparent gentlemen on our way down the alleyway.

"Have you finished mumbling?" said Chamberlayne, looking around. "Well, you've chosen a cheery spot."

"The graveyard's nearly always quiet. I was being practical." I nodded good morning to the headstone of an ancient, forgotten Bennet. "Now, I shall try to put that business with Lydia and Mr Denny out of my mind for the time being and focus on what you have to tell me. What do you know of . . ." I hesitated, not wishing to betray more information than he might possess.

"Of that bonnet of yours?"

I opened my mouth to speak, then closed it.

He was not smiling. At once, he looked older and more sensible. "The reason why I have to thank you – why I am indebted to you . . . How to explain?" He took a breath. "You came to The Bull. You heard something that made you come around to the yard at the back. You saw—" a flicker of emotion darkened his expression, "you saw Captain Ramton."

"That horrid-looking man with the brows and the frown?"

He nodded.

"Yes, I saw him there."

"But what you don't know, Miss Mary, is that you saw him before. That is – now it seems you did not." He shook his head. "I'm fumbling my way through this – the truth being that I lack comprehension of the whole thing – but you saw him hitting me." He looked away. "You saw the blood that ran down my face. You heard what he said about me." Chamberlayne's voice had become strained.

"But I did not."

"Just let me finish. You approached when Ramton left and crouched beside me where I was slumped against the wall. You asked me for a penknife which you then used to adjust something on your bonnet. I could not see what you were doing, one of my eyes was closing up and the other was streaming. You said: 'This will send you back three hours. Get yourself away from that man.' You put the bonnet on my head and everything went . . . *strange*. I thought it was all in relation to the blows I had suffered to my head but then you were gone. I was in my room. The bonnet was gone too. I checked my pocket watch and it was indeed three hours before the time it should have been. I felt a trifle unwell, though the pain had ceased, I could move freely once more without discomfort and I saw no sign of injury upon inspecting my reflection in the glass. Recalling your advice, I left The Bull at once and came into the high street, well before I might run into Ramton."

"I gave you the bonnet? I sent you back?"

"You did." He stared at a grave. "I knew he hated me. But I know now what he's capable of and will be prepared next time. I remember the pain. The humiliation. But *he* won't, will he?"

"No. Only the wearer remembers how time played out before." I said this as if it were a fact I had long known, such as the fact that the earth circles the sun.

"Which is why you do not remember?"

"Which is why I do not." My head was spinning so I sat myself down. He put his hand to my arm. "I am not faint, Mr Chamberlayne. I have *never* fainted and nor do I intend ever to do such a thing." He let go, looking askance at me with a half smile as he sat beside me. "Why does he hate you?" I asked.

He paused. "He hates men who are . . . different."

"Different?"

He got up, half turned away from me and rested his hand on a gravestone. "You heard what he called me once, in my recollection at least. I do not wish for you to hear it again."

"I'm sorry. I only wish to understand, not to offend you. I often say the wrong thing and I'm not aware that I'm doing it."

The darkness lifted from his face. "You did not offend me, Miss Mary. I hope that we shall be friends. Although you don't remember it, you have been more understanding than any friend I've known. If I can offer you any service, you only need to ask."

"If only you were Mr Denny."

"What?"

"You see, he's the officer I need a favour from." I told him all about the bonnet and how it had revealed Mr Thorpe's deception to me.

"Denny would never speak a word against his friend. But do you really think you need him? Why not stop Mr Thorpe from taking Netherfield in the first place?"

"And how do you propose I do that?"

He took the bonnet from my head and put it upon his own. "Come now, Miss Mary. I heard you mentioned as the most accomplished girl in Meryton. Surely you're not unintelligent?"

The storm had occurred on the fourth of August, the same date as Charlotte Lucas' birthday, two months and three days ago. I would need to unpick at least . . . I scrunched my eyes shut . . . one thousand, five hundred and eighty-four stitches to go back that far. There being four and twenty stitches to a petal and five petals to each flower of the bonnet's embroidery, I calculated that I would need to remove thirteen full flowers and one extra petal, after which, I should arrive at the fourth of August, close to midday. This would allow me plenty of time to prepare as Mr Thorpe had said that it was getting dark when his gig had got stuck close to Netherfield Park.

It puzzled me at first that the petal with the loose thread was fractionally smaller than I remembered it being but then I recalled the three hours Chamberlayne had gained. I smiled as I ran a fingertip over the petal. The event of me helping Chamberlayne no longer existed; he had removed himself from danger before it could occur again and the only memory of me unpicking those three stitches was held by Chamberlayne and the bonnet itself.

"How strange it is!" I said aloud with a laugh. "Yet there is a kind of logic to it. Now," I said, picking up Kitty's copy of *The Castle of Otranto*, "to research the strange and *illogical*."

I flicked through the novel, rolling my eyes at the ludicrousness of the horrors I found contained within it. In one scene, a giant plumed helmet falls, crushing one character to death, serving as a warning to the house's occupants that the place is not rightfully theirs. I laughed at this, though I sensed that such a response was not the author's intention. Then a thought came to me. There was a chest in the attic which contained the armour of an ancestor of ours from the civil war. Amongst the assortment of other oddities in that room was a stuffed cockerel with impressive rear feathers. It wouldn't take much effort to create a plumed helmet. If I could enact this bad omen in Netherfield in front of Mr Thorpe – without crushing anyone to death of course – he would surely recall the event of the novel and be terrified out of his wits, thinking that some spirit in the house wished him to be gone. His penchant for novels about the supernatural suggested that he would be susceptible to such a notion.

I congratulated myself on my own genius as I took out my little sewing box and began the lengthy process of unpicking. Once I had finished, I hesitated, taking a deep breath. "You can do this, Mary," I told myself before putting on the bonnet.

VOLUME I, CHAPTER IV
The Ghost of Netherfield Park

Sunday 4th August 1811

The same spinning sensation came over me as before, only this time it was more acute. The room shook so that I was convinced my window would shatter. However, it did not. The clear bright sky out of the window was supplanted by thick grey clouds and the air in the room hung close about me with oppressive stillness. The green outside had muted, as though a painter had covered each leaf and blade of grass with muddy grey. Feeling a twisting of nausea, I staggered to the chamber pot, into which I vomited, before being compelled to lie down until the dizziness subsided.

The bonnet would now be in the box along with the rest of the inheritance, all exactly as Great Aunt Gardiner had left it, except that thirteen flowers would have disappeared from the bonnet's embroidery as it sat waiting in the darkness. I had questions still, more than I supposed I would find answers to, but I would have to wait four days until Uncle Gardiner's arrival, at which time I could further investigate the workings of the bonnet.

After recovering sufficiently, I took myself up to the attic and heaved open a chest to recover the helmet of the fervent Cavalier, Captain Gordon Bennet, after which I amputated the tail feathers from the ancient, dusty cockerel which was nesting in an old cradle. "My apologies," I said, patting its head.

A moment of morbid curiosity led me to pick up the Captain's pistol from the chest and wonder how many Roundheads he had shot with it. I shuddered at the thought that duty and loyalty could compel one to commit such violence. After lowering it back to its resting place, I set about attaching the feathers to the helmet with string. Pursing my lips and tilting my head, I surveyed the result. The metalwork of the helmet was simple and tarnished, the face bars crooked. It was unlikely to impress with the same force as the giant helmet in Walpole's tale. However, now that it was festooned with black feathers, it conveyed a certain distinction – a distinction lost to that poor dead cockerel which now stared at me blindly, the very picture of helpless indignity.

After conveying the helmet and a ball of string to my room in a moth-eaten pillowcase, I went into the vestibule, tutting as I glanced up at the face of the clock. It would be several hours before I could set out to Netherfield and I would have to partake in the four o'clock family dinner before I could slip out of the house.

I had the advantage of suspecting that it was the cold partridge meat that had, in my first partaking of this meal, led Lydia and me – the only ones of the family to eat from this dish – to be violently sick in the evening. This time around, I took pigeon pie and vegetables instead.

"I suspect that the partridge is on the turn," I said to Lydia.

"Nonsense," she replied, landing a whole bird on her plate. "It looks absolutley fine."

I shrugged. It would not appear natural for me to press the point.

The start of the meal was accompanied by Mama's relation of all the information she had acquired about Colonel Forster, whom Aunt Philips had met when he was searching for accommodation in advance of the militia settling in the town. He was unmarried, wealthy, handsome and sociable, thus gaining Mama's interest at once.

"However," she said with a sigh, "it is rumoured that his affections are already engaged."

"Did not my aunt say he was upward of five and thirty? He's much too old for any of us, surely?" said Lydia, her mouth full of partridge.

"I would say that still makes him quite a young man," insisted Mama.

"Though it would make him elderly if he had the misfortune to be a lady," muttered Lizzy.

"To whom are his affections engaged?" asked Kitty.

"Oh, I really couldn't say," said Mama, "but my sister did see him looking at Miss Andrews, one of Mrs Long's unmarried nieces."

Lydia snorted. "I'd wager he was looking at her because she wears gowns so thin you can read through them. I must ask her where she buys her muslin."

"Lydia!" exclaimed Jane.

This prattling gossip made me yawn. Upon finding a gap in the conversation, I turned it in a direction that suited me.

"Mama, pray, what do you remember of Great Aunt Gardiner?" I said. "What was she like when she was younger?"

"Oh, poor Aunt Harriet. I had quite forgotten that she so lately died. She could be most opinionated and stubborn and had a way of knowing more than anyone else did about things which rather got on people's nerves, I'm afraid. I suppose that is why she never found a husband. Men do not like to be made to feel ignorant."

"No indeed," said Papa, a corner of his lips curling.

"But what were her interests, her accomplishments?"

"Papa said her opinion was vital when it came to ordering stocks and creating new designs, yet she always wore that old bonnet. Is it not strange that a woman with such an eye should keep such a thing? That is precisely what makes no sense to me. Perhaps she came to think her good taste superfluous with regards to herself, as she had no suitors or husband to please with it."

I did not pursue the subject. I should have known better than to hope for anything useful from Mama.

After the meal, we withdrew into the front parlour as the sunlight was too bright at this hour in the drawing room. Mama and my sisters played at vingt-un, Papa read and I sewed, listening out for the chimes of the clock.

At half past six, I got up. "If you'll all excuse me, I shall spend some time reading in my room."

"Why not bring a book down and read to us, Mary?" said Jane. Whilst kindly meant, her suggestion was far from convenient. "What is it you wish to read?"

"Er . . . Fordyce's sermons," I said, knowing that such lessons to young ladies would be less than appreciated by the majority of persons in the room.

"That's as dull as dust," said Lydia. "If you're going to read it aloud, Kitty and I will play cards elsewhere."

"There is no need," I said. "I would rather have some quiet to reflect on my reading."

"But the tea will be brought in soon," said Lizzy.

"I really had more than a sufficiency at dinner. I shall spend some time in quiet study but I am somewhat fatigued, so I believe I shall retire to bed before long. I'll wish you all goodnight now for I do not want to be disturbed."

Lydia snorted. Jane's eyebrows drew together in a look of concern; perhaps she thought my proposed isolation was the result of Lydia's incivility. I smiled at her, hoping that she would not feel the need to seek me out only to discover that I was not in my room, nor indeed anywhere else in the house.

Out of the sight of family and servants, I gathered my things, put on my old straw bonnet and black cloak and snuck out of the house. I had the best part of two hours before it started to get dark, more than enough time to walk the three miles to Netherfield and set the stage ready for Mr Thorpe's arrival.

What had started as a mist of drizzle grew to purposeful rain and, whilst this would ordinarily be disagreeable, I was glad that it allowed me to hide my face beneath my hood without looking strange. Noticing figures through a window at Lucas Lodge, I left the path which would have taken me right in front of their house and trudged through a field bordered by trees, avoiding being seen at the cost of the cleanliness of my boots.

As I neared Meryton, the wind whipped my drenched cloak and the fields around me darkened as clouds billowed above. I picked up my pace, the graveyard before me a miniature landscape painting framed by my hood. My vision thus restricted, I did not see the newly dug grave. My first knowledge of it was the lack of ground beneath my feet and the cry of alarm which escaped my lips. As I tumbled into the stony earth, pain burst at the back of my head.

An owl hooted. I woke with a gasp. All was dark. I couldn't feel my fingers. Rain battered my face, making it difficult to keep my eyes open, not that there was much to see. Once I had recollected where I was and why I was there and reasoned that the pain in my head must have been the result of my fall and the cause of a period of unconsciousness, I groaned and punched the wall of earth at my side. Mr Thorpe was likely already at Netherfield and I had no bonnet to go back in time with.

As I pushed myself up, one hand slipped through mud and knocked against a stone. My fingers found two round holes in it, beneath which was a smaller hole with a narrow top. I laughed. "How wonderful!" I said when I realised that it was not a stone at all but a human skull.

The clouds must have parted, for now the skull was illuminated with cold light as I held it in both hands. Sitting there in the grave, feeling rather like a more rational and hopeful Hamlet, I contemplated my situation. Nature had blessed me with a storm and a full moon and the gravediggers of Meryton had provided me with a skull. Perhaps I was not too late to haunt Netherfield after all, I thought, adding the skull to my bag, even though I did not yet know exactly how I was to use it.

With much more physical excursion than I believe I have ever been required to use before, I dug my fingers into the earth, pushing with my feet, crawling inch after rain sodden inch until I reached the land of the living. I tasted mud.

"This had better be worth it."

Plastered in dirt, I pressed on through the rain, determined not to waste this opportunity to 'shoo' Mr Thorpe out of Netherfield and provide the opportunity for someone better to move in. However, as I wound my way up the long drive to the great house, shivering and staggering under a wave of dizziness, I felt inclined to abandon my plan and simply seek shelter from the elements. I began to circle the building, hoping that Mr Thorpe had managed to light a fire somewhere. A flash of lightning revealed a large drawing room, white dust sheets over the furniture and, upon a sopha, a man lying asleep. A crack of thunder must have made him jump, for I heard something fall.

I knocked at the window. "Let me in!" I cried but he seemed not to hear me. Then I had an idea which caused my lips to curl even as my teeth chattered. Untying my cloak, I lifted the fastening above my head, hiding my face, and held the skull above me, the hood draped over the top of it. I peeked through my cloak – though it was too dark to see anything – and knocked again, louder than before.

"Who's there?" called Mr Thorpe, his voice just carrying through the window. "Shew yourself, d— it!"

Then, answering all my present hopes, a great flash of sheet lightning blasted the darkness from the sky. Mr Thorpe's face was a picture of unadulterated terror. No sooner had he seen the skeleton ghost at the window than he fell, whether stumbling in fear or fainting, I could not tell, and as he fell, there was a smack. I gasped, fearing he had hit his head on a side table as he went down. I hadn't thought I could feel any colder in summer than I had felt standing in the wind and rain but a chill pierced through my heart making me shudder violently. The room was silent and still.

Had I just killed Mr Thorpe?

VOLUME I, CHAPTER V
The Flame of Passion

I ran to the front entrance, rattling the door but it would not open. Racing around the house, I tried every door until I found the one by which I assumed Mr Thorpe had entered, a door which, judging by the large metal pot I knocked my elbow against, led into a kitchen. I stretched out my arms before me as I stumbled my way in the dark, winding through the house to the drawing room which Mr Thorpe had chosen for his repose.

I did not realise I had reached him until I trod upon something soft which groaned. In my fright, I had a sudden intake of breath which, due to my shivering, sounded as a rattling hiss.

"You're not dead," I said, though I did not sound like myself, the cold made my throat dry and my voice high and rasping. "You're not dead!" I repeated in hopes that I could improve the timbre of my voice. This I failed to do.

I stood over him and, in another flash of lightning, saw his face clearly. His eyes grew large as he looked up at me and, in the dark that then enveloped us, there was an ear-scraping scream.

"Sir, you have nothing to fear," I said. "I only want to inspect your head . . . Mr Thorpe?" He was motionless again. I shook him but he did not respond so, upon satisfying myself that he was still breathing, and that there was no obvious injury to his head, I left him where he lay and collapsed onto the sopha.

I laughed the hysterical kind of laugh which I assumed was known only to people who had got themselves cold and wet beyond imagining and who had made a man faint with fright at the mere sight of their face.

"I wonder which of us was more alarming," I said holding the skull before me and cackling until my throat hurt.

I cared less about the cold and the rain on my walk home. A euphoric giddiness inspired me to run, even though I had never taken pleasure in running before. Passing Lucas Lodge, I stopped. Someone appeared to be looking at me from an upstairs window. I hurried on my way, clinging to the hope that my family were neglectful enough not to have noticed my disappearance. I had not gone far before I heard footsteps behind me.

"Stop!" It was Charlotte's voice.

I froze.

"Mary, is that you?"

"You mustn't tell anyone you saw me," I said.

"You're wet through," she said, squeezing my arm and peering at me in the light of the lantern she held, "and covered in dirt. You look like some sort of vagabond, Mary. Where on earth have you been?"

"No one must know I've been out. Please Charlotte. *Please.*"

She paused. "Very well. Come with me. We'll take the back door into the kitchens and get you warm."

In the kitchens of Lucas Lodge, Charlotte lit a fire and helped me off with my wet things. Wearing little more than a blanket, I sat, watching the steam rising from my gown and cloak.

"You're not in any sort of trouble, are you?" she asked, drawing her chair a little closer to mine.

"No. Neither have I done anything wrong." I had made sure that Mr Thorpe was still breathing before I left him and I had returned the skull to its grave. I could think of nothing I had neglected to do.

"What were you doing out in this weather, Mary? And at this hour?" Soft firelight traced the edge of Charlotte's face and turned her brown hair into gold. Mama referred to her as plain in looks but I found I could not agree with her. Perhaps it was her look of concern, her evident kindness, which beautified her face.

47

"Perhaps I'll tell you someday," I said.

She tilted her head and frowned at me, though a smile then spread across her face. "You're an enigma, Mary."

When I made the short walk home, the rain had eased somewhat but the wind howled, attempting to blow me back the way I had come. Upon my approach to the house, something smashed by my feet. I clamped my hands to my mouth as I shrieked, realising that I had been two feet away from being killed by the falling roof tile. I was twice fortunate as the crashing of the wind and growling of thunder appeared to have masked my scream. At any rate, no one came rushing downstairs as I crept into the house. In the morning, it was quite evident that I had not been missed.

One morning, three days after I had inherited Great Aunt Harriet's bonnet for the third time, I decided to test it to see if it would reveal a distant conversation, as it had done in the instance of Mr Thorpe's revelation to Mr Denny. I put it on and focussed on what I wanted it to do for me but, for a long while, I could hear nothing. I concentrated harder. Then, eventually, soft voices emerged from the silence.

"Pass me my bonnet, Maria," said Charlotte. Her voice was muffled. Then silk swept against silk – she must have been tying her ribbons. "Does it shew where I mended it?" Her voice was resonant now.

"Hmm. No. It's fine," said Maria, her voice quieter than Charlotte's.

"Good."

It seemed that my bonnet was relaying the sound heard by Charlotte's bonnet and that her voice only sounded loud and clear because she was now wearing it. From this I inferred that I had only heard Mr Thorpe and Mr Denny so clearly because Thorpe was wearing or holding his hat. I laughed at the nonsense of this. How could items of millinery be linked in such a way? Yet, though sense was hard to find in this illogical phenomenon, I could not refute the facts of my experience.

When we gathered later that morning to walk home from church, Mama was in a flurry of nervous excitement.

"My dear Mr Bennet, girls, girls, you'll never guess what Mrs Long told me in church!"

"I hope, my dear, that you were not inattentive to the sermon," said Papa, sharing a smile with Lizzy.

"As important as the sermon no doubt was, you'll learn that it was *nothing* to what you are about to hear . . ." Mama paused, looking for signs of interest in her hearers. A slight movement of Papa's eyebrow appeared to satisfy. She continued. "Netherfield Park is let!"

So it was that I had not long repelled one man from Netherfield – one who, I found out later, left tales of the risen dead and ghosts of bitter spinsters in his wake – before another had come in his stead.

"Finally," continued Mama, "so long after the dear, old colonel, we are to have a new gentleman installed in that very house."

"You make him sound like a billiard table," commented Lizzy.

Mama ignored her. "His name is Mr Crawford and he is a single man with four-thousand a year, I am told, and a handsome estate in Norfolk."

"Why then should he take up a tenancy in this county?" said Papa. "If he already has an abode and a living elsewhere?"

"Mr Bennet!" Mama burst out. "I know you are not so simple-minded as you make out. Why else would he seek new society if not to meet a new set of young ladies," said she, gesturing to her offspring, "with the intention of marrying one of them?"

"What else do we know of this Mr Crawford?" I asked.

"He's rich and single," said Kitty, "all we need discover now is whether or not he is handsome."

"And if he is handsome, we might persuade him to join the militia when they're established here," added Lydia. "I'm starting to think that a man is rarely truly handsome unless he wears a red coat."

"He's bound to favour one of the girls," continued Mama, casting her gaze over each of us in turn. She frowned when she reached me. "Mary,

49

why do you insist on wearing that bonnet in public? It will do nothing to honour your great aunt's memory if you put off all the young men hereabouts and end a spinster."

"Aye, Mary," sneered Lydia. "It reflects badly on the rest of us if you make yourself look so dowdy and unfashionable."

"You wanted me to have this bonnet, did you not, Lydia? And in any case, do you not think rather that my plainness might do the rest of you a service by forming a contrast which helps to promote all your beauteous aspects and minimise the perception of your blemishes?"

Kitty put a hand to a pimple on her chin.

"You're starting to vex me with that kind of talk, Mary," said Mama, though I wondered if part of her was considering the validity of what I had suggested, if indeed she understood it.

"Sorry Mama," I said.

After Papa called upon the new tenant of Netherfield Park, he reported to the family that the gentleman was, as far as he was qualified to tell, a man of some handsomeness. "Though, Mrs Bennet, your informant was mistaken in his name. Whilst the gentleman pretended to be Mister Henry Crawford of Norfolk, a servant informed me that his name is, in fact, Monsieur Henri Choufleur of Normandy."

Mama put down her teacup with clattering force. "A *Frenchman?* Girls, if he asks you to dance at the Meryton ball, you must refuse. However devilishly handsome he may be, we cannot be seen to fraternise with the enemy! Just imagine what might happen – the militia could arrest us all!"

"I should not much mind that," declared Lydia with a laugh.

It was only when the evening of the August Meryton ball arrived that Papa informed us that Mr Crawford was as English as the rest of us after all. It was only his little joke to annoy Mama. At this news, Mama almost fainted with joy. Papa waved us off and, when we reached the assembly rooms, the hopes of my mother and sisters were met in the dashing form of the irrefutably English Mr Henry Crawford.

"Look at his nose," said Mama, "there's not a bit of French in it and his chin cannot be anything but English." She twittered with laughter when Sir William Lucas introduced him to us and, watching him lead Jane to the dance floor, she gripped my hand with such force that I feared my finger bones should crack.

Although Jane had the honour of the first dance with Mr Crawford, he shared his attentions liberally with the other handsome young ladies in the room. However, during my observant meanderings, I twice heard him ask people what they thought of Miss Bennet and, as hardly surprised me, her handsomeness was only surpassed by her goodness in the estimation of our friends and neighbours.

Mr Crawford accepted Mama's invitation to dine the following day and the evening ended in her blissful raptures of matrimonial expectations and the frenzied concerns about what meat and fish could be got on the morrow.

From Mr Crawford's dinner visit onwards, gaining Jane's affection was undeniably his object. The following weeks passed in a succession of dinners, card parties and country walks during which Jane and Mr Crawford were rarely apart.

"He possesses such humility," said Jane, as she and Lizzy were walking together down the Meryton road. I was listening from my bedroom with the assistance of the bonnet, which I was getting quite adept at using for this purpose. "He is always praising the virtues of others and telling of the effort it takes for him to chuse goodness and kindness over selfishness and vanity. He is too hard upon himself and exaggerates these traits whilst ignoring his virtues. But the fact that he wants to improve himself is praiseworthy indeed."

"I agree," said Lizzy. "As a general rule, men are far too apt to be blind to their own faults. Besides, with you as a guide, it would not take long for him to become a saint."

"Lizzy!" Jane laughed.

"Does not his sister visit him soon?"

"Indeed," replied Jane. "She is due to arrive tomorrow. I do so hope that—"

"Mary!" screeched Mama from the landing. "I wish for you to assist me in deadheading the roses. *Mary?*"

With an exasperated grunt, I took off the bonnet and so cut myself off from my sisters' conversation. "Coming, Mama," I said, stowing it under my bed before going downstairs.

Whatever it was that Jane was hoping for, I assumed her wishes were fulfilled for, after Henry's sister – Miss Mary Crawford – arrived at Netherfield, Jane was invited thither to stay for the course of a few days. Naturally, I listened in on Jane's visit at such times as at least one of the party had headwear at close enough range. All seemed promising and I congratulated myself on ridding the neighbourhood of Mr Thorpe and thus opening the door for Mr Crawford to come into our lives.

On the morning which ended Jane's sojourn at Netherfield, the three of them arrived at Longbourn, the Crawfords staying well into the evening. Mary Crawford declined Kitty's offer to play at cards, wondering if a more stimulating entertainment could not be thought of.

"Spillikins?" suggested Lydia.

"That is a game for children," said Mr Crawford.

"Then what would you suggest, brother?" said Mary.

"How about snapdragon?"

"I used to play that at Christmas time," said Mr Bennet, "when I was young and unmarried. Mrs Bennet does not approve of the game."

"And for good reason, my dear," said Mrs Bennet, "for I do so fear anyone getting hurt or the house burning down!"

"Trust me," said Mr Crawford with a touch to Mama's arm. "No harm will be done. It is a game commonly played."

"At Christmas," I said, though no one appeared to hear me.

"Oh do let us play it!" cried Lydia, "I so adore a bit of danger."

Mr Crawford spoke with the servants and gathered the required objects. In the centre of the table, he set down a large, shallow dish, into which he sprinkled a handful of almonds and Malaga raisins. Then he poured brandy into a ladle and held it over the fire until blue flames danced over the surface of the liquid.

Jane gasped as he poured the fiery brandy into the dish. "You would not suggest something that is not perfectly safe, would you, Mr Crawford?" she said.

"Quite safe, I should say, though perhaps not *perfectly* so." He smiled at her, his eyes flickering with firelight. "Where is the diversion to be found in absolute safety?" He whipped his hand in and out of the swirling flames, retrieving a juicy raisin which he popped into his mouth.

Lydia clapped and squealed with delight.

Mr Crawford glanced at Jane. "The person who gets the most treats from the dish can ask a favour of anyone in the room and they simply must oblige."

Lydia reached toward the dish.

"Oh no you do not, young miss," said Mama.

Mr Crawford caught himself a second raisin.

Papa snatched an almond, wincing at the snap of the flames. "It seems I am not as quick as I once was." He glanced at Mama whose gaze was as fiery as the brandy. "I believe you have beaten me, Mr Crawford."

"Mary?" said Mr Crawford.

A sudden urge to win overcame me and, if Mr Crawford would have the impertinence to address me by my Christian name alone, then I very much wanted him *not* to win. I plucked three treats from the dish in swift succession before noticing that Miss Crawford had also approached the table. Only then did I realise that Mr Crawford had been addressing her.

"Mary, you must desist!" exclaimed Mama.

The flames were starting to die out, so Mr Crawford added a little more flaming brandy but, in attempting to match my score, he flinched, flicking a spark onto Jane's gown. She shrieked. I was ready to race upstairs for my bonnet to stop us from playing the game in the first place but Mr Crawford had already dashed to Jane's rescue, catching up her muslin skirts with his bare hands and stifling the flames. No harm seeming to have come to her, I thought better of resorting to the bonnet. Jane's gown may have been spoiled but, if the drama of this event helped push the couple together, so much the better. As Mrs Crawford, Jane could have as many gowns as she wished for.

"Are you hurt?" said Mr Crawford, supporting Jane's arm as if she were about to faint, though I saw no sign that she might.

"I am not, sir, I assure you."

"I cannot apologise enough, Miss Bennet. I feel dreadful. Quite dreadful."

"But not *perfectly* so?" I muttered. Miss Crawford winked at me, quite taking me aback.

Mr Crawford brushed the scorched patch of fabric with his fingertips, then, seeming to realise that this was not the conduct expected of him, he took a step away from Jane. Papa frowned but Mama and Lydia smiled at one another, raising their eyebrows.

Mr Crawford sighed, shaking his head. "I ruined your gown."

"As long as you ruin nothing else," said Miss Crawford in such a low tone I barely heard her. The look the siblings shared unnerved me a little, though I could not quite tell why.

VOLUME I, CHAPTER VI

A Cavalry of One

It seems that a month is more than enough time to fall in love for those who are disposed to do so. One day, Mr Crawford arrived at the house, unexpected, and requested to speak privately with Jane. This was a swift affair, as was his following interview with Papa, and the couple were engaged before the breakfast things were cleared.

"Mr Crawford invites me to join him and his sister at his house in London," said Jane, looking up from her letter the next day. "He has some business there relating to his Norfolk estate and says that he and his sister much desire my company. However, he understands that this may be inconvenient as they must leave the day after tomorrow."

It did not matter that Jane appeared not to have made up her mind. Mama busied herself about selecting what Jane should take.

"You must travel in your sprigged muslin gown," Mama decided, "Lizzy will not mind you taking her pink muslin as it suits you better than the blue. And you should be sure to wear the embroidered net over it. You must not go without your gold trimmed silk gown for eveningwear; Sally will mend the sleeve in time, to be sure."

The following morning, satisfied at my achievements in contributing to the future wellbeing of my family, I allowed myself to spend time in my old habits of study, without concerning myself with any thoughts of my relations. I practised the pianoforte with the intention of perfecting a tricky section that threatened to defeat me. It contained such chords and trills that I wished I had much longer and more dexterous fingers than God had seen fit to give me. Pausing from my playing, I had a sudden impulse to put on the bonnet but I told myself to concentrate on my music.

"Whom would I want to listen to anyway?"

Despite my determination to focus, my fingers kept on tripping over one another, so I abandoned music for reading, a book on moral philosophy to be precise, but I found myself having to keep on restarting the same page over and over again.

It would not do.

I went to my room and put on the bonnet. Before I had even decided upon whom to listen to, I heard birdsong and the regular rhythm of gravel crunching – the footsteps of two people.

"Well you seem to have succeeded in selecting a woman with the natural goodness you need in a wife," said Miss Crawford.

"It would be a marriage of perfect balance, do not you think?" I could tell from his tone that Mr Crawford was smiling.

"Do not misinterpret my words, Henry. Her goodness would not balance out your vices but it would serve to help you into better habits. That business with Mrs Rushworth—"

"You need not mention it, Mary."

"But, consider, what if your clandestine affair with that woman becomes common knowledge here? What if Mr Denny speaks of it?"

"He will not. He is a friend and a gentleman. In addition, he knows that I am aware of even more of his indiscretions. I am not the only man in Hertfordshire to have had a dalliance with a married woman."

"Still, if you wish to marry Miss Bennet, brother, I think you ought not risk delay."

"Thank you for your advice. Now come, let me shew you where I have had the archery target placed and I can perfect my aim before dinner."

I took off the bonnet and contemplated what I had heard. Mr Crawford had a sinful past with a married woman, one Mrs Rushworth. If this was behaviour he repented of, it was likely in Jane's nature to forgive him but would she *marry* him? For a moment, I considered keeping this information to myself. Jane could be happy if she married

Mr Crawford. As Miss Crawford suggested, she might be a good influence on him. Her future would be secure, any children she might have would want for nothing and the connection would be more than useful to the rest of us. But she ought to know the truth, a voice within me stated. She should not be allowed to base her choice of husband on a false image of his character.

"Bother!" I said. "I must go to Netherfield at once."

"Miss Mary," called Mr Crawford as I rode up to the house. "To what do I owe the pleasure?" He looked around as if expecting more Bennets on horseback to arrive.

"I have come alone, Mr Crawford," I said. "A cavalry of one." I dismounted. A servant approached to take the reins but I pulled them back from him. The horse, Nelly, made to bite the man but he leapt away just in time. "She will not need stabling. I shan't be here long." The disconcerted servant backed away.

"Cavalry you say?" Mr Crawford smiled, shewing off his neat, white teeth. "Ought I to be afraid?" I stared at him until his smile twitched, his expression less self-assured.

"Not necessarily," I said. "I wish to speak to you of . . ." I threaded the ribbon of the bonnet through my fingers. "This is rather awkward, Mr Crawford. But, regarding your engagement to my sister, I am not indisposed to approve the match."

"Excellent. I am pleased to—"

"Pray, let me finish," I said, holding up a hand. "I do, however, have reservations about letting the engagement continue without Jane being made aware of your character."

"My character? What can you have to say against that?" he laughed. "Cavalry indeed! Ought I to be carrying a shield?"

"I speak of Mrs Rushworth, Mr Crawford, and your . . . *dealings* with her."

He hesitated momentarily. "I do not know this woman you speak of."
I raised an eyebrow.

His voice lost its light tone. "With whom have you been talking?"

Having expected this question, I cleared my throat. "I made Mrs Rushworth's acquaintance recently when I visited the daughter of my old pianoforte master in another county."

"Which county?"

"That is not important. At any rate, I made her acquaintance and she confided in me enough to provide me with information about your – forgive me – less than gentlemanly behaviour. However, it was not until recently that I recalled the name of the man she spoke of and, considering all the other information she disclosed to me, knew it to be you. I wrote to her and she repeated all of this in her reply. I have written proof," I lied.

His face reddened. "What— How—?"

"Mr Crawford, do not mistake me. I wish not to sabotage your chances with my sister. For all your faults, I think you may be her best chance and a welcome connection for our family. A man can survive scandal where a woman cannot. However, I insist that you inform Jane of your past with that woman. If it were one of my other sisters, I might not mind so much but she deserves to know and to base her decision on a fuller understanding of your nature. You will find her more forgiving than you expect."

"And if I do not?"

"Find her forgiving?"

"No. If I do not tell her? You will, I suppose."

"Indeed. And so . . . shall you?"

He looked down with his brow creased for some moments. "I think she may look upon me with forgiveness if I have the time to explain and if she has time to talk alone with my sister. If she were to come to London with us tomorrow morning as planned, I promise you I will tell her while we are there. Should she wish to break off the engagement and return home, our carriage and servants will be at her disposal. If not, she will have time to . . . adjust her feelings before returning to her relations. I hope I can trust you not to speak of this to any of them."

"I do not think such a revelation would be advantageous to any of us, sir." I bobbed my head before turning to Nelly. "Thank you, Mr Crawford, for seeing things from my perspective."

He bowed. "Do you wish me to assist—?"

"I can manage quite well with a mounting block, thank you," I said.

He signalled for a servant to fetch one.

As I rode off, I was sure I heard him mutter, "Maria Rushworth, friends with Miss Mary Bennet! Zooks!"

The following morning, after we had breakfasted, I could not settle into any mode of study and, wishing to be left alone to listen in on the Crawfords' conversations, I decided to take a walk.

"I expect I shall be back before you leave, Jane," I said. "However, if not, I wish you well on your trip."

"Thank you, Mary," said Jane, her smile even more radiant than usual.

I put a hand to her shoulder. "Happiness becomes you, Jane," I said. "Let us hope it lasts."

On my solitary walk, I overheard Miss Crawford talking with another young lady about home theatricals and I swelled with dread that she might intend to bring this custom to our household, when and if the Crawfords should join our family.

The ticking of a clock informed me that Mr Crawford was elsewhere. His hat must have been placed at no great distance from him as I heard him making arrangements with servants for his departure. A male servant mentioned something about sending his regards to a Joseph Paisley, "a most obliging man, for a Scotsman", according to him. In time, I heard the snort of a horse, then gravel displaced by rumbling carriage wheels.

All should be well, I told myself. Mr Crawford had been most reasonable when I spoke with him. I breathed in the cool, earthy air and walked in dappled light under arching boughs, hearing Mr Crawford greeted at Longbourn before he said something about he and Jane stopping at the Kings' house, where they would collect his sister on their way to Town. The family said their farewells and the couple left to the fading sound of Mama's prattling advice and hopes that they did not get attacked by highwaymen.

At some point on their drive, Mr Crawford asked Jane to whom she was waving.

"Old Mrs Pepperstock. That's her cottage there. She is quite a poor lady. From time to time, we bring her a joint of pork or a basket of fruit. The dear woman is most partial to gin as well and owes her longevity, she says, to its medicinal properties."

Mrs Pepperstock lived a good way north of the Kings' house. I wondered if Mr Crawford's driver were lost and, after a while, Jane made such an enquiry to Mr Crawford.

"Do not worry about my sister, Jane. The thing is, I wanted to talk with you alone. You have no need to blush, we are engaged and therefore such a thing is not unseemly."

"But your sister is expecting us."

"She is not. She will stay in Hertfordshire. Jane, I do not deserve such an angel as you."

"Mr Crawford—"

"No Jane, you are an angel. I find I have given my heart to you completely. I only hope that one day you might do as much for me."

"I have done, Mr Crawford. Why else would I have accepted your proposal?"

"Then let us be married as soon as may be."

I stopped, as still as the tree trunks surrounding me. He was not going to tell her.

"Well," said Jane, "it need not be many weeks for us to prepare and for the banns to be read."

"But what a fine thing it would be for us to return to Longbourn, not from London but from Scotland!"

"Mr Crawford! Are you suggesting that we—"

"Marry at once? To be sure. We love each other – there is nothing to stop us, is there?" Oh yes there is, I thought. "I care not for the meaningless pomp and frivolity of weddings now-a-days. All I wish for is to be your husband and love you all my days. What say you to that notion?"

"To the latter notion, I have already agreed. But by 'marry at once' – do you mean – *elope*?"

"Technically, yes. Though we'd not be like those couples who elope because their families wish them not to marry. There would be no scandal about it, nor anything for you to worry your pretty head about."

"Yes, there would be," I said, balling my hands into fists. "They would return to Hertfordshire stinking of scandal."

"I do not know," said Jane. "Why cannot we marry at Meryton with my family alongside us to witness the event?"

"Don't you see, Jane?" he said, his tone increasingly urgent. "It does not matter where we marry. Only that we become man and wife. But you look pale. There is an inn coming up. Let us stop for some refreshment and we can discuss this further when you feel stronger." There was a tapping which I assumed was a signal for the driver to pull in.

Mr Crawford had gone too far, speaking as though dragging Jane off to Gretna Green was the action of a chivalric hero. It most certainly was not! Selfishly tainting Jane's reputation in an unfeeling attempt to marry her on false pretences would not do. I determined to pursue them at once but, upon turning to rush home, I bumped into Charlotte.

"Did you not hear me, Mary?"

"I am sorry. My mind was elsewhere."

"Are you quite well?"

"Indeed. I did not hurt you, I hope?" I said, regarding her foot which I had trodden on.

"No, to be sure. But Mary, is something wrong? You look pale."

"I am not blessed with the best of complexions. Forgive me, Charlotte but I must go, I have little time to lose." I turned from her and started in the direction of home.

"You appear to have a weakness for leaving without explanations," she called after me.

"I am sorry, Charlotte." I repeated, glancing at her bemused expression and wishing in that moment that I could confide in her, though now was not the time to judge the wisdom of this. I headed back to Longbourn, stopping periodically to catch my breath, pressing a fist into a stitch in my side. Determining to spend more time in future reaping the benefits of regular exercise, I sped home and ordered the stable boy, Thomas, to put the side-saddle on Nelly.

As a Fury of the underworld, taking revenge on man for broken promises, I thundered northwards, breaking my steely expression only upon greeting Mrs Pepperstock as I passed her by, declining her offer of a cup of gin.

"I used to have a bonnet like that!" she called.

"Not quite like this, I expect," I said, not looking back.

VOLUME I, CHAPTER VII

The Gentleman in the Blue Coat

It was difficult to hear Jane and Mr Crawford now. The assorted voices in the bonnet, presumably from within the inn he had spoken of, as well as the pounding of Nelly's hooves, almost drowned them out.

The first inn north of Meryton was a small one but full as a ballroom. Grooms were assisting customers in changing horses, maids were serving refreshments and suffering the indignities of pinching from some of the more inebriated travellers. I looked around but could see neither Jane nor Mr Crawford.

A gentleman in a smart blue coat came up to the innkeeper and enquired as to whether he knew of any estates in the county which were vacant. I squeezed past him and turned a corner to see Jane and Mr Crawford sat at a table.

"Why, Mary!" Jane smiled up at me. "Fancy you being here!"

Mr Crawford scowled, looking at me askance.

"Mr Crawford, this is not the way," I said.

"What do you mean?" said Jane when he failed to respond.

"I mean," I said, still talking to Mr Crawford, "that injuring my sister's reputation only to delay the general understanding of your own is not the conduct of a gentleman." The man in the blue coat looked over at us and his smile dropt to a frown.

"What?" said Jane. "What is this about?" this directed to her betrothed.

Mr Crawford became very interested in the button of his cuff.

"He has caused scandal before. He had an inappropriate relationship with a woman – one Mrs Rushworth – whose husband was very much still alive."

"You must be mistaken, Mary," said Jane. "Mr Crawford cannot have done such a thing. Can you? Mr Crawford?"

"The fact is he did. See, he does not deny it. It is well known in his home neighbourhood in Norfolk I presume. Why else would he have sought a bride from a county that knows so little of him, with the exception of his friend, Mr Denny?"

"I have changed my ways, Jane," he said, leaning towards her across the table and grasping her hand. "Your goodness has changed me."

"You could still marry him, Jane. Only not like this. If you elope rather than marry him in a respectable fashion, you will damage the chances of our sisters. You must see that."

Jane looked hurt. "Even with little time to think, I had quite determined not to do something so foolish as to elope, whatever Mr Crawford said. I wish to marry in a respectable fashion with my family beside me. However, because of what I now know – what you did – yet it is so hard to believe – I feel that I do not know you, Mr Crawford. I hate to cause you pain but," and here she drew her hand from his, "I wish to be released from our engagement. It was too hastily made; I see that now." Tears spilled down her cheeks. "How could I have made such a foolish mistake!"

"But Jane, I love you and I promise to be faithful to you, always!"

"It is no use, sir. It would be wrong of me now if I were to give you false hope. I cannot marry you." Jane sobbed, drawing the attention of several customers around us. She stood and made to move away but Mr Crawford gripped her arm. "Pray, release me, sir."

"Jane, I will not let you go," he said.

"Excuse me." The gentleman in the blue coat came closer. "Is this man causing you any distress, madam?"

Tears sparkled in Jane's eyes as she looked up at the gentleman beseechingly. He put a hand on Mr Crawford's shoulder. "I think you had better unhand this good lady. Let her go," he added firmly.

Mr Crawford glared at the gentleman but released Jane.

"And I think you had better leave. I shall see to it that the ladies have all the assistance they require for their journey. If they will allow me?" He made a bow in our direction and we nodded in response.

Mr Crawford did not move at first. "Jane?" He softened his voice and features in a way that I knew would make this hard for her. She seemed incapable of speech and was using all her effort to suppress her sobs.

"It's 'Miss Bennet' to you now, sir," I said, "and my sister wishes for you to leave." Jane held my hand then, giving me a quivering smile.

"You heard the lady," said the blue-coated gentleman. "It's time for you to go." He gripped Mr Crawford's arm but Mr Crawford flung the stranger's hand away.

"Very well," Crawford shouted. "I'm leaving." He lowered his voice as he spoke to Jane but he did not look at her. "My man will fetch your case."

Whispers and sniggers followed him as he marched out of the inn, head down.

"My driver can take you home whenever you are ready," said the gentleman, "wherever that may be. And I can accompany you if that is your wish."

"I came on horseback, separately," I said. "And our home is but a short ride from here."

"Then why do I not borrow a saddle and ride your horse alongside you as the two of you sit in my carriage. Does that not sound agreeable?" He smiled at Jane.

"Thank you, sir."

"Pray, will you tell us to whom we are so obliged?" I asked.

"Forgive me. My name is Charles Bingley," he said with a bow. "And I am at your service."

When we reached Longbourn, Mr Bingley helped us descend from the carriage, his hand holding Jane's a little longer than was quite necessary. I took in the sight of the two of them as they took in the sight of one another. Mr Brook, having noticed our arrival, brought Thomas to see to Nelly whilst he took Jane's case.

"Would you like to come in?" I asked.

Mr Bingley looked from me to the house to Jane. "I think," he said at last, "that you have had a trying day and would most likely value the respite of being alone with your family. I shall therefore take my leave. It has been a pleasure making your acquaintance Miss Bennet," he bowed, "Miss Mary."

Goodbye, Mr Bingley, I thought to myself with regret, having been much impressed by the gentleman's attentive manner as well as his fine carriage.

It was most unfortunate for Jane that, being seen alone with Mr Crawford in a carriage travelling north when it had been put about that they were to head south to London, the gossips of Meryton guessed at an intended elopement. The wagging of their rumour-mongering tongues turned the business at the inn into a brawl. Limbs were broken, hairy chests bared, blood was shed in this fictional frenzy of violence. In short, at least a dozen stories sprang up, painting Jane by turns as a tease, as a rejected victim of a rake and a bookkeeper for gambling on the outcome of fights at a number of inns in the county. None of these depictions did Jane any favours, regardless of how false our close friends believed them to be. I had failed at saving her reputation but it occurred to me that there was something I could do to redeem it.

Friday 9th August 1811

Stitches unpicked, bonnet donned and nausea quelled, I met with Mr Crawford when he was inspecting Netherfield with a view to renting it, before he had met any of us.

"You should think again, Mr Crawford," I said, surprising myself with the depth of authority in my voice. He was walking in the shrubbery and whipped around to face me, almost slipping over, the ground being wet from the storm of the previous evening. "Your scandalous treatment of Mrs Rushworth and her poor deceived husband is well known in this neighbourhood. You may wish to leave before I decide to let word of your shameful behaviour spread throughout the entire county."

He gaped at me, his face white, his expression such as one might present to a mythical augur of unknowable powers. Even though I did not win at snapdragon in this version of reality, I still considered I was owed my reward, a favour from one of the players. That favour would be Mr Crawford's leaving Hertfordshire. "Good day," I inclined my head in a mockery of a bow and left while he stood there as silent and unmoving as one who had beheld the face of Medusa.

When the day came again that had once held Jane's abduction, I took myself to that same inn and left an advertisement of my own creation with the innkeeper.

"My dear Mr Bennet," said Mama, only days after my outing. "Have you heard that Netherfield Park is let at last?"

At last, I thought, smiling behind my book.

VOLUME I, CHAPTER VIII

The Impact of an Admirer

Michaelmas had passed and, along with it, the date upon which Mr Bingley settled himself at Netherfield. However, despite this happy event, Mama had fallen from heights of elation to irritated pessimism. The reason for this decline in her spirits was that Papa shewed no inclination to call upon Mr Bingley, a circumstance which boded ill for our chances of developing an intimacy with the gentleman. Though, since he had called upon Mr Thorpe and Mr Crawford, at least in my own recollection, I had no doubt that he would likewise visit and, in due course, introduce us to Mr Bingley.

One particular day, Mama's nerves had little respite. Or, rather, we had little respite from them. She shouted at Mrs Hill for charring the toast, at Lizzy for joking about ending up an old maid and at Kitty for coughing, something Kitty assured Mama that she did not do for her own amusement. That evening, I sat reading, hoping not to do or say anything that would upset her further.

Lizzy sat close to me, trimming a hat with pale green ribbons. "What do you think, Jane?" she asked. Jane complimented the decoration. "Why *do* you wear that old bonnet, Mary?" Lizzy turned to me, a sparkle in her dark eyes. "It's not as though you have nothing better."

I hesitated. "I think our great aunt would have wanted it to be used," I said at last, keeping my eyes on my book.

"But there's nothing to stop you from trying to improve it at any rate," she continued. "Why do you not take it to Pratt's shop next time we're in Meryton? He or his wife may be able to correct its shape somewhat.

For that matter, I think I could do a fair job of it myself." She drew out a large pair of scissors from the sewing box and made a sharp snip with them in the air, the sound cutting coldly through me.

"No!" I blurted out, reaching for my bonnet which I had felt compelled to keep close by me, hanging from the back of my chair. "I do not wish for it to be altered." I should have kept it in my room. As I drew it to my lap, I could have sworn I felt its ribbons tremble. I wondered then if I should tell them all about what the bonnet could do so that they would not inadvertently harm it. I could even shew them its abilities, as I had shewn Chamberlayne, and then they would understand why it had to be protected.

"No one will think you frivolous or less accomplished than you are, just for wearing something that looks as though it comes from this century." Lizzy smiled and caught Papa's eye. "If nothing were ever changed, there would be many exhausted horses on the roads and many bored dance partners at a ball." There was a flicker of amusement in both of their faces. I knew this shared look too well, as well as the warmth in my cheeks which followed it. Lizzy had long practised taking up arms, shooting her witticisms alongside Papa so as to escape the line of fire herself.

"And I dread to think of the state of the guard at St James's Palace," added Papa, "if people refused for things to change."

Lizzy snorted.

I felt smaller as they spoke, shrunken under yet more words of ridicule and misunderstanding which joined with those I had collected over years past, threatening to bury me alive.

"But you see . . ." I began. I could tell them now, I thought, I could make them understand the power that I possessed but, as I looked at the bonnet, I feared that the consequences of my telling them might bring untold injury.

"Yes?" said Lizzy.

I clutched one of the bonnet's russet ribbons, its silky fabric smooth between my thumb and forefinger. "Never mind," I muttered.

Fortunately, Lizzy's feeble attempt at wit seemed to inspire Papa and he turned the conversation in another direction, beginning to tease Mama about how she should introduce Mr Bingley to Mrs Long at the next Meryton ball.

Mama exclaimed how this was quite impossible, her not being acquainted with the gentleman. She glared at Papa and tugged her embroidery thread so hard that it snapped.

"How *can* you be so teasing?" she cried.

Papa smirked and continued in the same vein, suggesting that *he* could introduce Mr Bingley to their friends. What with his previous jokes about Mr Thorpe's gout and Mr Crawford's Frenchness, I was not in the least surprised when he revealed that he had, in fact, called upon Mr Bingley, unbeknownst to any of us. I nearly jumped out of my chair then as Mama's laughter battered my eardrums, the others joining in her excited reaction. A smile played at one corner of Papa's mouth when he noted Lizzy's appreciation of the joke. I tried to appear as though I had been taken in as well but the arrangement of my facial features cannot have been quite right, for they merely served to prompt Jane to ask if I were feeling quite well.

At the Meryton ball two weeks later, Mr Bingley appeared even more pleased with Jane than he had during the incident with Mr Crawford, an occasion which only existed in my own memory now. He brought with him his two sisters, Miss Bingley and Mrs Hurst. Mr Hurst, apart from being both the most intoxicated and spherical person in the room, was quite forgettable. Lizzy caught the eye of Mr Bingley's friend, Mr Darcy, a more interesting personage by miles. He was tall, handsome and the degree of his fortune – ten thousand a year – was a fact that the whole assembly became acquainted with before the gentleman had progressed five steps into the room. He seemed disinclined to meet any of the eyes that were consequently drawn to him and, rather than seeking introductions as his friend did, he lingered around the periphery of the room, preferring to station himself near windows and doorways. Perhaps he comforted himself with the thought that he could make a speedy departure through either, if the occasion called for it.

When Mr Bingley tried to persuade him to dance with Lizzy who was sitting alone due to the lack of available gentlemen and her preferring not to dance with a girl, I overheard Mr Darcy say, "She is tolerable; but not handsome enough to tempt *me*."

I snorted at this, then turned away when it appeared that Mr Bingley and Mr Darcy had heard me. Lizzy had drawn herself up several inches at Mr Darcy's words, blinking rapidly. Of course, it would have been better for a man as eligible as Mr Darcy to take an interest in my sister but, seeing how unlikely that was, I considered that a dose of pride-ruffling might do her some good.

My mood was lifted all the more by overhearing Charlotte talking about my family to one of Mr Bingley's sisters and saying that I was the most accomplished girl in the neighbourhood. All in all, I found the ball one of the pleasantest I had yet attended.

Straight after breakfast the following morning, I took my book into the shrubbery. There being a considerably sized holly bush between the benches where we sat, Lizzy and Jane had not noticed me and I felt no need to hint at my presence.

"Well, he certainly is very agreeable, and I give you leave to like him. You have liked many a stupider person."

"Dear Lizzy!" laughed Jane.

"Oh! you are a great deal too apt you know, to like people in general. You never see a fault in anybody."

I nodded, thinking of how Mr Crawford spoke of his faults, albeit with affected humility, yet Jane refused to suspect the truth of them until I revealed all to her. At least Mr Bingley had proved himself – through his actions and manner during that episode – to be a true gentleman, although of course Jane was unaware of this proof of his character.

After this, the subject of their conversation turned to trivialities, casting my attention off, like a boat, allowing it to drift into my own reflections. I was only vaguely aware that they were discussing ways of dressing hair. I sighed as I surveyed the house, its deep red bricks crisscrossed with dark ones; the crooked chimneys; the vegetable beds; the trees, one of which still bore the old swing we played on as children; Asian chrysanthemums and South American fuchsias blooming beside one another in English flower pots. After Papa died, all of this would go to a male relation of ours whom we had never met, with whose father Papa had been on the most disagreeable terms.

I shivered and drew my shawl around my shoulders. The heir to Longbourn was not likely to allow we female Bennets to continue living in his property. It was, therefore, of vital importance for us to establish good connections through marriages. Recalling the sight of Mr Bingley dancing with Jane, I allowed myself to hope that this occupant of Netherfield would be the one to set our family's prospects on a secure trajectory. Then I thought of Mr Darcy, whose wealth was at least double that of Mr Bingley – but I shook my head – more chance of finding a Viking treasure hoard in the little wilderness at the end of the lawn.

Whilst contemplating how different life would have been had we had a brother, I froze. *Chamberlayne*. It was the day after the ball – the day I had previously rescued him by lending him the bonnet. I startled Jane and Lizzy by leaping to my feet.

"Were you here all this time?" said Lizzy.

I did not answer. Determined not to neglect my friend in his hour of need, I hastened towards the Bull Inn, surprised at the energy I found for such brisk exercise.

I considered that, once again, I would, in sending Chamberlayne back in time, go back in time myself and forget my knowledge of doing anything for him. Perhaps I had *already* gone back in time and Chamberlayne was, even now, safe from danger due to my help. My head hurt as I tried to unwind this tangle of logic.

At least the bonnet knew the truth of things, I thought. This idea calmed me considerably and I recalled that the evidence of the bonnet's knowledge was in the stitches. Someone who had only given the bonnet a cursory inspection before and after the event might not have noticed any change. However, I knew the placing of each stitch, having studied them assiduously. I knew the numbers of complete flowers and the stitches of the only incomplete one. Three stitches were missing from it. Three hours had been gained, though not for me. Therefore, instead of making for The Bull, I met Chamberlayne at Clarke's library. We had even more to discuss than the first time I met him there.

Several days later, we attended a party at Lucas Lodge. I sat on a sopha, watching as Mr Darcy turned away from Miss Bingley. Mrs Hurst and I both took particular note of him in that moment, for instead of seeming bored, looking vacantly into the air or through a window as was his wont, his gaze was caught and in his look I perceived admiration. I sought for whatever painting or gilded ornament had drawn his attention but saw, instead, my sister Lizzy. Mrs Hurst's face fell and she whispered something to her sister, whose nostrils flared. Lizzy was now speaking with Colonel Forster and Mr Darcy moved so as to be near enough to overhear their conversation.

"I've noticed too," said Charlotte, sitting beside me.

"Noticed what?"

"That Mr Darcy looks at Lizzy a great deal. Promising, is it not?"

I laughed bitterly. "I only wish it were. Lizzy has been determined to dislike the gentleman ever since he told Mr Bingley that he did not wish to dance with her at the Meryton ball. She swears that she will never dance with him, even if he asks her." I tutted. "Would she somehow think herself victorious for refusing him? I ask you! If fine looks, good breeding, an estate in Derbyshire and ten thousand pounds a year were to acknowledge a moderate prettiness, low connections and no fortune, the latter should win nothing by rejecting the former or making him the object of her attacks of wit. Sometimes she is too much for me to bear, Charlotte." I sighed. "And she calls *him* proud."

"I think he has a right to be proud," said Charlotte.

"Perhaps. At any rate, Lizzy judges him too harshly. Pride is a very common failing I believe. Human nature is particularly prone to it, and there are very few of us who do not cherish a feeling of self-complacency on the score of some quality or other," I considered Lizzy's self-assured air, "real or imaginary," I added.

"And a person may be proud without being vain," said Charlotte.

"Exactly. Pride relates more to our opinion of ourselves, vanity to what we would have others think of us."

Charlotte nodded. "I certainly receive the impression that Mr Darcy is not wanting in integrity. There is a lack of affectation in him which I find quite refreshing. He does not seem to feel the need to change anything about himself just to please others. Not unlike yourself, I think."

Over breakfast a little over a week later, I felt a swell of pride within me at Jane's receiving an invitation to dine at Netherfield with Mr Bingley's sisters. Hiding a smile as I sipped my tea, I flattered myself that this development was due to my efforts in ridding Netherfield of inappropriate rogues and nudging Mr Bingley into taking on the tenancy. Even though Jane was only dining with the women, as the gentlemen were dining in Meryton with the officers, a connection was developing between Jane and the Bingley family which might be likely to bear fruit.

"Can I have the carriage?" asked Jane.

Papa considered for a moment. "I believe the horses are needed for the farm," he replied.

"But that will not do," said Mama. "It will create a much better impression if we can send Jane in the carriage. Oh, let them use the pair of chestnuts on the farm if they must but that still leaves Nelly and you can send Thomas to rent a second horse from The Bull to pull the carriage. There, now everyone is happy with the arrangement."

Papa raised his eyebrows but kept his eyes on his food and said not a word about the matter. I supposed his mind to be engaged in calculating the expense of renting a horse for the day and thinking of how much more work will fall on the remaining servants at Longbourn if Thomas or Mr Brook were to be absent in attending Jane with the carriage. However, he did not argue with Mama upon this occasion. I had noted the quantity of wine he had taken the previous evening and deduced that his head was not up to disputing with her.

No sooner had Jane set off for Netherfield that afternoon than a west wind intruded uninvited into our corner of Hertfordshire, bringing with it darkening clouds. The deluge that followed could have floated Noah's ark and put paid to my intention of visiting Charlotte. She had invited me over that day to practise a duet she had recently acquired. Instead, I occupied myself with the embroidery of roses on a cushion cover.

It was still raining by the time Sarah and Sally lit the candles. As the evening drew on, I rested from my sewing and leant back in my chair to observe the domestic scene before me. Something was missing apart from Jane. Then it dawned on me that there was a noticeable lack of disharmony. Papa was engrossed in a book and a glass of wine, as was Lizzy. I preferred their understanding to be exercised in silence rather than their wit in vocalisations. Mama, Kitty and Lydia were playing at vingt-un without squabbling or shrieking at the vicissitudes of the game. The glow of candlelight softened their features and I felt a surge of affection for them all, even for Lydia. Perhaps it was unfair of me to keep our great aunt's secret to myself. Surely the others might benefit in ways I would not have considered if they were aware of the possibilities it afforded.

"There's something I think I should tell you all," I said at last but, as I spoke, wheels crunched on gravel outside and footsteps raced to the front door.

"What's that commotion about?" said Mama, leaping to the window. The front door banged shut and Jane flung the parlour door open and, wailing, rushed into Lizzy's arms.

Lizzy cradled Jane's head. "What is it, Jane?"

"Oh, Lizzy!"

"Whatever can have happened?" said Lydia.

Jane's cheeks shone with tears. "The carriage – the rain – he was there on the road – the wheels skidded in the mud." She spoke in staccato, interspersed with sobs. "It's my fault! It's my fault!" She buried her head in Lizzy's shoulder.

Mama stood frozen, mouth hanging open, eyes bulging. Kitty darted to the table to fetch the smelling salts.

"What do you think is your fault, dearest?" asked Lizzy.

"I killed him!" she cried between sobs. "I killed Mr Bingley!"

VOLUME I, CHAPTER IX

Dark Clouds

Jane plummeted from sobbing to unconsciousness. Kitty looked from Jane to Mama and seemed so shocked that the former had fainted, rather than the latter, that she lost the use of her limbs. I snatched the smelling salts from her, used them to revive Jane and, after three cups of strong coffee, which Mama insisted on lacing with brandy, she was in enough control of her faculties to explain to us in greater detail what had happened.

She told us that the carriage which had borne her had wound down the narrow road from Netherfield, its wheels skidding in the treacherous mud as they came around a bend. Unfortunately, Mr Bingley and a servant were standing in the road seeing to some problem, be it with wheel or horse.

"I knocked at the window and cried out and he looked up at me. I'll never forget how his face changed in that moment, his mouth falling open, his eyes widening in horror. He pushed his servant out of the way – how brave he was! – but it was too late for him. Our wheels skidded again and the carriage hit him squarely on the head. When I saw him next, his body was lying there in the mud." Jane buried her face in a handkerchief.

"Oh, Mr Bennet!" wailed Mama in a flutter of nerves. "What will become of us now? Shall Jane have to testify in court? Should we flee the country?"

"If you please, Ma'am," said Mr Brook, "as I told Miss Bennet repeatedly – though my words did not appear to break through, as you might say – the gentleman wasn't dead. I stopped the carriage and told Miss Bennet to stay inside while I went to investigate. The gentleman's friend had got out of their carriage and was attending to him. He informed me that Mr Bingley lived, though he was at that time unresponsive. I assisted them in carrying him into the carriage and righting their stuck wheel and they went on their way."

"There, Jane," said Lizzy. "He'll likely be resting at Netherfield now with the physician called for. He will be well again, I have no doubt."

"But it was my fault," Jane repeated. "If he does recover, what shall he think of me?"

"It was an accident, Jane," Lizzy consoled her. "There was no way anyone could have prevented its occurrence."

There was a frustrating truth to Lizzy's words. How could I unpick these events and change things to stop them from happening in the first place? It was impossible to halt the incessant rain and thus improve the condition of the road and I had no ideas regarding how to alter the time that either Mr Bingley or Jane left their dinner engagements. However, perhaps Mr Bingley would make a full recovery and this event might even serve as an anecdote that he and Jane would in time laugh about when retelling it to their grandchildren. There was nothing to do but wait and observe the unfolding of events.

Papa called at Netherfield the following day and, although he ended up speaking only to Mrs Nicholls, the housekeeper, he ascertained that Mr Bingley had recovered his consciousness the previous evening but was keeping to his room upon the advice of his physician, Mr Jones. The next day, Jane wrote to Miss Bingley to ask after her brother and received in reply a rather short note which indicated that he had regained sufficient strength to go out shooting with the gentlemen.

At church that Sunday, the Bingleys seemed not to see us, even though our pew was just across the aisle from theirs. Upon leaving the church, we saw Mr Bingley staring at a gravestone while his sisters spoke with the vicar, Mr Palmer.

"I am pleased to see you so recovered, sir," said Jane to Mr Bingley.

He did not look up. "To think how close I was to joining the ranks of such as these, their faces now forgotten, their voices never to be heard again, their bodies nought but dust."

There was a pause.

"You were lucky," said Jane.

He turned on her. "Lucky?" he said, frowning. "You call me that?" He laughed bitterly. "How can you think me anything but the victim of misfortune? Ever since that night, I have dreamt of calamity haunting my steps and behind me, always, the sound of carriage wheels." He began walking away. "I should never have come to Hertfordshire."

Jane's face went white. "Mr Bingley—" she breathed.

"Come along, Jane," I said, drawing her away from the invisible shadow that radiated from Mr Bingley, a mocking contrast to his previous inexhaustible supply of sunshine. "Mama insists that you take the carriage rather than walk."

Jane wrote to Miss Bingley a number of times over the next week, and received brief replies in response to about half of them. She even took advantage of a dry day and walked to Netherfield with Lizzy, only to hear from the housekeeper that the family were not at leisure to accept callers. She returned, disappointed and subdued, and not even my best performance of her favourite pieces could cheer her.

"I hope my dear," said Papa to Mama at breakfast, "that you have ordered a good dinner to-day, because I have reason to expect an addition to our family party."

Jane froze, looking up at Papa with barely suppressed hope.

"Who do you mean, my dear?" said Mama. "I know of nobody that is coming I am sure, unless Charlotte Lucas should happen to call in, and I hope *my* dinners are good enough for her. I do not believe she often sees such at home."

"It is a person whom I never saw in the whole course of my life." He took a large bite of toast and we all paused in our eating as we waited for him to continue. "About a month ago," he said at last, "I received this letter, and about a fortnight ago I answered it, for I thought it a case of some delicacy, and requiring early attention. It is from Mr Collins, the son of my first cousin, who, when I am dead, may turn you all out of this house as soon as he pleases."

"Oh! My dear," cried Mama, "I cannot bear to hear that mentioned. Pray do not talk of that odious man. I do think it is the hardest thing in the world, that your estate should be entailed away from your own children."

Papa read out the letter in which Mr Collins spoke of his uneasiness at the disagreement between his late father and Mr Bennet, which had long kept their branches of the family apart. In addition, being newly ordained and blessed with a parish under the patronage of the Right Honourable Lady Catherine de Bourgh, he felt it right to set the Christian example of the offered olive branch. Regarding his feelings as to being heir to Longbourn, he wrote: *I cannot be otherwise than concerned at being the means of injuring your amiable daughters, and beg leave to apologise for it, as well as to assure you of my readiness to make them every possible amends.*

Every possible amends. I had guessed at what that implied long before Jane wondered aloud what his meaning could be. The only way he could 'make amends' for inheriting our father's estate, would be for him to marry one of us. It would be very difficult for him to cast out a widow and fatherless daughters from their home if he was in fact married to one of those daughters. This seemed to me a most interesting development and had the potential to bring with it security for my family's future. I admitted to myself then how I dreaded the thought of leaving my home.

"I do not know what to make of him by his letter," said Lizzy. "There is certainly something rather pompous about his style."

"And there is a lack of originality in his figurative language," I said. "The olive branch, particularly, is much overused. However, I do not judge him ill for his writing style. The important thing is the sentiment behind the words. At any rate, it would be foolish to be prejudiced against him when we know so little of his character."

Whilst our heads were filled with the implications of this expected visit, an unexpected guest arrived who snuffed out any hope that I had nurtured with regards to Jane's chances with Mr Bingley. When Miss Bingley was shewn into the front parlour, she told us of her and her sister's unease regarding their brother. Since the collision, he had been irritable, melancholic and short tempered when once he had been calm, amiable and kind.

"He sent Mr Darcy away when they disagreed about which county furnished sportsmen with the best range of birds to shoot," said Miss Bingley. She sniffed and held a handkerchief to her nose. "And he says Mr Darcy will never again set foot in the house." With a shake of her head she declined Mama's offer to ring the bell for tea. "No, I shall not stay," she said, getting to her feet.

"Is Mr Bingley still planning to have a ball at Netherfield?" asked Lydia.

Miss Bingley hesitated before answering "He is."

"Hurrah!" cried Lydia.

"I quite long for a ball," chimed in Kitty.

"But," here Miss Bingley swept an icy gaze over all of us, letting most of the frostiness settle upon poor Jane, "my brother has decided that it shall be a small affair. I regret that we have not the space to include your family in the party."

"What?" I said. "But Netherfield is huge. How can there not be enough—"

"He also wishes for no more cards to be left or letters to be sent to any of us, filled with questions regarding his health."

Jane coloured at this, gripping Lizzy's hand as she fought back tears. She held out until Miss Bingley took her leave but was soon forced to restrain her emotions again for, at that moment, several officers arrived.

"Oh!" cried Lydia. "I quite forgot to tell you I'd invited Denny and

Sanderson to take tea with us."

"I do not much mind such surprises," said Mama, neatening her lace cap and fluttering her eyelashes as three red-coated gentlemen marched in.

Mr Denny bowed. "I hope you do not mind that I extended your invitation to Chamberlayne here," he said.

"Not at all! Not at all!" cried Mama, laughing. "The more the merrier, is that not what you always say, my dear?"

Papa coughed. "If it is not a phrase I tend to say, it must surely be a sentiment that the female population of the house surmise from nothing at all but my generally obliging manner."

"Indeed, indeed," said Mama. "That is quite what I mean."

After tea was brought in and the gentlemen had taken their fill of cakes and other dainties, Kitty suggested a turn about the garden and we were all inclined to take the air but Papa who preferred the dustier air of his library.

"So, Miss Mary," said Chamberlayne, his voice low. "Have you been on any of your *travels* lately?"

"What do you mean, Chamberlayne?" asked Lydia, appearing at his side all of a sudden.

He looked uneasy.

"Within the library, he means," I said, "books being the vehicles that carry us into different intellectual spaces." I saw Lydia's attention drift as soon as I'd said the word 'library'.

"Is not this pleasant?" she said to Mr Denny when he strode up to us. "You must all come to visit like this very often and bring as many of your friends as you wish."

"I'm glad that you enjoy regimental company so much, Miss Lydia. It was by happy chance that Chamberlayne joined our party, as he happened to be at Sanderson's lodgings."

"I thought you were staying at The Bull?" said Lydia to Chamberlayne.

"I am," he replied, "only I visited him yesterday evening and got soaked in all that rain. I had to stay the night to let my things dry. Are you alright, Miss Mary?" he said then, turning to me and putting a hand on my arm. "You're not ill, I hope?"

"I am quite well," I replied, "but I must return to the house."

"Then I shall accompany you," he said.

"No, stay with us," said Lydia. "She'll only be going off to read some deep book or other. Sanderson is busy talking with Lizzy but we and Kitty will make two pairs for battledore and shuttlecock. Last time, I hit Kitty right on the nose – how we laughed! Well, I did at any rate."

"Are you sure you are quite well?" Chamberlayne whispered.

I winked at him. "I have some *travelling* to do. I thank you for giving me the idea."

His eyes lit up with a mix of comprehension and intrigue. "Then I wish you luck," he said with a bow.

As I raced to my room, I calculated how many hours I needed to gain in order to salvage Jane's relationship with the Bingleys then, sitting on my bed, I carefully unpicked the stitches.

Tuesday 12ᵗʰ November 1811

After donning the bonnet, I found myself, as I had hoped, sitting at the breakfast table as Sarah brought a letter to Jane. As she read it, I leant towards Mama so that our heads were almost touching.

"If that is an invitation to Netherfield," I whispered, "Jane should ride on horseback, for it looks like rain and if her clothes get wet, she will have to spend the night and will then spend more time with Mr Bingley."

"Hmm," she said, her attention fixed on Jane. I crossed my fingers under the table, hoping that my words had found home. Then I uncrossed them, reminding myself that there was no rationality to such a superstition.

"It is from Miss Bingley," said Jane who then read the letter aloud.

Mama's disappointment that the gentlemen were dining out caused her to drop a slice of bacon on her gown.

"Can I have the carriage?" asked Jane.

"No my dear, you had better go on horseback, because it seems likely to rain; and then you must stay all night," said Mama.

"That would be a good scheme," said Lizzy, "if you were sure that they would not offer to send her home."

"Oh, but the gentlemen will have Mr. Bingley's chaise to go to Meryton; and the Hursts have no horses to theirs."

"I had much rather go in the coach," reiterated Jane.

"But, my dear, your father cannot spare the horses, I am sure. They are wanted in the farm, Mr. Bennet, are not they?"

Papa acknowledged that they were and, due to the determination of Mama, which I had quite depended upon, it was agreed that Jane would ride to Netherfield on horseback.

I felt a little sorry for Jane and for Nelly as I watched them disappear down the Meryton road towards the swelling grey clouds. Few minutes passed before the onslaught of rain began and I watched as Mrs Camfield rushed about getting her washing in, Mr Camfield likewise watching her through the window, his arms crossed.

"This was a lucky idea of mine, indeed!" said Mama, taking the credit for my suggestion. Though I did not, in fact, deserve all the credit. I would not have thought of this without Chamberlayne having said what he had about getting soaked through and being forced to stay the night at Sanderson's lodgings.

A servant arrived the following morning at breakfast with a letter from Jane to Lizzy and it transpired that getting wet through had led to Jane feeling poorly.

"Well, my dear," said Papa to Mama, "if your daughter should have a dangerous fit of illness, if she should die, it would be a comfort to know that it was all in pursuit of Mr Bingley, and under your orders."

I kept my eyes on my cutlery as he spoke.

"Oh! I am not at all afraid of her dying. People do not die of little trifling colds. She will be taken good care of. As long as she stays there, it is all very well. I would go and see her, if I could have the carriage."

Lizzy was tapping on the table.

"I am afraid that the horses cannot be spared today either," said Papa.

"I will go to her," said Lizzy, "I shall walk."

"In all this dirt!" cried Mama, gesturing around as if the mud had somehow made its way into the house and over all the furniture.

I felt heat rise into my cheeks. "I admire the activity of your benevolence," I said to Lizzy, "but every impulse of feeling should be guided by reason." I did not see how Lizzy arriving at Netherfield in a muddied gown would serve to promote Jane in the estimation of the Bingleys. "Would this exertion of yours be in proportion to what is required? You surely do not think Jane dreadfully ill when all she complains of in her letter is a sore throat and a head ache?"

"I think we all know Jane well enough to know that she would make light of her symptoms so as not to worry us."

I had nothing to say to this but sat there chewing my lip, feeling yet more uncomfortably warm.

"I think that walking three miles is certainly in proportion to what is required," she continued. "Jane would wish me to be with her even though she would not ask it." She excused herself from the table and went to get her bonnet.

"I have no reason to think that Jane will suffer greatly from this. No, indeed," I said before taking a bite of toast which edged down my throat like a stone.

VOLUME I, CHAPTER X

Blooming Affections

My thoughts turned to the visitor whom Papa expected – although he would not be revealing this fact to the rest of the family for some days. I knew little of Mr Collins except that his name was William, that he was a second cousin of mine whose father had been on bad terms with Papa – though no one alluded to the cause of this enmity – that he and his two brothers formed the totality of our male relations on Papa's side and that he would, after Papa's demise, inherit our beloved Longbourn.

No sooner had I returned the bonnet to my head than I heard whom I assumed to be Mr Collins talking with another man. His hat was presumably close at hand.

"But Stephen, you do not think anyone has evidence do you? Letters, witnesses of anything clandestine, that sort of thing? If any of this were to reach the ears of *Lady Catherine*—"

"Calm yourself, brother. That is not what I meant. I only referred to the rumours we are both aware of as a possible reason for Mr Bennet's ill feeling towards us. Imagine what he must think, supposing he believed us, or at least you, not to be the natural son of our father. Imagine him on his deathbed, suspicious that the very person who would take his place and rid the house of his loved ones, for all he knew, was in fact no true blood relation of his. Salt in the wound, William, do not you see?"

"And should any evidence against our legitimacy come to light . . . ?"

"Even in that unlikely scenario, we cannot be considered anything but legitimate heirs by law."

"At times such as this," said William Collins, "it is a great comfort to me that you went down the law line."

"And it is apt that it has fallen to you, as a clergyman, to be the peacemaker. Good thing Frederick was not the eldest," said Stephen.

"Indeed. He's best off where he is, shooting at the French."

"Quite. But Napoleon's not infiltrated Gibraltar surely?"

"No. I forgot to mention," said William, "I received word that his garrison has been sent to Cádiz to support the Spanish resistance there."

"Ah. I do not envy him marching about the country. Well, I had best take my leave now, though I might just indulge in one more piece of marzipan for my journey, if I may?"

"You had better leave it for me, I have little left since Frederick packed for Spain and I can see that you're growing rounder by the day. A little marching might do *you* some good."

"But I need to be able to deliver the *heavy* arm of the law! Now, I may not see you again before you go into Hertfordshire," said Stephen Collins through a mouthful of – presumably – marzipan, "so I shall take this opportunity to advise you now – take a wife from amongst the Bennet daughters. The entail is secure but it will be easier for you and them, when the time comes, if you can step into the role of benefactor rather than invader."

"Thank you, Stephen. I see every reason to be optimistic and Lady Catherine will be most pleased, I am sure, that I will have found a wife in a way that heals the discord within the family. She vehemently disapproves of family discord."

"Any way our family can curry favour with Lady Catherine, the better. She has much influence at St James' court and could be prevailed upon, in time, to recommend me to the position of judge, then we'll both be well established gentlemen, me at the Old Bailey and you at the old family seat. And once you've fathered an heir and a spare, the Collins branch will be firmly rooted at Longbourn where it belongs."

This conversation left me with confusing feelings with regards to the Collins brothers. Yes, Mr William Collins might marry one of us and that would add to our security. However, he might inherit Longbourn and not be a trueborn heir. That was not right, despite what his brother assured him about the legalities. If the correct way of things could be subverted in such a way, what was the point of the entailment of property? How could it be better for a man potentially unconnected to us by blood to inherit Longbourn rather than the women who were born and brought up here? However, they spoke of rumours, and rumours did not mean fact. Perhaps he had every right to our beloved home. Perhaps.

"After all of Lizzy's concerns and Papa's morbid jokes about Jane's health," I said as Charlotte and I strolled down the garden, "we have been most fortunate in that she has not become so ill as for us to be alarmed but that her mild fever and fatigue was deemed sufficient for her to stay on at Netherfield until she gains strength."

"It certainly provides an opportunity for Mr Bingley's regard for her to grow through his caring for her," said Charlotte. "And it is most thoughtful, is it not, that he has invited Lizzy to stay as well?"

"It shews his hospitality but that does not surprise me, from what we have seen of him heretofore."

"But more than that, it indicates his attentiveness to Jane's comfort, for she will no doubt benefit by Lizzy's presence in the house."

"True," I said.

"And I wonder if Mr Darcy's gaze will be drawn to Lizzy as frequently as at our recent party."

"Interest from that quarter would be more luck than I think our family deserves."

"But do you consider that a reason to object to it?" she asked, smiling.

I laughed. "No indeed."

"No. We must embrace all the good fortune we can, I say, for who knows when our luck might turn."

We continued our walk down to the end of the lawn where blackbirds were darting in and out of a hazel thicket.

"Look there," I said pointing to a small tortoiseshell butterfly, "I didn't think I'd see another this year. A late butterfly on a late rose."

"All our roses have long since faded; you are lucky."

"It's a China rose called 'old blush'. They tend to flower into the Autumn but this last bloom has exceeded my expectations."

"Perhaps it does not adhere to the rules of time as the rest of them do."

I gave Charlotte a sidelong glance but she seemed unaware of any greater significance to her words. I wondered how she would respond if I told her about the bonnet.

"Charlotte," I began.

"Zooks!" she exclaimed, "I had quite lost track of time. Mama expected me home long since to make the mince pies for dinner."

It was probably as well that she had interrupted me. She would think I was out of my wits if I told her.

"You are not dining here?" I said.

"I regret not. We have invited some of the officers to dine."

"Oh. I could help you with the mince pies."

She squinted at me. "And how are you at making pastry?"

"I do not know. I once asked Mrs Hill if she could teach me to cook something but Mama reprimanded me before she could answer. 'You're not a servant,' she'd said."

"No," said Charlotte.

I noticed her expression change. "Have I said something wrong?"

"No, indeed, Mary. Mrs Hill and Sarah produce excellent dinners; there's no need for any of you to help."

"I was only saying what Mama said. I didn't offend you, did I?"

"Of course not, Mary," she said, linking her arm through mine. "The truth is, I wish that the king had not honoured my father with a knighthood after his service as mayor."

"Really?"

"Well he gained a title and an elevated social position but that very

89

status led him to abandon the trade which had enabled him to prosper enough to become mayor in the first place. If he had not been given a title, he would not have seen fit to give up his business and we might have been able to keep a cook, not to mention Maria and I might have had dowries. The ways of society often strike me as nonsensical."

"I suppose they can be. But, regarding the mince pies, I really would like to come and help you. May I?"

"What would your Mama say?"

"She doesn't have to know," I whispered.

Charlotte laughed and we walked on together.

On our way to Lucas Lodge, we returned to our discussion of the Netherfield household. When I mentioned Jane's friendship with Miss Bingley and Mrs Hurst, the bonnet conveyed to me the conversation presently taking place where those ladies were, presumably forming a connection with Mrs Hurst's lace cap. She and Miss Bingley were criticising Lizzy's arrival in muddy attire. I hoped that I had not been right in advising her not to go. They appeared to think her traipsing about the countryside rather odd.

Charlotte was talking of the sisters now but I struggled to attend to her words.

"Ah," I said, hoping that would do.

"It shews an affection for her sister that is very pleasing," said Mr Bingley. I only just heard him; he must have been positioned across the room from Mrs Hurst.

"I am afraid, Mr Darcy, that this adventure has rather affected your admiration of her fine eyes," said Miss Bingley smugly.

"Not at all," came Darcy's voice, deep and clear, "they were brightened by the exercise." This was a rather satisfying response, I thought. However, the speech which followed it was most certainly not.

"I have an excessive regard for Jane Bennet," this from Mrs Hurst, "she is really a very sweet girl, and I wish with all my heart she were well settled. But with such a father and mother, and such low connections, I am afraid there is no chance of it."

" . . . That's what I told her anyway," said Charlotte, referring to what, I could not say.

I made a small laugh. "Quite so."

The sisters then spoke ill of us having one uncle who was an attorney in Meryton and one who was in trade in Cheapside. I had heard from Charlotte that the Bingleys' fortune came from some mill or other in the north of England. How was it that they could look down their noses at others whose income came from trade? It made no sense at all.

"If they had uncles enough to fill all Cheapside," cried Mr Bingley, "it would not make them one jot less agreeable." My spirits rose. If I were to make a list of men I held high in my estimation, Mr Bingley's name would be at the top.

"But it must very materially lessen their chance of marrying men of any consideration in the world." This from Mr Darcy. I respected his keen observation; what he said was simply a fact, after all. However, I should have preferred it to be a fact that he was unaware of or, at least, one he did not feel the need to state.

I tried to block out the speech of Mr Bingley's sisters as they left the gentlemen to attend to Jane, speaking to her in tones of cloying sympathy. I was doing better at conversing with Charlotte now, despite the distraction, but lost no time in removing the bonnet as we approached Lucas Lodge.

On the fifth day after Jane got wet through, she was well enough to attend church and there we met the Bingleys and were able to transfer Jane home.

"We shall see you again soon, I hope," said Mr Bingley as he gave Jane his hand to assist her into the carriage, "and we shall have a ball at Netherfield to look forward to once you are fully recovered. I may have to consult you on how you would have me decorate the ballroom; I am quite at a loss regarding such things. I shall see if we can get hothouse flowers in, should you like that?"

Judging by the way Mr Bingley smiled at Jane and talked of Jane and waved at Jane as the carriage rode off, I felt somewhat encouraged that his sisters' and Mr Darcy's discouraging words had not appeared to lessen his regard for her. With great satisfaction, I wondered what else I could achieve with the use of the bonnet.

VOLUME I, CHAPTER XI

Saving Time

That evening, after the rest of my family and the servants were gone to bed, I stole downstairs with the bonnet, a candle, a needle and thread. The last stair creaked and I froze – but no one emerged from their rooms. I continued, creeping through to the vestibule where I knelt in front of the big, old, long-case clock. Setting my candle down before it, the glow of the flame danced across the smooth mahogany casing. My heartbeat fell in time with the ticking as I stared up at its face. In a matter of seconds, the clock was due to ring out twelve chimes to signal midnight. Taking my needle, I made one yellow stitch into an embroidered flower, tied it off and then placed the bonnet on my head.

A shock jolted me and I likened the sensation I felt afterwards to that of swift locomotion, as when riding a galloping horse or tripping over, unable to stop oneself from falling. It might be how I would feel if I were shot from a cannon, though if such an unlikely event occurred, I assumed the explosion of gunpowder would have killed me so, more likely, I would have felt nothing at all.

I planted my hands on the floor to steady myself, even though I was kneeling and unlikely to go anywhere. Then, when the sensation subsided, I looked up at the clock again. The second hand continued its steady ascent but the hour hand had shifted. One o'clock struck, the sound vibrating through the floor and into my fingertips. One stitch gained, one hour lost. My suspicions had been correct; a rule contrariwise to that written within the bonnet applied to a forward motion through time. I decided then to make this part of my daily routine, to lose an hour or two of sleep in order to build up a reserve of time, an investment to give me security against the unknown vicissitudes of the future.

I took myself back up to my room and blew out the candle. Getting into bed, I kept one hand on the bonnet as a child might a doll, my fingers resting over the stitches. It struck me then that beneath my hand were hours of time. Not anonymous, abstract, meaningless hours but hours of my great aunt's life, hours she had given to the bonnet.

Did she know that she would not reclaim them for herself? Did she intend to do so but died before she had the chance? Had she meant to pass them on as part of her legacy? I could not answer any of these questions but I did, from that time on, have a greater respect for each and every stitch.

"What the deuce—!" Lydia's exclamation made me jump but my alarm was nothing to hers. To her it would have looked as though I had appeared out of nothing, like a fairytale witch. Her gaze was fixed on me, her mouth gaping.

I took off my bonnet and held it behind my back. "What are you doing in my room?" I asked.

"What am I doing? Not black magic, that's what I'm *not* doing! What the dickens are *you* doing?"

I could hardly tell her that I was stitching away odd hours here and there, now having replenished several patches of unpicked flowers.

"Why are you trying to hide your bonnet? Is . . . is that what did that *thing* just now?" She waved her hand around in a vague gesture.

I said nothing.

Clamping her hands to her mouth, she stared at me. "It is, isn't it! Your bonnet is *possessed*! Great Aunt Harriet was some sort of witch and *you* . . . you're an *aberration*!"

"That's a very big word, Lydia."

"You have to get rid of it, or I'll tell Mama."

I sat on my bed and crossed my arms, holding the bonnet tight against my chest. "You may be her favourite, but if she thinks you're going insane, at the very least she will not let you leave the house. And be assured, if you start talking about a magic bonnet or witchcraft, people will think you're mad, even Mama and Kitty. You say a word to anyone and you will regret it. Mama won't run the risk of you displaying your witless mind to the neighbours or any potential suitors."

She huffed, stamping her foot. "I will destroy it. Burn it or something!"

I put the bonnet behind me, like a mother cat defending her young. Straightening my spine, I mantled myself with seeming confidence and smiled. "Oh, but you can't do that. Great-Aunt Harriet told me how the bonnet works. If anyone destroys it, they will be cursed."

Her eyes grew wide but fear had not completely replaced her anger. "But I can still get rid of it."

"Threats work both ways, Lydia. You touch my bonnet and I will tell Papa that I saw you kiss Mr Denny. He wouldn't let you near an officer again."

"You wouldn't!"

I blinked slowly, then stared at her, wearing the face of a formidable warrior statue.

She kicked my chair and snarled at me, slamming the door behind her as she left. Laying back on the bed, I laughed, congratulating myself on my ability to outmaneuvre the sister who had, for so long, seen me only as an object of ridicule.

The knowledge that she was aware of the power I held over her gave me a thrill and I felt sure that, if she were to try anything stupid, I could certainly outwit her again. However, with hindsight, I ought to have relinquished this flattery of my pride and gone back to remove the event of her discovery from existence. How painful it is when wisdom comes to us too late.

VOLUME I, CHAPTER XII

Sermons & Scandals

"Mr Bennet, Mrs Bennet, my most humble salutations," said Mr Collins, bowing to each of them before he was fairly out of the carriage.

Lydia made a moue of disappointment after surveying him. In truth, he was not a handsome man.

"Ah! These must be your amiable daughters." He bowed to us, looking up with an unreadable expression.

"Welcome," said Papa, his lips sealing shut again after this single word.

Mama curtsied. "I do like a visitor to be punctual and you have the punctuality of a clock maker sir."

"Such compliments are more than I had expected and must be evidence of your genteel graciousness, madam." Mr Collins bowed again, much lower than seemed necessary.

"Shall we go in?" said Papa.

Mr Collins followed Papa and Mama into the house, turning his head as he walked so as to cast his eye upon the rest of us and to smile at Jane in particular. Paying little regard to his footing, Mr Collins stumbled over the threshold, causing Lydia to snort. However, he recovered his composure and began complimenting the house, from the construction of its windows and staircase to details such as the choice of wallpaper and the straightness of the skirting boards. Mama received these comments with a smile, though not the kind that lasted long upon the face. Perhaps she wondered, as I did, if his observations were triggered by the notion that the house would be his one day.

However, his compliments of her daughters occasioned greater enthusiasm in Mama.

"The beauties and charms of these most sweet and accomplished ladies have rendered me utt-er-ly speech-less," he said, failing to keep all traces of spittle within his mouth as he emphasised the last words. Lizzy cringed in Jane's direction and Kitty mimed being sick, resulting in herself and Lydia being quite incapacitated by giggles. "I do not doubt that you shall see them all, in due time, well disposed of in marriage," added Mr Collins.

"You are very kind, sir, I am sure," said Mama as they sat together upon the sopha, "and I wish with all my heart it may prove so; for else they will be destitute enough. Things are settled so oddly."

A line creased Mr Collins' brow, an expression that looked rather rehearsed to me. "You allude perhaps to the entail of this estate." He leant towards Mama and they spoke in low tones, cutting the rest of us off from their discussion. However, judging by Mama's smiling, her hanging upon his every word and the excited giggles that punctuated her speech, I supposed that she found much in his conversation to please her.

Over dinner, Papa's amusement at Mr Collins' sycophantic praises of Lady Catherine de Bourgh and her daughter prompted him to question our cousin about his patroness. However, the effort of engaging in conversation with Mr Collins soon appeared to bore him and so, after the meal, he suggested that Mr Collins, who seemed happier to talk than to be quiet, read to the family. Papa brought from his library a selection of novels and books of poetry but Mr Collins found, from a dusty shelf, a much neglected copy of Fordyce's *Sermons to Young Women*.

Most of us gave at least the appearance of attentiveness for the first couple of pages.

"As for you, my *fair* pupils," read Mr Collins, looking around at the younger generation of females, "we no doubt wish you to possess such fortitude as implies resolution, wherever your virtue, duty, or reputation, is concerned. But along with that we expect to find, on other subjects, a timidity peculiar to your sex; and also a degree of complacence, yieldingness, and sweetness, beyond what we look for in men."

Lydia and Kitty began whispering together, not seeming to notice Mama's subtle cough.

"Neither do we," continued Mr Collins, "so far as I know, ever rank amongst feminine qualities, valour, strictly so called. A woman heading an army, rushing into the thickest of the foe, spreading slaughter and death around her, or returning from the field of battle covered with dust and blood, would surely to a civilized nature suggest shocking ideas."

"Shocking indeed," I said.

Mr Collins nodded his agreement. "Your best emblem, beloved," here he glanced at Jane and her face fell, "is the smiling form of peace, robed in white, and bearing a branch of olive."

As he read on, Mama's eyelids drooped.

" . . . men of sensibility desire in every woman soft features, and a flowing voice, a form not robust, and a demeanour delicate and gentle. These are considered—"

"Do you know, Mama, that my uncle Philips talks of turning away Richard," said Lydia, speaking of our uncle's servant whom she often attempted to provoke into a reciprocation of flirting but who had never as yet allowed her to succeed.

"Lydia," reprimanded Lizzy, though with the flicker of a smile.

Lydia did not seem aware that she had acted improperly. "And if he does, Colonel Forster will hire him. My aunt told me so herself on Saturday. I shall walk to Meryton tomorrow to hear more about it, and to ask when Mr Denny comes back from Town."

"Lydia, Mr Collins may wish to continue," said Jane.

However, Mr Collins put the book down with a sniff. "I have often observed how little young ladies are interested by books of a serious stamp, though written solely for their benefit."

Lydia appeared not to hear him and, in this, I could empathise with Mr Collins.

The following morning, Mr Collins accompanied my sisters into Meryton and I took the opportunity to walk to Lucas Lodge. Charlotte had said that she could shew me how to bake a cake, as I had not done badly with the mince pies but, knowing Mama would not approve of my working in a kitchen, I kept the real reasons for my visit to myself and pretended to be swapping sheet music to copy.

"And so, you disapprove of him?" asked Charlotte as she handed me an egg to crack.

"Not disapprove exactly. One cannot know a person after only a day. It might be that he has hidden qualities of which we are unaware." I cracked an egg, then fumbled to fish out a slippery piece of shell from the bowl. "I only mean that he has not fitted into the household as well as he could have. But then it is not as if he were alone in that." I made a hollow sort of laugh and tried to mask it with a smile.

"You know, you are always welcome to come here," said Charlotte, "whenever you like." She placed iron disks onto the scales to weigh out the flour. "All families are different. I get on well enough with Maria but we do not have the closeness of Lizzy and Jane."

"We chuse our friends," I said, passing her the bag of flour when she reached for it.

"That we do."

I paused, feeling as though there were the ghost of something unsaid between us and it frustrated me that I did not know what it was. The subtleties of relationships often eluded me.

"I think that Mama may soon have to hint to Mr Collins that he has a rival in the form of Mr Bingley," I said in order to break the silence.

Charlotte's eyes widened. "Mr Collins wishes to court Jane?"

"To be honest, I think he would be happy with Jane or Lizzy. It would be convenient for him, help secure his position as heir of Longbourn and heal the old upset between our families if he were to marry one of us."

"And what do you think of that?"

I cracked another egg. "If truth be told, I cannot see Jane or Lizzy wishing to marry him. My sisters all have such romantic ideals. Yet, if he married into the family, I could not imagine him throwing us out of Longbourn when Papa dies. An offer from him would be an offer of security for us all."

"So Mr Bingley may prove an obstacle to Mr Collins' hopes of Jane but what do you think of Darcy? Might not he be deemed a rival for Lizzy's hand?"

"Admiration is one thing, a proposal of marriage quite another."

Charlotte handed me a whisk. "And you're sure Mr Collins is limiting his sights to your elder sisters?"

"I have noticed him regard my younger sisters with some disapproval and, conscious of my plainness in contrast to the others, I am far from expecting a marriage proposal from any man. Truth be told, I hope that my sisters make good enough matches so that I do not need to enter into matrimony myself." I shrugged. "I do not think much is expected of me in that regard anyway."

Charlotte sighed. "I think you are fortunate. Expectation is indeed a burden."

Lizzy embracing the option of becoming Mrs Collins and the remote chance that she were to become Mrs Darcy were possibilities that receded into a distant horizon as Mr Wickham sauntered into the foreground.

He was a new officer of the militia, brought into the fold by Mr Denny – of course it would be him! – on his return from Town. Judging by the low calibre of his friends Mr Thorpe and Mr Crawford, I wondered with some unease as to what we had in store with Mr Wickham.

"By gad, I declare that the women of Meryton are the most amiable and handsome I have ever met with," said Mr Wickham when we were gathered at Aunt Philips' house to play cards one evening. He already had the full attention of the group of ladies encircling him, including Lizzy, Lydia and Kitty, and I could not but observe a subtle yet distinct shift in the attitudes of the other women in the room, their gazes glancing towards him. Where he had positioned himself, the candlelight softened his features, made his straight, white teeth glint in their smile and his eyes sparkle with animation.

"I said, are these muffins not delicious?" repeated Mr Collins to Lizzy.

However, Lizzy was too preoccupied to take notice of Mr Collins or his muffins, walking past him to join Lydia and Kitty at a table near Mr Wickham who promptly joined them.

"I believe my aunt is looking for a fourth for whist, if you should wish to oblige her," I said to Mr Collins, hoping that this invitation would smooth over the awkwardness left by Lizzy's inattention.

"I confess, I know little of the game. However—"

I crossed the room to the coffee table and poured myself a drink. My motivation was curiosity rather than thirst, if truth be told, as from here I was able to overhear parts of Lizzy's conversation with Mr Wickham. I learned from what he said that he had grown up with Mr Darcy at Pemberley in Derbyshire being, as he was, the son of old Mr Darcy's steward. Old Mr Darcy had, according to Mr Wickham, loved him as his own son and planned for him to take orders. I did not hear much more of their conversation as Mr Collins kept commenting on the room's decor as he came back and forth, fetching coffee for those at his table.

I could not imagine that Mr Wickham's story was as interesting as Lizzy's rapt attention suggested. She was probably just flattered that he had spoken solely to her for so many minutes together. All I was likely to have missed was his explanation of why being a clergyman would not have suited him. It was no surprise to me that he was of the sort who preferred red to black, marching songs to hymns and firing guns to giving sermons.

After Lizzy and Mr Wickham had been talking for some time, Lydia interrupted them, insisting that Mr Wickham join in the game of lottery tickets and seeming most pleased when he moved his chair closer to hers. To think what might have been if Mr Wickham had been a clergyman! I could not decide if Lydia would have ignored him because of his occupation or if, due to his charms, she would all at once have developed an appetite for sermons.

Four incessantly rainy days passed by in which only the servants ventured out and only for such necessities as food for the pantry and roses to decorate my sisters' shoes for the approaching ball at Netherfield. Lydia and Kitty, who were quite itching to get out of the house, let alone rest their eyes upon an officer, found more things than usual to argue about, such as which of them looked better in pink, whether Mr Wickham preferred Lizzy's company or Lydia's and who stole who's hair pin. The atmosphere of irritation was by no means lessened by Mr Collins' quoting from James Fordyce in attempts to inspire my younger sisters into meekness.

One afternoon, having been in a state of restless petulance since breakfast, Lydia scowled at the rain through the window.

"At least the garden will benefit," I said, looking up from my book.

She squinted at me. "You don't have anything to do with this, do you?" she said.

"What? To stop you flirting with the officers, you think I've summoned the rain?" I laughed. "Have you any notion of how deranged that sounds?"

"What sounds deranged?" asked Kitty, coming into the front parlour.

Lydia hesitated, looking from Kitty to me. "Oh, Mary thinks it would be improper to the point of insanity to refuse Mr Collins if he wanted to dance with us at the ball."

I relaxed a little. She had not told Kitty of what she had seen or what she suspected about my bonnet. Perhaps she never would. There was a good chance that she would not become the obstacle to my endeavours that I had feared.

Kitty shuddered. "Lord, however improper refusing him might be,

I'd not dance with him for the world!"

When the day of the ball arrived, the relief was tangible. Tension and squabbles melted away and harmony, at least for a little while, reigned once more. We were all of us pleased as we walked about the ballroom dressed in our finest, amongst our friends and neighbours, all of whom seemed disposed to enjoy themselves, except perhaps Mr Darcy who looked as out of place as an eagle in a dovecot.

I stood nearby as Lizzy and Charlotte talked.

"But Mr Wickham is not here?" asked Charlotte.

"Mr Denny says he has business in Town," I followed Lizzy's gaze to Mr Darcy. When he caught her eye, she looked back at Charlotte and sighed.

"Never mind," said Charlotte. "At least you'll not want for a partner these first two dances."

"Don't remind me." Lizzy rolled her eyes. "My only hope is that once these dances with Mr Collins are over, he will not ask me again."

"You may be surprised. He might dance well."

"Even if he does, which I doubt, his other oddities, his pomposity and unnatural obsession with his patroness, would be more than enough to make me ill-disposed to be his partner."

"You see no advantage to adopting a . . . more *favourable* attitude towards him?"

"Charlotte, such a task would be impossible. I cannot persuade myself that he is anything other than ridiculous! There is no way that—"

"My fair cousin," said Mr Collins, appearing all of a sudden. "The first dance is imminent."

"Sir, this is my friend, Charlotte Lucas. Charlotte, this is Mr Collins," said Lizzy, reddening.

Miss Bingley was leading the dance with Colonel Forster, though her consistency in looking at Mr Darcy led me to surmise that she wished to have been asked by him. I smiled to myself as I saw Mr Bingley dancing with Jane. After watching two dances, I felt the need to stretch my legs.

Walking past the doorway to the dining room, I breathed in the aroma of freshly baked bread rolls and a mingling of other dishes which made my mouth water. Then I came to another doorway and peered inside. There was little furniture in this room except a cabinet and a chaise longue, the principle purpose of this small room being to display the fine works of art which presumably did not fit along the upstairs gallery.

I was studying the hunting scenes, the still life pieces and the Canalettos when my attention was caught by a small double portrait I recalled seeing before at a ball held by Colonel Harpenden. On the left side sat a young woman from the previous century, with fresh rosy cheeks, but it was not her beauty that drew my eye but what I saw in her hands. It was mostly out of frame but I did not doubt that the woman in the portrait was holding my great aunt's bonnet. Perhaps it was even she herself. I tried to recall the features of the aged lady's face and decided there was a resemblance.

"So here you are!"

I turned to see Charlotte in the doorway.

"Do you not dance this evening?" she asked.

"I do not expect a partner. Besides, there are more women than men and I do not mean to compete for attention."

"There is no need to. We could dance together. Other women are doing so for the exact reason that there are more women than men." She shrugged. "But I understand if you do not wish to." She glanced at me before fixing her eyes on a painting.

It surprised me that some gentleman or other had not secured her for more dances. Though I was not much of a dancer myself, I wished for her to enjoy the ball, so I bowed and, imitating a gentleman's voice, I said, "It would be my pleasure, ma'am."

She laughed and took my arm but before we entered the ballroom again I glanced back over my shoulder at the portrait. In the foreground, the top of a circle, like a rainbow of red, white and blue, caught my eye. It looked as though the artist had included, just in frame, a tricolor cockade. Had my great aunt been a supporter of the revolution in France? Impossible! Besides, I reminded myself, it might not even have been her. The other figure in the portrait drew my attention now. She was a woman with brown skin who wore an ornate golden bangle, an emerald ring and had her head wrapped in cloth of green and gold. Light from an unseen source gave a lustrous sheen to the gold fabric and glinted in her dark, intelligent eyes which looked directly at me. Their story was merely hinted at in this image; characters and events tantalisingly close but out of reach, as from a forgotten dream.

As Charlotte led me to join the throng of dancers, I tore my thoughts away from the mysteries of the painting. It had been a long time since I had danced and it took a few minutes for me to perform the movements with ease.

"Good, Mary," said Mama when the dance was over. "You see? You can make the effort. Now come with me. Unfortunately, Colonel Forster is quite devoted to Miss Andrews this evening, some say they may be soon engaged, and 'tis a pity for he can usually be depended upon to dance with anyone. However, there are some young men over here and I should think that if you were to walk along near them, one of them may ask you to dance."

"*Mama—*"

"Off you go," she said, giving me a push. Several people had turned to look, having heard Mama's words, including some of the gentlemen she had referred to. Not knowing what else to do, I turned to face the direction she had indicated and edged one foot in front of the other. A scattered female audience looked over in my direction. Several men took note of my approach and turned away. Earlier, it had not mattered that no man asked me to dance but being slighted like this twisted something inside me. Too many people had heard Mama and were watching me fail her. My eyes stung and my face became overheated. Then I heard a cough behind me.

Mr Chamberlayne bowed. "Will you do me the honour?"

"Thank you," I whispered, placing my hand in his. "It is most kind of you to ask me when there are so many other women to chuse from."

"But, my dear, there is no other Miss Mary Bennet."

As he led me down the dance, I made a small squeak, unable to hide my surprise.

"What is it? Did I tread on your toe?" he asked, before taking the hands of the lady next to me and turning about with her.

"My sister Lizzy," I said, when he was opposite me once more. "She's dancing with Mr Darcy."

He squinted over at them. "What of it?"

To me, the look shared by Lizzy and Mr Darcy might either betray a mutual desire to partake in a duel or to make straight for Gretna Green. "She always said she would never dance with him."

"Women are always changing their minds about one thing or another," he said, rolling his eyes. "Not at all like men."

I glared at him. "Lack of obstinacy is hardly a flaw. However, you won't find me being so changeable."

"Of course not," he said, smile lines creasing at his eyes. "You never change anything, do you?"

I continued in conversation with him at supper and Charlotte came to sit opposite us.

"You surprise me, Miss Mary," said Chamberlayne. He made to pour me wine but I placed my hand over the glass. "I thought you would be an advocate of Mary Wollstonecraft's ideas."

"What I mean is that there are certain roles we adopt in society and certain boundaries within which we navigate that have been established for our own good and to ensure stability."

"You just want to be careful that a boundary does not become a noose," he said.

"Whatever do you . . ." my words trailed off as my attention was drawn to Mama who was toasting Jane's good fortune with anyone who would clink glasses with her. Her boasts rang out across the room that Jane would soon be engaged to Mr Bingley and that this piece of good fortune would throw the rest of us into the way of other men of wealth. I clutched my cutlery, feeling the heat rise in my cheeks.

Chamberlayne glanced at her. "Can I serve you some chicken, Miss Mary?" he said, spearing a slice from the dish in front of him.

I ventured to look at Mr Bingley who, thankfully, appeared not to have heard Mama. Mr Darcy, on the other hand, was regarding her with an expression of unconcealed alarm. Lizzy, too, had gone quite red and even whispered to Mama in an attempt to prevent further inappropriate speeches of unfortunate volume.

I assumed that Lydia's cheeks were merely rosy from the amount she had had to drink, rather than from any kind of embarrassment, for she chattered away merrily, holding out her glass to be refilled by an obliging officer.

"It is a most elegant room," said Charlotte, taking in the high ceilings and fine windows. "Mr Bingley has found himself a most charming residence, do not you think?"

"Indeed," said Chamberlayne, grasping the subject with enthusiasm. "Though I admire older buildings. Your house is Elizabethan, is it not, Mary?"

As I looked up from my plate, I realised that my friends were trying to draw me out of my mortification. "It is."

"A manor built in the traditional E shape, for the queen," said Charlotte.

"Indeed," I said, "though I like to think of it as an M. It could be an M you know, if seen from another perspective."

"How whimsical! Is that because of your own name?" asked Chamberlayne.

"No. You see, at the age of six, when a historical book taught me that Queen Elizabeth had had her cousin Mary executed, I considered that, from another angle, the E shape might look like an M. So, in my mind, our house has been M shaped from that time, in solidarity with the unfortunate queen who lost her liberty and her birthright, followed by her head, of course."

Chamberlayne laughed. "She did try to have Elizabeth assassinated, though."

I shrugged.

When supper was cleared away and people began to get up from their seats and mingle about the room, Mr Bingley tapped his glass with a spoon.

"I should just like to thank you all, once again, for joining me at Netherfield this evening. I for one am having a most agreeable time." A grin stretched across his face. "All there is left for me to wish for is a song. The pianoforte awaits! Whom can we persuade to sing for us?"

The gathering had quietened to listen to Mr Bingley and the muteness continued in the general tentativeness that is generally felt when no one wishes to push themselves forward as the focus of attention. In the lull, a twittering of laughter could be heard. I looked towards a door which must have led to the small room with the paintings. There was another burst of giggling but louder this time.

"Surely we can prevail upon somebody?" said Mr Bingley.

Miss Morris, a girl I did not know well, looked frantically about the room, then rushed over to open the door. The doorway framed the room inside like a theatre curtain drawn back to reveal a scene from a licentious play. Mr Denny sat in a too relaxed posture on the chaise longue and Lydia threw her arms about him and kissed him on the lips. Catching sight of their scandalised audience, Mr Denny moved Lydia aside.

"Miss Morris, allow me to explain. I did not know that Miss Lydia was about to—"

"We're meant to be engaged!" wailed Miss Morris as she fled the room to the accompaniment of shocked gasps, piteous comments and accusations.

Mama had been struck into silence, which was quite something. Papa went white. Lizzy was crying with humiliation and Jane looked close to fainting when Miss Bingley swooped upon her saying, "You will get your family out of this house at once. At *once*, Miss Bennet."

Through the doorway I could see the painting of the woman holding the bonnet and the other standing behind. It seemed almost as though they were looking at me, willing me to do something.

"We're going." Lizzy gripped my arm, frowning at me. "Mary, I do not see how you can be smiling at a time like this. We need to leave. *Now.*"

Tearing my gaze from the portrait, I looked at Lizzy. "I'll get my bonnet."

VOLUME I, CHAPTER XIII

A Performance & a Proposal

One hour would be plenty. While Lizzy steered Lydia through the front door and down the drive where our carriage and Thomas awaited us, I snuck behind a curtain in the vestibule, took out a tattered needle case from my reticule and unpicked one stitch from the bonnet.

"Come along, Mary!" growled Papa.

"I am ready," I said, putting on the bonnet and finding myself back at the supper table. In my mind, I had already eaten my fill but my stomach, empty once more, grumbled. A few moments of steady breathing were enough to quell the queasiness I felt and then, for the second time, I indulged in white soup with crusty bread, slices of pink roasted beef, chicken, buttered carrots and leeks, followed by a bowl of summer berries and cream. I had no nerves putting me off my food. I had already decided what was to be done.

Unfortunately, I could do nothing about Mama embarrassing her nearest relations but, as soon as Mr Bingley mentioned having a song, I rushed to the pianoforte. I could never have imagined putting my well-honed skills to better use than this. Blessedly few seconds of quiet had elapsed before I commenced my song: 'The Lass of Richmond Hill', a piece I had copied from Charlotte's collection.

I struck the keys with more force than the composer had intended and, just as the sounds betokening improper flirtation began in the next room, I filled my lungs like a pair of bellows and started to sing with exceptional volume. Being preoccupied with how loud I was singing, I was not always quite accurate with the melody. Yet, on I sang:

> *Ye zephyrs gay that fan the air,*
> *And wonton through the grove,*
> *O whisper to my charming fair,*
> *I die for her I love.*
> *How happy will the shepherd be*
> *Who calls this nymph his own!*
> *O may her choice be fix'd on me!*
> *Mine's fix'd on her alone.*

Planting my fingers down on the last chord, I looked askance at the door. Discerning muffled tones, I lost no time in launching into my next piece, selecting some verses from the song of deplorable domestic captivity, 'Alcanzor and Zayda'.

As well as being pleased that my plan to hide Lydia's scandalous behaviour was succeeding, I felt that I was also gaining some resonance as well as volume, so I played and sang with increasing enthusiasm. However, I began to doubt the latter cause for satisfaction when I saw Lizzy's face. Her obvious mortification at my performance was an arrow piercing through me. She did not consider that I was singing well and, by almost shaking her head, raising her eyebrows which drew together, opening her mouth in shock and by other subtle means, she displayed to me her wish that I would desist. I looked down at the keys, glanced at the door again, and pressed on into the next verse, my voice faltering:

> *Canst thou think I thus will lose thee?*
> *Canst thou hold my love so small?*
> *No! A thousand times I'll perish!*
> *My curst rival too shall fall.*
> *Canst thou, wilt thou, yield thus to them.*
> *O break forth and fly to me;*
> *This fond heart shall bleed to save thee,*
> *These fond arms shall shelter thee.*

Lydia slipped back into the dining room with a grin, her cheeks flushed. Thus released from my duty, I ended the song upon the closing of this verse to a thin scattering of applause, chiefly from Charlotte and Chamberlayne. I coughed just then and it seemed that Papa and Lizzy mistook this for clearing my throat, ready to sing again.

After they exchanged a look, Papa stood up and said, "That will do extremely well, child. You have delighted us long enough. Let the other young ladies have time to exhibit."

The sight of people's discomfort at his words humiliated me more than the words themselves. Lizzy looked sorry, Jane and Mr Bingley awkward. Charlotte had a pained expression and dropt her gaze to the floor. I got up, shakily, and Mrs Hurst took my place at the instrument. Returning to my seat, I focussed on my breathing, willing myself not to shew any sign of emotion, having to remind myself of my great accomplishment – I had saved my family from shame and much greater chagrin than now persisted. This was indeed the lesser of two evils.

I held my chin high when I got into the carriage that evening for, thanks to my intervention, far from being the first family to leave, we were the last to depart and, Mr Bingley assured us, we had been more than welcome to stay longer had we wished to.

As I had expected, Mr Collins was not planning a lengthy courtship of Lizzy. The teapot from the next morning's breakfast had not yet cooled before his proposal of marriage was offered. However, his expectations, as well as Mama's, were disappointed.

Ignoring Jane's chiding, Lydia, Kitty and I listened in at the library door after news of the refusal had spread through the house. Mr Collins had sought the sanctuary of the garden, leaving Mama and Papa to use their influence on Lizzy.

"An unhappy alternative is before you, Elizabeth," said Papa. I should have liked for him to continue with: 'a life married to someone you lack affection for or the prospect of becoming an old maid, haunted by the knowledge that you had disappointed your family and deprived your mother and sisters of the prospect of a roof over their heads in the event of my death' – but he didn't. "From this day you must be a stranger to one of your parents." He paused. "Your mother will never see you again if you do *not* marry Mr Collins," he said, "and I will never see you again if you *do*."

I ground my teeth, aware that no amount of unpicking could change this situation. Lizzy had always said she would not marry without love. If only she had less sensibility and more rational prudence. The prospect of protecting herself, her mother and sisters from becoming destitute ought to be enough of an inducement for her to marry!

Later that day, I saw Lizzy, Jane and Kitty shuffle out of the breakfast room and ease the door shut.

"Are you escaping our cousin?" I asked.

"Aye," said Kitty with a shudder. "I'm terrified that he'll pick another one of us to ask. Lydia's brave though, she wants to stay for the entertainment of his conversation with Mama."

"And Charlotte," said Lizzy.

"Charlotte?" I said, my brows drawing together. "*She's* in there?"

"She just arrived," said Jane. "Oh, I hope she does not feel awkward with such a discussion going on."

"She had the chance to leave with us," said Kitty, shrugging. "Perhaps she's as nosey as Lydia!"

I took myself to my room and back to my bonnet. *Mama's lace cap, Mama's lace cap*, I thought, concentrating as best I could.

"But we are all liable to error," came Mr Collins' voice. "I have certainly meant well through the whole affair. My object has been to secure an amiable companion for myself, with due consideration for the advantage of all your family . . ." From here his words could no longer be discerned through Mama's crying, a pitiful sound which I cut short by whipping the bonnet off my head again. I thought it odd, both that they were discussing this sensitive matter in front of a visitor and that Charlotte had staid in the room to hear them.

Charlotte spent the day with us and was most useful at dinner in listening to Mr Collins prattle on about Lady Catherine of Rosings Park. The way he talked of her elegance and condescension, one might think the woman were an empress. He hinted that her patronage might extend to assisting his brothers in their careers – both Captain Frederick Collins in the army and Mr Stephen Collins, a barrister at the Old Bailey. As tedious as his conversation was, Charlotte was polite enough to seem interested and Mr Collins was diverted from other subjects of conversation which might have been awkward for more than just Lizzy.

Her kindness in tolerating Mr Collins' conversation extended through much of the day. I gave her opportunities to have a period of respite from him – drawing him away to take a turn about the shrubbery whilst I asked him about Fordyce's sermons; walking down to the end of the garden to discuss the flora and fauna that thrived there and taking in views of the house from the side so that I could point out the reconstructed parts of the southern end of the house which had suffered damage in the civil war. However, each time I attempted to give Charlotte a rest from him, she accompanied us as well, seeming not to understand my intention, despite my hints.

The next day, I joined my sisters in a walk to Meryton, keen to escape the atmosphere at home which Mama's nerves and the cloud of resentfulness which surrounded Mr Collins were making less conducive to study or leisure.

Lydia was determined to go to The Bull to see if Mr Wickham had returned from London.

"Is this a Bennet I see before me?" We all turned to see the very gentleman Lydia sought, dazzling red cutting through the dull, dusty colour of the street. "No indeed, it is five – how fortunate, by gad!"

Lizzy laughed more than Mr Wickham's adulterated Shakespeare quotation deserved. Her face was animated, fixed on his, a flower facing the sun. Oh, Lizzy! You had better not have refused Mr Collins for an officer without wealth, property or prospects, I thought.

I went into the milliner's shop so that I could pretend to be looking at the bonnets in the window display whilst I was in fact studying the faces of my companions on the street outside. Lizzy, in her posture, movements and glances, navigated the careful dance between flirtation and decorum with regards to Mr Wickham. His features were open and pleasing but there was a hint of vanity in the way he appeared unsurprised at Lizzy's admiration.

"These are very fashionable in London at the moment, miss," said Mr Pratt, indicating the large silk flowers decorating a straw bonnet.

"I beg your pardon?" I said.

"They're quite the thing this season in London."

"Is that so?" I nodded, barely attending to his words.

"Indeed. If I may be so bold, might I suggest something like this one." He held up a neat, little straw bonnet, trimmed with pink ribbons. "Something a little more," his eyes were fixed on my bonnet, "à la mode, shall we say, compared with. . ."

I raised my eyebrows at him.

"That is to say . . ." His eye twitched.

"I find you are too bold, Mr Pratt," I said, turning from him.

"F-forgive me, miss. I only meant—"

But I left the shop before I could hear the rest of his blathering.

"I hear from your sisters that our friend, Miss Lucas, has been making herself most useful," said Chamberlayne, taking his place beside me as we walked home. He had joined our group as we walked about Meryton high street and Lizzy had invited both he and Mr Wickham to take tea with us at Longbourn.

"Since Lizzy refused Mr Collins, things have been rather awkward at home," I replied. "By drawing him away from Lizzy's company and the unpleasant subject of her rejection of him, Charlotte has shewn much thoughtfulness."

"Hmm. Thoughtful perhaps." Chamberlayne did not sound convinced. "But opportunistic may be closer to the mark."

"What do you mean?"

He was about to respond when Lydia linked her arm through his and steered him away.

"Kitty heard the most amusing rumour about Sanderson – you must tell me if you know whether it's true or not!" she exclaimed. "I should ask Wickham but he is too much occupied in *serious* conversation."

Mr Wickham turned with smiling eyes directed at Lydia before returning to his tête-à-tête with Lizzy.

Chamberlayne's hand brushed the hilt of his sword, an unconscious gesture of defensiveness I thought, and there was a nervous edge to his voice when he answered, "What rumour, pray?"

"Why, that he's been seen wearing ladies' clothes! What a fine joke that would be if it were true!"

He grinned and gestured to Lydia's gown. "Who would not wish to be in possession of such pretty garments as you chuse to wear, Miss Lydia? Such taste! Such style! Such effortless elegance! I know not about Sanderson but I would have you pick out my wardrobe. Miss Mary may chuse the bonnet though." He winked at me.

"Ha! But she has no eye for such things! No, I would chuse you a delicate, straw bonnet with green ribbons to match your eyes. How fine you would look!" She laughed and joked the rest of the way home, quite monopolising my friend's attention.

VOLUME I, CHAPTER XIV

Odd Behaviour

Lizzy introduced the officers to Mama and Papa, no doubt hoping for them to see the potential of Mr Wickham as a match but, though the gentleman might, with his looks and red coat, charm Mama, I did not suppose that Papa would be so enamoured. After the etiquette of introduction and tea being called for, Jane received a letter from Netherfield. She took it to a corner and was quite motionless as she read it. Folding it up small, she clutched it in her hand and turned to join our conversation, her face paler than beforehand.

Later, after the officers had taken their leave, I discerned an unspoken communication between Lizzy and Jane and the pair of them surreptitiously absented themselves from the drawing room. No one else appeared to notice that anything was amiss. I waited a few moments before leaving as well, creeping up the stairs in time to see them go into their bedroom.

Mrs Hill was polishing the banister so I could not get away with eavesdropping in the conventional way, so I went to my own room and put on my bonnet. Unfortunately, their speech was faint. I could picture one of their bonnets, which mine had formed a connection with, sitting on a shelf in the closet, muffled by muslins. I could only make out snatches of their conversation, some of which, I assumed, was read directly from the letter.

". . . her equal for beauty, elegance and accomplishments and the affection she inspires . . . hereafter our sister . . . most kindly to put me on my guard . . . wants him to marry Miss Darcy . . . you cannot seriously imagine . . . A thousand things may arise in six months!"

I was able to infer more from this fragmented information than we were later told by Lizzy and Jane. They informed us that the Bingley family had left Netherfield to spend a period of time in London. Whilst this in itself was an unfortunate, though not catastrophic obstacle, the possibility I was aware of, namely that of a potential match between Mr Bingley and Miss Darcy, was such news to shrivel the hope I had dared to nurture.

After all I had done to bring Jane and Mr Bingley together, I felt this blow keenly and it made me resent Lizzy's refusal of Mr Collins all the more. Opportunities to secure the future of our family were few and not able to be guaranteed. Oh, why had Mr Bingley left when he had clearly been developing an affection for Jane?

I found it difficult to hide my annoyance at Lizzy and, more than once I pretended not to hear her when she asked me to pass her an item at table when we dined with the Lucases that evening.

Charlotte was as surprised as I was at the departure of the Bingleys but tried to reassure Jane that the sisters' wishing to remain in Town did not prevent the brother from returning into Hertfordshire.

I wanted to have a moment alone with Charlotte to tell her what Miss Bingley had written regarding Miss Darcy, to confide in her my fears and my disappointment. However, when an opportunity arose for the two of us to converse in a corner of the drawing room, Charlotte glanced at me awkwardly, then left my company to sit at a card table with Kitty, Lydia and Maria, before I had the chance to say a word.

I happened to look through the window of the oriel rather early the next morning, having woken from an unpleasant dream and not been able to return to sleep, and I leant closer to the glass at the sight of Mr Collins walking from the house towards the Meryton road, his stride swift and posture purposeful. What could he have been about at that hour?

Later, I walked out to Meryton with Kitty and Lydia, though

once we got to the high street they abandoned me for a gathering of officers. Glad to have some time to myself, I borrowed some books from Clarke's before wandering past the shops. A blue printed muslin in Mrs Dyer's, the dressmakers, caught my eye. Mrs Pepperstock emerged from this shop, which puzzled me as I did not think she had the means to purchase anything from Mrs Dyers. She tucked a cloth over something in her basket before entering Mr Pratt's shop. I crept closer, watching her through the window, half hidden by a row of gentlemen's hats. She scanned the shop, passing her hand over some rolls of ribbon.

"Careful!" shrieked Mrs Pratt from around a corner in the back part of the shop.

Mrs Pepperstock froze and Mr Pratt, who was carrying a large stack of hats, dropt them so that they rolled across the floor.

"What is it, my dear?" he called.

"Careful not to drop anything on the floor. You haven't swept it yet."

Mr Pratt mouthed an obscenity – at least I think that's what he mouthed – and, while he was picking up the new and now dusty stock, I caught a glimpse of green in Mrs Pepperstock's hand. Then it was gone. Had she just stolen from Mr Pratt? I laughed, still watching her as I made to walk on, my attention so caught up that I walked into the vicar who dropt a handful of letters.

"My apologies, Mr Palmer," I said, helping him pick them up, snatching up an envelope marked with ink blotches before it blew into a puddle. I only took in half of what Mr Palmer was saying about requests for Christening dates and for banns to be read. Instead, I looked back into the shop. Mrs Pepperstock had gone.

"Here you are." I pushed the last of the letters into Mr Palmer's hand.

We were all at home again long before Mr Collins returned and, when Mama asked him of his whereabouts that morning, he was evasive in his answers. He brought back no purchases and his boots shewed no signs of mud, so he could not have gone far. All that was different about him was an ink smudge on his thumb and a lightness of spirit which exhibited itself in his whistling merry tunes and being unexpectedly civil towards Lizzy to whom he had, since his rejection, adopted a coldness of demeanour. Twice he began sentences which he cut short, putting his inky hand to his mouth and exhibiting an air of smugness.

I accounted for his behaviour by considering that he was making the effort to end his visit on good terms, being careful not to say anything to spoil that outcome before he left the next morning as planned. With the proximity of his departure, we found an increase in our own civility towards him, knowing that we would not have to put up with his presence much longer.

"You are most welcome to visit us again at Longbourn in due course, Mr Collins," said Mama as we said our farewells that evening in anticipation of his early departure.

"Thank you, Mrs Bennet. Indeed, now that the branches of our family have reunited, I hope to take the liberty of trespassing on your hospitality again very soon."

A stunned silence followed this statement and I for one retired to bed with not a small degree of bemusement.

"Mary!" Mama exclaimed in a half whisper before coming into my room that night. "I must speak with you. It is my belief that Mr Collins plans such a hasty second visit as a compliment to you."

"Pray, what do you mean, Mama?"

"Why, that he may plan to make you an offer of his hand of course!"

I froze where I sat, on the edge of my bed. "Perhaps he still hopes that Lizzy will change her mind?"

She sighed. "I think Mr Collins is finally aware of Lizzy's stubborn nature. But you do not dislike him as much as your sisters do; that is quite clear."

"I . . . well . . . I feel sorry for him when I know that others are ridiculing him. Now and then he makes observations about life and human nature which are not without merit, even if they are not original. He is not as stupid as others make him out to be but he can only ever be my inferior in that regard and— to *marry* him?"

"Think about it, Mary. If you married him, you would single-handedly rescue us from destitution. We could keep our home." She held my face in her hands and smiled. I wondered if she meant to embrace me then, something she had not done for many years, but then she made for the door. "Think about it," she repeated before leaving me to go to bed.

Did being the saviour of my family outweigh the repulsion I felt at the idea of being Mr Collins' wife? My sleep was fractured that night as my waking and dreaming mind dwelt upon this question.

Mr Collins had left before any of us were about, excepting the servants, and all the evidence of his presence that remained was a letter on the side table in the vestibule dated from the preceding day.

Friday 29th Nov 1811

My dear cousins,

Please accept my profuse thanks for your hospitality. I beg that you forgive my benefitting so much from it and I apologise for these ink blots. It seems that none of the available pen nibs where I sit here writing match the quality of those at Longbourn. My stay has brought me immeasurable satisfaction and I flatter myself that it was a happy thought indeed that led me to heal the longstanding ill feeling between our families. Lady Catherine de Bourgh would approve, not only of this action but of your good selves when I regale her with accounts of your kindness. I shall miss the comforts of Longbourn when I reach my humble abode but, rest assured, I shall return before long. More of this later, but for now, I take my leave.

Your humble servant,
W. Collins

Charlotte came by later that day and, though she answered my greeting, she did not meet my eye. When she handed Mrs Hill her bonnet, I noticed spots of ink like black freckles on her wrist. I was about to point these out to her in case she were unaware of them but she turned from me and asked Lizzy if the two of them might speak alone. Lizzy walked with her into the front parlour. I could not listen at the door in secret, nor could I use my bonnet to hear them, neither of them carrying any headwear. I went to the window seat upstairs and reflected upon all of my latest interactions with Charlotte, trying to work out what I had done or said to have made her so uneasy in my company. In this I was unsuccessful.

About ten minutes later, Charlotte stepped out onto the drive. She stopped and turned to look up at me, her expression blank. Then she walked away, her bonnet lowered against the wind.

VOLUME I, CHAPTER XV
Knots in the Thread

"Miss Mary," said Sally, trotting through the shrubbery to where I sat, her arms wrapped around herself in lieu of a shawl. "Bit chilly to be sitting out, isn't it, miss?"

"At least it's quiet. Or was," I muttered. "What is it, Sally?"

"My mistress told me to fetch you to the front parlour."

I looked up from my reading. I had been attempting to open my mind to one of Christopher Wyvill's works defending political reformation in England, hoping that this topic might engross me. However, I found that my mind frequently reverted to thoughts of Charlotte's puzzling visit of that morning.

"What does Mama want me for?"

"Sir William Lucas is here."

"I'm sure he would not object to my remaining where I am. I should like to finish this today."

"I believe he wants to talk to all of you, if I heard right."

"All of us? Is something wrong?" I studied Sally's face but saw no signs of agitation. In fact, she sniffed in so nonchalant a manner that it bordered on the vulgar.

She shrugged. "I couldn't say, miss."

I abandoned my reading and went to the parlour where I sat by the window and took up my sewing, trying to convince myself that dread was not gnawing at my insides. I refused to put my fears into words.

"I, on behalf of my family, have come to offer my compliments to you all, my dear neighbours, whose society and fellowship we value to so high a degree," began Sir William, "as to make this proceeding but a natural progression of our intimacy. I congratulate myself that the connection between our households will soon be more than that of friends but of family."

I stared at him, noting the cheerful ruddiness in his face and a kind of nervous energy about his fidgeting fingers.

"Would you be so good as to enlighten us as to your meaning, my dear Sir William?" said Papa.

"Why, our families are to be joined by the union of your cousin, Mr Collins, and my daughter Charlotte."

I stopped breathing in that moment. It was as if the air had been punched out of my lungs. This could not be. It could not.

"Excuse me, Sir William," said Mama, glancing first at Lizzy, then at me, "but I do not know how— That is, I am afraid you must be mistaken. Entirely mistaken!"

"I . . . do not think so, madam."

"Good Lord! Sir William, how can you tell such a story?" said Lydia, laughing. "Do not you know that Mr Collins wants to marry Lizzy?"

Sir William's colour deepened and there was something of discomfort in the way he coughed. He looked with confusion at Lizzy before addressing Mama. "I believe that there can be no mistake, madam, the fact being that I have spoken on the subject with the persons in question. My consent was applied for and I saw no reason why I should not grant it."

"It is so," said Lizzy. "Charlotte told me of her engagement this morning," there was a stiffness to Lizzy's smile, "and I heartily congratulate you and all your family, Sir William."

The clock ticked and the air felt thick and heavy.

"Indeed," said Jane, who could always be trusted to recall what was due to civility, though the rest of us had lost the use of both words and movement. "Congratulations, sir. I am sure they will be very happy. Mr Collins is a man of excellent character, to be sure." There was a moment of quiet after this statement which lasted slightly too long. "And the distance from Hunsford to London," she added, "why, that will be a most convenient thing for Charlotte." Another pause. "For shopping and such."

I excused myself and slipped out of the front parlour without attracting much attention. Safe in my own room, I slumped against the door, trying to control my breathing which came in uneven bursts. How *could* she? How could she want to *marry* him? Did she not consider that Lizzy might still be persuaded to change her mind? Or that Mr Collins might be brought to hope that another Bennet might suit him as a marriage partner? How could she do this to me? I knew I had to do something. I had to speak with her before Mr Collins went out that morning on his secret errand which, by now, had all mystery stripped from it.

I fumbled for my needle, slipped it under a stitch and pulled. But the thread resisted. I pulled harder, the needle bending at the end with the force I put on it. The thread must have been knotted somehow and caught in the fabric. With stinging eyes and the sight of blurring stitches before me, I threw the needle to the floor and my hands became a vice, strangling the bonnet before I sent it flying as well.

"The blasted thing!"

A sob shook through me but I stopped myself, recoiling from this shapeless emotion. The very shock I experienced at the feeling made me freeze and I stared ahead, into the air, failing to comprehend it.

VOLUME II

VOLUME II, CHAPTER I

The Art of Mending

Perhaps my burst of irrational sentiment had been due to my having hoped, more than I had realised, that Mr Collins would provide future security for our family. But was that enough to elicit such a reaction? I gripped my rationality with greater firmness. Of course this was a shock – Mama and Lydia were not at all lacking in astonishment either – and the suddenness of it might naturally affect one's nerves. This explanation, whilst comforting in its justification of my response, made me shudder. Would I soon need smelling salts to hand at all times, just like Mama?

My logical mind must take charge of my emotions, my physicality and my actions. I retrieved the bonnet from under the bed where I had thrown it, determined to go back and talk to Charlotte. Perhaps she regretted accepting Mr Collins. His proposal was so sudden that she may have answered without giving it due consideration.

As I prepared to unpick a part of the embroidery which I hoped did not contain knotty thread, I paused, feeling a loose patch of the plain woollen fabric on the inside of the bonnet's crown. My fingertips slid against a silky surface beneath the wool. I must have torn an inner hem when I had mishandled it. Holding it now as if it were the fragile egg of some rare species of bird, I turned it over to inspect the damage, biting my lip as I imagined what my great aunt would have thought of my carelessness. Stitches had come away in a line about three inches long, a gash that would, quite literally, take many hours to mend.

"What have I done? I'm so sorry." Taking in what I'd said, I shook my head. "I'm apologising to a bonnet. I must be losing my wits."

Just then, sunlight glinted on something. I eased the wool down a little from the damaged hem, revealing a fabric beneath it – a gleaming, iridescent gold. My fingertip hovered above it before brushing it. I could have been tracing my fingertip over water, the workmanship was so fine. I wondered how my great aunt had afforded or acquired such silk. Why she had concealed it, was less of a mystery. Perhaps I could ask about it at Pratt's shop, or Mrs Dyer's, the dressmakers – but would that elicit unwanted questions?

Bringing myself back to focus on the present situation, I worked out how many hours I would need to go back before Mr Collins' proposal to Charlotte. Then I counted the tiny indentations in the golden silk which shewed how many stitches I had inadvertently torn out. Icy threads trailed through me then as I realised that the number of stitches I had lost corresponded precisely with the number of hours I required to go back. An uncanny question crept through me, one which would repeat itself like a running stitch throughout my life. Was I in control or was the bonnet? I sat there – a statue of myself – the seconds slipping by without me. Eventually, I seized the moment and put it on my head.

Friday 29th November 1811

I was trapped in darkness, feeling my way around a room. Stone scratched against my hands, chilling my fingers. I found no way out until thread-thin slices of light appeared, outlining the shape of a door. Stumbling over to it, I reached about for the handle and gripped it. Iron rattled but the door staid shut. The light beyond the room flickered and I knew that someone was on the other side holding a candle.

"Open the door," I cried. "Please, open the door!" But nothing happened. It came to me then that there was something important I needed to remember, something about Charlotte. I had to get out of this room.

As I woke, pieces of my memory stitched themselves together bit by bit. When I remembered what I had come to do, I leapt out of bed and dressed myself hurriedly, trying to ignore my queasiness due to the leap of time. Upon leaving my room, I heard a humming from Mr Collins' room. Thank goodness. He had not yet left.

"Where's Charlotte?" I asked Maria when I arrived at Lucas Lodge. She looked alarmed.

"Is everything alright, Mary?"

"Yes, of course, I just wish to talk to your sister about a book we've both read."

"Oh," Maria looked confused. "At this hour?"

"Is she about?"

"She's upstairs at the moment but I can fetch her."

"There's no need," I said, making my way upstairs. Charlotte's voice led me to one of the spare rooms where I discovered her helping a maidservant fold a pile of bed linen.

"Edward!" she cried, turning to her youngest brother, a boy of eleven. "Stop tormenting poor Euphemia." A couple of ink drops spat onto her hand from the pen she snatched away from him. "She should claw you for throwing pens at her, now pick up the others." She tutted and stroked the poor frightened cat. "Spoiling the nibs too," she muttered. "Mary!" She turned to me with a look of surprise and a smile. "How lovely to see you. Unexpected . . . but lovely."

"I can help you with those," I said, pointing to the sheets. "Can we talk alone?" I added in an undertone.

Charlotte's smile dropt. "That will do for now, thank you Molly." The servant bobbed a curtsey before leaving and Charlotte sent Edward out of the room. I took up two corners of a sheet, Charlotte taking up the others, and we stepped apart.

Her brow furrowed. "Is something wrong?"

"Now that I am here . . . this is difficult to say." One corner of the sheet fell from my hand and I bent to reach for it again. "I . . . that is, do you have any idea of Mr Collins' intentions?"

"Towards whom?" she said, looking down at the sheet.

"You."

A tangible silence filled the room before she responded. "He is a man who wishes to settle down in life. And he is not the sort of man whom Lizzy would ever accept."

"She might change her mind."

She raised her eyebrows at me.

I sighed. "You are right. She won't. But he meant to chuse from us Bennet girls because he is to inherit Longbourn. Such a match would guarantee that we had a place to live after Papa's death."

"However, he will not be accepted by Jane, who may still have a chance to make an excellent marriage to the man she cares for and Kitty and Lydia would elope with a soldier and disgrace the family sooner than marry a clergyman. We've already established that Lizzy will not have him. So, what about you?"

"Me?"

"Do you wish to marry him, Mary?"

The thought was sensible, rational and prudent and I'd had some time to consider it. So why then did the idea still make my skin crawl? "I don't want you to marry him."

"That wasn't what I asked. Besides, he hasn't even proposed to me."

"But if he should."

"And why – if none of you would accept him – why should I not?" She snatched up the folded sheet and added it to a pile. "What else is there for women like us? If we were independent we would have no need of marriage but that is not the case. I have no illusions about matrimony being a path to romantic happiness. I confess I feel little attraction to the idea of the married state," her gaze focussed on a point in the air, "or to men in general." She shook her head and found another sheet for us to fold. "But the hope of marriage is the only preservation I have. I am twenty-seven. If I were to have any chances left, I would be lucky. My parents already fear that I will end an old maid. My little brothers too, though they joke about it without understanding what it means for them. Can you imagine what it would be like to live to be dependent upon the boys whom I helped care for as infants? To live to be resented by them?" Her face screwed up for a moment, as though something had stung her. "And, should they have families of their own to support, I might sink into poverty. I have never been considered handsome. If I were to receive an offer of marriage from anyone, I would be foolish to expect that, should I refuse, another offer might be made to me in future. I'm not a fool. I don't want to become the poor relation. I don't want that shame. Cannot you understand that?"

"But there are rumours about him. Some suspect his mother of . . . that is, they think he could be illegitimate. If he is no true Collins, he does not deserve to be my father's heir. Would marriage to a man in that position not also bring shame?"

"Such gossip is beneath you, Mary."

I looked down at my feet, my face uncomfortably hot. There was no evidence and I could not even explain to her where I had heard this rumour. Tears were hot in my eyes and I blinked them back. "But he is inferior to you. Your mind, your sensibilities are something apart from his, residing in different worlds. You cannot love him."

"This isn't about love," she snapped. Her tone silenced me for some moments. I felt like a scolded child.

"No," I whispered, an ache swelling in my chest. "I see that for you it is not." Outside, a broad brimmed, black hat bobbed along behind the hedge. "He is here."

Charlotte looked pale as she turned to the window. "Here?"

I nodded. "Go to him. You're the one he's come to talk to. Go."

She abandoned the laundry and surprised me by holding me in her arms. I felt her warmth and breathed in the scent of bread. She must have been helping in the kitchens early that morning. "Forgive me," she whispered. Then she was gone.

Quiet and discreet as a servant, I left through the back door, unnoticed by anyone.

I wished that time would stay still. However, December arrived and Mrs Hill hung a wreath on the door for Advent, the anticipation of Christmas which, for me, was tainted by the knowledge that within a week of twelfth night, Charlotte would become Mrs Collins.

One afternoon, Mr Wickham, Mr Denny and Chamberlayne had come from visiting at the Kings' house in the village next to Longbourn, to persuade my sisters to walk with them into Meryton. I hung back as they prepared to set off, not considering myself to be amongst the number invited on this excursion.

Chamberlayne came up to me with a mock frown. "What might be ailing Miss Mary?"

"Nothing."

"Then you will have no reason to stay at home. Come, the sun is out – not something to be sniffed at on a winter's day – so we should be out likewise."

"I have reading to do."

He assumed a tortured expression and leant upon the table as though he might collapse otherwise.

I laughed. "You belong on the stage, Chamberlayne."

"I like to think so. Do come with us."

He drew from me a faint smile. "Very well."

"Good," he said, flashing his teeth in a grin. "You'd better fetch your bonnet then."

We walked into Meryton, Lizzy and Jane either side of Mr Wickham, Lydia and Kitty with Mr Denny. Chamberlayne and I slowed to lengthen the distance between us and the others.

"It is difficult to picture, that is true," he said, "our Miss Lucas with your cousin."

"Yes, well . . . it is not the match she deserves."

"No. But there is some comfort to be taken from the fact that she will be provided for."

"It occurs to me all of a sudden that women are put into a most unfair position when, in order to prosper, or even survive, they must sell themselves into marriage."

"That is the most revolutionary talk I've heard from you, young lady. Soon you'll be chopping heads off left and right in the French fashion."

"I hope not," I said, surprised he had been able to make me laugh a second time. "If it's a choice between society as we know it or a reign of terror, I chuse the former."

"But it's only natural that things change."

"True, but I believe the most profound changes are the ones that occur gradually. Lamarck writes that the physicality of animal species changes a little over time through habits and efforts, relating to their environment, and these changes are then passed on to the next generation. Perhaps it is the same with the English – with regards to society I mean."

"Well, if Lamarck comes over when the French invade, I'll be sure to discuss it with him, if I'm not too busy crossing swords with his compatriots." He laughed at the notion before regarding me. "Miss Mary—?" He frowned. "Are you quite well?"

We were parallel to Lucas Lodge and I found that I had stopped. Chamberlayne put my arm through his and I was able to continue. He asked me questions about trivial things and, eventually, I found myself talking away. I spoke of how Kitty shewed no sign of giving up her habit of reading ridiculous novels; of witnessing Mrs Pepperstock thieving in the high street and I even revealed to him how I had found the strange gold silk of the bonnet's inner lining.

"That is most fascinating," he said. "Could its powers be derived from that fabric, do you think? Whoever made the bonnet clearly took pains to hide it."

"I cannot say," I replied, "but I think the stitches I make or unpick must pass through the gold."

"Then isn't it the logical conclusion that the power resides within the gold silk?"

"Oh, Chamberlayne, there is nothing logical about any of this. More's the pity. I could do with things making at least the smallest bit of sense."

135

On the high street, we passed Mr Klein's, the jeweller's shop. Young Miss Klein, who was about Kitty's age, was about to step out into the street but, upon setting eyes on Mr Wickham, she blushed and went back indoors. Mr Wickham did not seem to notice but was busy laughing at something Lydia was saying. I shot a puzzled look at Chamberlayne. However, he did not look the least bit surprised.

"Look here," he said, grinning as he pointed through the doorway to the church. The vicar, Mr Palmer, was talking to a group of ladies and no one but Chamberlayne and I noticed Mrs Pepperstock rifling through some sacks and fishing out a pair of thick, green woollen gloves and a matching muffler before disappearing discreetly through the side door.

"Well, I suppose it's not exactly stealing," said Chamberlayne. "Those things were going to be distributed to the poor anyway."

"But they're not meant to just come and take their pick. If they all did that, it would be chaos. I'd wager she'll conveniently forget that she's received a winter gift already when Mr Palmer's charitable ladies come to call."

"Mrs Pepperstock is, what you might call, a survivor," said Chamberlayne. As we turned to follow the others who were crossing the street, the smile on his lips faded. His expression became frozen, making me think of doors being shut and bolted. He had stopped at the side of the street. Ahead of us was Captain Ramton and Mr Wickham went over to talk with him, Lydia and Kitty at his elbows.

"Come," I said, taking Chamberlayne's arm and steering him into the church. "I'm suddenly very interested in viewing the stained glass."

I gazed up at a window depicting the prophetess, Deborah, as I breathed in the smell of dust and cold stone. I did not ask Chamberlayne to confide in me but let the air hang silently between us.

"Mary?"

A shiver ran through me.

"Miss Lucas," said Chamberlayne. "Good day. I see you're getting involved in the vicar's charitable scheme."

"Mama volunteered us for mending the clothing donations that required it."

"Well, that is most admirable. Is it not, Miss Mary?"

I finally looked up at Charlotte's face. She was looking at mine intently.

"If you'll excuse me, ladies, I shall pay my respects to Lady Lucas and Miss Maria." Chamberlayne left us and I was only vaguely aware of his merry tone of greeting from across the nave and Maria's ascertaining that Kitty was outside and going off to chat with her about a novel.

Charlotte put down her bag of mending and reached into the pocket of her cloak. "Here," she said, holding out a small cloth bundle tied with ribbon. "I've carried this with me for my walks into Meryton for some time now, in hopes that I might see you. I made you something and I did not wish to wait until Christmas." She put it into my hands.

"You shouldn't have."

"Open it."

I pulled the ribbon and the cloth fell open to reveal a tiny leather-bound book. However, upon opening it I realised it was in fact a needle case, fashioned to look like a book.

"You made this?"

She nodded.

"It's beautiful. Why did you stitch a letter 'E' on the cover? Were you planning to give it to Lizzy?"

She laughed and turned it the correct way around.

"Ah. I see."

"Just like the shape of Elizabethan Longbourn, you need to see it from the right angle for the 'E' to be an 'M'."

"You remembered."

"Also, I noticed your felt needle case is looking a bit worn and, well, I know how you love books."

"It's perfect." I traced the stitched edges of the case with my fingertip. "You don't know how perfect. I'm sorry I don't have anything to give you."

"Your friendship? Your forgiveness?"

I took her hand, feeling a lump in my throat. "There is nothing to forgive unless it's you forgiving me for my behaviour. My friendship you will always have."

VOLUME II, CHAPTER II

Checkmate

Mrs Pepperstock's cottage smelt of cabbage. Old cabbage. Back at Longbourn, Jane was in bed with a severe chill. She had asked me to visit Mrs Pepperstock in her stead, as the old woman would be expecting our contribution to her winter supplies. If the request had come from anyone else, I might have found a way to refuse.

I set the basket on the table and took out bottles, jars and cloth-wrapped bundles. She wiped two cups with a rag that might once have been white and, no sooner had I put her medicinal gin on the table than she was pouring what she called 'a healthy dose' of it into one of the cups.

"You?" she said, pointing at me with the gin bottle. "You look as though you could use some."

"I don't drink," I replied. "I prefer to keep a clear head."

"Is it clear now?"

It wasn't. It was far from clear. I had spent the whole walk to Mrs Pepperstock's cottage worrying about how life would be for Charlotte when she married and wondering when I might next see her after the event took place. Still, despite my sombre mood, I felt no inclination to touch the bottle which Mrs Pepperstock planted on the table before me.

"My friend is going to be married," I explained.

"Ah." Mrs Pepperstock nodded. "He's a violent man, this man she's to wed?"

"No."

"A poor man then?"

"No."

"Then – I don't understand – why are you sorry that she's to be wed?"

"She doesn't love him and, whilst I wouldn't like to call him a fool . . ."
I sighed. "He's a fool. He'll never understand her nor value her true
worth."

She drained her glass. "Will she have a roof over her head? Food on
her table?"

"Yes. Of course she will."

"Have I ever told you my story, young missy?"

I shook my head, realising how little I knew of this woman,
excepting her poverty, her tendency to thieve, her old vegetable aroma
and her penchant for gin.

"My father was a gentleman." She straightened her back, sitting
tall, chin raised. "There, I see that I have surprised you. I was indeed
a gentleman's daughter, such as you yourself are. Being his only child
to have survived infancy and possessing a degree of prettiness, I had
as large an array of admirers as I could have wished for. I got engaged
to a colonel with golden hair. He danced with the lightness of foot of a
spring lamb. I imagined marrying him and our son one day inheriting
my father's estate. However, before I had the chance to marry or beget
an heir, the extent of my father's debts was revealed and he died, some
say of too much good company."

"But you still married the colonel?"

"Not that fickle b—d, no." She laughed, shewing her few remaining
teeth. "Oh, your face, miss! I should think that's a word you've never
heard let alone said. Why don't you give it a try?"

"No thank you." I gave her a hard look. Illegitimacy was not
something I wished to think about. However, I could not help my
thoughts drifting to Mr Collins and the suspicions about his parentage.

She laughed a dry, crackly laugh. "Anyway, the estate passed to a
distant male relation I never knew I'd had and the colonel skulked off.
This relation took no pity on me but forced me to leave the property.
I staid at one friend's house, then another's, then another's until my

whole acquaintance disowned me. Down to my last few coins, I was forced to go about the streets of Wapping begging. Then one day a pedlar comes by and the next thing I knew was that we were married."

Here I expected her story to reach a happier point. Her message to me was surely going to be that adverse situations are bound to improve. "So he was Mr Pepperstock? He owned this cottage?"

"Oh no, missy, not he. He was Mr Prince. No woman in history ever emptied the piss pot of a more overbearing, vile creature as he was. Still, he put a roof of sorts over my head. I had no wish for him to sell me."

"*Sell* you?" I gaped at her.

"To Mr Pepperstock." She sloshed more gin into her cup. "One day Prince put a rope about my neck and dragged my sorry bones to the market square where he met Mr Pepperstock. Money changed hands and from that day on I was Mrs Pepperstock and Prince was free to marry another poor creature."

"But that's not legal!" I exclaimed.

She shrugged. "I'm not the first wife to be sold in such a way and I doubt I'll be the last."

"But Mr Pepperstock," I said, determined for this story to have a positive ending, "he was a decent man, was he not?"

"Well, he made a pretty decent prize fighter when we lived at Wapping, though he spent more than he won. In time, he stole a horse and took it into his head to be a highwayman, which turned out well at first." She took another gulp of gin. "Until he was caught and hanged, that is. I fled from his creditors, taking enough of his business profits to purchase this place."

I looked around at the cottage bought from the proceeds of theft, violence and probably murder.

"For a long while, it was just me and the cat. Of all my companions in life, he was the one I loved the most and the one who shewed me the most love in return. Until the day he ate a poisoned rat and died."

At this, I grabbed the bottle of gin and took several long gulps, the drink burning its way down my throat.

"You see, no matter how bad things are, they can always be worse."

"I see. I am much obliged to you, Mrs Pepperstock," I said hoarsely, picking up the basket. "Your riches to rags tale was most edifying. Enjoy the calf's foot jelly, it'll spare your few remaining teeth."

"I prefer drink to food," she said raising her cup to me before I closed the door.

I left in a greater fog of low spirits than I had arrived in, seeing in Mrs Pepperstock's story how easily one's fortunes can spiral downwards. Still, poor as she was, she had made herself a woman of property.

The next time I saw Charlotte, she looked somewhat pale, her hands clasped rigidly in her lap as we witnessed the marriage of Mr Denny and Miss Morris. It would be fair to guess that her mind was preoccupied with thoughts of her own marriage in a month's time.

I lost sight of her as we left the church and joined the well-wishers in seeing the happy couple off in their carriage.

"Kiss the bride!" came from someone in the gathering, a cry that was taken up by other voices and, obediently, Mr Denny planted a small, delicate kiss on the new Mrs Denny's lips.

I chuckled. "I suppose that sort of kiss is modest enough for holy ground. Quite different to the sort practised in alleyways though, wouldn't you say, Lydia?"

Lydia turned on me with a face like a vengeful devil. I did not think anyone else had heard me but noted, to my discomfort, that Mr Wickham looked between the two of us with a puzzled expression that danced between a smile and a frown, a look that did not go unnoticed by Lydia.

"I don't know what you're blathering about, Mary." Lydia's voice was unnaturally high. Gripping my elbow, her hand a tiny vice, she whispered in my ear. "You'll regret that, Mary. Just you wait."

"Oh dear," I said, my voice flat. "I'm really scared." I couldn't help my sarcastic tone, yet I realised that annoying Lydia further may not be conducive to my own peace of mind. Still, surely our awkward stalemate would continue. Lydia would not wish for Mama and Papa to hear how well she had known Mr Denny. I wondered then if even I knew the extent of their acquaintance, though perhaps it was better not to know.

Over the next couple of days, my mind was distracted from concern about Lydia's threats by thoughts of Charlotte's pallor at the Dennys' wedding. I decided to go to see her again on the pretext of lending her some sheet music to copy and so, after breakfast, I went into the drawing room with a view to making a selection from my pile of music.

Lydia was sitting at the pianoforte. She noted my entrance, then bashed out a few discordant notes that stung my ears.

"What are you doing, Lydia?"

"You know, it was really very foolish of you to say what you did in front of Wickham."

A chill ran through me and I thought of my bonnet, high up in my closet and hidden amongst blankets, where I had left it the previous evening.

"You don't think he already knows that you're an outrageous flirt?" I said.

"You made me sound worse than that. You practically painted me as a harlot!"

I said nothing but a slight movement of one of my eyebrows made Lydia's face screw up in reddened anger.

"Well! Just you know that I have no regrets in doing what I've done. In fact, the thought of it gives me much pleasure!"

"What do you mean?"

A wry smile spread across her face.

"What did you do, Lydia?" I demanded.

She just looked at me smugly.

"But you wouldn't. You knew I could tell Mama and Papa about you kissing Mr Denny."

"But he's married now. Even if they believed you, they'd have no need to fear that it could happen again."

"What have you done with it?"

Lydia stood and went over to the mirror to neaten her curls. "I'll leave you to your tinny little pianoforte now, Mary. I have some outrageous flirting to do."

I stepped back from her, shaking my head, then raced upstairs. Tossing blankets onto the floor, my hands met empty space and the wall behind. I shoved aside linens and bandboxes, gowns and nightclothes, my heart racing, chills streaming through my veins.

It was gone.

My bonnet was gone.

VOLUME II, CHAPTER III
Mr & Mrs Collins

Christmas came and went and, along with it, a visit from my aunt and uncle who took Jane back to London with them for an extended sojourn. I had my old, straw bonnet on as I watched her leave. As Jane waved and the carriage set off for the London road, I stood twisting the lifeless bonnet ribbons, my hands tight fists, frustrated that I would have no way of overhearing what occurred in London or of adjusting events, if required, to help Jane and Mr Bingley meet again.

I had searched the entire house for a place that Lydia might have stowed the bonnet, from cluttered, dusty attic to spider infested broom cupboard. I wondered if my earlier fabrication that it would curse anyone who destroyed it would have been sufficient to prevent Lydia from doing anything terrible to it. I had inspected all the fireplaces and the dust heap for signs of it having been burned but I found no such evidence. That was a mercy anyhow. My hunt took me through the garden, poultry yard, pig sty, stable and even through the ditches and copses around the land farmed by our tenants. I was not foolish enough to harbour any hope of extracting information from Lydia about what she had done with it.

Grey clouds rolled above as I walked back from yet another exploration of the Camfields' barn. As the sky spat beads of ice at me, the heat of my anger sank into cold despair. What was the point of longing to get the bonnet back? It was lost. I might as well face that fact. Lydia had probably thrown it into the river.

I woke most nights, my stomach in knots, having dreamt of

drowning, as though I were tied to the bonnet as it descended into a watery resting place, powerless to save myself. Sometimes in my dreams, my sisters and Mama were drowning too, all giving me venomous looks – even Jane – blaming me for their fate. Occasionally, Charlotte appeared in these dreams but she was not angry like the others. In her face, I saw resignation and acceptance. Somehow this was worse.

"It is my duty to drown," dream-Charlotte would say.

The day of her wedding was now fast approaching and there was no way to avert it. She was bound to her decision and I could no longer blame her. I understood that her options were few but I felt for her, imagining the sacrifice of giving up her singleness for such a man as Mr William Collins.

It was in a state of precarious nerves that I spoke with her when she visited the day before the ceremony. After talking with my family and giving thanks for their congratulations, despite the cold delivery of Mama's, she joined me at the pianoforte where I was flicking through sheet music, an action which occupied my hands and gave the impression of holding my attention.

She sat beside me on the piano stool, her gaze skimming me before resting on the black and white keys. "I will write to you."

I nodded, rummaging through another pile of music.

"I wondered if – in the Spring – if you would come to stay with me at Hunsford."

I felt the involuntary smile take hostage of my face.

"I am not likely to leave Kent for some time I believe," she continued. "Only come if you'd like to," she added, looking at her hands. "Papa and Maria are coming, so you could travel with them. It would give me great pleasure to have that to look forward to." She sat stiffly. Her brow held a delicate crease. I could only imagine how she must be feeling now that her wedding was imminent.

"Of course. I shall ask Mama and Papa if I may go."

The ceremony on the following day was a modest, quiet affair, the rain having put off a number of townsfolk from coming. Charlotte dressed simply, her only adornment being my gift to her earlier that morning. I had found a cluster of winter aconite beneath the trees at the far end of our garden. Though the stalks were short and the flowers nought but yellow beads, I arranged them with sprigs of rosemary and other pieces of foliage to turn them into an attractive posy, if a diminutive one. Charlotte said little after leaving the church and smiled even less. The carriage rumbled away, conveying her and her new husband to their life together.

She did not look back.

During the following weeks, I kept my sights on the day I would set off for Hunsford. With no means of stitching them away, the hours crawled by, lengthened by the mundanity of domestic squabbles, visiting and balls, until, at last, the appointed day in March presented itself. I had barely slept the night before, I found it hard to eat, my heart raced at an unprecedented speed and I could not focus on one task for any length of time. From what my mutinous sensibilities sprang from, I did not understand. I recalled reading a recent article from the Royal Society, by a Dr Parry, in which he describes his treatment of a woman suffering from nervous affections, with symptoms such as head-ache, laboured breathing, mania and convulsions, arising from a violent impulse of blood into the vessels of the brain. He applied pressure with his thumbs to the woman's carotid arteries until the symptoms ceased. I tried this now, pressing either side of my neck.

I did not consider the experiment successful and began to doubt the professed intelligence of our eminent scientists. Despite several attempts, I remained in a state of excitement. However, with much effort of concentration, I unpacked and repacked my case so that I was able to bask in the satisfaction of my perfect arrangement of belongings, confident of minimal creases and a convenient, though not excessive, selection of clothing.

"Salutations, dear family!" called Mr Collins as Sir William Lucas, Maria and I got out of the carriage at Hunsford parsonage. "You are most welcome to my humble abode and I trust you shall see for yourselves how comfortable our dear Charlotte is in her new establishment and how she wants for nothing and how the condescension of my patroness, Lady Catherine de Bourgh, honours her as well as myself."

"Indeed, Mr Collins, I thank you," Sir William cast his eye over the house. "It is a larger dwelling than I had expected."

"All thanks to the benevolence of Lady Catherine's ancestors. Rosings has always taken care of its clergymen. Look," he said, pointing, "beyond those trees, you may just make out several of the chimneys of the great house."

"Rosings!" cried Maria, standing on her toes and craning her neck, though that could do little to improve her view.

"You're here!"

I turned.

Charlotte hurried up the drive. "You're earlier than I was expecting. I was helping Martha feed the chickens. A sweet girl but she needs much guidance. I hope your journey was not uncomfortable?"

My initial impression was that she seemed just the same as ever she was and I wondered that I should have expected her to be altered. I observed no obvious signs of regret or misery but of course she would wish to make the best of things. However, if I did notice a change, it was perhaps an increase of confidence that must have come from running her own household.

After we had settled into our rooms and taken some refreshment, Mr Collins shewed us around his garden.

"My dear Charlotte is most pleased with the arrangement of these flower beds," he said, waving his arms about as if he were conducting an orchestra. "Lady Catherine said they should be just so. And she finds the shrubbery much to her taste, do you not, my dear?"

"What's that, my dear?"

"And it is a great pleasure for her to offer guests our own honey for their bread. Can you see the hives? They're over there, behind the cucumber beds. The cucumbers grow rather well in that spot. Last year, Lady Catherine herself made a point of admiring their girth . . ." Mr Collins' prattle trailed off as Charlotte and I had slowed our pace, allowing the others to get ahead of us.

"According to your husband, you must be very contented indeed," I said.

"He is keen to impress my father."

"But it is a lovely garden. He has every right to enthuse about it."

"True," she said. "He spends much time in the garden."

"And do you?"

"I more often take the air on walks in the woods. I know little of how to care for plants and I think Mr Collins knows even less. He pruned these rosebushes while we were still getting frosts and killed off all the new leaves, look. Still, I confess I pretend to bow to his superior knowledge, the easier to encourage him to be frequently out in his garden."

"I see."

We ambled on, catching up with the others who had paused by another flower bed. Mr Collins was talking of the contrast in colours that would be most attractive when his purple columbines were to bloom in the summer beside the pale pink roses. I peered over at the plants he thought to be columbines, inspecting the shapes of their leaves.

"I do not wish to discourage your husband in his horticultural endeavours," I whispered, "but I hope he washes his hands well after attending to the plants he calls columbines."

"Why particularly those?"

"Because they are aconites, also known as wolf's bane. Unlike the winter aconites in your wedding posy, these are rather poisonous."

"How dreadful! I cannot imagine what the previous resident of the parsonage had been about! Do not fear, I'll be sure to disillusion him in this instance."

VOLUME II, CHAPTER IV

Good Breeding

By the creaking of steps as people rushed about and the tones of surprise I discerned, I wondered if something distressing had happened to one of the household of Hunsford parsonage.

Maria battered at my door. "Mary! Make haste and come downstairs!"

"What's the matter?" I asked.

"You'll never guess!" she called from the landing.

Involuntarily, I pictured Mr Collins, in an attempt to impress Lady Catherine with his extensive vocabulary, falling from the ladder in the library after reaching for a copy of Dr Johnson's dictionary, or perhaps collapsing in the dining room, choking on an insufficiently boiled potato.

"Is anyone unwell?" I said. Upon opening my bedroom door, I noted the expression of excitement in Maria's face and deduced that no one had met with an untimely death. However, I could not be quite certain that, if Mr Collins had met his end, Maria's visage would not appear similar to how it did now.

"Oh, no, it's nothing like that."

"Ah. . . . Good."

I followed her to the dining room where we had a view of the front gate. Two women in a phaeton had pulled up beside it and Charlotte and Mr Collins were rushing out to meet them. The younger woman contrasted with the other by her pallor, her petite build and her fine attire.

"I suppose that is Miss de Bourgh," I said to Maria. "Who's the other lady?"

"That is Mrs Jenkinson, her old governess, now companion. Charlotte said that Lady Catherine has not let her daughter drive out alone ever since Mrs Jenkinson spoke of seeing some gypsies in a nearby field."

"I should not think any harm would come to her from gypsies. Highwaymen perhaps, though I doubt there are many of them frequenting the little roads around Hunsford."

When the phaeton moved on, Maria returned to her needlework and I sought out Charlotte to ask about her callers.

"Of course I did not say anything then! How would that have seemed?" Mr Collins' voice was raised. I hesitated outside the parlour door.

"I am sure she paid no heed to my appearance. In any case, you say that the de Bourghs like for dress to display the distinctions of rank."

"But to be wearing a filthy apron in the presence of Lady Catherine's daughter?" I flinched at the aggressive tone which I had never heard from Mr Collins before. "Next time I insist that you consider how your appearance reflects upon me. In all ways, we must shew the de Bourghs our respect." He opened the door to leave and started at the sight of me. "Oh, Miss Mary!" With a flurry of blinking, he regained his composure. "I must congratulate you on your very good fortune."

I frowned. "To what are you referring?"

"Why, to the fact that we are all invited to dine at Rosings on the morrow. Such affability and condescension!"

"Yes, it is all very condescending." I narrowed my eyes at him. "Mr Collins, I believe a stray dog has got into the front garden and befouled the lawn. I do hope that Miss de Bourgh does not drive past this way on her return home and notice the unsightliness."

"Good gracious! I must see that it is taken care of."

"Are you alright?" I said to Charlotte when we were alone.

"Oh yes." She busied herself with rearranging her writing things on the desk. "So, tell me how things are with your sisters. We've had little chance to talk properly yet. Is Jane still in London?"

"She is. Lizzy is staying with my aunt and uncle for a short visit there too."

"And does she still have eyes for Mr Wickham?"

"I think not. Kitty tells me that his attentions have diverted to Miss King, who has lately come into her inheritance of course."

"How convenient for him," she said, smiling. "And how did Lizzy respond to that?"

"Much better than I would have anticipated. I think that, whilst she was flattered by him, her affections cannot have been deeply involved."

"I wish that something more had come of Mr Darcy's attentions to her," said Charlotte. "That dance at the Netherfield ball! I shall never forget how he looked at her."

"Nor I."

"It is such a shame that she had decided to dislike him. However, just as her attachment to Wickham did not prove to be well formed, perhaps her disdain for the other gentleman might be equally fleeting."

"That may be but my main concern in the matter is whether Mr Darcy's admiration of my sister might be strong enough to overlook the vulgarity of my mother. And Lydia," I added.

"I wouldn't say that about your mother, Mary."

"You heard her at the Netherfield ball. More significantly, so did Mr Darcy."

"Well, that was some time ago. He may have put the episode out of his mind. Do you expect Lizzy and Jane will see Mr Darcy and Mr Bingley in Town?"

"Lizzy wrote to Papa a few days ago that she, Jane and our aunt had walked to Fortnum's and, along the way, had happened upon Mr Bingley who was just coming out of Boodle's club. The outcome of it all was that they, as well as my aunt and uncle, were invited to dine at his house."

Charlotte's face lit up in a smile. "That is most promising."

"And most timely. I was starting to worry that, with all the distractions of London, Mr Bingley might forget how happy he had been in Hertfordshire. I am glad that he shall meet my aunt and uncle too, then he will see that they are not the vulgar relations Miss Bingley might paint them as."

"Though you do not know whether Miss Bingley truly expressed such an opinion."

"No. To be sure," I lied. "Only it would be congruous with my perception of her character."

"I think that his absence from Jane might prove to have been all for the good," she continued. "Now that they are reunited, he will no doubt feel how empty his time had been without her."

I nodded. "Time does feel empty when we are apart from those we care for."

Even from a distance, Rosings struck me with its imposing grandeur, as cathedrals must have made medieval mud hut dwellers gaze in awe. It cut across the landscape, holding its many chimneys aloft, a pronged crown on its head. The place glared at us through glittering windows, sitting enthroned amongst rising lawns and framed by ancient woodland. The belittling effect of such greatness made me unconsciously touch my bonnet but, upon remembering that it was not the one bonnet that could give me a feeling of confidence, I hung my head.

"Do not make yourself uneasy, my dear cousin, about your apparel," said Mr Collins as we walked up the serpentine drive. "Lady Catherine will not think the worse of you for being simply dressed."

"That is a comfort," I replied. "Indeed, I have no wish to muddy the boundaries which distinguish one rank from another."

A steward led us through an antechamber into a cavernous room, then bowed so low I feared his wig would fall off. The panelled walls were decked in oil paintings of well-dressed men, women and children, most bearing noticeable resemblances, so that we seemed to be surrounded and scrutinised by the ghosts of the de Bourgh family. Shafts of sunlight gave a pearly sheen to marble table tops and glinted off gilded legs. Japanese vases sat beside Roman busts which half bowed in deference to the greatness around them. In the midst of all this splendour sat a tall woman with sharp eyes and a prominent nose which Mr Collins would no doubt call aristocratic. So here sat the commander of Rosings Park.

"Lady Catherine, Miss de Bourgh, Mrs Jenkinson, this is my father, Sir William Lucas," said Charlotte, "my sister, Maria, and Miss Mary Bennet, Mr Collins' cousin."

Lady Catherine rose to receive us, though of course it was out of the question that she should return our curtseys. Sir William would not stop bowing until Charlotte caught his eye. As we sat down, the silence was punctuated only by a clock ticking and I wondered who would be next to speak.

Mr Collins leant forward, perched on the edge of his seat. "Your ladyship, I—"

"Do you approve of your daughter's new home?" said Lady Catherine, turning to Sir William.

Sir William stammered his way through an affirmative answer.

"Mrs Collins, I hope you have followed my instructions and got rid of those Rosecombs? You must make your poultry yard as efficient as you can and it's all about breeding. The Sussex hens are all very well but you must acquire Derbyshire Redcaps."

"I shall endeavour to arrange it, your ladyship."

"Speak to my steward and he shall find someone to assist you. Derbyshire Redcaps are the only hens worth keeping, being the strongest and healthiest in the country. My sister, Lady Anne Darcy, would not eat an egg from a hen of any other breed and, to honour her memory, neither do I. Though I do recall her criticism regarding the diminutive size of the cocks."

I caught Charlotte's eye, pursing my lips so that I could not smile. She covered her mouth and might have looked as though she were suppressing a sneeze.

When we sat down to dinner, I had to stifle a shock of laughter at the vast array of dishes. When I pulled a large shrimp from a crustacean pyramid, causing the pile to collapse and a langoustine to tumble with a plop into Miss De Burgh's soup bowl, Charlotte snorted into her napkin whilst I sat frozen, wide-eyed and blushing. The rest of dinner passed without much incident. I tried to talk to Miss de Bourgh but I struggled to break through her wall of timidity. After a syllabub and a selection of fruits, including oranges which I had tasted only twice before, the women took Lady Catherine's cue and retired into the drawing room.

"Your father's estate is entailed on Mr Collins," said Lady Catherine when we were sat down again.

"It is."

"My Anne suffers from no such circumstance. I see no occasion for entailing estates from the female line and, fortunately, it was not thought necessary in Sir Lewis de Bourgh's family."

"Is that so?" I said. "That must be of comfort to you, Miss de Bourgh."

Miss de Bourgh looked about to speak.

"Indeed it is," said Lady Catherine. "Her marriage shall be to secure the family line rather than to secure her own comforts. It is not so for most women, indeed. Do you play and sing, Miss Mary?"

"I do. It gives me much pleasure and I practise regularly."

She nodded her approval. "You must perform for us during your stay."

"I should be glad to. I see that you have a fine instrument here." I nodded to the pianoforte in the corner of the room.

"A Broadwood grand."

"Do you play, Miss de Bourgh?" I asked. Miss de Bourgh looked from me to her mother.

"My Anne's health did not allow her to pursue that accomplishment but she draws exceedingly well. Do you draw?"

"I am afraid not. I never learnt."

"I wonder at your parents not chusing a more accomplished governess."

"Oh, we had no governess. I daresay I should have liked to have had one but my parents did not think it necessary."

"Mary is, nevertheless, one of the most well-read and accomplished women in Meryton," said Charlotte.

"That is a most extraordinary outcome," said Lady Catherine. "But what of your sisters?"

"One plays and sings – that's my sister, Lizzy – and the others sew adequately enough."

"And are any of your other sisters out?"

"Yes, we all are."

"What? All five out in society? The younger daughters out before the elder are married? That is most irregular."

I nodded. "I quite agree, your ladyship." I thought of Kitty and Lydia who might have benefitted from more restrictions, less wine and fewer officers. "My youngest sister is only fifteen."

Lady Catherine leant back in her chair. "You seem to be a young woman of sense, Miss Mary and, considering your lack of formal education, much resourcefulness."

After playing at cards for a time, Lady Catherine ordered the carriage for us.

"She seemed to like you," said Charlotte when we entered the parsonage again. "Pray, what did you make of her?"

"She is proud but I see no reason why she should not be. My only criticism is that she speaks for her daughter. I do not think I heard Miss de Bourgh say a single word."

Charlotte nodded. "She has little chance of overcoming her shyness in the shadow of her mother's dominance. I even suspect that she is not so sickly as Lady Catherine makes her out to be. I once saw her leap from her phaeton and run, as fast as a horse, to catch a hair ribbon that had taken off in a gust of wind."

"Really?" I said. "I could hardly imagine it; she seemed so lacking in vitality, as though a small gust would make her keel over. However, perhaps her appearance and manner are evidence of her submission to her mother's opinion on the subject of her health." I was struggling to undo my bonnet ribbons which I had tied too tightly.

"Allow me," said Charlotte, coming to my assistance. "Lady Catherine's opinion holds sway over much." She glanced at Mr Collins who was humming as he walked about the front parlour.

"Indeed. And I think it likely that Miss de Bourgh has grown accustomed to taking her place in the scenery as it were, allowing her mother the prominent place in the foreground. She might as well have been one of the de Bourgh portraits rather than a living, breathing woman."

"Is that not a little harsh, Mary?"

I shrugged. "It is only with careful observation and reflection that we can presume to support those of our fellow women whom we are in a position to help."

Charlotte put her hand on my arm. "I do admire the impulse but I fear we cannot correct Lady Catherine's ways."

Sir William staid until the end of the week and, during the course of the following fortnight, time became a steady pendulum, passing in a regularity of events. Between breakfast and dinner, Mr Collins could either be found in his garden or his library which overlooked the road, whereas Charlotte, Maria and I tended to occupy ourselves in the back parlour if we were not out walking in the woods, tending the poultry or assisting with kitchen work. In reading, sewing, cooking and walking with Charlotte, I took such pleasure that the days passed like hours.

One afternoon, Mr Collins rushed into the house, red and puffing, his brow coated in a sheen of sweat.

"Mr Darcy has come to Rosings!" he said when he had regained the use of his voice. "Saw his carriage going up the drive." With one hand, he supported himself on the edge of the table, with the other, he pointed in the direction of the road. "I shall call upon him—" another intake of breath, "directly."

"Are you in a fit state to call upon anyone?" I asked.

"Mr Collins," said Charlotte, "it would be more courteous to allow him time to settle in. Why not delay calling on him by a day?"

"I suppose so. But—"

"Lady Catherine would not approve of too early a visit," she added.

"Ah, yes, indeed."

Mr Collins visited Rosings the next day and returned with not one cousin of Miss de Bourgh's but two. Mr Darcy and his cousin Colonel Fitzwilliam paid their respects to Charlotte as a recent bride and new neighbour to their aunt.

Colonel Fitzwilliam looked at me. "Bennet?" he said after Mr Collins introduced us. "Did I not hear you mention a Bennet family, Darcy?"

Mr Darcy congratulated Charlotte on her marriage, seeming not to have heard his cousin. His remarks were concise and few, unlike the colonel's chatter which rambled about in many directions, punctuated by smiles and laughter.

The others crossed the room to hear Mr Collins elaborate on Lady Catherine's attentiveness in having them rearrange the furniture just as they saw it, leaving Mr Darcy and myself quite apart from the rest of the group.

"Are your sisters in good health?" he asked.

"Which of the sisters are you enquiring about?" asked Colonel Fitzwilliam, breaking away from his conversation with Mr Collins.

Mr Darcy did not wait for my reply but moved across the room to look out of the window. A blush, contrasting with his snow white cravat, rose from his neck into his cheeks.

I gave him some time, then joined him at the window. "Have you been in Town, Mr Darcy?"

"I have."

"Are the Bingleys well?"

"Quite well, I thank you."

"Have you happened to see my elder sisters in Town?"

"I was present for a dinner which Miss Bennet attended."

"But not Lizzy?"

"Miss Elizabeth sent her apologies via Miss Bennet who said that her sister had hurt her ankle from too much walking. If I remember correctly." He looked sceptical.

"She is overly fond of walking, so that surprises me not. She would have been disappointed to have missed out on the visit though." I thought I caught in his eyes a questioning look before he appeared to become more interested in a selection of objects on a side table. "So, you've only seen *Jane* in London? From my family, that is."

"Quite so."

Mr Darcy kept his wall of formality as impenetrable as possible but there could be no mistaking the meaning of that earlier blush.

VOLUME II, CHAPTER V

Taking a Turn

Having such superior guests at Rosings, our company was not required for some days, but eventually, we were honoured by an invitation to join the great family for an evening of card playing.

"I hope that my aunt will invite you all to dine tomorrow," said Colonel Fitzwilliam, laying down a card. He and I were proving a fortunate pair at whist against Mr Collins and Miss de Bourgh. "I like to hear plenty of voices around a dinner table. Some have a tendency to monopolise the conversation." With a jerk of his head he indicated the other card table at which Mr Darcy, Charlotte, Maria and Lady Catherine were seated. Mrs Jenkinson happened to be abed with a slight cold, though I wondered if Lady Catherine had arranged this so that there might be two tables of four for whist.

"But Mama is dining at Rotherby Hall tomorrow," said Miss de Bourgh. "We will have to chuse another evening."

"That is true," said Mr Collins, "I remember her saying as much to me when she condescended to take tea with us at the parsonage last week."

"But you can invite them as *your* guests, Anne," said the colonel.

Miss de Bourgh shot a glance at her mother.

"Darcy you must pay a visit to Sir Reginald during your stay," directed Lady Catherine, her voice carrying shrilly over those of the others. "He will be quite put out if you do not."

Mr Darcy played a card without replying.

"I should like to," said Miss de Bourgh, "but Mama . . ." her words trailed off and she appeared most intent on studying her cards.

"Another time, I am sure," I said, hoping to lessen her discomfort. It seemed that she was not permitted to act as hostess of her own accord.

"Come to think of it, I might be late for dinner tomorrow anyhow," said Colonel Fitzwilliam. "Did you not say, Collins, that the cricket match is tomorrow?"

"Indeed," Mr Collins answered with a frown. "And it means much work for me. The lower orders are apt to let a half holiday make them quite giddy and lead them into the most improper behaviour."

"Of what nature?" the colonel asked with a smile.

Mr Collins muttered inaudibly.

"Never mind, Collins. Eh, Darcy," he turned to address his cousin, "did you know the Hunsford village cricket team are playing against Swinhurst tomorrow? You recall the times we joined them when we were boys?"

Whatever reply Mr Darcy gave, his words were swamped by those of Lady Catherine who declared, "If I had known you were behaving in such a way at the time, I should have put a stop to it. To think of my relations mingling with persons of questionable rank at such a vulgar event as a cricket match! Darcy, I forbid you to go and you too, Fitzwilliam."

Mr Collins took advantage of the completion of our game by leaping from his seat, as if to dissociate himself from the impropriety of Colonel Fitzwilliam's juvenile misadventures. He took a seat near Lady Catherine whereupon he proceeded to agree with every word she said and compliment her on every card she played.

The colonel ignored both Lady Catherine's comments and Mr Collins' uncivil departure. "Well, we could play vingt-un now perhaps?" he said, shuffling the deck. He leant forward with a conspiratorial smirk and lowered his voice. "It's a mightily good thing I did not mention the time *you* played in a match too, Anne."

The colour deepened in Miss de Bourgh's cheeks. "Though you chuse to mention it now, cousin."

161

"How old were you then? Eleven? Twelve?"

Miss de Bourgh gestured for him to speak more quietly.

"You played cricket with boys?" I asked.

"She was frightfully good at it too, I remember." His laugh drew Lady Catherine's attention. "The Swinhurst fielders were quite done for at the end of her turn as batsman. Took them completely unawares."

"Cousin George, *please*." Miss de Bourgh, who was already petite, appeared smaller as she shrank into her seat.

"Did you enjoy playing?" I whispered.

She hesitated before nodding. "I remember . . . I felt like a different person out there on the pitch."

"What are you talking of now?" demanded Lady Catherine. Miss de Bourgh gripped her seat and looked at us pleadingly.

"We were talking of the poor of Hunsford, ma'am," I said, "and how Charlotte and I plan to take baskets around to some of the local cottagers tomorrow. I was wondering if Miss de Bourgh might like to join us." Miss de Bourgh and the colonel regarded me with surprise. Perhaps I looked too accustomed to telling falsehoods.

"You did not mention this plan, my dear," said Mr Collins to his wife.

"Didn't I?" said Charlotte sending a questioning look to me. "I must have forgotten to."

I smiled at her, giving the barest of nods.

Mr Collins studied Lady Catherine's features in order to determine his opinion.

After a pause, her ladyship said, "A very appropriate thing for a clergyman's wife to do."

"Indeed," concurred Mr Collins. "Exactly what I was about to say. Ooh, marzipan, how fine!" he added when servants brought in the coffee and plates of delectable items.

"However," continued the great lady, "I am in no way convinced that it is something my daughter ought to involve herself in, particularly as I shall not be free to accompany you, nor Mrs Jenkinson who is indisposed with a chill."

"I am sure you are quite right," I said, to which her ladyship nodded. "It is interesting to observe, however, that where charity is practised, there is a greater degree of harmony between social ranks. One does not have to go back far to the time when discord and terror reigned across the channel. And I heard recently that in our own country, in some northern city or other, poor folk smashed factory machines to pieces. Inappropriate as that behaviour was, I cannot help but wonder if it might have been avoided had they been shewn pity and had their poverty been alleviated a little by those in the area who were more fortunate."

"That is most logical, Miss Mary," said Colonel Fitzwilliam.

"Indeed," agreed Charlotte. "The surest way to sow discord is through lack of understanding or of compassion."

Lady Catherine shifted about in her seat; I had succeeded in stirring up the common anxiety that many aristocrats in England had felt since the revolution in France.

"Now that I consider it more fully, I think that Anne should join you," she said.

"My dear wife and Miss Mary shall be most attentive to your daughter, your ladyship," said Mr Collins, "of that you can be assured."

I managed to share a few words with Colonel Fitzwilliam, out of earshot of the others, before Lady Catherine sent for a carriage to convey us back to the parsonage.

Charlotte took the baskets from Martha who bobbed a curtsey and returned to the kitchen. "Are you sure about this, Mary?"

"The colonel seemed to think it a good idea," I said, relieving her of one of the baskets. "We may be supposed to honour our parents but no one should be afraid of them."

"But surely everyone's afraid of Lady Catherine?"

I laughed and, taking Charlotte's arm, walked with her to the drive. "I will not allow *you* to fear her."

Maria joined us when the carriage approached.

"Oho!" called Colonel Fitzwilliam, waving from the barouche as he and Miss de Bourgh arrived. Jumping out, he assisted us into the carriage. "I brought *my* man to drive us. We can be assured he won't talk."

"Why should we be concerned about servants talking?" asked Miss de Bourgh.

"Well, my dear cousin, our destination is to be kept secret from other members of the Rosings household."

"We're not going to feed the poor?" she asked.

"We shall take these things to the cottages that border Hunsford and Swinhurst," said Charlotte, resting her hand on one basket.

"And this is coming with us to the cricket match." I opened the other to reveal bottles of drink, cheeses, bread, a large pork pie, a jar of pickled vegetables and a fruit cake.

 Miss de Bourgh gaped at us. "But Mama—"

"Doesn't have to find out," I said.

"I do not like this plan one jot," said Maria. "Why did you not tell me of it, Charlotte?"

"Please, Maria—"

"No. I shall not be party to it," she declared, hopping out and fleeing back to the house.

Charlotte bit her lip, blinking as Maria slammed the parsonage door shut.

I shrugged. "All the more picnic for the rest of us."

"Mary!" Charlotte tried not to laugh.

Later on, I was quite determined to remove from my mind's eye the scenes of rural squalor we encountered in the nearby cottages. I did not wish to think of crying, hungry children, of old women working their tired limbs to the point of exhaustion, of waspish quarrels that stemmed from longstanding want. Charlotte shewed more practical kindness than even a clergyman's wife was expected to and encouraged Miss de Bourgh and myself to make ourselves useful. Still, I could not help but shudder as we left each dwelling.

As the match began, we seated ourselves on a bank where the sun's warmth drew out the sweet fragrance of earth and flowers, and watched Colonel Fitzwilliam play remarkably well. For quite some time, Miss de Bourgh declined to eat any of the picnic and I feared that my scheme had only resulted in triggering some sort of nervous complaint. However, mid-way through the match, one of the sportsmen fell into a patch of mud and she fell into fits of laughter. Finally at her ease, she watched with rapt attention and ate the whole pork pie without assistance from either Charlotte or myself. She even drank the majority of the wine we had brought with the colonel in mind.

"Are you glad we brought you here, Miss de Bourgh?" I asked.

She took another swig of wine. "You know? I rather think that I am. In fact," she said, getting up, "I wish to take a turn."

I stood, thinking she wished to take a turn along the common and back and might appreciate a walking partner. However, I was mistaken.

A batter had just limped away from the pitch. Before I knew what was happening, Miss de Bourgh was in his place, holding the bat ready. Most of the players froze, casting bemused looks at one another, and there was whispering amongst the spectators but, whether people recognised her as the daughter of the lady of Rosings or whether they were simply shocked at the sex of the batter, I could not be sure. However, the bowler, a wiry looking man with a greying beard, appeared to suffer no disconcertion. He bobbed his head in a bow, then bowled.

A clap filled the air as she struck the ball. It soared far, the crowd gasped and Miss de Bourgh hitched up her dress and ran as though that were the sole purpose her body had been designed for. With the runs she gained for the Hunsford team, she secured their victory.

Colonel Fitzwilliam ran up to her, expressing his amazement but Miss de Bourgh simply took his arm and allowed him to escort her from the pitch as if she were walking to a formal dinner. Players ran up to her to convey their gratitude and congratulations and she nodded to each, exchanging words with a few.

"I think I've just had a vision," said Charlotte.

"Of?"

"Of the future lady of Rosings. Look at her! I did not know that sport could look so dignified."

"And the villagers seem to love her," I said. "If that does not give her confidence, I do not know what will."

I squinted at a small, red-faced man marching towards us before realising that it was Mr Collins.

"Charlotte! How dare you bring Miss de Bourgh to this place," he yelled. "You know her ladyship would not approve."

"It was I who brought the ladies here."

Mr Collins turned, his nose level with Colonel Fitzwilliam's chest.

"Y-You, sir?"

"Yes."

"And do you mean to suggest," said Miss de Bourgh, "that I lacked the ability to refuse to come if I had not wished to join them?"

"Er . . . no, of course, it's just that Lady—"

"Good." She turned to Colonel Fitzwilliam. "Now will you help me into the carriage." This he did, though by now we all knew that such assistance was a mere formality, not based on any physical disadvantage of hers. At this point, I would have thought Miss de Bourgh capable of clearing the barouche in one leap.

Mr Collins hung his head like a sulky, chastised dog. "Lady Catherine will be most displeased," he mumbled.

"Only if you tell her," I said. "But I would not advise it."

"Why ever not?"

"Do you think when Miss de Bourgh comes into her inheritance, she will afford you the same benevolence the present lady of Rosings does if she looks back on instances of you thwarting her pleasures or causing friction between herself and her mother? You may at last have learnt the rules of whist, Mr Collins, but you would do well to learn to play your cards better, in the figurative sense." Feeling rather pleased with my turn of phrase, the more so for punctuating it with a dignified turn of head, I climbed into the barouche.

Mr Collins followed us on horseback and, given the sufficient distance between us and him, we were able to form a merry party on our way home.

"Do you know, Mama does not allow me to drink," said Miss de Bourgh.

"Is that so?" I said. "Why not?"

"She says it would be injurious to one of my slight build."

"That wine seemed to do you no harm," Charlotte pointed out.

"Quite the reverse," I said.

Miss de Bourgh put her hand to her mouth, stifling a laugh. "Once," she said, "I was so frustrated at Mama's not letting me take wine at Christmas, that I put vinegar into every bottle of her favourite blackcurrant wine."

I could not remember when I had laughed so much or when Charlotte had looked so happy and it occasioned great satisfaction in both of us finally to see the real Miss Anne de Bourgh.

That evening Maria retired early, professing still to be unsettled by our actions that day, though the maid, Martha, told us she had chased the carriage after we had left, waving for us to stop so that she might come too. I sat with my sewing on the sopha opposite Mr Collins who was snoring with his book on his chest.

"Thank you, Mary." Charlotte's voice was little more than a whisper as she topped up her husband's glass of wine. "That was truly thoughtful, what you did for Miss de Bourgh today." She returned to her seat beside me and I handed her back the embroidery ring she was working with.

"She is your friend, naturally she's important to you. That makes her important to me."

Ready to add some rose buds to the cushion cover I was decorating, I reached towards the sewing table for a spool of red thread but knocked it to the floor when Mr Collins woke with a porcine snort.

Charlotte shared a look with me, rolling her eyes, then retrieved the spool which had rolled to her foot, placing it in my hand, her fingertips brushing my palm.

I glanced up at her face, her steadfast gaze, then looked down. "I think I shall retire," I said, tidying away my sewing.

"And I," said Charlotte.

Mr Collins yawned, "I too."

"But, my dear, you have not finished your wine," said Charlotte.

"Ah. I shall follow you in due course then, my dear."

Charlotte did not return his smile. We left him imbibing a Lady Catherine-approved, patriotically English elder wine. As we stepped into the dark vestibule, a draught carrying heady scents from the garden blew out my candle.

"Here, light it from mine," said Charlotte.

However, the candle refused to light, so I walked close beside her up the stairs, sharing the same candle. Once in my bedroom, she found a spare in a drawer and lit it against hers, the flame leaping as it caught on the wick. Her face was close to mine, all shadow and gold, its expression indiscernible.

"Goodnight," I said, taking the candle holder.

"Goodnight."

The seconds stretched, Charlotte and I both holding the newly lit candle, our fingers just touching. Then she left.

At breakfast, Martha brought me a letter with news from Mama of Jane's engagement to Mr Bingley. I had been holding my teacup as I read and, in a moment of joyous distraction, let its contents pour onto Mr Collins' hand. I felt as though the sun itself shone for the sole benefit of the Bennet family. Whilst Mama had been inappropriate in talking of it openly at the Netherfield ball, I too considered how this happy event might make good marriages for my other sisters all the more likely. I received everyone's congratulations with graciousness and smiles and breathed out a happy sigh before returning to my food.

I heeded no more of the conversation at breakfast, my mind full of the fact that my actions, when I was in possession of the bonnet, had led to this triumph. Lifting my teacup, I made a silent toast to my poor bonnet, now lost to me. You served my family well, I thought. Your work was not in vain.

When Colonel Fitzwilliam and Mr Darcy visited and offered their congratulations as well, I began to think that Mr Darcy might learn to think better of our family in general, since his close friend would be joining it. If it was possible that he might consider tolerating our oddities and low connections for the sake of his friend, then this might make a match between Lizzy and himself a more valid possibility. Before they left, he wished me to send his regards to my family when next I wrote, a comment which made me wish, all of a sudden, to dance a reel. If Jane were to marry Mr Bingley and Lizzy Mr Darcy, our family would be provided with the most astonishingly secure future when we eventually lost Papa and Longbourn. Whilst such an expectation would be irrational, I confess I did allow myself to hope for it. However, it frustrated me that I was powerless to promote Lizzy's chances with Mr Darcy, the absence of the bonnet manifesting as a dull ache throughout my entire body.

"It's a little breezier than I thought," said Charlotte, buttoning her pelisse as we left the parsonage for a walk. "I think you could do with taking your shawl."

Goosebumps spread across my arms and I nodded. "Yes. I'll just be a moment."

Maria was sitting in the little parlour, trimming a bonnet.

"You're sitting on my shawl, Maria."

"Oh, sorry," she said, dislodging it from beneath her. "What do you think?" She turned her bonnet, embellished with ruffles. "I hope Lady Catherine would not disapprove of it."

I shrugged. "I thought it looked well enough before."

"Perhaps she prefers young ladies of lower rank than her to wear plainer, simpler bonnets like yours," she said, frowning. "I think I'll unpick the ruffles and start over." She looked up at me then. "Your bonnet suits you well, Mary. I'm glad you gave away your old one. What would Lady Catherine have thought of that, I wonder!"

"Gave it away?" My tone caused her to stare at me, alarmed. "Why do you think I gave it away?"

"It was in one of the collection bags at the church. The last collection before Christmas."

I grasped her shoulders. "Where did it go after that? To whom was it given?"

She leant back, away from me. "Let go of me, Mary. You look quite wild and strange – what is *wrong* with you?"

"I need to know where it is!"

"I don't know. Mr Palmer distributed the last bag of donations. Mama said we had done our charitable duty and there was so much to do before Christmas and the wedding and everything."

I let go of her. "Thank you, Maria. You've been of much assistance."

She stared at me wide-eyed, mouth open like a fish as I smiled and left the room.

"Is all well, Mary?" called Charlotte from the doorway.

"Yes," I replied. I still did not know who had the bonnet but I had a clue with which to resume my search. "I think everything will be well after all."

VOLUME II, CHAPTER VI
The Secret Revealed

Which household from amongst the poor of Meryton, I wondered, had benefitted from possibly the most valuable object in the country, let alone the parish? If I found the new wearer, could I tempt them to sell it back to me with what little pin money I had saved? But what if they had unearthed its secrets and were unwilling to part with it? Might I then have to resort to theft? Would it even count as theft if the bonnet was rightfully mine?

Pondering these questions as Charlotte and I walked in Rosings Woods, I twice knocked my foot against tree roots and once ducked too late, receiving a face full of bud laden twigs. After adjusting my bonnet, I continued in my train of thought, an idea coming to me that made me smile at first – then my smile became a heavy sigh. If I managed to get it back, could I bring myself to do what might further the prospects of my family – even if it meant a sacrifice for myself – yet may merely be a waste of many stitches?

". . . whole leg of mutton or not. What think you, Mary?" came Charlotte's words, finding a gap through the cloud of my thoughts.

"Forgive me, what was the question?"

Charlotte laughed. "I've been talking of it for some time. Have you not been listening?" She paused as her gaze fell upon my face. "Mary, is something wrong?"

I could have lied, reassuring her that all was well but in that moment, the weight of what I felt to be my imminent decision pressed down on me and I knew that she could sense it. She would know I was not telling the truth if I tried to put on an act. However, a small part of the truth would be nonsensical to her.

With a steady look into her deep, trusting eyes, I realised I was about to tell her everything.

"Here," I said, gesturing to a fallen tree, "let us sit a while." We sat down. "You may think that I am running mad," I said, making an effort to regulate my breathing and pressing my hands onto the rough bark to keep them still.

"Tell me. What is it?"

I hesitated, taking in a slow breath. "My old bonnet, the one that belonged to Great Aunt Harriet, well it is not any ordinary bonnet . . . it has the power to manipulate time."

She blinked rapidly, a puzzled expression spreading across her face, but her impulses were not to mock or judge. "Go on," she said.

I then narrated the story of my discovery of the bonnet's power and what I did with it in ridding Netherfield Park of Mr Thorpe and Mr Crawford and, on a number of other occasions, altering the trajectory of my family's future. I told her how Lydia had stolen the bonnet and how I had, just now, discovered where she had taken it.

She was silent for so long that I frayed the end of my bonnet ribbon as I twisted it. I expected her to laugh, to ridicule me or accuse me of insanity but all she said was, "I believe you."

"When I return to Meryton, discovering its whereabouts and returning it to my possession will be my sole object. If I am fortunate enough to succeed in this . . ." I paused.

"You want to go back in time and ensure that Lizzy comes to Hunsford too so that we can take advantage of Mr Darcy's proximity?"

It was my turn to blink in amazement at the rapidity of her mental faculties. "Yes. I would go back to when you asked me to Hunsford—"

"And suggest that I invite Lizzy too," finished Charlotte, nodding. "That is an excellent notion." She smiled at me but the edges of that smile began to fade. "But would that mean—"

"That things will happen differently and you will forget all that happened this time."

She thought about this. "Will *you* forget?"

"No."

She shook her head and began to laugh. "This is madness! I finally understand why you came back home in the storm last year! Oh, Mary, to think you have carried this secret alone for so long."

"Not exactly. Chamberlayne knows."

She sat more upright. "You told Mr Chamberlayne and not me?"

"I had to, to save him from . . . something."

"What?"

"I don't remember. That is, I cannot. He says I put the bonnet on him to send him back in time. Therefore, he remembers what occurred and I do not. I did want to tell you about the bonnet and almost did so on a number of occasions."

"Then I suppose I shall have to forgive you. But I find I do not like the idea of you removing these weeks we've spent together," she said, looking up at me, her tone sinking into solemnity. She took a refreshing, deep breath and resumed her practiced cheerfulness. "However, you shall still come to Hunsford. You may find that much is repeated. I certainly hope that the cricket match will be."

"And I too, if only to see once more the look of shock on Mr Collins' face."

"I only hope you're not bored reliving it all."

"I could never be bored of it," I said. "However, I may not even succeed."

She gripped my hand. "You have to try, Mary. I have every faith in you."

I saw no need to change my plans and leave immediately, despite the fact that I would need to use up more stitches to go back to the start of the year, if I was indeed successful in regaining possession of the bonnet. I remembered that there were plenty of flowers on it and, in any case, leaving straight away for Longbourn would mean leaving Maria to travel alone and goodness knows where she would end up.

Also, if I returned early and failed to achieve my goal, I would have missed out on the last week of my stay at Hunsford for nothing. So I savoured every last moment of my visit, excepting those spent solely in the company of Mr Collins.

"My dear cousin," said he. It was the eleventh of April, the last morning of my visit and I was looking for books I had left in the parlour. "I am sure that, when you speak of us to your family, you will have nothing to report that is not favourable. You have seen how comfortable we are here in our quiet way, how our lives are enriched by the society Rosings offers and how Lady Catherine honours your friend with attentions that are beyond kindly."

I raised my eyebrows.

"My dear Charlotte and I have but one mind and one way of thinking," he continued whilst I reflected that, if they had but one mind, it was all Charlotte's. "There is in everything a most remarkable resemblance of character and ideas between us. We seem to have been designed for each other."

I did not know if mirth or annoyance was my most prominent emotion in response to these last words, but both welled up within me and I was grateful to be spared issuing a reply.

"Ah, my dear," Mr Collins said to Charlotte as she passed by the doorway, a saccharine grin on his face as if to emphasise his last point. "I asked Martha to buy a trout for our dinner when she set out for Hunsford village."

"But—"

"No," he said, holding up his hands, "you need not thank me. Any little thing I can do to lessen your domestic cares is a pleasure to me."

"But I cannot eat trout," said Charlotte, rolling her eyes. "I've told you this. It brings me out in hives."

His smile dropt as swiftly as it had formed. "I am sure you did not tell me so, my dear."

"And I am sure that we agreed that I was to take charge of the ordering as befits the mistress of a house." She sighed and continued

174

down the corridor.

"How am I to know that you do not eat trout unless you tell me?" he called after her before turning to me with a nervous laugh.

"If you'll excuse me," I said, "I must finish my packing but, rest assured Mr Collins, it will by my pleasure to inform my family of the full extent of your matrimonial harmony."

His eye twitched.

I bowed and left the room.

VOLUME II, CHAPTER VII

Prize Fighter

I do not wish to dwell upon my feelings at parting with my friend but part we did and, as planned months ago, Maria and I went to stay with my aunt and uncle in London for a short visit.

"Either both of you can share Great Aunt Harriet's old bedroom or one of you can sleep there and the other share with the twins in the next room," said my aunt as the footman carried up our travelling cases. "Do feel free to take a look at the rooms and freshen up and, when you're ready, there will be a pot of tea waiting for you in the parlour," she said with a warm smile before going to attend to one of her children.

"My Great Aunt Harriet's ghost is said to haunt her old room," I said, seizing the opportunity to tell Maria this while we were briefly alone. It was a lie of course but Maria looked about to faint at the notion. I knew she had read the same silly novels as Kitty had and supposed that she might be as easily frightened.

"Oh, Mary! What are we to do?"

"Oh, I do not much mind taking her room, if you're happy to share with the children, that is?"

"Oh, quite happy, yes."

I considered that it would not do to have Maria telling anyone of what I had said. "You know, I probably should not have mentioned the—" here I mouthed the word 'ghost'. "In all the stories, it is when the living speak of them that they tend to appear. We may be fortunate that in mentioning it just the once, we are spared any unwanted visitations."

Maria trembled. "I hope so."

"Not that we need give such tales any credence. In truth, I think it all nought but nonsense."

"Oh, indeed. There's no such thing as . . . . Which is the twins' room?"

I reclined on the spacious bed and smiled, gazing about me at white walls, wooden furniture, a patterned rug, embroideries decorating the walls and the lack of other people to disturb or annoy me. My perfect tranquillity did not last long, though its interruption was not unwelcome.

"Mary!"

"Hello, Jane."

She embraced me. "Are you well? How was your journey from Kent?"

"I'm quite well. I do not need to ask if you are; it is quite clear that you are more than well. Congratulations on your engagement."

She beamed, demurely lowering her gaze and I thought then that I had never seen her look so beautiful, her complexion radiant with a rosy glow. "I never dared to hope, let alone expect, that I should be so happy."

"You deserve to be so, Jane. Mr Bingley is a most fortunate gentleman."

"You shall see him at dinner tomorrow. He, Miss Bingley, Mr and Mrs Hurst and Miss Darcy will be joining us."

I spent most of the next day deliberating over ways I might shorten our visit or justify travelling alone, so anxious was I to begin searching for the bonnet again and so little did I care for the amusements of London. My mind was so occupied that I did not heed much of what my aunt said as we walked down Cheapside.

"And this shop here is our oldest client, stocking Gardiner hats and bonnets for generations."

"What's that about bonnets?" I asked, catching up to my aunt who was walking beside Jane.

Just then an old woman entered the shop my aunt had indicated which was situated across the street. Other people were walking by and I did not have the best view of her.

I squinted, shielding the sun from my eyes. "Was that Mrs Pepperstock?" and, more importantly, was she wearing my bonnet?

"What would Mrs Pepperstock be doing in London?" said Maria. "Surely she hasn't the money to travel."

I marched across the street, narrowly avoiding a passing carriage, and entered the shop. However, there was no sign of her or, indeed, of any old woman.

Little could rouse me from my perplexity but I found myself able to put it to one side when Mr Bingley and his party arrived to dine with us. Miss Darcy was a small girl of comely proportions and a sweet disposition, as evidenced by her smiles. The little unease she felt appeared due to shyness, rather than snobbery. The reverse could be said of Miss Bingley and the Hursts.

"Maria and I had the pleasure of your brother's company and that of Colonel Fitzwilliam when we were in Kent," I said to her at dinner.

"Yes, of course. I hope Fitzwilliam was well when you parted?"

"He was, I believe," I said. "Mr Darcy came to Town about the same time as us and I had wondered if he might be here this evening."

Miss Darcy stirred her soup. "I believe he has much business to attend to at present."

I wondered if Mr Darcy was too proud to accept an invitation to Gracechurch Street. However, if his friend and his sister gave him good reports of the genteel manners of my aunt and uncle and their fondness for my family's company in general, I hoped that we might be somewhat elevated in his estimation. To that end, I made a point of engaging Miss Darcy in conversation, asking her questions about herself and her favourite aspects of London and complimenting her performance at the pianoforte, even though I noted her playing three incorrect notes and wobbling through a trill.

"What a pleasurable evening that was," said Mr Gardiner the next morning as we joined him for breakfast. He had started early and made his way through much of 'The Sporting Magazine'. "I would be very glad to see at least two-fifths of the party again."

"My dear," said my aunt, in a reprimanding tone.

Uncle Gardiner chuckled as he folded his paper but before he put it aside, to better engage in conversation with the rest of us, something in it caught his eye.

"How strange it is," he muttered.

"What, my dear?"

"Oh, I was just looking at this report of female boxing. How ladies can bring themselves to fight in that way, I do not know."

"Heavens! That is most shocking," said Jane. "What if they get injured?"

"It reads: 'I, Miss Emma Wood of Wapping, renowned prize fighter, known in these parts as 'the Lady of Steel', challenge Miss Jenny Fairfax of somewhere up North – who dared to vex me by attributing this latter title to herself – to attempt to defeat me in the yard of The Anchor, Wapping, on the thirteenth of April, for the prize of seven guineas.' Astonishing, is it not now?"

"My dear, I do not think we wish to hear of such things at breakfast," said Aunt Gardiner.

"Oh, I think we are ladies of a little more 'steel' than you give us credit for, aunt," I said.

There was something about the letter from 'The Sporting Magazine', something that triggered a memory, though I could not put my finger on what it was. At length, I recalled a past conversation with Mrs Pepperstock, in which she had said that her husband, Mr Pepperstock, had been a prize fighter and that they had lived in Wapping. If she was in Town with the bonnet, this was as good a place as any to commence my search.

That evening, after coffee, I excused myself from the drawing room on the pretence of retiring early for bed. I retrieved my boots and cloak from the boot room and my straw bonnet and reticule from my room, then peered over the banister. Light poured into the hall downstairs. A servant must have opened the drawing room door. Even if I was fortunate enough to cross the length of the hall without my family or Maria seeing me, they would likely hear the front door opening and shutting as I left.

"D—" I muttered.

I heard an intake of breath. Five year old Matilda was standing behind me on the landing in her white nightgown, her mouth a forming a wide 'O'.

"Couthin Mary, that'th a *bad* word!" she said.

"I was referring to the collapse of the Puentes dam in Spain. Now go back to bed, Matty, or I'll tell your Mama that you're up and about."

Her bare feet pattered as she rushed to her room and I returned to my own. I could not get to the front door or the back where the servants might see me. How else was I to leave? The edge of the curtain waved beckoningly in the breeze. Looking through the window, I judged that the stable roof was about five feet below the window ledge. Whether or not there was a way down to the ground below, I could not ascertain from my current viewpoint.

Bonnet and cloak on, I opened the window and clambered through it, clinging onto the narrow ledge as I felt for the tiles with my feet. After finding my footing, I stumbled, making a thud which I thought might carry down the street. I lay flat on the rooftop, scratching my hands as I clung to the tiles, waiting for voices.

But none came.

The sun was low in the sky, the shadows deepening, but a slice of light struck a ladder laid out below the window I had just descended from. It folded in the middle with a hinge.

"Thank you, Harriet," I said, glancing upwards, realising that I was not the first person to have left the house in this manner.

My hands sticky with cobwebs and gritty with old evidence of passing birds, I descended the ladder at the back of the stables where I would not be seen and made my way to the streets, heading east along the north bank until, about half an hour later, I reached Wapping.

"Pray, Madam," I said, addressing a straggler from a group of gaudily dressed women. "Could you direct me to The Anchor?"

"Lord, how *genteel*!" laughed one of the other woman. *"Pray, Madam!"*

The person I had spoken to scrutinised me with her gaze. "Fallen on hard times, darlin'?" she said in her broad East End accent. "Happens to the best of us. You're better off trying your luck up Ratcliff Highway – that's where we're heading."

"I know not what you mean. But I am looking for someone who may be at The Anchor, a Mrs Pepperstock."

"Is *she* back in these parts?" growled a woman of around fifty years of age.

"What you got against her, Meg?" said another.

"People talked. The things they said she got up to! Just you watch yourself with that Pepperstock woman," she added, squinting at me. "The Anchor's down that way. At the corner of Cinnamon Street."

Being in possession of the knowledge that respectable ladies were not to be found in taverns or alehouses, I had already decided that, if asked my name, I should say I was Miss Taylor, thus protecting the collective Bennet reputation.

The tavern smelt of wood smoke, ale and meat. It was a riot of male voices – chatter; laughter; drunken singing; hot-headed boasting and bursts of violent argument – with a peppering of female voices – bold waiting maids putting customers in their place; giggling women in very low cut gowns perched on men's knees; the awkward laughter of two lodgers unsure how to respond to unwanted attention as they made their way upstairs. I crossed the threshold into the fray, my heart racing. I felt like a kitten amongst a pack of wolves and thanked my plain looks that I received bold and puzzled stares rather than lewd remarks like those bombarding the escaping lodgers.

A gentleman wearing a green waistcoat, whose face was framed by unfashionably large side whiskers, wove about the room taking bets for the upcoming fight.

When he reached me, he looked up and grinned, shewing more gaps than teeth. "You'll place a bet, I'm sure?" he said. "Two to one for our Miss Wood; four to one for Miss Fairfax."

Heat rose to my face. "I, er—"

"I'll put two pounds on Miss Jenny Fairfax."

I turned around to see Mrs Pepperstock in the tavern doorway behind me. She was wearing the bonnet. Part of me wanted to reach out for it but, instead, I stole out of sight of her, hiding behind a corpulent gentleman contentedly gnawing on a goose leg. Whilst she remained in the doorway, I considered that she might all too easily slip away and then go back in time in order to elude me should she realise that I wanted the bonnet back.

"Are you sure, Mrs Pepperstock? You want to bet against the true 'Lady of Steel' and with such a sum as that?"

"Life is a gamble, Mr Gribes." Mrs Pepperstock chuckled and tightened the bow of the bonnet ribbons.

Mr Gribes announced the imminent commencement of the fight and the crowd filtered through to the yard. I followed, at a little distance behind Mrs Pepperstock, my head lowered with a hand half concealing my face.

The crowded yard smelt like straw, sweat and unemptied chamber pots. The spectators gathered around a circle chalked on the ground. Jostled and shoved, I was forced to the opposite side of the ring from Mrs Pepperstock, despite my efforts to get closer to her. With toes sore from being trodden on and shoulders tender from being knocked about, I watched as two women entered the ring and I could not help but blush at the sight of them dressed in little but small bodices and short petticoats, exposing their shapely calves and muscular upper arms. They stood facing one another, each glaring into the eyes of their opponent and holding herself up to her full height. One jutted out her chin menacingly. The other spat on the ground.

"Allow me to present," called Mr Gribes from within the ring, indicating the boxer with brown skin and wiry hair tied back like a dark halo, "for your diversion, and the victor's glory, a paragon of fighting prowess, a woman of courage and spirit in accepting the challenge laid before her, ready to defend her honour, I give you, Liverpool's Miss Jenny Fairfax!"

A cheer rose from the crowd and Miss Fairfax smirked, glowering across the ring at Miss Wood with her piercing, dark eyes.

"And the Champion of Wapping, the Undefeated, the Breaker of Noses, our very own 'Lady of Steel', Miss Emma Wood!"

This elicited louder cries from the spectators, some of whom began clapping and chanting 'Lady of Steel – Lady of Steel – Lady of Steel!' but red haired Miss Wood, whose face was strewn with freckles and scars, hardly seemed to heed them.

So the fight commenced and I stood transfixed by the explosion of violence before my eyes. Miss Wood threw a punch but Miss Fairfax deflected it and thrust her fist into Miss Wood's side. While her opponent's arm was raised, Miss Wood jabbed at her ribs. Miss Fairfax stumbled backwards, receiving a rain of blows to the face and shoulders. Staggering, she looked about to fall but righted herself and, with lightness of foot, ducked and dodged so that Miss Wood repeatedly missed her mark. Then, with some swift footwork and hefty punches, the champion of Wapping appeared to gain the upper hand once more. The fight progressed with cheers and gasps from the crowd, the fighters alternately gaining the position of dominance.

"Unfair! Unfair!" I shouted when Miss Wood pulled Miss Fairfax's hair. Surely that must be against the rules.

Then Miss Fairfax scratched Miss Wood's arm, breaking the skin.

Realising how distracted I had become, I looked about for Mrs Pepperstock and, when I had spotted her, I edged my way closer. When I reached the spot where I thought she had been, she was no longer there, and so I wove about the throng in search of her.

The fight was reaching its conclusion with Miss Wood sprawled on the floor, Miss Fairfax above her, panting. Mr Gribes lifted up the champion's hand to a mixture of cheers and groans. One spectator laughed a crackly, gleeful laugh and I followed its sound to find Mrs Pepperstock punching the air in delight.

"Two pounds at four to one," she crowed to herself.

"Using the bonnet to cheat? Have you no moral standards at all?"

She froze, then looked over her shoulder at me. "Miss Mary," she croaked, her face pale as chalk.

"I suppose similar activities gained you the funds to travel to London."

"This is no place for the likes of you," she said. "What are you doing here?"

"I think you know. It belongs to me and I've come to take it back. I can pay you."

"Not as much as I can earn with it." She narrowed her eyes at me. "You'll have to fight me for it."

"Fight you? But you're ... *ancient.*"

Before I knew it, she had lunged and I felt as though a small boulder had been thrust at my stomach. I doubled up, coughing.

"Experienced in hasty departures though!" she cried as she ran off.

Catching my breath, I sprang after her, running across the yard. She went through an open gate, flinging it behind her so that it clicked shut, delaying my pursuit as I fumbled with the latch.

"Stop! Cannot we come to some kind of arrangement?"

She ran down the street and I pursued, gaining on her. Then she turned, disappearing down the side of what looked like a warehouse at the edge of the river. I saw her turn right as she reached its far corner and I dashed around the building from the other side.

She shrieked as I collided with her. I snatched the bonnet from her head and she grasped it too, tugging like a dog trying to pull a branch from a tree.

"Stop, you'll damage it," I said.

"*You* stop!" she countered.

"You're too close to the edge, Mrs Pepperstock," I warned.

"Give it back, missy!"

"But it isn't truly yours; it was bequeathed to me by my great aunt, Miss Harriet Gardiner!"

As I uttered the name, the bonnet ribbons rotated, like spiral staircases rising through the air. First one *snap*. Then another. I thought the bonnet had ripped but, at Mrs Pepperstock's cry of pain as she let go, I realised that the bonnet had lashed out at her and the force she had used to pull the bonnet now served to propel her backwards. At once, she disappeared. Then came a splash followed by crazed laughter.

"Mrs Pepperstock! Are you alright?"

She continued to laugh maniacally, her gown ballooning around her giving her the appearance of some crone-like, mythical water demon.

"It chose you, missy," she said. "It's yours, fair and square."

Scanning the area, I spotted a mooring rope and threw it down to her. I successfully pulled her to the edge of the river but she was still several feet below the dockside and I had not the strength to drag her higher.

To my aid came a group of women that reminded me of the one I had encountered upon my arrival in Wapping, with their colourful gowns and exaggerated fineries.

"Here, love," said one, gesturing to the rope.

With six of us heaving, Mrs Pepperstock ascended to the dockside and I wrapped my cloak around her. She coughed and spluttered but her nerves appeared to be unaffected and she got to her feet with remarkable sprightliness.

"Lucky those doxies were passing by just then," she said after our good Samaritans had gone.

"Those what?"

"Doxies . . . *prostitutes*," she added at my puzzled expression.

I gaped at her. "They were— Good heavens! Are you sure?"

We returned to The Anchor where Mrs Pepperstock gained her winnings from Mr Gribes and secured a room for the night.

"I got a bottle of gin too," she said, after making her arrangements, "for your shocked innocence and my chilled bones. Care to take some?"

"You know what? After the events of this evening, I think I will."

The maid left the small room, having lit the fire, and the door creaked shut behind her.

"Your people don't know you're out?" she said, leaning towards the crackling, flaming logs.

I shook my head.

"I never took you for the rebellious sort, missy," she said between sips from her cup of gin.

"Yes, well, me neither." I clutched the bonnet tightly in my hands.

"Don't worry," she said, "I've enough respect for that thing's power than to cross it when it's made its will quite clear."

"Mrs Pepperstock, I must be correct in assuming that you know what it has the power to do."

"Oh, yes," she replied. "Though it was quite by chance that I discovered the first of its powers. I was doing some . . . *shopping*, shall I say, at Pratt's, when—"

"Can we save the story for another time?" I said, knowing her tendency to prattle on. "I am planning to go back in time, much further than I have done before, back to the eighth of January. I realise that at that time, you will have the bonnet, not me, but it will serve me for my sister to think that it is quite lost to me."

Mrs Pepperstock nodded. "And you'll want to find me then and get it back?"

"Yes. Ideally without a fight."

"You'll find me in Meryton that week. I will have just returned from my first lucrative trip to London." She chewed her lip. "I know now that the bonnet has chosen you and I accept that. However, the me from January may be a trickier customer."

"You amaze me. So what shall I say to you?"

"The truth. Tell me exactly what you know happened. Tell me about how you found me, fought for it and won."

"And you'll just willingly give it back? Judging by your actions this evening, you can hardly expect me to believe that."

She poured herself another cup. "Goodwill goes both ways, missy. You might let me borrow it to allow me to live in the manner to which I am growing quite accustomed."

"Fine. But only on occasions when I have no need for it and only for the unpicking of an agreed number of stitches. I don't want you unravelling any important work I've done with the bonnet."

"Can't say fairer than that. I have people who inform me of opportunities as they arise. When I wish to capitalise on any, I will send someone with a note for you and we can talk terms. Best we meet at Pratt's."

"Why there?"

She looked at me strangely. "Why, convenience, to be sure," she replied. "Of course, you will need to remind me of all these details."

"Yes, I know. But are you sure that you will believe all I say, that you will not think that I am tricking you by saying 'your future self agreed to this plan and so should you'?"

She paused, drumming her fingers on her cup. "I know. I shall tell you a secret that I have told no other living soul. Repeat it back to me in January and I'll agree to the arrangement, I have no doubt about it."

She poured me a cup of gin. "To the bonnet," she said, tapping her cup against mine.

"To the bonnet."

VOLUME II, CHAPTER VIII

Lydia's Revenge

Wednesday 8th January 1812

"What's the date, Sarah?" I asked, waking up to see the bright-eyed maidservant bringing a ewer of warm water into my room for me to wash with.

"Wednesday the eighth, miss."

"Of January?"

She turned, regarding me with a bemused smile. "Aye, January. You've a sleepy head this morning."

"That I do," I croaked, pressing my cool hands over my throbbing temples.

I had returned, as calculated, to the morning of the day preceding Charlotte's wedding. Soon she would call and invite me to Hunsford and I could set the mechanism in motion which I hoped would lead to the lottery win of all marriages and to the best possible fortunes for my whole family.

"Thank you, bonnet," I said, into the thin air after Sarah had departed. Not only had the bonnet conveyed me once more to when I wished to go, it had done so without the jump in time making me nauseous. The initial head-ache was already easing. "Perhaps, as a sailor gets his sea-legs," I said to myself, "I am getting my time-legs, as it were."

I grabbed the chamber pot from beneath the bed, taken unawares by a surge of vomit. I had spoken too soon.

After my queasiness had been quelled, my bedroom door opened and standing in the doorway was the last person I felt inclined to converse with.

"Why have you come into my room, Lydia?" I asked.

"I thought you'd be up by now. I just wanted to see how you're doing without your ugly, possessed bonnet."

I suppressed a smile. "Will you never tire of crowing over your victory?"

She picked up an embroidery hoop and pulled a sour face as she looked over my work. "I don't think so, no."

I got out of bed and washed my face. "What I do not understand, Lydia, is where this bitterness in you comes from. It's not just that you were afraid of the bonnet. It goes much deeper. You delight in having beaten me. Why is that?"

"You're always boasting about how you're the cleverest one," she said, an ugly expression on her face.

"No, I'm not—"

"And I thought it would serve you right to shew you that I am capable of outwitting *you*."

I paused, studying her face. "It's more than that. It must be." I did something then that I had never properly done before. I used my analytical mind to construct a view of life from Lydia's perspective.

"What are you doing?" said Lydia. "Why have you got your eyes shut? Stop it, Mary. You look like a lunatic!"

I opened my eyes again. "I think I understand," I said, exhausted at my mental effort, stepping closer to Lydia as I spoke. "As we grew up, our parents adored beautiful Jane and witty Lizzy was Papa's favourite. Jane and Lizzy were always inseparable and prefered playing together to playing with us. I learned to occupy myself in my studies and accomplishments. Kitty gained the most affection from Mrs Hill who would read her stories when she was young. Yes, you became Mama's favourite, you and she being so alike, but that was never enough for you. You were jealous of Jane for the respect she gained from Papa and of Lizzy for the affection she received from him but you could never take out your bitterness on Jane who, we all agree, is practically an angel, or Lizzy who would strike you with a barb of wit at the first opportunity. Kitty became useful to you in doing everything you wanted her to do and so you began taking out your ill feeling on me and, for that matter, seeking male attention elsewhere, though in ways that were beyond improper."

Her face resembled a giant beetroot. "You presume to . . . How *dare* you!" She threw herself at me and I shoved her away. I did not mean for her to fall but she landed on her backside with a thud.

"Oh, my poor Lydia!" cried Mama, flustering down the corridor. She must have witnessed my shove, though not what had provoked it.

Lydia chose this moment to begin sobbing. "Mary s-struck me!"

"She's fine. She's overreacting," I said. "Besides, I was defending myself."

"Just you stay in your room young miss until we think of how to punish such behaviour," said Mama, pointing a finger at me. "Come now, my dear girl, let me get Hill to make up a cold compress."

Lydia sniffed. "And some biscuits for the shock?"

"Of course, my sweet one."

Lydia got up to embrace her, bestowing upon me a satisfied grin from over Mama's shoulder.

Charlotte came by as I knew she would and invited me to Hunsford.

"I should dearly like to visit," I said, "in fact, nothing would give me more pleasure, but would you favour Lizzy by asking her too? The two of you have been particular friends for so long; I know she would appreciate it."

Charlotte looked a little surprised. "In truth, I am not certain that she would agree to come. I fear she may find it awkward."

"I am sure she would not," I said, shaking my head. "And even if there is any awkwardness regarding all that passed with Mr Collins, is it not better that it be dispelled soon by a lengthy visit, rather than be left to grow from extended separation?"

"I think you most insightful, Mary." She squeezed my hand. "Yes, I shall ask her as well."

After we had taken tea, Charlotte bade us farewell. As she turned to leave, a shadow fell across her face and her smile faded. Poor thing.

"Well, it seems I shall be visiting Hunsford in March," said Lizzy with a sigh.

"I do not envy you!" exclaimed Lydia. "I've had just about enough of Mr Collins."

"I too," seconded Kitty.

"Charlotte also invited me," I said.

"Why ever did she do that?" said Mama. "We all know that *Lizzy* is her closest friend. Are you sure you did not mishear her?"

"Quite sure," I said, sitting up taller. "I may go?"

"Well . . ." Mama contemplated the question.

"After the violent scene she enacted upstairs this morning?" cried Lydia. "Why should she be allowed to go off on an extended visit?" There was a flicker of satisfaction in her eyes which told me that I had betrayed my dismay. "You told me you would consider how best to punish her, well here we are! She should stay home. Besides, we cannot risk her losing her temper in front of Lady Catherine de Bourgh, can we?"

"That is true, my dear," said Mama. "Besides, now I think of it, the house will be quiet enough with both Jane and Lizzy away. I shall inform Miss Lucas, or Mrs Collins as I will shortly have to get used to calling her," she added, rolling her eyes, "that I cannot spare both of you and that only Lizzy shall be going."

"But, Mama, please! It's not fair!" I wailed. "You can't just—"

"Your father and I decide what's fair, I think you'll find." She looked to Papa, as did the rest of us.

He shrugged. "I'll be in my library," he said. "Such screeching may inspire pride in the parents of seagulls but the ringing in my ears and my subsequent irritation remind me that I am no such creature."

My eyes began to sting so I ran to my room, determined not to allow Lydia the satisfaction of seeing me cry.

VOLUME II, CHAPTER IX

More Lost Than Pin Money

My visit to Mrs Pepperstock went as smoothly as I could have hoped. I took a seat opposite her so that she could see that I meant to talk rather than to snatch and run. Of course, she did not wish to part with the bonnet. Who would? However, it seemed I had the ability to persuade.

"And what secret did my so-called 'future self' confide in you?" she said with a snort of laughter.

"The golden-haired colonel. Mr Prince. Mr Pepperstock's creditors: a butcher, a landlord and a book-keeper."

Her jaw dropt.

I nodded. "I know you poisoned them all."

I left her cottage with the bonnet stowed and covered in my basket.

I felt the keys of the pianoforte beneath my fingertips, closed my eyes and let the music sing of my blended joy and disappointment. Yes, I had the bonnet, but I would not be going to Hunsford.

"*Lord*, Mary!" yelled Lydia through the vestibule. "We *are* assembling for breakfast. Now will you stop playing that dreary dirge or you'll put us off our food."

I joined them in the breakfast room, though I had little appetite.

"Mama, can we not have the pianoforte moved to another part of the house?" said Lydia. "It carries so where it is and I for one am finding it increasingly vexing in the mornings."

"Particularly," muttered Kitty under her breath, "when you've taken too much wine the night before."

"I do not see why it cannot be moved up to Mary's room," said Mama. "She has the space for it. And I would so like to put a chaise longue in its place. It would make the room more serviceable for entertaining."

"But music entertains, does it not?" I said.

"*Some* people's music does," said Lydia. "Besides, it's a dreadfully tinny old thing. Who wants to listen to that at a party? Kitty can learn to play the harp, can't you, Kitty?"

"What?" This from Kitty, through a mouthful of cold ham.

"It's not tinny in the least." This was all the argument I had energy for and so I was not surprised that it held no sway and that, later that day, Mr Brook and Thomas carried the instrument up to my room. The move was no compliment to my pianoforte or my playing but its being in my room gave me more excuse to remove myself from my family's company which, in turn, gave me more opportunities to use my bonnet in peace.

I had got so used to the April days of light and new life and walking out in Rosings Woods with neither gloves nor muffler, that plunging back into January with its short, grey days of frosts and rain was rather a shock and resulted in my catching a cold complete with throbbing head and red, swollen nose. The only benefit of this was that, not wishing to catch colds themselves, my family left me to myself which enabled me to risk making more stitches in my bonnet than I otherwise would have.

It was a bleak season, knowing what I had given up. However, what got me through was the hope that, through my sacrifice, Lizzy would have a chance of winning Mr Darcy's heart and hand.

Time unfurled, bringing March along with it once again, and I stood with Mama, Papa and my younger sisters watching Lizzy leave for Hunsford in my place. She was to pay a visit to our aunt and uncle in Cheapside to break the journey and see Jane before continuing on to Kent.

Days passed and I expected we should soon receive a visit from Mr Bingley to ask for Papa's permission to marry Jane.

"I do so wish that Jane should meet a rich colonel in town," said Lydia. "Then we could stay with her and have a constant supply of officers to dance with."

Kitty giggled.

"I'd wager that Jane shall be engaged to Mr Bingley before the week is out," I said.

"Oh Mary," cried Mama, "for Heaven's sake, don't tempt fate!"

"How much would you wager?" asked Lydia.

I smiled to myself. "A pound."

Kitty gaped at me. "What! Are you in earnest, Mary?"

I nodded.

"I'll take that wager," said Lydia. "I'll spend your pound on some new shoes and a pair of silk stockings as I've danced holes in all my others. Kitty, why do you not take that wager also, then we can shop for shoes together!"

"It is most unlike you to wager so, Mary," commented Kitty. "Anyone would think you'd had word from London. Whilst the chances of an engagement within the week are low, it is not impossible and I for one should not like to risk losing a whole pound."

"I should not have thought to rank Kitty amongst the sensible half of the family," said Papa as he peered over his newspaper.

A week from that day, Lydia came to sit in the oriel where I was reading and rested her feet on one of my library books.

"Get off, you'll scuff the cover," I said.

"Oh. My apologies," she said, not sounding the least bit sorry, keeping her feet there until I noticed her new shoes. No doubt her stockings were also new. I wondered if she had spent the whole pound she had reminded me to give her first thing that morning.

"Are they not pretty?"

"They don't look particularly practical."

"I forgot. You don't understand what pretty means," she said, jumping to her feet.

"At least I have more uses for books than as foot rests."

Lydia smirked and skipped away, flaunting my failure as embodied by her ridiculously thin-soled, bead trimmed, silk slippers.

"Kitty," she called, "you can have my old blue ribbons. I've bought myself some new red ones with the money I won from Mary."

I chewed my thumbnails as I sat there, unable to ease the knot of anxiety in my stomach. What if Lizzy's long visit to London, the one that no longer existed, had been necessary for Jane and Bingley to resume their courtship? What if the couple's fortuitous reunion outside Boodle's club had only occurred because Lizzy had suggested they walk to Fortnum's that day? Had my actions, springing from my intentions for Lizzy, ruined our hopes for Jane?

I found myself snapping at Hill that morning for burning the toast, criticising Kitty's taste when she told us of the new novel she had borrowed, and my irritation at Lydia's and Mama's giggles and gossip grew to such a pitch that I almost stuffed my ears with pound cake so as to block out the sound.

Despite the state of my nerves, there was one thing which made me hold firm to the belief that I had done the right thing in sacrificing my visit to Hunsford and risking Jane's happiness. Lizzy and Mr Darcy would meet in Kent and, if the spark of attraction I had witnessed at the Netherfield ball were rekindled there, they might become engaged. That match would be invaluable to our family and might increase the likelihood of Jane's marrying Mr Bingley anyway . . . unless he married Miss Darcy first . . . and unless Mr Darcy, without his friend's being engaged to Lizzy's sister, failed to overlook the inferiority of our family connections. I buried my head in my hands. What had I done?

At odd occasions during the weeks that followed, I used my bonnet to catch snippets of what passed at Hunsford parsonage and Rosings.

"I fear I must remark upon your conversation with Lady Catherine, this evening," said Mr Collins, carriage wheels rumbling in the background. There was a pause. "I feel it is my place, as a clergyman as well as your cousin, to point out that openly disagreeing with her ladyship regarding such matters as the inappropriateness of your younger sisters being out in society, trespasses into the territory of disrespect."

"I imagine that Lady Catherine is secure enough in her point of view to weather a little variation of opinion," said Lizzy, "though being disrespectful was never my intent."

I tapped my fingers on my dressing table as I sat listening to this conversation, considering how, if her ladyship expressed a negative view of Lizzy to Mr Darcy, she might influence his opinion. However, a conversation some days later between Colonel Fitzwilliam and Mr Darcy alleviated my anxiety.

"And how did you find the ladies?" said Colonel Fitzwilliam. There was a pause in which I heard their footsteps and imagined them to be walking in the woods of the park.

"Miss Bennet alone was there. The others had gone to the village."

"Indeed? They did not think to leave a chaperone with one so pretty and charming?" The colonel laughed.

"Why do you say that?"

"Don't look at me like that, Darcy, it was a joke. Though it needn't be, if you catch my meaning."

Mr Darcy cleared his throat. "Fitzwilliam, do you mean that your intentions with regard to Miss Bennet are—"

"My intentions are only to express what a fool I'd be to wait for some other man to propose to her, if indeed I were in a position not to need to marry for money."

"Do you . . ." Mr Darcy's voice was gruff, making him sound uncomfortable, "do you care for her? You have failed to explain your intentions to me with any degree of clarity."

"I admire her, I do not deny it, but she's not for *me*." There was another pause. "I suppose I am simply congratulating myself on my superior taste."

Well, this was interesting. I turned their words over in my mind, attempting to analyse the tones used and the thoughts that might have filled the pauses in speech. It seemed pertinent that Mr Darcy had called at the parsonage without his cousin, something he had not done during my visit. Of interest to me too was his discomfort during the conversation.

From this point on, I listened with more regularity, my bonnet ribbons often twitching in anticipation until I had put the bonnet on. As I could only hear sounds caught by other items of headwear, it was, more often than not, country walks that I overheard and, in the days that followed, I often heard Mr Darcy out walking, even when rain pattered through trees.

One day, when my bonnet was conveying to me the sounds caught by his hat, I heard Lizzy say: "I did not expect to meet with anyone in this part of the woods; it is a favourite haunt of mine." I could not tell whether she was hinting that she wished to be alone or was providing him with information which would allow them to meet together on subsequent occasions. Whatever she had meant, they did meet in the woods several times that week and, whilst their dialogues were far from extensive, Mr Darcy did make the effort to ask Lizzy a number of questions. If this particular one were not suggestive of his feelings, I did not know what was. He said: "Do you like solitary walks... or do you prefer having a partner to walk with?" One could not pretend to be deaf to the double meaning. He might as well have asked if she were of a mind to seek a husband.

As the day of Mr Darcy and Colonel Fitzwilliam's planned departure from Kent loomed, I grew so nervous that I ate very little. However, no one but Mrs Hill noticed and inquired as to my state of health. I listened via Charlotte's bonnet as the party from the parsonage arrived at Rosings and, just before hats and bonnets, spencers and pelisses were taken away by servants, I heard Mr Collins muttering: "Lady Catherine will be most disgruntled."

"Really, Mr Collins," said Charlotte, "I'm sure she shall understand when we explain that she has a head-ache."

"Miss Bennet is unwell?" said Mr Darcy who must have met them in the vestibule.

"Just a trifling head-ache," said Mr Collins, "such as women are wont to give in to."

"I see."

"Shall you be joining us for tea, sir?" asked Charlotte.

"I am afraid not," said Mr Darcy. "I have some arrangements to make before our departure the day after tomorrow. Fetch me my coat, Blakeney. Yes, the green one."

My suspicions led me to try listening in at the parsonage again and, before a quarter of an hour was through, my curiosity was rewarded. Fortunately, a bonnet had been left in the parlour, from which I caught a rap at the door. Although I missed the first few words that were spoken, I recognised the tones of Mr Darcy's voice. There followed a pause which made me wonder if he had left. However, at last he spoke again.

"In vain have I struggled. It will not do. My feelings will not be repressed. You must allow me to tell you how ardently I admire and love you."

Lizzy did not speak. I did not breathe.

"I have attempted to conquer my passion. The disparity of our spheres of life, the expectations of my family, the inferiority of yours, my own rational mind – all these things oppose an alliance between us. But I love you and that overcomes all. I ask that you will end my torment and accept my hand in marriage."

Eventually, Lizzy replied. "In such cases as this, it is, I believe, the established mode to express a sense of obligation for the sentiments avowed, however unequally they may be returned." My heart sank. I felt as though I were teetering over the edge of a cliff. "It is natural that obligation should be felt, and if I could feel gratitude, I would now thank you. But I cannot— I have never desired your good opinion, and you have certainly bestowed it most unwillingly. I am sorry to have occasioned pain to anyone." No you're not, I thought, my jaw clenched, my nails biting into my palms. If you were sorry, you would not speak so coldly to him. "It has been most unconsciously done, however," she continued, "and I hope will be of short duration. The feelings which, you tell me, have long prevented the acknowledgment of your regard, can have little difficulty in overcoming it after this explanation."

Foolish girl! D— foolish girl! My insides boiled, my rage swelling more and more with each tick of the clock.

After a painful silence, Mr Darcy spoke again. "And this is all the reply which I am to have the honour of expecting? I might, perhaps, wish to be informed why, with so little endeavour at civility, I am thus rejected. But it is of small importance." The latter remark was delivered in a tone so bitter that only a fool would suppose the information he sought did not much matter to him.

"I might as well enquire why with so evident a design of offending and insulting me, you chose to tell me that you liked me against your will, against your reason, and even against your character? Was not this some excuse for incivility, if I *was* uncivil? But I have other provocations. You know I have. Do you think that any consideration would tempt me to accept the man, who has been the means of ruining, perhaps forever, the happiness of a most beloved sister?" Lizzy's tone grew heated. "I have every reason in the world to think ill of you." Oh, stop being melodramatic! "No motive can excuse the unjust and ungenerous part you acted there. You dare not, you cannot deny that you have been the principal, if not the only means of dividing them from each other, of exposing one to the censure of the world for caprice and instability, the other to its derision for disappointed hopes, and involving them both in misery of the acutest kind." *I* was in misery of the acutest kind. I had sacrificed so much for this opportunity and Lizzy, irrational, unreasonable, hot-tempered Lizzy had, with the swift eloquence of a guillotine, destroyed my hopes. "Can you deny that you have done it?" she asked.

"I have no wish of denying that I did everything in my power to separate my friend from your sister, or that I rejoice in my success," he said. "Towards *him* I have been kinder than towards myself."

"But it is not merely this affair on which my dislike is founded."

For God's sake, Lizzy – *enough*! "Long before it had taken place, my opinion of you was decided. Your character was unfolded in the recital which I received many months ago from Mr Wickham." Not that preening performer again. I thought you no longer cared for him. "On this subject, what can you have to say?" Thanks to Lizzy, I was now suffering from a head-ache too.

"You take an eager interest in that gentleman's concerns," growled Mr Darcy.

"Who that knows what his misfortunes have been, can help feeling an interest in him?"

"His misfortunes! Yes, his misfortunes have been great indeed." His sarcastic tone did not escape me.

"And of your infliction," cried Lizzy. "You have reduced him to his present state of poverty, comparative poverty. You have deprived the best years of his life, of that independence which was no less his due than his desert." Honestly, Lizzy, why are you not more concerned about *our* lack of independence? "You have done all this and yet you can treat the mention of his misfortunes with contempt and ridicule."

"And this is your opinion of me! This is the estimation in which you hold me! I thank you for explaining it so fully."

I did not.

Even through the blurred vision of teary eyes, I could see that there was not enough embroidery on the bonnet for me to go back again and not persuade Charlotte to invite Lizzy to Hunsford. I knew it, though I felt the compulsion to look again. I listened as Lizzy continued to burn the bridges between herself and the most eligible man any of us were ever likely to meet, she attacking him with fiery arrows of condemnation, he defending himself with icy walls of pride.

With a roar of anger I threw myself onto my bed and pounded my pillow over and over again until the seam burst open and a shower of feathers floated down all around me like ashes. Unable to move, I just lay there, grinding my teeth.

VOLUME III

VOLUME III, CHAPTER I

Birdcage Walk

In a band box, under a travelling case, behind a pile of folded bed linen, on the top shelf of my closet, my bonnet was shut away from the world. I had lost my touch. Whilst once my use of the bonnet had been blessed with good fortune, now I felt the thing to be a curse. I had failed to take Lizzy's dislike of Mr Darcy seriously and had therefore not only wasted my time and stitches but had, inadvertently, ruined Jane's chances of happiness with the man she loved.

Jane's stay in London was drawing to a close. What if she did not see Mr Bingley at all? What if he never returned to Netherfield? Or, worse, what if he did return but with Miss Darcy as his bride?

Days passed and life returned to a simulacrum of normality. I devoted more time to reading and playing the pianoforte than I had for some months. I might not be able to do anything to improve my family's lot but I could continue to develop my accomplishments. Over these pursuits I had at least some degree of control.

One day, I joined Lydia and Kitty on their daily walk into Meryton so that I could change some books at the library. Noticing that Clarke's had just acquired a copy of the latest Philosophical Transactions of the Royal Society, I flicked through it.

"My dear," said Mrs Palmer to her husband, the vicar, "I have just received a note from poor Mrs Smith at Bower Green, requesting our pastoral attention."

Mr Palmer rolled his eyes. "That's the whole day gone."

Lydia and Kitty's chatter outside diverted my attention from B. C.

Brodie's article: 'Experiments and observations on the different modes in which Death is produced by certain vegetable poisons'. I looked through other items new to Clarke's and, after selecting Germaine de Staël's *The Influence of Literature on Society*, I left the library to witness the most flagrant flirting on the part of Lydia and Kitty with a group of officers, most of whom were unknown to me. It was not merely giggling and come-hither eyes that they utilised. Kitty pretended to swoon so that one officer caught her in his arms and Lydia, on the pretence of lacing her boot, hitched up her dress to shew the men a long stretch of her silk-stockinged leg. Several townsfolk muttered derogatory comments as they passed by, Mr Palmer stared and even servants busy about their errands tutted. Poor Mr Sanderson, the officer closest to Lydia, blushed to match his regimentals.

"You two are exposing yourselves to the derision of the town!" I told them on our way back home.

"Did you see Johnson's face!" laughed Lydia, paying no heed to my words.

"And Sanderson's!" said Kitty.

"You cannot flirt as you did back there and not expect to become objects of ridicule. Who will take you seriously when you behave like that? What man would want to marry a woman who garners so much disrespect from her neighbours?"

"You're just jealous that the officers like us and not you," sneered Kitty.

"Believe me, I'm not."

"No, Kitty," said Lydia, "she's just being a bishop as usual and making herself feel superior by dishing out a sermon."

"Can't you see, I'm trying to help you and, in so doing, to be of some good to our family?"

"And how much good are you doing the family," said Lydia, "reading books no one will talk to you about and playing music no one wants to hear? At least we shew some interest in marrying someday. You were born a spinster!"

Kitty lowered her eyes but, if she thought Lydia had gone too far, she shewed no intention of saying as much. Of course, it was true that I wished to evade the fate of marriage, despite it being a sure way to find security for the future, and it was also true that, of late anyway, I had done more harm than good for the family. Whilst they would never be aware of what my actions had led to, I reprimanded myself enough for it.

I hoped to have a more peaceful trip into Meryton some days later as Lydia and Kitty were sleeping off their sore heads, having been to a May Day party the night before. It was Mrs Forster's first time hosting a party since marrying the colonel and of course Lydia had to be there. She had been quick to visit the new bride after her wedding in March and swiftly developed an intimacy which secured her invitations to all social events involving officers of the regiment.

Any sense of tranquillity I had felt during my outing was short-lived. As I left the library, I overheard Colonel Forster talking with Mr Denny.

"It's a b— shame," said the colonel. "I thought him a gentleman and a decent officer."

"Poor Chamberlayne," said Mr Denny.

"I fail to see how he deserves any sympathy after what he's involved himself in."

My stomach dropt. "What's the matter?" I demanded. "What's happened to Chamberlayne?"

Turning, they regarded me with surprise. Colonel Forster filled the silence with a cough. Mr Denny's mouth twitched in a way that might have conveyed either sympathy or amusement.

"Nothing that need concern a lady such as yourself," said the colonel at last, before bowing and taking his leave.

"Mr Denny, please," I said, pulling at his sleeve to stop him from turning away. "Tell me what has occurred."

Fortunately, Mr Denny allowed ladies greater breadth of topics of conversation than Colonel Forster did.

"This might come as a shock. Shall we find somewhere to sit down?"

"I am not at risk of fainting, Mr Denny. Just tell me."

"Mr Chamberlayne has been arrested. I'm sorry. I know that the two of you are friends."

"Arrested? Why?"

"He was sent to London to negotiate with Colonel Harwell regarding the acquisition of ensigns to join our regiment. That was two days ago. The ensigns arrived this morning but Chamberlayne did not accompany them as expected. A letter they brought Colonel Forster contained news from Colonel Harwell of the arrest." He hesitated.

"Go on."

"He was in the wrong place at the wrong time. If you have – forgive me – an attachment to him, this may be difficult to hear."

"He's my friend; that is all. Please do not withhold anything you know about what happened. If I can help him, I shall."

"I fear there's nothing to be done. Last night, a molly house was raided. The woman in charge of it and several of the men who were there were arrested and pilloried. Chamberlayne was one of them."

"A *molly* house?"

"It's a—" Mr Denny cleared his throat, "a place frequented by certain men. Men who prefer the company of other men."

I digested this information for some moments. "It was raided last night, you say? What time?"

He squinted at me. "What *time*? I do not know."

"Well where is the molly house in question?"

"As the regiment found out about it so quickly, I presumed it was not far from the barracks at St James' Park."

"And when did the ensigns last see him before the raid?"

"I cannot say," he shrugged.

I fixed him with a hard stare.

"Well, we know that he dined with the regiment. But beyond that, I—"

"Thank you, Mr Denny. I can see that your usefulness is limited. I shall simply have to find Chamberlayne *now* in order to find him *then*." Abandoning etiquette, I turned without bowing my head, paid no heed to Mr Denny's confusion and made straight for home and the stables.

"The horses are needed on the farm, miss," said the stable boy.

"I don't need Nelly for long, Thomas." I mounted the chestnut brown mare. "By evening, this excursion will not exist anyway. Good day to you." I nodded to him before kicking Nelly and riding out of Longbourn and down the London road.

Grey clouds churned above me before breaking but on I rode, only stopping for directions. When I knew I must be close, I dismounted and went into a shop.

Rows of tall, black hats, black bonnets, black gloves and veils indicated the specialist nature of the place. However, I pushed aside the looming sense of foreboding it conjured.

"My sympathy for your loss," droned the woman minding the shop, a phrase I supposed to be her customary greeting.

"Thank you but I have not suffered a loss. In fact, I am lost myself. Could you assist me in navigating my way?"

Nelly and I wound through a network of streets until we reached a broad road which, if the shopkeeper had been correct in her directions, was named 'Birdcage Walk', the road to the south of the royal park where King James was said to have kept an extensive aviary.

I had not ridden far down this street before I joined the rear of a jeering crowd. Ahead, pillories had been set up on a raised platform and my gaze was arrested by a scarlet jacket.

"Chamberlayne!" I dismounted, tied Nelly to a post and pushed through the crowd. "Let me pass. Get out of my way, imbeciles!" I growled as I became squashed between two burly men and had to elbow them both to dislodge myself. Panting, I clambered up to Chamberlayne. I almost did not recognise him at first. His head and hands, locked in place by the wooden blocks, were besmirched with filth and one of his eyes was swollen shut. I had to crouch to allow him to see me. "Chamberlayne?"

"Miss Mary?" he croaked. He smiled and I could sense him searching for some joke to utter but, instead, his eyes filled with tears.

VOLUME III, CHAPTER II

Mrs Clapton's House

Something smacked against my face then and my hand came away muddy when I touched it.

"You must go. *Please*," said Chamberlayne.

"Not until you tell me how long ago the raid was and how I can get to the molly house?"

"Are you going to save me, Mary?"

I gripped his hand. "Of course I'm going to save you, you blockhead."

Friday 1st May 1812

One petal plus a few extra stitches unpicked and I had given myself plenty of time to get to Chamberlayne before the raid. However, this time I needed an excuse for my lengthy absence.

"I forgot to mention," I said at breakfast as I loaded my plate well, knowing I would need my strength, "I bumped into Mr and Mrs Palmer yesterday and they invited me to Bower Green Village Hall for a series of lectures on moral philosophy. Would anyone be interested in joining us?"

It was a question that merely served to add credence to my story. As expected, no one wished to come to the fictional gathering.

"May I take Nelly?"

"If the Palmers invited you, they must have meant to transport you there and back," said Mama. "There'd be room for you on the back of their cart."

"They did not offer to take me and I had rather not be presumptuous."

"Nelly is needed on the farm today as Thomas tells me that Nora is lame and must rest," said Papa. "I am afraid you will have to be presumptuous if you wish to go."

Ah, well, I had enough pin money to take the mail coach and a hackney carriage. I left in a hurry and only just made it in time for the coach's departure to London, finding space enough to sit, wedged between two large gentlemen with stubble on their faces. They snored loudly and smelled as though they had been travelling for weeks without stopping to wash.

A hackney carriage took me from the coaching inn to my destination. Then, rather than waiting and wandering about London for hours, I made some stitches in my bonnet, causing a cat to hiss at me when I appeared all of a sudden out of nowhere.

I walked up to the door at the address Chamberlayne had given me and braced myself before knocking, not knowing what shocking sights to expect, but I told myself not to think of my own discomfort. I was here for Chamberlayne, my friend who needed me.

A buxom woman opened the door and squinted at me suspiciously, her hand on her hip. "Can I help you?" she croaked, as if she had no intention of doing so.

"I need to find a friend of mine. A Mr Chamberlayne. He should be here. This is the molly house, isn't it?"

"Shh!" The woman checked up and down the street before pulling me inside. "You want to be careful what you say."

"I'm sorry. I didn't . . ." Around the room, men and women were sitting around tables drinking tea. The scene was shockingly ordinary. Then I noticed that one of the women had sideburns and another wore surprisingly large boots.

"Mrs Clapton!" called a gentleman across the room and the woman went off to clear up a tea spillage.

Not seeing Chamberlayne anywhere, I took a seat at an empty table and a gentleman came to sit next to me.

"May I say, you look extremely like a woman."

I blinked at him. "I should hope so, *sir*, for I am one."

He coloured. "Oh, I do beg your pardon. I must have drunk far too much . . . tea." He bowed and left.

"Miss Mary?" Chamberlayne had followed another red-coated officer into the house.

"You're back, Chambers!" cried a young man who grinned before embracing him. Another man, swaying too much for someone who had only taken tea, placed on Chamberlayne's head a white wig of the Marie-Antoinette style and, with quick circular movements of his fingers, rouged his cheeks.

Chamberlayne froze as he regarded me, his cheeks no longer requiring artificial colouring. "What in Heaven's name are you doing here?"

"Trying to be just about convincing as a woman, it seems." I shot the embarrassed gentleman a cold look. "But listen, you're in danger of arrest. You have to leave."

"What?" he said, removing the wig, his hair sticking out in all directions. "Have you seen it? In the future?"

"I've seen you pilloried and I do not want that to happen to you. They would throw you out of the militia. You might even be sent to prison. You have to leave now before the raid." I took his arm and made for the door.

"No. We cannot abandon the others to that fate."

"What do you expect me to say to them? I have come from the future with my magic bonnet to warn you of a raid?"

"No because you're cleverer than that. You just need to be a stitch bolder."

"They could be here any minute, Chamberlayne."

"So we must be quick about it."

I held his gaze for a moment, then climbed up onto a table.

"Listen, everyone." My voice came out unusually high pitched. One or two men looked up. I stamped my foot. "I said, *listen!*" The chatter died down, apart from Mrs Clapton fussing about the varnish on the table. Scanning the dozens of faces turned to me, I knew then that I wanted to save them just as much as Chamberlayne did. I realised too that how I went about it was of vital importance. "You have to leave in as discrete and orderly a manner as you can. One at a time."

"What the devil are you going on about, miss?" asked Mrs Clapton.

"There's going to be a raid. If you all leave at once, it will look suspicious and you may get caught or suffer your companions to get caught."

"How do you know there's going to be a raid?" the woman asked.

"I can't explain now, there isn't time and you would not believe me anyway. I'm not going to shew you the disrespect of making up a falsehood. I came here to rescue my friend, Chamberlayne, and he wishes that you should all be saved, as I now do."

"Do you trust her?" the other officer said to Chamberlayne.

"Wholeheartedly."

Everyone got to their feet and, despite their obvious anxiety, waited to be directed.

"Is there a back door?" I asked the mistress.

She nodded.

"Good. Those at the back four tables, follow Mrs Clapton to the back of the house but be sure to leave one at a time and not to all go off in the same direction and, for goodness' sake, leave dresses and wigs behind! The rest of you, line up at this door."

"After this, I'm going to dress you in regimentals and get you to join the militia," said Chamberlayne, his comment getting several laughs.

"And I'm sure she would be a fine officer," said the gentleman who had mistaken me for a man. "More competent than most."

"She'd be an admirable general, rather," said Chamberlayne.

I nodded to him as I ushered the first gentleman out of the building. When it was only Chamberlayne and myself left, the mistress of the house returned to the front room.

"Go now," she said. "They can't touch me for owning an empty house."

"Thank you for your hospitality, Mrs Clapton," said Chamberlayne with a bow.

I was about to leave when I looked back at her. "Why do you do it? Why run the risk?"

"The world out there, miss," she said, gesturing outside, "is full of deceit and concealment. We only have to open our eyes. So-called gentlemen feed on the sweat and blood of workers who are little more than slaves, wilfully blind to the real source of their wealth; business exchanges are sanctified as holy matrimony and the flamboyance of the royal court masks disease and insanity. At least the world in these four walls is a place where people can live honestly, without shame, where they find fellowship and don't have to hide within themselves."

"Thank you, Mrs Clapton," I said. "It has been an honour and an education. You seem to be a woman of remarkable insight. I'd never have guessed."

"Would that insight buttered the parsnips!" she said with a half-smile. "Be off with you now."

The low sun cast long shadows as Chamberlayne and I walked the cobbled streets.

"Will you go back to the regiment?" I asked.

"All the arrangements are made, the monies for the ensigns paid to the colonel. I was going to ride back to Hertfordshire this evening."

"I plan to go by post," I said.

"Then you'd have to wait until tomorrow. You will have missed the mail coach, I'm afraid."

"Oh. Cannot I ride with you?"

"Oh, Mary!" he said, raising his hands to his face in mock alarm, "You and I on horseback together? If only my horse could accommodate a chaperone for us too. Really, the ways you risk my reputation!"

"And rescue it."

"I know, Mary," he said, putting my arm through his as we walked to where his horse was stabled.

He set me down on the Meryton road so that it would look as though I had walked back from the Palmer's house.

"Mary," he said, "I cannot say how much I am—"

"Chamberlayne! Are you coming too?" said Kitty. She and Lydia were making their way from the direction of home.

"You're not going are you, Mary?" asked Lydia. "Mrs Forster did not invite you, surely?" I had forgotten that Lydia and Kitty had been invited by Mrs Forster to her May Day party. The Forsters, who were renting the house next door to that of my aunt Philips, loved company and gossip and Mrs Forster had, of late, sought both from Lydia in particular. "Lord, Chamberlayne, why are you wearing rouge? What a good joke. I know! We shall dress you up to pass for a lady and see if we cannot fool Wickham and Denny when they arrive – how we shall laugh!"

Chamberlayne kept up a steady supply of laughter as he was paraded around that evening in the best muslin and lace that Aunt Philips' wardrobe could provide but, when I caught his eye, I saw his mask slip. There was an ignorance to Lydia's idea of a joke that had its basis in mockery. Chamberlayne seemed only to be playing along and laughing *with* the others so as to seem not to be laughed *at*. In the gathered party, I observed little but a variation of the crowd at the pillories of Birdcage Walk.

VOLUME III, CHAPTER III

Logic & Logistics

I embraced Jane, glad to see her after her long stay in London. Only in her absence did I appreciate how her presence was an oasis of peace and kindness in a desert of disharmony and inconsideration. In her smiles I saw that she was not unhappy to be home but there was a shadow at the corners of her expression which stabbed me with guilt.

"Welcome home, Lizzy," I said, though I left her to initiate a fleeting embrace. Still angry about her refusal of Mr Darcy's marriage proposal, I could not keep the edge of coldness out of my voice. However, she appeared not to notice.

When we gathered to dine, the Lucases joining us, I was keen to hear the news and stories of the travellers but Lydia, interested only in her own small world, preferred to regale us all with her inconsequential anecdotes and opinions.

"Pass me the potatoes, Mary," she said. "Oh! Mary, I wish you had gone with us."

"Really?" I said, not without sarcasm. The dish of potatoes made a thunk as I placed it between us.

Lydia described, not for the first time, how Kitty and herself had taken the carriage to meet Jane, Lizzy and Maria Lucas at an inn to convey them home. "We had such fun! As we went along, Kitty and me drew up all the blinds and pretended there was nobody in the coach and I should have gone so all the way if Kitty had not been sick. And when we got to The George, I do think we behaved very handsomely, for we treated the other three with the nicest cold luncheon in the world."

"Which we had to pay for," muttered Lizzy under her breath.

"And if you would have gone, we would have treated you too."

I rolled my eyes, wondering if she said this for Mama's benefit or because Jane had asked her whether or not I had wanted to come.

"And then when we came away it was such fun!" she continued. "I thought we never should have got into the coach. I was ready to die of laughter. And then we were so merry all the way home! We talked and laughed so loud, that anybody might have heard us ten miles off!"

"Far be it from me, my *dear* sister," I said, "to deprecate such pleasures. They would doubtless be congenial with the generality of female minds but I confess they would have no charms for me. I should infinitely prefer a book. Besides, it should have been most uncomfortable if I had gone, there being barely enough room for the five of you with all the luggage. How can you not have considered that inconvenience when you set out? A servant might have collected them from The George and they should have had a comfortable ride home. Besides, it's all very fine your saying that I should have gone when you had ample opportunity of asking me but chose not to." It had been quite early on in my speech that Lydia's eyes had glazed over and she was now engrossed in loading her plate with a second hefty wedge of pigeon pie.

"I still cannot believe that you bought that ugly bonnet," said Kitty.

"Well, *you* tried on two in the shop that were much uglier," said Lydia. "You don't mind if I use some of your pink satin to trim it with? Once I've done that, I daresay it'll be tolerable."

Kitty snorted. "And as you said, it matters little what one wears this summer, what with the regiment leaving for Brighton."

"Oh! If one could but go to Brighton!" Lydia caught Mama's eye and both sighed with the same expression of mingled dejection and longing.

Lizzy glanced over her shoulder, checking that no one was nearby but Jane. As the two of them walked down and drive, they had no notion that their conversation would be overheard. As I sat on the window seat, watching them set off on their walk, I put on my bonnet.

"You do not blame me, however, for refusing him?"

Jane put a hand on Lizzy's shoulder. "Blame you! Oh, no."

"I do," I muttered.

"But you will blame me for having spoken so warmly of Wickham."

"No." Jane's voice was comforting, reassuring, making me think of Charlotte. I so missed the loss of the occasion when I had confided so extensively in her. I wished I were at Hunsford with her now to tell her all about the bonnet once more and to confess to her how I had botched things. Perhaps I could tell Chamberlayne. "I do not know that you were wrong in saying what you did," Jane added.

"But you *will* know it, when I have told you what happened the very next day."

I leant forward, pressing my forehead against the window.

"Why?" Jane was as intrigued as I was. I had one glimpse of her wide-eyed expression before the two of them disappeared around a bend in the Meryton road.

"I avoided my usual walk, recalling the number of occasions I had happened upon Mr Darcy on that route. Yet he found me, in a grove at the edge of Rosings, and presented me with a letter."

"What did it say?" I breathed.

"What did it say?" Jane asked.

"He wished to defend himself against my accusations in relation to his treatment of Mr Wickham and— oh, Jane!— nothing could have prepared me for what I read. We knew already that Mr Wickham was the god-son of Mr Darcy's father. Wickham was truthful in relating to me that Darcy's father loved him well and wished for him to be provided for. Old Mr Darcy left him a thousand pounds in his will and made his wishes clear to his son that Wickham should be supported in starting out in a career and, if he took orders, a family living should be offered to him. Darcy felt that Wickham's character was not suited to the church and was not surprised that he asked for money in lieu of the living. The sum of three thousand pounds was agreed upon and Wickham professed an intention of studying law. How he spent his time and money, we cannot know and perhaps we should not wish to, but he did not progress in the law and, when a parish living became available that Darcy had the power to give, Wickham used the memory of old Mr Darcy's affection to try to get Darcy to give it to him. He refused."

As well he should have after giving him three thousand pounds!

"It surprises me that Mr Wickham wished to take orders after being so disinclined towards the profession," said Jane.

"I think it can have been no love for the church that led him to such a dishonourable reappearance in Mr Darcy's life. He needed money and, after receiving nothing, he left greatly embittered, so much so that he later tried to elope with Mr Darcy's sister, Georgiana, who has a fortune of thirty thousand pounds."

"What? I cannot believe it!" said Jane. "Though surely Mr Darcy would not construct such a lie that involved his sister. But he might have viewed the situation through the tainted lens of prejudice. Surely Mr Wickham would not do such a thing out of malice or greed! Perhaps he loved Georgiana and, fearing Mr Darcy's disapproval, he considered that elopement was the only way that either she or he could be happy. Though it would have been foolish and inappropriate."

Really, Jane, that is too much, even for you!

"But Georgiana was only fifteen, little younger than Lydia!" said Lizzy. "We already know Wickham was desperate for money and there was this young, wealthy girl he could manipulate and take advantage of and, in so doing, make himself rich, as well as hurt the man who refused to bend to his will. How could his actions be viewed in any other way than with abhorrence? You never will be able to make both of them good. There is but such a quantity of merit between them to make one good sort of man. For my part, I am inclined to believe it all Mr Darcy's."

Interesting.

"I do not know when I have been more shocked," said Jane. "Wickham so very bad! It is almost past belief. And poor Mr Darcy! Dear Lizzy, only consider what he must have suffered. Such a disappointment! And with the knowledge of your ill opinion too! And having to relate such a thing of his sister! It is really too distressing. I am sure you must feel it so."

"Oh! No, my regret and compassion are all done away by seeing you so full of both. I know you will do him such ample justice, that I am growing every moment more unconcerned and indifferent."

I tutted. It was just like Lizzy to obscure her true opinions with light repartee. Her opinion of Mr Darcy must have changed. She pretended her regret and compassion were fading but, in making such a remark, I considered that she betrayed the fact that she was regretful and that she did feel compassion towards Mr Darcy. What a change from the day of his proposal!

After agreeing that it would be inappropriate to reveal Mr Wickham's true character to others, as it must necessarily involve the exposure of Georgiana's past, Jane and Lizzy's conversation moved on to talk of pleasanter topics, in particular, the trip that Lizzy was planning with Aunt and Uncle Gardiner to the Lakes.

The discovery of Mr Wickham's reprehensible behaviour towards Mr Darcy and his sister interested me much less than the signs I had noticed in this overheard conversation that Lizzy's view of Mr Darcy had shifted. I had no way of knowing how his letter might have addressed her condemnation of the way he had separated Jane and Mr Bingley. Perhaps he had managed to explain his actions in a way that cast them in a better light. He had certainly done this with the Wickham issue. At any rate, Lizzy's opinion of him seemed so altered that, if the future held another proposal from that quarter, she might be able to give him an affirmative answer. Though how likely was a renewal of his offer? If the couple happened to be thrown into company with one another tomorrow, no such happy event would likely be wrought. There would be too great a prevailing of Lizzy's confusion of feeling and Darcy's stinging resentment of her rejection of him for any degree of openness between them. However, if Lizzy's good opinion of Darcy were given time to establish and Darcy's wounded pride allowed to rally into an emergence of new hope, and if at such a time they were thrust together, I could believe it possible that the match of all matches, that which I had already invested in, the marriage to save our family might be made.

My renewed positivity was enhanced the following week by Lydia's receiving an invitation from Mrs Forster to journey with herself and Colonel Forster to Brighton. Whilst she delighted in prattling on about the town's huge camp full of soldiers, I rejoiced in the prospect of her absence. Her mind was so preoccupied by the clothes she would take and the flirting she would do, that I began to feel less anxious that she might find my bonnet. Besides, she would still think it in the possession of one of Meryton's deserving poor. On one occasion, the relaxation of my vigilance must have led me to leave my closet door ajar, something I would not have ordinarily done. Yet I cannot be certain that I did so. However, it seems the only explanation for a particularly bizarre occurrence.

The Forsters, Mr Wickham, Mr Denny, Mr Sanderson and Chamberlayne came to dine with us on the day prior to their departure for Brighton. I asked the colonel, who was sitting opposite me, if he knew anything of how the war was faring in Spain, not realising that this question would trap me into having to listen to him go on and on about those of his acquaintance in the regular army and where they were all stationed. He described the siege of Badajoz, which had occurred several months previously, in such detail that he might have been there himself.

"The curtain wall was now breached in three places and Wellesley gave the order to storm the town. Of course, the French knew full well what was coming and immediately rained musket fire down on those brave souls at the base of the breaches."

"What's that about breeches my dear?" said Mrs Forster. "Oh, yes please Wickham, a little drop more would be lovely."

"Then our men were facing great blasting barrels of gunpowder . . ."

"No one wants gunpowder in their breeches," muttered Chamberlayne so that only I heard. He nudged me and I couldn't help but snort as I took a sip of water, near choking myself.

It was then that a tiny movement caught my eye. Something poked into the room from beneath the door. It looked like a dark, paper-thin snake. Flicking about and quivering, it withdrew, then emerged again with another just like it. The door creaked open. Mrs Hill could not have shut it properly.

"Indeed?" I said, feigning interest as I pretended to attend to the colonel's description of the battle. "No, really? . . . Ah . . . How awful." My stomach spun as I saw a shadowy object through the small gap in the doorway.

"Perhaps we of the gentler sex ought to leave you gentlemen to such unpleasant topics," said Mama, getting up, "until you are ready to join us for coffee."

I had to get to the door before the other women made for the drawing room. I got up, knocking my cutlery which clattered on my plate. "Pray, excuse me," I said, "I have come over somewhat indisposed." I curtseyed and rushed to the door which was creaking again, opening wider.

"Really, my dear, you must learn that most ladies do not like to hear of bloodshed at dinner," I heard Mrs Forster say to her husband.

Snatching my bonnet from the doorway, I ran to my room.

"What the dickens are you doing?" I said to it.

The ribbons fidgeted as if someone was tugging them and then I heard a small voice coming from inside it. I did not lose any time in putting it on.

"I daresay the wording was not well chosen for its intended purpose." It was Colonel Fitzwilliam's voice. "Whilst honesty is essential, it could be possible to be both truthful and kind. Women do not respond well to insults."

"Yes, thank you, Fitzwilliam," said Darcy gruffly.

"Whatever her family may be like, you must admit that birth does not necessarily equate to true gentility of character. Consider our aunt. How many times have we been ashamed of the words issued from her mouth? And if Miss Elizabeth Bennet comes from a family with an array of defects, how infinitely more impressive is it that she should emerge from it as the pinnacle of female perfection?"

"I need not look so far as Rosings for an example of our family's lack of true gentility."

"Steady on," Colonel Fitzwilliam exclaimed.

"No no, I meant myself." He paused, sighing. "She said that the mode of my declaration merely spared her any concern she might have felt in refusing me had I behaved in a more gentlemanlike manner."

"B— hell, Darcy!"

"Indeed. I did not realise what I had become. It is she who has reminded me of what a true gentleman is, namely a man who commands as much respect as he bestows upon others. It is that which I must strive to be. I may have lost her but I will hold onto what she has taught me."

"But it need not follow that you have lost her forever. Your letter will go a long way to altering her opinion of you for the better and if, in time, she understands your true character and if you present your best self to her, then why not ask her again?"

"I fear that—"

"Well fear not! Happiness was never gained through fear. Rally yourself, man."

"You think I still have a chance?"

"Why not talk to Georgiana? She may advise you better on the ways of a woman's heart."

"I don't know. Perhaps. I shall be seeing her in August, so I may discuss it with her then, though I do not care to burden her."

"As you do me." The colonel laughed.

"Quite."

"Oh! You are not going to Pemberley before my brother's wedding to Miss Frances Beaufort I hope?"

"When's the wedding to be? I forget."

"The third of August."

"My business in Town should be completed by the end of July but I should like to be in Derbyshire as soon as possible afterwards."

"I know you and he are not so very close but he would wish you to be there, as would I."

Darcy paused. I guessed that he was unused to changing his plans to suit others. "As you please. I shall stay to witness the ceremony but I must journey north straight after."

As they discussed their opinions of Miss Frances Beaufort, soon to be Lady Fitzwilliam, there was a knock at my door.

"Mary? I just wanted to see if you're quite well."

I whipped off the bonnet and stuffed it in my closet. "Come in, Jane."

Her smiling face emerged from around the opening door.

"Thank you, I am much better," I said.

"Everyone will be leaving soon. Lydia's staying over at the Forsters' house before their early start tomorrow and I knew you would want to say farewell to her."

"I would take great pleasure in doing so."

"Very good," she said, innocently.

As I walked downstairs, ideas came to me in rapid succession. With each step I took, my brain hummed with increasing excitement.

"Is anything wrong, Mary?" said Chamberlayne.

Jane gave me an odd smile, looking from Chamberlayne to me before leaving the two of us alone in the vestibule.

"What was that supposed to mean?" I said, imitating her expression.

"Perhaps she thought that you and I—"

"Never mind, there's no time to ponder that," I said, waving away the topic. "Chamberlayne, I must ask a favour of you!"

I just managed to say all I needed to before the rest of the party emerged from the drawing room. Mr Brook stowed Lydia's luggage atop Colonel Forster's carriage and, after she had dashed to her room to make her last few preparations, she almost danced out of the house.

Kitty was crying, though not at the idea of missing her sister. "It is most unfair," she remarked, pulling a sour expression.

Mama was bouncing on the balls of her feet as she squeezed Lydia's hand through the carriage window. "To think of the amusements that await you, my dear! You must be sure to enjoy yourself as much as possible."

This brought on another outpouring of Kitty's tears.

"I'm sure I shall. Lord! Just think of how gay Meryton has been since the regiment came here and how much more so Brighton shall be with a whole camp full of soldiers. I daresay every street is lined with officers, dazzling in scarlet!"

Kitty looked about to burst.

"Goodbye, Lydia," I said, smiling as the carriage drove off.

Upon returning to the house, I breathed deeply, feeling as though a storm had blown itself out, making way for gentle sunshine. This feeling continued over the following weeks and, as Kitty's grief at the loss of the regiment began to ease, a sense of harmony spread throughout the household. For myself, the only thing which caused anxiety was wondering if the task I had given Chamberlayne would meet with success.

One day, in the last week of June, a letter arrived for Lizzy and another for me when we were sitting at breakfast. Even before either had been opened, I anticipated the satisfaction which would unfold from the contents of both.

"I'll open it later," I said, "It'll be a response to my request that the circulating library strives to acquire more books on scientific topics." This was sufficient to kill my family's curiosity.

"Oh dear!" said Lizzy as she read her letter. "My aunt Gardiner writes that we shall not be able to leave for the Lakes when we had planned to."

"Why ever not?" said Mama.

"Business of my uncle's has meant that we must leave a fortnight later than planned and the extent of our trip is to be curtailed as he must return to London later in August. As this would not leave sufficient time to explore Cumbria and the Lakes in the leisurely manner we had wished, they propose that our tour should go no further north than Derbyshire and the Peaks."

Well done, Chamberlayne, I thought as I smiled into my teacup.

After breakfast, I walked out to the hazel thicket in the garden to enjoy the sunshine and sit in solitude to read Chamberlayne's letter.

Preston Barracks, Brighton, 23rd June 1812

To the indomitable Miss Mary Bennet,

I hope this letter finds you in good health. It was a pleasure to offer my services in the manner you requested and I have good reason to hope that my efforts will meet with success. I must say I rather enjoyed writing in the role of a textile broker with an enthusiasm for the fashionable world. My portrayal of this fictional character led me seriously to consider joining some theatre company or other when my service in the militia has come to an end.

I shall here summarise the correspondence between myself and your uncle or, should I say, between Mr Garrick and your uncle. That esteemed tradesman has arranged to meet Mr Gardiner at his warehouse on 27th of July, after his meetings with Lancashire mill owners. Unfortunately, this has meant that Mr Gardiner's northern tour will have to be delayed. Should you witness the meeting you would note in Mr Garrick's visage a resemblance to a gentleman you met with briefly at a respectable tea room near Birdcage Walk. I can assure you that this Mr Garrick can be trusted to present himself well and will no doubt reassure Mr Gardiner that their plan to meet again on the 27th of August will be likely to result in the acquisition of quality stocks at most reasonable prices. After this date, Mr Garrick must journey to Manchester.

However, I foresee from my knowledge of Mr Garrick's penchant for port wine, that an agonising attack of gout will lead to the cancellation of his meeting – at rather late notice – and to his subsequent retirement from the world of textile broking with its requisite quantity of travel. He shall, having decided to take orders, receive the patronage of a certain Lord Fortescue, with whom he shares a preoccupation with the alcoholic aspects of the Eucharist.

Having dwelt, in my second letter to Mr Gardiner, upon the beauties of the north, in particular the county of Derbyshire – which happens to be the county in which my uncle Chamberlayne and his family resides – I hope to have helped inspire the ideas which your plan requires.

I have enacted all this in good faith that you will explain to me further how this may help your sister achieve an advantageous marriage and that you shall keep me abreast of further developments.

Your humble servant,
E J Chamberlayne

I did not wish to tempt fate but I was so desirous to share my hopes with Charlotte, that, in my next letter to her, I told her of Darcy's proposal to Lizzy, her refusal, the letter that changed things and of my hopes that they might meet in Derbyshire or, at least, that Lizzy might visit his great estate of Pemberley. I explained how their going there was far from a guaranteed success. The main thing my plan hinged upon was the hope that Lizzy and my aunt and uncle would stay for a time at Lambton. Not only was this the town where my aunt grew up, it was also the one that was closest to Pemberley.

"Do you have fond memories of your childhood at Lambton?" I asked my aunt. The time of the trip had arrived and they had come to Longbourn to stay the night and leave their children in Jane's care before setting off with Lizzy the following morning.

Aunt Gardiner leant against a sopha cushion and looked wistfully ahead at something only she could see. "Ah, I do indeed, Mary. The memories of that time bless me whenever I turn my mind to them."

"Do you still have acquaintances in the town?"

"There are some school fellows of mine who are most likely still residing there. Though it is so long since I corresponded with them that I cannot be certain."

"Is not Pemberley nearby?"

"Only a stone's throw away. Now *that* is a house beyond comparison."

I sat a little closer to her. "I can imagine. So, you've looked inside the place?"

"I know it's strange, having lived there so long, but I never saw inside 'the big house' as we called it."

"Would you not be intrigued to see its fineries?"

"I should not object to the idea but what would draw me most are the gardens. They are said to be exquisite."

Lizzy came over then. "Would you like more coffee, Aunt?"

Her coming over to us and asking about the new fashions in London quite disrupted my topic of conversation but I flattered myself that I had sewn sufficient seeds that a definite plan to stay in Lambton might soon sprout, growing into the notion of visiting Pemberley.

Over the following days, I listened in on their conversations from time to time and kept track of their route. They visited Blenheim Palace, staying at an inn in Oxford, spent a night at Warwick, from where they toured the castle of that city and the one at Kenilworth, and staid a night in Birmingham, visiting Aston Hall, a cathedral and a busy coffee house. They reached Derbyshire sooner than I had anticipated and, over the next four days, took in the sights and splendours of Matlock, Chatsworth, Dovedale and points of picturesque grandeur at the Peaks, reaching Lambton on the third of August. My heart leapt as

I thought how Mr Darcy would soon be travelling north. I just hoped that, if Lizzy did get to Pemberley, it would not be before his arrival.

"Is Pemberley not a very fine place?" I overheard Lizzy say.

"It is ma'am," said a girl with a northern accent, "as all about here would tell you."

"And what family lives there?"

This comment focussed my attention. What cause did Lizzy have to pretend ignorance?

"Their name is Darcy, ma'am."

"And are the family home for the summer?"

"No, ma'am. I hear they're at their London residence just now."

"Ah."

"Do you plan to visit the place?"

"My aunt and uncle talked of a visit tomorrow, should my head-ache not persist. I think we shall go. Thank you for the hot water, Edith."

"You're welcome, ma'am. I'll bid you goodnight then."

From this conversation, I gathered that Lizzy was indeed curious to see Pemberley but anxious at the idea of seeing Darcy. I'd wager her head-ache was one of convenience but, upon discovering that the house was empty of its residents, she might cancel her head-ache and see the house of which she might have been mistress.

It would perhaps be beneficial for Lizzy to see the Darcy estate as it might go some way towards making her regret her refusal of Darcy's proposal. However, how much better would it be for them to meet there! I ground my teeth in frustration at the fact that Lizzy would be there the day before Darcy was due to arrive, assuming he left straight after the wedding, breaking the long journey by two nights on the road, as would be probable.

If only he had not had to stay in Town for that blasted wedding!

VOLUME III, CHAPTER IV

Pride & Promiscuity

The impact of Pemberley's beauty was felt even by myself, despite the fact that I could not see it. The responses of Lizzy and my aunt and uncle as the housekeeper, Mrs Reynolds, shewed them around the place, were enough to paint a vivid picture of grandeur, beauty and taste. How I longed to ensconce myself in Pemberley's cavernous library with a pile of books by my side and a view through the window of the sweeping lawns and the woodland beyond.

When Mrs Reynolds spoke of expecting Mr Darcy to arrive tomorrow with his sister and a large party of friends, I knew that Lizzy would be relieved that their visit had not been delayed by a day. I, on the other hand, was left to regret that I could not have done more to allow them to see one another. I had got so close but Fortune seemed only to turn her wheel partly in my favour. However, Mrs Reynolds' praise of Mr Darcy was more than I could have wished for and it could not but have helped Lizzy to see the gentleman in a favourable light.

"If your master would marry, you might see more of him," said my uncle.

"Yes, Sir, but I do not know when that will be. I do not know who is good enough for him."

"It is very much to his credit, I am sure," said Lizzy, "that you should think so."

"I say no more than the truth, and what everybody will say that knows him," replied Mrs Reynolds. "I have never had a cross word from him in my life, and I have known him ever since he was four years old."

In thus manner she continued in his praises for a while, then all I heard were soft footfalls and the occasional creaking, suggesting the vastness of the room they walked in. Then Mrs Reynolds picked up the thread of this topic again.

"He is the best landlord and the best master that ever lived. Not like the wild young men now-a-days who think of nothing but themselves. There is not one of his tenants or servants but what will give him a good name. Some people call him proud; but I am sure I never saw anything of it. To my fancy, it is only because he does not rattle away like other young men."

"This fine account of him," my aunt whispered to Lizzy, "is not quite consistent with his behaviour to our poor friend." She could have meant none but Wickham.

"Perhaps we might be deceived," said Lizzy.

There was much of a positive nature which I could draw from Lizzy's time at Pemberley. I felt that she must at least respect Darcy now and possibly even like him. It was not incredible therefore that, nudged by the charms of her surroundings, she might allow these feelings to grow into something more substantial. Indeed, there was much to satisfy me with the visit and I considered that mine and Chamberlayne's work and planning, as well as the performance of his friend in London, had been worthwhile. However, hearing Darcy as he arrived the next day and following his and Lizzy's separate comings and goings, their paths frustratingly close but never crossing, I found myself more irritated than I could bear.

The following day, I cast a wider net, seeking information about Darcy and his connections. I listened to Lady Catherine reprimanding Mrs Jenkinson for allowing Miss de Bourgh to go out without a shawl and advising her on the number of drops of laudanum to add to her daughter's daily tonic. I heard Colonel Fitzwilliam and Mr Bingley at Boodle's club where the former lost a great deal of money in a card game. I heard Lord Fitzwilliam, the colonel's elder brother, talking to a servant about what needed to be packed for his wedding journey. I even listened to Lady Frances Fitzwilliam, née Beaufort, as she took a walk.

"I had to marry him, do you not understand?" This was a surprising beginning from Lady Fitzwilliam.

"No, I do not. I cannot. Were we not happy?" This the voice of a young man.

"Of course we were!" Her voice became hoarse with emotion. "I have never been happier than in those blessed moments when I have lain in your arms." I froze in shock. Had she been promiscuous with someone prior to her marriage? With my hand clamped to my mouth, I listened attentively. "But happiness is not enough and such pleasures have consequences. I am carrying your child, Robert. Oh, why did you have to be already married?" Oh *my*. "Do you not see, it was not because Lord Fitzwilliam will be an earl one day that I became his wife; I might have married anyone. It is simply that he was the first to ask me. Well, perhaps the second - the first gentleman to propose, one Mr Thorpe, was far too presumptuous in offering me his hand."

"Dear Frances, what can I do?"

"There is nothing you can do. I asked to meet you simply to say farewell. I shall never see you again. I cannot." Stifled sobbing followed.

How vexing it was, when I considered it, that Mr Darcy might have arrived at Pemberley on the day that Lizzy had visited had not he felt obliged to attend the marriage ceremony of this woman who was using Lord Fitzwilliam as a means to launder her reputation.

I whipped the bonnet off my head and started unpicking seventy-two stitches.

Sunday 2nd August 1812

I found myself at the pianoforte, stopping mid-sonata to brace my stomach against the swell of nausea. It was noon of the day before Lord

Fitzwilliam's wedding. I went straight to Papa's library and knocked on the door, hoping that he would be in an agreeable mood.

"Enter."

"Papa, may I have Nelly? I have just heard that a friend I met at the lectures in Bower Green is ill."

"Which friend is this?"

"Er . . . Miss," Hill walked behind me with a pile of pressed petticoats, "Petti," my eyes fell on Papa's snuffbox, "snuff. Miss Pettisnuff."

Papa paused for one long moment. "Very well, go about your good deeds and do mine for me while you're about them, if you would."

"Thank you, Papa. I certainly shall."

I hurried to the stable, told Thomas to saddle Nelly, then off I rode to London, bracing myself for the discomfort and fatigue of the journey.

On my way, I attempted to locate the characters in this drama from the sounds caught by their headwear but failed to deduce where Lord Fitzwilliam or the woman he considered his good lady might be. However, when I targeted Colonel Fitzwilliam, I heard him enter a building which contained sounds of male banter which had become quite familiar to me. Upon reaching London, I asked an obliging coachman for directions to Boodle's club to which place I hastened.

"Miss, I regret that you cannot enter. This is a gentleman's club," said the doorman, a balding man with very little chin.

I was still catching my breath after my journey. "Can I not just come in to talk with someone? It won't take long."

"I regret that such a thing would contravene the rules of the club."

I glared at him. "If you truly were regretful then you might consider changing the rules."

The man frowned.

"But as that seems too revolutionary for you to contemplate, would you inform Colonel Fitzwilliam that a lady waits to speak with him."

"And whom shall I say gave this message?"

"It's 'who' in such a context – but never mind. Tell him, Miss M—" I stopped myself from saying my name when I recalled that, whilst I had

232

a clear recollection of meeting and conversing with the colonel, he had never met me, in this version of reality at any rate. "Miss Bennet awaits him," I said.

The doorman gave a curt nod, then closed the door on me. Some minutes later it was reopened and the colonel stepped out.

"Miss . . . Bennet?" I did not miss the slight look of disappointment and confusion which, well-bred as the colonel was, he masked sufficiently by a polite bow.

"I think you know my sister Elizabeth."

"I do indeed, and which sister are you?"

"Oh, that matters not. I will not take up much of your time. I only wish to do a service to you and your family."

A smile pulled at one corner of his lips. "Indeed? How obliging."

"Your brother, Lord Fitzwilliam is due to marry Miss Frances Beaufort, is he not?"

"He is. What of it?"

"I am afraid you must prepare yourself for a discomforting revelation. I overheard Miss Beaufort – and knew it to be her from hearing her name spoken – walking in the park with a gentleman. The couple conversed with an intimacy of manner which I would expect only to observe between a husband and wife. I expected that the gentleman was her betrothed until I heard her say that she could not see him anymore and that she was carrying his child."

Colonel Fitzwilliam went white. "This is a grievous accusation. Are you sure you heard correctly?"

I nodded. "I thought it only right that Lord Fitzwilliam should be told."

"If I can be sure that what you say is true, he shall be. But I cannot believe it!"

"I can have no reason to lie and I have nothing to gain by seeking you out to inform you of what I heard." My mouth became dry, making me cough. "I believe you to be a friend of my sister and, therefore, a friend to our family. My coming here is purely from a desire to do what is right."

I had to hold my hands to stop my fingers from fidgeting as he hesitated. In this pause, my mind wandered to imagining what the future had in store for Miss Frances Beaufort, pregnant and cast off from society. I tightened my hands as if I could crush this thought between my palms. What was the evil in ending a relationship that was based on a deception? And, in any case, this might be necessary to bring about a marriage between Lizzy and Mr Darcy. It was surely worth the cost.

"She called the gentleman Robert, should that help you in your enquiries."

"Robert?" Now the colonel's complexion gained too much colour and he glanced back towards the interior of the club. "Thank you, Miss Bennet. I appreciate your sense of what is right and humbly request that you keep this knowledge to yourself."

"I assure you I shall. The sense of honour which brought me to you shall forever silence me on this subject."

"I thank you. Good day, madam." He bowed, his brows drawn together and nostrils flared as he spun around and marched back into the club.

I did not hear his conversation with either Robert or Lord Fitzwilliam, though I supposed that at least those two uncomfortable discussions had taken place for, when I was back home that same afternoon, I heard Mr Darcy preparing to set off for Pemberley as I had hoped, a day earlier than last time. He told a servant that he planned to stay at an inn in Oxford and another north of Leicester before the last stretch of road which would take him to Pemberley.

"Should you wish to travel with me, Georgiana?" he asked.

"I had been prepared to leave with you tomorrow," replied his sister, "and I have an engagement with an old school friend this afternoon which I feel bound to honour."

"You shall accept the Bingleys' offer then, to travel with them?"

"I shall."

I hoped that Miss Darcy's wish to travel with them did not betoken an attachment to Mr Bingley. Still, one concern at a time, I thought.

As I listened to all of these arrangements sliding into place, I caught myself bouncing on the balls of my feet. Then, recalling that doing so was a habit of Mama's, I stopped. However, I needed some vent for the excitement of my feelings, so I skipped about my room before playing a Scotch reel on the pianoforte.

I had some little thought about the woman whose cancelled wedding and soon to be swelling belly would cause her disgrace, unless she were able to catch another gentleman and soon, which she might well do. Perhaps Mr Thorpe would ask her again if she encouraged him. However, luck might not be on her side. Despite the benefit of wealthy relatives, she could become an outcast, forced into seclusion from the world.

It was unfair that the man called Robert would not share half the public derision she could be expected to suffer, even if his behaviour became generally known. However, I comforted myself that Lord Fitzwilliam might kill him in a duel and that the lady would have learnt a valuable lesson which should lessen the stupidity which got her into the situation in the first place.

I hummed to myself as I put on my night clothes, brushed my hair and climbed into bed, taking up my bonnet and the needle case from Charlotte. By the light of the candle I made a stitch, as was my nightly custom, for at this time of evening, no one would notice my hour of absence. It was after eleven and everyone but Papa had retired for the night. All was quiet but for the ticking of the clock downstairs and the call of an owl across the field behind the house.

Putting on the bonnet, my expectations of continued domestic quiet in the following hour were upturned.

Mama was wailing.

There were hurried footsteps in the house.

Hooves in the gravel outside.

I reached the window but all I saw of the departing visitor was a swinging speck of light from a lantern.

My bedroom door was ajar, not shut as I had left it. Rushing from my room, I followed the sounds of commotion and discovered Mama in the vestibule, crying and clinging to Papa who stood as pale and stony faced as a statue, a letter in his hand. Jane appeared with Mama's smelling salts and Kitty hovered in the shadows.

"Oh, where were you, Mary?" said Jane when she saw me. "I could not find you."

"What's happened?"

Mama howled. "Oh, my poor, poor Lydia! My most precious girl!"

"Is she—?" I was prevented from voicing my assumption of her death by Jane who came up to me and explained the situation in as clear and calm a manner as could be expected.

"An express came with a letter from Colonel Forster. Last night, Lydia ran off to Gretna Green with Mr Wickham. They were not missed until the morning."

"What?!"

The front door cannot have been properly closed after the departure of the express for it now swung open, letting in a blast of wind that cut through my nightgown, threading my skin with ice and blowing out the candle I held. As no one else moved, I went and heaved it shut, turning the key in the lock. I was not one to look to nature for signs and omens but I scowled through the window at the weather outside, fighting against the sense of foreboding that the chill gust brought with it.

VOLUME III, CHAPTER V

Taking the Sea Air

Mama babbled incoherently, her speech interspersed with tears. Eventually, distinct words became discernible. "My poor girl! How she shall be unjustly censured for this and what shall she have to live upon when she is married I do not know! For Wickham has little to call his own and Mr Bennet can give her barely anything! Oh, my poor Lydia!"

"It may not be the most prudent of matches with regards to fortune," said Jane. "However, the fact that he chuses to marry her must shew that his affection is untainted by pecuniary interest. His character is shewn in an unexpectedly good light through this, is it not?"

"Like many young men, he chose his bride impetuously, without giving due consideration to his future," said Papa. "He has been thoughtless and indiscreet and will no doubt learn from his mistakes when it is too late to remedy them. I had never dared hope for such a son in law. I am sure he will provide much entertainment for me and numerous observations on vice and folly for Mary."

"Be serious, Mr Bennet! This is no occasion to joke!"

Papa's face was still ash white and I saw no hint of a smile, despite the humour of his words. As he glanced at me, I wondered if his thoughts had led to as grave a prospect as mine had. Although it was assumed a marriage would take place between Lydia and Mr Wickham, I could not be easy until it had.

I spent much of the next morning pacing my room, considering how best to handle the situation, thinking through the possibilities, wondering how I could stop Lydia from running away with Mr Wickham in a way that would prevent her from simply doing so at a later time. I had as much inspiration as I had breakfast – which was none. I was too agitated to eat and drank so much coffee that when a carriage arrived I could not tell if I shook from nerves or from too much of this beverage. When I recognised the usually cheerful but now sombre face of Colonel Forster, my stomach twisted into a knot and I froze at the window, watching him progress up the drive, torn between rushing up to him to demand news of Lydia and burying my head in sopha cushions so as not to hear what he might say.

No word had passed his lips but already his manner and expressions filled me with dread.

"What news have you?" said Papa, before Mr Brook had closed the door.

"I fear what I have to relate will cause you alarm but you must be informed. After sending the letter to you by express, one of my officers, Mr Chamberlayne, repeated to me something he had heard from Mr Denny. He believed that Wickham had no intention of going to Scotland or of marrying Miss Lydia at all."

I collapsed into a chair and let my head fall into my hands.

Mama only just suppressed her bout of hysterics enough for Colonel Forster's raised voice to be heard.

"I left immediately, with the intention of tracing their route. Making enquiries, I learned that they took a chaise from Epsom to Clapham where they removed to a hackney coach. All I could discover from those at the coaching inn was that they were seen going down the London road. None of my other enquiries in that town brought any enlightenment and so I made for Hertfordshire, stopping at the inns in Barnet and Hatfield and thus determining that they had likely not come that way. I believe them to be in London still."

"Where they can be easily hidden," added Papa bitterly.

"Good heavens!" Jane shook her head in disbelief.

A marriage between Lydia and Mr Wickham might be irresponsible and an elopement would have fostered a degree of scandal that would not have left the rest of us untainted. However, the idiotic couple had now raised their value to the gossip-mongers higher still. They were last seen in London. There was no indication of them travelling further north, specifically towards Scotland where they might legally marry without Papa's consent or banns having to be read. They would be living together, unmarried, hidden from good society and with every minute that they passed in that reprehensible state, they darkened our family's future more and more.

Colonel Forster's words became muted by the fog of my thoughts but the clock's ticking was as clear to me as a driver's whip. Just then, I had a vision of Mama in black and Mr Collins casting the Bennet women out of Longbourn for good. With naught but a pittance to live on and no decent man wanting anything to do with a family that had produced a fallen woman such as Lydia, we would be left to slip further into poverty, despair and the increase of vexations, quarrels and general irritation with one another that this state would surely cultivate. I pictured Lydia, pregnant and abandoned, like the unfortunate Miss Frances Beaufort but without the wealthy relations to alleviate her suffering.

"Fetch me my smelling salts, Mary," said Mama.

"No," I said, making my shock-frozen limbs move. "If you'll pardon me, I can do better than that." I made for the stairs, ignoring Colonel Forster's wide-eyed surprise, Papa's disapproving squint, Jane's bemused look and Mama's and Kitty's incredulous stares. They might think my behaviour rude, disobedient and unsympathetic to our cause but I refused to let that rankle with me. I knew where my duty lay and that was of greater consequence to me than their misjudged opinions. Besides, I thought as I reached my room and started unpicking stitches from my bonnet, soon enough this moment will not even have existed – for them at any rate.

Saturday 1st August 1812

"Pray, make my excuses to Lady Lucas, I recall she invited us to take tea with her, but I must go to Bower Green to visit my ill friend again."

"Again?" said Mama as she sat in front of her dressing table, Sally behind her arranging her lace cap. "When were you off visiting the sick before?"

In the mirror's reflection, I caught my look of consternation. My first pretended visit was on the second of August and so, for Mama, had not happened yet.

"Back in May, when I went to the lectures with the Palmers, we visited her. I'm sure I mentioned it at the time."

"Oh, yes," said Mama and I smiled at how we were neither of us speaking the truth. "Now I recall. Miss . . . what was her name?"

Something to do with undergarments was it? "Her name?"

"Yes."

Did Papa's pipe help me come up with the name? No, his snuffbox!

"Miss . . ." Chemise – bodice – stays – corset – drawers – petticoat – *petticoat!* "Miss Snuffpetti – I mean, Pettisnuff." My triumph at remembering the name was somewhat marred by the consideration that I could have given any name – Smith, Jones, Dalrymple – it would not have mattered. "I expect to be out all day and will dine there. Indeed, should I be asked to, I may even stay the night."

"She sounds like one of these irritating people who are always fancying themselves ill. What is her complaint?"

Poor Miss Pettisnuff's complaint was the first one that came into my head, one which, thankfully, I had had as a child and therefore would not catch. "Scarlet fever."

"Scarlet fever?" Mama turned to face me. "Are you quite sure that you wish to go? It seems to me that you are taking your philanthropic sensibilities a little too far."

"I merely wish to develop myself, both in terms of virtue and accomplishments. If I gain practice as a nurse, I may be better equipped

240

to be of assistance should any of my own family become ill."

Mama looked thoughtful and nodded. "There is logic there. Very well. Will you need Nelly?"

"No thank you, Mama. It is a fine day and not three miles to Bower Green. I shall walk."

My excuses made and a basket of food and drink prepared by myself and Mrs Hill as gifts for the invalid, I set off for Meryton. The mail coach left for London at half past eight that morning and I was on it, squeezed between sour-faced Mrs Camfield, a piglet on her lap, and incessantly talkative Mrs Pratt, who took up most of the seat, several of her little Pratts opposite us, fighting over a bag of buns.

After reaching London, I was directed to the mail coach bound for Brighton and reached it just in time. We were not much south of Croydon before my backside ached. By Reigate, where we changed horses, my back began to plague me with discomfort and by the last stop, at which we gained a fresh driver as well as horses, I felt so jostled about that I was quite astounded that I had not brought up my dinner of pork pie, bread, cucumber, strawberries, cherries and pound cake.

I shielded my eyes as I emerged from the coaching inn yard onto a busy Brighton street, the low sun suitably radiant as the town's prefix advised. It was not long until I spotted an officer of my acquaintance.

"Good Lord, Miss Mary! Are all the Bennets come down to Brighton?" said Mr Denny.

"No, sir." However, I could not say that I had come here alone. "I came with my aunt and uncle to try the benefits of sea bathing. I have read much about it. Though we are only stopping here for refreshment before we take the mail coach to Worthing."

"And is Miss Kitty with you?"

"She did not wish to come this way. She's had quite enough of officers. Now, if you please, can you inform me where my sister Lydia is staying?"

"With the Forsters."

With a jerk of my head and a pointed look, I encouraged him to elaborate.

"They've taken rooms on Church Street, near Prince George's Marine Pavilion. Number one hundred and twenty."

"And what direction is that, pray?"

He indicated the way. "You may find them not at home. They went to inspect the soldiers' camp in Hove, though they're due to return soon as they're hosting a supper for a number of the officers in about an hour and a half."

"Mr Wickham has been invited, I suppose?"

"He has." There was an uncertain flicker of movement about Denny's eyes which made me wonder what he guessed about that so called gentleman but any concerns he had, he masked with his customary smile.

"And Mr Chamberlayne, where is he?"

"I just left him at the billiard table at the Royal Circus," he nodded towards a modern looking three storey building fronted by pillars and topped with a Pegasus sculpture, "but he should be at the Forsters' shortly. I'm sure the colonel would extend the invitation to you and your aunt and uncle if you—"

"That won't be necessary. We shall be leaving soon." I bowed. "Goodbye."

Across the street, I made for a door on the left side of the building, the side bearing a painted sign for 'Billiards'.

"I regret that ladies are not permitted—"

"Why does everyone say they regret excluding ladies whilst displaying no sign of that sentiment whatsoever? Tell me, what do you think shall happen to our language if words are continually selected which bear no relation to the truth?"

The doorman's mouth fell open but he had nothing more to say and I was left to peer through the windows in the hope of spying my friend. Making my way to the other end of the building – the location of a coffee house – a group of red coats caught my eye. I hurried in, pushing past the doorman on this side before I could hear any further regrets. However, a scattering of women at the tables made it clear that I would not be unwelcome here.

"Miss Mary!" Chamberlayne broke away from his group. "Where did you come from? Or should that be 'when' did you come from?" he laughed, making creases at the corners of his eyes. "We'll have two coffees here please, young man."

"Certainly, sir."

He pulled out a chair for me. "So, tell me, how did our little scheme go? Has love been kindled in Derbyshire?"

"Oh Chamberlayne," I said, ignoring the curious glances directed our way, "I thank you for all you did and it might all have gone very well had not something happened which ruined everything!" I could not speak for a time. He offered me a handkerchief. "No thank you, I am not about to cry." I drained my coffee cup. "I came here from Monday."

"Today is Saturday, is it not?" he asked.

"Goodness, Chamberlayne. You could at least keep track of the day. Yes it is Saturday. Tonight, around midnight, Lydia is going to run away with Mr Wickham."

Chamberlayne's cup clattered on its saucer. "What?"

"That is, unless we can stop them."

"They plan to elope?"

"Whilst I think that to have been Lydia's belief, it cannot have been what Mr Wickham intended. They were traced to London but there was no sign of them having gone to Scotland. They were living together there in such a manner as will wreck all my family's prospects when it is known."

"And you plan to stop them before it happens."

I nodded. "I shall attempt to speak to Lydia alone. I do not wish to make my presence here known to the Forsters. Mr Denny knows of it, unfortunately, but he thinks my aunt and uncle and I are on our way to Worthing."

"You're getting quite practised at spinning tales."

243

"That is from necessity," I said, reddening, "and I don't always spin them with skill. However, back to the matter at hand. Will you talk with Wickham?"

He hesitated, looking into his cup. "I shall. Of course I shall but I cannot claim to have any degree of influence over him. In the past, I have advised Wickham not to gamble so much but I've heard that his gaming debts have soared since our arrival in the town."

"Better and better," I said, slumping in my chair.

He smiled at my sarcasm but his expression soon melted into one of concern.

"If he'd listen to anyone, it would be Denny but he's not the sort to interfere in any gentleman's business."

"The more's the pity." I sat in thought for some moments, absently stirring my coffee. "If Wickham's financial situation is so very dire, that might explain why he plans to leave Brighton," I suggested. "Perhaps his running away with Lydia was a secondary plan, a spontaneous one that we might easily thwart. Then he would leave the town to escape his creditors and she should be out of danger from him."

"We can but hope," he took one last sip of coffee and placed coins on the table. "We must do what we can. I shall go now to the Forsters' house, before the other guests arrive and do my best to express to Colonel Forster my concerns about Wickham's intentions. When alerted to the danger, they shall be sure to keep a close eye on your sister which should prevent her being able to get away."

"Yes," I took his hand. "Thank you. They are sure to pay heed to you. And you will try to talk with Wickham?"

He took a deep breath. "I shall, for your sake, though I cannot see it doing much good." We proceeded directly to Church Street together, Chamberlayne entering the house and I waiting around the corner.

After a few minutes had elapsed, I spied Lydia stepping out of a carriage. She slipped a little on the step, taking Colonel Forster's arm and flying into a fit of giggles, her cheeks rosy, her laughter carrying down the street.

"I'm sure the soldiers were quite heartbroken that I could not stay with them for supper and cards," she exclaimed. "But I could not disappoint our dear officers now could I? Have we time to change? I am determined to wear my new silk gown." So she prattled on as she entered the house on Church Street.

I crept around the building, spying through windows. I passed a boot room where a maid stood over a basin of brown water, scrubbing dirt from the household's footwear. Moving on, I ducked just in time before the butler saw me on his way down the stairs. Then I came upon a room which was mostly taken up with a billiard table. Colonel Forster froze after striking a ball and looked up at Chamberlayne who was speaking to him. The colonel mirrored Chamberlayne's grave expression before shaking his head. With no hats near them, I could not hear what they said but I trusted that Chamberlayne would do his best.

Next, I came to a parlour where Mrs Forster was arranging flowers in a vase. The door burst open and Lydia joined her, dressed in cream silk with gold trimmings, her cheeks flushed, a parody of a blushing bride. The window was a little ajar, allowing me to hear their words.

"What say you?" asked Lydia, twirling. "Do I not look well in it?"

"Indeed you do, my dear. Though I still cannot believe you spent near all of your money on one gown," said Mrs Forster.

"How Mama would laugh! But I liked it so well, I could hardly deny myself!" she said.

I rolled my eyes.

"I only wish I had better shoes to match," she continued.

"Why not try on my cream silk slippers? They may fit you. I'll just be a minute." Mrs Forster shuffled out of the room and I seized my opportunity.

"Lydia!" I tapped on the window.

"What the dickens are you doing here?" cried Lydia. She gave me and my bonnet a look of incredulity, peppered with venom.

"Lydia, I have to warn you about Mr Wickham."

"Just you go away, Mary! I'm having the jolliest time I've ever had in my life, by gad, and I'm not about to let you spoil it!"

"You want to be married and you think he'll elope with you if you run off with him tonight but ask yourself this: what would a man such as Wickham gain from a union with you? He who pursued Mary King for her fortune, who has no particular wealth of his own, only a large amount of debt it seems. He may appear charming but, count on it, he will not marry you Lydia."

"What would you know about it? You know nothing of men's hearts. Wickham loves me and I shall do what I like. Now, get away before Mrs Forster returns."

The door opened again and I ducked out of sight.

"Oh," said Mrs Forster. "I thought I heard talking and wondered if any other officers had arrived."

"Oh. I must have been talking to myself."

"Ah, there you are my dear," came Colonel Forster's voice. "Might I have a private word with you in the front parlour. Pray excuse us, Miss Lydia."

Lydia came back to the window. "I care not how you got here, Mary, or what you hope to achieve. If you wish to go sea-bathing, you can go to another town, only leave me alone. Understand?" She shut the window just as I was about to respond, trapping my finger before I whipped it away, wincing.

I returned to the window of the billiard room and tapped, whereupon Chamberlayne opened it.

"Thank you for speaking with the colonel," I said.

"He did not wish to believe my concerns to begin with," he said, "but he left me with the assurance that Mrs Forster's maid will rouse her mistress if Lydia attempts to leave her room in the night. Poor girl, I hope they pay her extra for being on the night watch."

"Good," I said. "You've achieved more than I have. I spoke to Lydia, little good it did though."

"What are you to do now?"

"I must wait until night time and stop Lydia if she tries to leave. Though I need not wait hours. I can stitch myself along a bit."

"You can *what?*"

"Never mind that now, I hear riders," I said, my voice low. "The other guests are arriving, I believe, so I will go." I whipped out my needle case and made three stitches.

"Where?" he asked.

I grinned at him. "To the future." I put on the bonnet and had one last look at his amazed face before all became dark. The sun had disappeared as swiftly as a candle being blown out. A gust of wind crashed into me, teasing lengths of my hair out from under my bonnet and whipping them into my eyes. I pulled up my shawl around my shoulders but the chill air threaded through my clothing, snatching away any warmth it could find. An oak across the road moaned in a long, low creak, the street lamp a few houses away casting sinister shadows across its bark.

"Come on, Lydia," I said. "If you're coming then do so now." The house on Church Street remained deathly quiet. I shivered as a barn owl screeched in the distance. As I rubbed warmth into my arms, I heard the tap of shoes on stone and jumped.

Lydia was on the doorstep, easing the front door shut behind her.

D— Mrs Forster's maid or whichever servant it was, I thought. Surely Lydia could not have got out without someone's contrivance, even though she cannot have paid them much, having already spent most of her pin money.

She lingered on the doorstep and I could just make out the creak of her shoes as she bounced up and down. I thought of Mama. The pair of them were so alike, it was not surprising Mama indulged her. If only Papa had cared enough to keep her behaviour in check, things might not have led to this.

Soon, a carriage rolled up outside the house. With a sharp click, the door opened and footsteps pattered towards it.

"NO!" I cried, rushing at Lydia. I grabbed her arms, pinning them behind her back. "You will not go with him. You will not ruin our family's reputation, our sisters' chances of good marriages, our whole future."

"Get off me. You're insane!"

"You must know the truth of him." She struggled a little less but I rushed through my list of his vices in case she should break away from me. After she knew all, her intentions would surely be altered. "He accepted three thousand pounds from Mr Darcy in lieu of a parish living which he did not want but when the money was gone, he demanded more. Selfish, bitter and malicious as he was, he told the world that Darcy dishonourably refused to acknowledge his father's wishes for him but the dishonour was all his—"

"What does it matter what he said about that horrid Mr Darcy! Wickham loves me and treats me well. Let me go!"

"He went after Mary King for her money and apparently took such liberties with her in his desire to exert power over her that her family took her away to be safe from him. Before that, he tried to elope with none other than Mr Darcy's sister, to spite him and gain her thirty thousand pounds. He cares not about the reputations of women. He only thinks about himself, his pleasures and how he can take advantage of others. He gambles, leaving a trail of creditors in his wake. He wants money and he delights in bolstering his vanity. You serve the latter purpose for him but once he's tired of you, your inability to satisfy the former will be his reason to abandon you."

"I don't care what he's done or not done," she said, pulling away from me. "He was never in love with those girls as he's in love with me."

"Wake up, Lydia— he will not marry you!"

"Yes he will!" she said through gritted teeth. "Get OFF!"

She got one arm free and in my reaching for it again, I only grasped a handful of fabric. There was the tight sound of it ripping.

I didn't see the back of her head coming towards me but I felt its impact. All at once, my nose burst with pain, as though it had been struck by a hammer.

"You clumsy cow, Mary! I care little about the gown that tore last night but this one is new!"

I tasted iron as warm blood flooded my mouth. I must have let go of Lydia for now she ran from me, leaping into the carriage which bore her and Wickham away into darkness. I heard her laughter long after the carriage was out of sight. I might as well have tried to keep hold of the battering, salty air as keep Lydia from doing as she pleased.

Part of me wanted to collapse to the ground but I stood tall, hands as fists, face resounding with pain so that I could not think of anything else in that moment but how I damned Lydia for a fool.

VOLUME III, CHAPTER VI

Drastic Measures

There was nothing to be done but to unpick stitches and return to the morning of the day Lydia ran away. I would blot out my pointless venture to Brighton and, in so doing, return the pin money I had spent on my journey back to my purse and fix my broken nose. However, financial replenishment, lack of major facial dissymmetry and blood-steeped neckline notwithstanding, this journey back in time had its disadvantages. I doomed myself to wait through Saturday and Sunday, anticipating my family's shock at the letter that would arrive on Sunday night.

In the tumult of this drama, I had almost lost track of Lizzy and Mr Darcy.

I had a decision to make. Should I relive my visit to Colonel Fitzwilliam on the Sunday afternoon, thus causing Lord Fitzwilliam's wedding to be cancelled and allowing Lizzy and Mr Darcy to meet at Pemberley or should I not do so? Would not Lydia's actions eliminate all hope of a union between the pair? In the end, I reasoned that it would not do to lose hope entirely, so pay the visit I did. What had I to lose?

That night, my heart sank as I heard the express arrive. Anxiety spread through the household like a fire, though an odd one which drew out all the warmth from one's person. It was most unbearable. Then, the following day, I was made to relive Colonel Forster's visit and his revelation to us which, remaining quite unaltered from the first occasion of it, was even more painful to me than it had been.

Anger swelled within me – at Lydia – at Wickham – at myself for failing to stop them.

I spent much time that day in my room in the pretence of studying. Kitty shook her head at me in exasperation, calling me unfeeling in carrying on as normal and thinking of no one but myself but, in truth, my duty to my family was my primary motivation. Kitty continually expressed how unfair it was that Papa was angry at her for hiding her knowledge that Lydia and Mr Wickham were, according to Lydia, desperately in love. She dwelt on how much better she would have behaved should she have been allowed to go to Brighton. She took no time to care for Mama in her state of distress but lingered as usual about her toilette, arranging her hair, applying lotions to her face and spending long hours reading absurd novels, no doubt fantasising a romance for herself.

Jane's care of the Gardiner children and of Mama, who would not leave her room, cast her actions in angelic light, radiating for all to see, whereas my superior intelligence, my most effectual gift to my family, required time and space for the development of a solution to aid us in our distress. It might be frustrating but I had not the time to care that my service was, as Thomas Gray's poetic flower, 'born to blush unseen'.

My curiosity led me to hear how things passed for Lizzy, though I all but tore my hair out in frustration when I heard her meeting Mr Darcy and followed the signs of their budding relationship. It was tragic. Mr Darcy would surely not connect himself with such a family as ours once Lydia's shame became known. My success at bringing them together was all for nothing. The heights of expectation, which Lizzy's attentions from Mr Darcy had nurtured in me in the first instance, merely emphasised the devastation that lay before our family as we began our plummeting descent.

Perhaps I should not have listened. Each day brought an increase of bittersweet distress but listen I did. Darcy's manner towards my aunt and uncle, though knowing them to be in trade, was nothing but affable. He spoke with great civility, inviting Uncle Gardiner to fish in his trout stream, but a request he made of Lizzy was a clearer indication of his wish to strengthen their relationship.

"There is also one other person in the party who more particularly wishes to be known to you. Will you allow me, or do I ask too much, to introduce my sister to your acquaintance during your stay at Lambton?" he said as they walked together in the grounds, my aunt and uncle's footsteps some way behind them.

Who could have inspired his sister's desire to meet Lizzy but he himself and how else but with words of great admiration?

The next day, as Lizzy, my aunt and uncle were just returned to the inn at Lambton after taking the air, Mr Darcy and his sister called upon them, followed soon by Mr Bingley. Thankfully, upon Lizzy's removal of her bonnet, she kept it somewhere close by which enabled me to hear much of what passed. Mr Darcy was more talkative than I had ever heard him which must have betokened his desire to please.

At one point, Mr Bingley asked, in a quiet tone, "Are *all* your sisters at Longbourn?" If this were not a discreet enquiry after one who had inspired his affections, I knew not what could be, and it gave me all the more reason to grind my teeth at the thought of how things might have been if Lydia had not been so ... *Lydia*.

I knew Jane to have written to Lizzy. At any moment, she would find out what had occurred and the dream would fade to nothing. I had little hope that she would have the opportunity to secure Mr Darcy in an engagement before she heard the news, and she lacked the art to hide her distress and seek to deceive him after her discovery. I respected her honest nature, though it was rather inconvenient in this instance.

The following morning brought no letter from Jane, which surprised me. Lizzy and my aunt called upon Georgiana whilst my uncle went fishing with the gentlemen of the party. Later, they joined the ladies and the visit did not end before Mr Darcy and his sister expressed their wish of having Lizzy and the Gardiners to dine at Pemberley before they left the county.

Finally, upon the next morning, Jane's letter arrived. Two in fact, if I heard correctly. I did not envy Lizzy the revelations that would now manifest themselves to her.

"Good God! What is the matter?" I heard Mr Darcy exclaim. What a moment for him to visit! She would certainly not be able to hide the truth from him. His response to Lizzy's narration of events shewed compassion as well as shock.

"I am afraid you have long been desiring my absence," he said at last. Did he actually mean that he wished to remove himself from her company? Had the taint of scandal repulsed him already? "Would to heaven that anything could be either said or done on my part, that might offer consolation to such distress." But no. Of course he could offer us no consolation. He could not marry Lizzy and raise us up again without dragging himself down. "But I will not torment you with vain wishes, which may seem purposely to ask for your thanks. This unfortunate affair will, I fear, prevent my sister's having the pleasure of seeing you at Pemberley today." Was that a question or a statement? I could not tell whether he wished to un-invite Lizzy or, out of civility, make it easier for her to withdraw her acceptance of the invitation.

"Oh, yes," said Lizzy. "Be so kind as to apologise for us to Miss Darcy. Say that urgent business calls us home immediately. Conceal the unhappy truth as long as it is possible. I know it cannot be long."

"Of course, you can rely on my discretion. I cannot tell you how sorry I am and I wish that your present distress will not remain so acute. May the conclusion of this business be happier than there seems reason to hope at present. Please relay my compliments to Mr and Mrs Gardiner."

There was silence. Then the tapping of footsteps and the click of the closing door as he left. I felt instinctively then that she would never see him again.

A large moth fluttered about my window, seeking an impossible escape. I reached out, thinking at first to push the window ajar, but I paused. With care, I cupped the trembling creature in my hands and removed to Lydia and Kitty's room, then unoccupied. I gave the moth a new residence in Lydia's closet with a selection of her undergarments and stockings.

"Do your worst, little one," I said. "Lord knows, that is all that *I* have left to do."

I knew then the path I must take to save my family from destitution. We had lost all hope of decent marriages. We could not lose Longbourn. All that could help us now would be the deaths of the Collins heirs. Lydia had lost her virtue, destroying our family's hopes. If I had to lose mine to restore them – albeit in a different manner – I was ready to make that sacrifice. Perhaps this was why the bonnet had come to me. Perhaps, all this time, I had been destined to be both the saviour of my family and a murderess.

Lizzy arrived home the next day and I sat beside her at dinner. Jane would have known how to shew her, in the subtlest of looks, how sorry she was for Lizzy's personal and our collective loss, but I was bound to get it wrong so I rarely lifted my gaze from my plate.

I sighed, sentiment swelling so within me that I felt I had to express my feelings of regret and my concern for my family. "This is a most unfortunate affair and will probably be much talked of," I said.

I thought of how we four remaining Bennet girls would live the rest of our lives together in spinsterhood, a prospect hitherto unimagined. Oh, the dreams that foolish girl had killed – the security, happiness, the marriages and children that might not exist because of her! Kitty ate her way through a whole plate of potatoes. Poor thing! Such overindulgence could only spring from her dejection.

"But we must stem the tide of malice," I continued, though I knew it would be a good while before I could forgive Lydia, "and pour into the wounded bosoms of each other, the balm of sisterly consolation."

What would they think if they knew what form I meant my consolation to take? What a burden I meant to shoulder for their sakes! No one else spoke, so I continued to follow my own line of thought.

"Unhappy as the event must be for Lydia, we may draw from it this useful lesson: that loss of virtue in a female is irretrievable." I thought then of my own virtue which I was preparing to defile. "That one false step involves her in endless ruin." Or ruin that only ends with the gallows. I shivered. "That her reputation is no less brittle than it is beautiful."

I felt a warmth of love for my sisters which I did not often feel. If I were to be caught and hanged— but no. It would not serve to contemplate that outcome. They were looking at me strangely now and I hoped that no hint of my private thoughts had come through into my speech. Picking up the threads of my words, I ended: "And that she cannot be too much guarded in her behaviour towards the undeserving of the other sex." There were too many such men around, in my opinion. The male Collinses were, in my view, undeserving of Longbourn – most likely being illegitimate – and I must be most guarded and cautious in my dealings with *them*.

"Mary, pass the bacon," said Kitty.

On Sunday, our hopes for a letter from Papa in London were disappointed and my uncle left to join him and aid him in his search for the couple. Tuesday did bring a letter, though it contained no promising news. Every day that passed worsened our anxiety. The others were concerned about Lydia's fate but I had quite given up on her. She had already cast us all into the dirt. The subject which occupied me and kept me awake at night was how I might kill the male Collinses and get away with it.

Shortly after the delivery of my uncle's letter, Aunt Philips came by.

"Oh, Mary! Is this not the most horrendous thing! How I pity you all!" she said as we walked upstairs together to Mama's room. "Oh sister!" she cried when she saw Mama who was propped up in bed by many cushions, wrapped in shawls, a tray of smelling salts and medicinal port wine within her reach. "I have come to console with you and offer what comfort I can. Look, I've brought some of these little boxes of marzipan to cheer you. Mrs Long brought them back from her trip to Bath as she knows how I love Molland's marzipan but I decided they would be of more benefit to you."

"Oh, yes. Mr Collins quite ate us out of marzipan when he staid with us and Hill has not taken the initiative to make more. Oh, sister, no one in this house thinks about me."

Aunt Philips sat on the bed and gripped Mama's hand. "Oh! I have heard such things about Mr Wickham, you would not believe! He left Meryton with such debts, both from extravagant purchases and imprudence at the gaming tables."

"Oh, my poor Lydia!" Mama wept.

"And it is said that the reason why Miss Mary King was removed by her family to the north was because Mr Wickham had taken such liberties with her in unchaperoned moments as no gentleman would do."

"Oh, what a fiend! He had better make an honest woman of my poor girl. If he does not, Mr Bennet will fight him and be killed and then Mr Collins will turn us all out of the house!"

Not if I get to him first, I thought.

I made to leave the room, there being only so much of Mama's despair I could endure without my head splitting, but I looked back before crossing the threshold. The boxes of marzipan scattered on the bed caught my eye and gave me a rather interesting idea.

VOLUME III, CHAPTER VII

Tutor & Pupil

My head a whirl of ideas, my heart hammering, my blood running now hot – now cold, I raced to Mrs Pepperstock's cottage on Nelly.

"Afternoon, missy" she said, opening the door and noting with clear disappointment that I brought her nothing.

"Mrs Pepperstock, I have a rather unusual request. Can I trust you?"

Unconsciously tapping my fingers on her dust-covered table, I related to her all that had passed regarding Lydia and Mr Wickham.

"I hardly need explain the implications of this," I said.

She shook her head. "But you have a plan, or you would not have come to talk with me like this, nor would you be so agitated."

"I do. But I need your help." I looked into her eyes. "You will not tell," I breathed.

"Not a soul. You carry a secret of mine; you can trust me with yours."

"I plan to . . . dispatch the male Collinses, the heirs to the Longbourn estate. Then the house will stay with us. There are no other heirs."

"Quite right and proper," she said, unperturbed.

"If you can help me make marzipan – and poisoned marzipan at that – then I will attempt to locate the Collinses and present them with our creations. The only difficulty is Frederick Collins who, I believe, is fighting in Spain. We may be lucky though," I shrugged, "and he may die at the hands of the French."

"You fear going to a place of war?"

"Well—" I half laughed. "It might be rational to experience fear at such a prospect but I have not the means to travel so far and, even if I did, I do not know how I would explain my absence to my family for the length of the sea voyages and I know not what."

"Sea voyages?" she said, squinting at me. "Are you not forgetting? Are the candles lit but no one at home? You might travel direct to the nearest town, silly girl, providing it has a milliner's shop."

"What are you talking about?"

She laughed then. "You do not know! You had the bonnet for I don't know how much longer than I had it and you did not discover—" she interrupted herself with yet more laughter.

"What do you mean by 'travel direct'? Are you saying I've been needlessly travelling to London and Brighton on horseback and by coach, enduring hours of discomfort," I put my hand to my posterior, "not to mention wasting precious time? Stop laughing, Mrs Pepperstock, and tell me what you know."

VOLUME III, CHAPTER VIII
Shopping Spree & Confectionery

"Right, men, get up. We march on. Some of you lucky b—ds will sleep in proper beds tonight. I know I intend to."

"But Captain, will it be as easy as all that?"

"Rest assured, Harrington, it won't be another Badajoz and it's sure to be easier than Salamanca. King Joseph Bonaparte fled Madrid with the royal household days ago. Most of the civilians evacuated along with a swathe of soldiers. They'll have left a garrison to be sure but it'll be swatting flies, no more than that. The civilians who are left will be delighted to be liberated, I have no doubt."

"Sir – Frenchies! Over that hill!"

"B— hell! Where did they spring from?"

"Looks like only three, stragglers or cowards."

"Or scouts."

"D—! Where did they go?"

A shot rang out, jolting me so that my bonnet nearly fell off. My heart was galloping in my chest. I was sitting on my bed but I could almost imagine myself to be in Spain, being shot at along with these soldiers I was listening to.

"F—!"

My eyes widened in shock at the language the bonnet had allowed me to hear. Then the crack of the musket was followed by a second and a third, the blasts echoing in my ears, more shocking even than the soldier's expletive. Heart racing, I gave in to irrationality, diving into a crouching position between my bed and chest of drawers as though I were also being fired at, even as I rebuked myself for such ridiculousness.

"Captain? Captain Collins? Are you alright, sir?" This voice was muffled.

Perhaps Captain Collins was dead. I might have no need to see to his demise myself.

There was a cough, though its sound, like the last remark of the soldier, was faint. "D— Frenchies! Completely ruined my hat."

His *hat*? D—, I thought in agreement with Captain Collins.

"Well," he said, "may it belong to whichever b—d finds it."

No! How was I to keep track of his movements if he left his hat behind? I was forced to put that question aside, along with my bonnet, as my family would be expecting me at breakfast. I made myself eat about as much as usual. It was bound to be a trying day, requiring sufficient fortification, but the twisting sensation in my stomach and the dryness of my throat made it difficult to eat.

My family believed I was going on another charitable visit to my most useful creation, Miss Pettisnuff, but instead I walked to Pratt's shop in Meryton to carry out Mrs Pepperstock's directions. I entered the shop, ignoring Mr Pratt's greeting, and turned back around to face the door, my eyes shut. Apart from the nervously humming Mr Pratt and myself, the front room of the shop was quite empty of people but, as I concentrated on the place I wished to go, I began to hear the chatter of customers and shop assistants. It sounded as though business was better in Hunsford.

Thinking of that place, listening intently to the sounds from the other shop and crossing my fingers, I opened my eyes. The shop around me remained unchanged but the view outside, extending before me as I pushed open the door, was certainly not Meryton. Rather than landing on a sound-muffling hard packed earth surface, my shoes tapped on the cobbles of a narrow street.

A dog barked at me, jumping about in agitation and a small child only a yard or two away from me pulled at his mother's skirts, saying:

"How did she do that, Mama? Is she the wicked witch?"

"I do apologise," the woman said to me. "Don't be rude, Horace!"

Turning, I looked into Hartley's, the milliner's shop in Hunsford. The window displayed a range of bonnets of the styles I had seen Lady Catherine and her daughter wearing, as well as the gaping faces of several customers who stared at me unblinkingly. I winked at them before going on my way.

When I reached the lane that led up to the parsonage, I put up my parasol so as not to be recognised, then crept into Mr Collins' garden. I saw Charlotte through a side window as she sat in her parlour, sewing a quilted blanket. Her eyelids appeared heavy as she looked up and she sighed, putting aside her work as though it weighed the same as a stack of dinner plates. I edged closer, longing to know if the rosy tinge in her cheeks might be a sign of good health or fever.

Feeling a crunch beneath the sole of my shoe, I winced, realising I had killed a poor snail. Whether from this sound or some other cause, Charlotte looked out in my direction but I ducked behind a laurel bush just in time.

At that moment, Mr Collins, humming a hymn, strolled down the shrubbery and began deadheading the roses. How I could extricate myself from the garden now without being noticed, I did not know. However, my dilemma did not last long. A carriage trundled by causing Mr Collins to jump, dropping his pruning shears as he rushed through to the front of the house, bringing Charlotte with him to welcome whoever it was that was visiting.

I let out a deep sigh and made my way to the flowerbed where once I had seen a healthy cultivation of aconitum, also known as monkshood, wolf's-bane and queen of poisons. My stomach dropt. In its place was an empty bed. I could not account for it as my warning to Charlotte of the plant's toxicity had not occurred for her since Lizzy had taken my place at Hunsford. There was nothing I could do but return to Meryton. I did not know the location of any other poisonous plant and neither did Mrs Pepperstock. I would be forced to abandon my plan.

As I was retreating back down the lane, my eye was caught by a plant with dark, shiny berries and bell shaped, purple flowers. It was within a little wilderness which edged Rosings Park, where the trees gave way to clusters of nettles and weeds. I laughed to myself at the different levels of appropriateness of this plant as the potential means of fulfilling my plan after all.

Firstly, it seemed ironic that Mr Collins' downfall would come from the land of the woman he worshipped as his noble patroness. In addition, it felt significant that the plant in question was deadly nightshade, also known as atropa belladonna. It was named after Atropos, Greek goddess and one of the three fates, whose name meant 'she who may not be turned aside'. Through my actions, we Bennet women would not be turned aside or sent from our beloved home into poverty. The fates wove the threads of life and Atropos cut them to mark a person's death.

I approached the plant, ignoring the stinging nettles and thistles that bit at my legs. "Well met, Atropos. I know a little about threads too," I said. Kneeling down, I slipped on my gloves and used the knife I had brought to claw at the earth, prising stones away, until the pale brown roots of the plant came into view. After sawing away some gnarled lengths of root, I wrapped them up in a cloth and bound it with string, unwilling to risk touching this most poisonous part of the plant.

"What on earth are you doing?"

Miss de Bourgh appeared through the trees at the edge of the grounds of Rosings. Using her parasol, she pushed aside the branches of a sapling to get a clearer view of me.

"Who are you? Do you know that that plant is poisonous?" She spoke with more authority than I had been used to hearing from her in the company of others. Perhaps it helped that I was a stranger, possibly even a trespasser, depending upon whereabouts the boundary to Rosings lay. "It ought not to be there and I shall see that it's removed. Why are you taking a cutting from it?" Her eyes widened. "You *know* it's poisonous. You don't mean to . . . to do something horrid?"

"It's my intention to leave Hunsford quietly without harming a soul." For now at least. "Say nothing of this and I shall say nothing to your mama of your spoiling her blackcurrant wine with vinegar." It seemed cruel to speak in such a way to someone I had a degree of friendship with, in my own recollection at least, but it was necessary in this case.

"How on earth did you—?" She frowned as she slid behind her customary veil of shyness. "Very well," she said, frowning.

With a swiftness that gave me just enough time to shield my face, Miss de Bourgh picked up a stone and threw it. It soared like the cricket ball I had seen her hit, landing, to my relief, far from me.

"I saw Mr Collins approaching," she whispered. "He's the vicar here. I wasn't throwing it *at* him you understand, I only meant to distract him. You should go now, before you're seen."

"Thank you," I said, as shocked as she must have been confused. It was most convenient that her instinct was to preserve our secrets, rather than to relieve her curiosity by asking how I knew what she had done. If we had continued longer in conversation, she might not have seen Mr Collins approach and I might have had to explain my presence here to him.

In Hunsford village, I purchased the items from a list that Mrs Pepperstock had dictated to me. Almonds and sugar I bought at the grocers, rosewater and a bottle of laudanum I acquired from a druggist.

Upon entering Pratt's shop, I saw the proprietor surrounded by a mess of hats and bonnets, his face ashen as he stared at me, one eye twitching.

"Did I hear you dropping things again?" came his wife's voice. "Clumsy fool."

"Did you . . ." piped Mr Pratt. "D-did you disappear earlier then reappear just now?"

"That sounds most irrational, Mr Pratt," I said.

He blinked rapidly. "So it does. My apologies, miss," he added with a little bow before proceeding to pick up his merchandise with trembling hands.

"Oh, Mary, I didn't think you were in town," said Kitty who came over from a display shelf with a handful of ribbons. "I had to get away from Mama's nerves for a bit and thought I'd see if they had the ribbons I was admiring last week."

The bell above the door tinkled as Mrs Pepperstock entered.

"Look," Kitty shewed me the strips of pale green silk, "they would have cost thruppence more had I bought them last week, is it not lucky that I waited? But I thought you were paying a visit to your sick friend, Miss Pettiscruff?"

"Pettisnuff," I said. "I was going to ... but—"

"She died," said Mrs Pepperstock, nodding gravely.

"How awful," said Kitty.

"Yes," I agreed, glaring at Mrs Pepperstock, "and quite a shock it was. She had been so useful to others during her lifetime."

"Well, your basket of *charitable gifts* need not go to waste," she said, shuffling out to the street. "You can carry it for me, Miss Mary."

"How bold she is!" exclaimed Kitty. "I do not like her one jot. You do not have to give her those things, surely?"

"I might as well give them to her as to anyone."

"You'll join me for dinner, missy?" said Mrs Pepperstock, winking.

"What will it be? Toad stew and snake fritters?" muttered Kitty.

"Tell Mama and Papa that, even though I am no longer at Bower Green, I will be not be back for dinner," I said.

"Better you than me," she said, pulling a face of disgust.

I flinched at the tickle of cobwebs on my face as I walked to the far end of the old cottage. The window sills, floor and table were peppered with mouse droppings and coated in sheets of dust which did not move even when the draft from the open door stripped a vase of flowers of its remaining petals.

"I think this environment," I said, waving my hand in the air, "is lacking in the necessary cleanliness for food preparation."

"Oh, really!" said Mrs Pepperstock, raising her eyebrows at me as she sat herself down. "It's so filthy it will make your poisoned confectionery unfit for consumption?"

"A point well made. Well, let us get to work. I'm afraid I did not acquire the aconitum but I found something that I think will do just as well, if not better perhaps."

"What is it? Hemlock? Arsenic? Henbane? Poisonous mushrooms? Laurel water?"

I stared at her for a moment, both impressed and disturbed by her knowledge. "Atropa belladonna."

"Ah!" She leant back in her chair. "Berries?"

"Roots."

She smiled crookedly. "You know your deadly nightshade."

"I know a lot about botany, as well as many other subjects, though I would not consider myself to be an expert in the field of poisons. I leave that title to you."

She directed me in grinding almonds and deadly nightshade root, pounding sugar into a powder and mixing particular quantities of all the ingredients.

"I've got something for you," she said as she tipped a few drops of laudanum into her second cup of gin.

"Do you honestly think I would drink any of that even if I didn't have to keep my wits about me?"

She rolled her eyes and took a small bottle from a cupboard. "Yellow dye. Picked it up in town earlier." She tossed it over to me and my heart leapt to my throat as I just caught the fragile glass container.

"Mrs Pepperstock, what if I had dropped it?"

She shrugged.

I squinted at her. "And by 'picked it up in town' do you mean you stole it?"

She laughed before taking a sip of her 'medicinal' concoction. "Is now really the time to discuss the moral implications of petty theft?"

"Well . . ." I studied the label which indicated that the dye was made from weld, also giving the Latin name: reseda luteola. "Suitable for

265

dying wool, linen and silk, it says. Can it be used in food?"

"It's sure to turn it yellow. If it causes a stomach upset, that symptom will no doubt be alleviated by the belladonna." She hunched over, caught up in a fit of cackling.

After colouring the mixture, I bent over my work, painstakingly shaping pieces of raw marzipan into delicate flowers, so that they resembled the stitched blooms on my bonnet.

"Rather poetic, I'd say," said Mrs Pepperstock, rocking back and forth like an impatient child. "Right. Put them in to cook!"

"Wait. They have to look perfect, tempting," I said as I pinched the petals to make them look more realistic.

"Ah, temptation," she said with a twinkle in her eye. "You know, that is my only weakness."

I raised my eyebrows at her. "Very droll."

In the absence of an oven, we baked them in a covered pan over the fire. In a reversal of moods, I was itching to check on them but Mrs Pepperstock made me sit and wait. At last, once baked and cooled, the marzipan flowers were just firm enough and the sight of them made my mouth water just as much as the ones Mrs Long had purchased from Molland's in Bath had done.

From my basket, I retrieved three boxes, lined with crêpe paper and inscribed with 'Molland's Marzipan', each designed to fit a single item of confectionery. Mama had emptied these within minutes of receiving them, as well as making good progress into a large box which contained, along with the famous confectionery, a goodly number of jellied sweets and sugared almonds. Using a cloth, I transferred the baneful bonbons, one into each box.

Mrs Pepperstock was eating sugar by the spoonful while I finished my preparations. When all was ready, I loaded my basket and took a deep breath. "Wish me luck."

"Good luck," she said, spitting sugar as she spoke.

VOLUME III, CHAPTER IX

Sweet Seduction

"Excuse me, Ma'am, these rooms are out of bounds to the public."

I recognised Mr Stephen Collins' voice even though it had been close to a year since I had last chanced to hear him. I thought of his conversation with Mr William Collins back then, recalling the rumours they had mentioned about their being the offspring resulting from their mother's affairs and, as I listened in on him as he worked, I marched down the road from Mrs Pepperstock's cottage, dwelling upon the structure of rules and laws which, like many others, served to favour undeserving men over accomplished and virtuous, though disadvantaged women. "Good Heavens," I thought, halting, "I think I have become a revolutionary!"

Back to Mr Stephen Collins.

"Ma'am, I just said—"

"Oh, I heard you. But I am not one of those persons to whom such barriers apply."

What Lady Catherine was doing at the Old Bailey I had no idea. A horsewoman approached on the road between Mrs Pepperstock's cottage and the high street so, once I had turned a corner, I darted into the woods to avoid conversing with her. I could not afford to miss this conversation. My bonnet must have thought similarly when I had first put it on after saying farewell to Mrs Pepperstock for, whilst I was thinking generally of the Collins brothers, I had not expected to eavesdrop on any of them at this time. However, my bonnet had clearly decided to form a connection to the brother who worked as a barrister in London, presumably using his wig.

"I take you for a lady of quality but why has no servant entered to introduce us?" he asked.

"I did not require it."

"You did not wish for your presence here to be known?"

"In my long experience, there are few servants who know their place sufficiently as to uphold the virtue of discretion. You are Mr Stephen Collins, brother of Mr William Collins of Hunsford Parsonage, are you not?"

"I am."

"I am Lady Catherine de Bourgh."

"Lady Catherine! I have heard much of your benevolence to my brother, your unsurpassed affability and condescension." He was flustered. "It is an honour, Ma'am, an honour. Is there any way that I might be of assistance to you? Any legal matter regarding which you require the benefit of my advice?"

"You are for the prosecution in the case of Mr John Griffiths, are you not?"

"That is no secret, though how your ladyship acquired such knowledge, I do not know."

"That is not your concern."

"No indeed. My apologies."

"I require for him to be found not guilty."

"But he robbed a man, your ladyship. Not only that, he had his accomplice knock him to the ground before striking him violently and repeatedly. Why should you wish for such a man get away with his crime?"

"Because otherwise this whole unfortunate episode will be talked of and printed in the newspapers and it may not be long before Mr Griffiths' unfortunate connection with my family were to become known. I cannot allow that to happen."

"He is . . . connected to—?"

"Understand that if, in due course, I believe you to have betrayed my confidence, I shall use my influence with the Right Honourable, the Lord Chief Justice with regards to your career, or subsequent lack of one."

"I assure you, I shall be as silent as death."

That comment made me laugh.

"Very well," said Lady Catherine. "A cousin of mine shamed her family by a most inappropriate marriage. I was, at that time, soon to marry into the de Bourgh family and was anxious that news of this connection did not reach them. I used my influence with her parents and, as was quite right and proper, they disinherited my cousin. We never spoke of her again. Mr Griffiths, her husband and the father of the accused, sank into debt, depravity and death. Before my cousin likewise passed away, she told her son the truth of her own Fitzwilliam parentage and, before long, he made contact with his maternal grandparents, demanding an allowance. It was granted to him with the understanding that all transactions would cease should his relation to the family become known. If he faces the gallows and has nothing to lose, he might reveal the truth our family has striven to hide, bringing shame upon the Fitzwilliams and, by the connection of my own marriage, the illustrious de Bourghs."

"That would be most pitiable and I know how my brother would feel it acutely. I confess to being quite amazed at what you have related and I thank you for being so candid. I hope that you will believe me when I reiterate that this knowledge will not be disclosed by me to another soul."

Except mine.

"Now, tell me, Mr Collins, do you consider that the case against him can be weakened?"

There was a pause and a tapping sound, a quill nib upon a desk perhaps. "I believe it can, your ladyship. And, now that I think on it, justice can only really be served by him *not* being sentenced. He stole a snuffbox for goodness' sake! And cast it aside as he ran. Who's to say that the unknown accomplice was not the main person behind the assault? I shall speak with Mr Timothy Lane, a principal officer of Bow Street and the man who apprehended Griffiths. If he can be persuaded to doubt that he got the right man, the jury will likely side with the accused."

"You think he can be persuaded?"

"I know Mr Lane, Ma'am, back from his days as a corrupt thief-taker, setting up supposed crimes merely to apprehend gullible men and collect rewards. He would certainly be susceptible to persuasion of a," he coughed, "pecuniary kind."

Paper rustled.

"Will that be sufficient?" asked Lady Catherine.

"Indeed it will."

"Very well then. I shall now take my leave of you."

A little later, I heard Mr Stephen Collins leave and take a hackney carriage to Bow Street. There was a period of quiet but for the distant sound of carriages and passers-by. Then he spoke.

"Mr Lane?"

"Mr Collins, sir."

"If you would be so kind, would you meet me at my house in Bedford Square? Number fifty. I need to discuss the Griffiths case."

"The snuffbox robbery? The lad who can't pronounce his 'R's? Just to be clear, I said 'R's, not—"

"Mr Lane, I'll thank you not to utter vulgarisms. But yes, that is the person to which I refer."

"Of course, sir. But why your house? Why not here or at the Old Bailey?"

"It's more convenient, that is all. More private."

"I see. I have to follow up a report about a pickpocket but could be there in an hour, if I – er – had the money for a hackney coach."

"There."

"My thanks, sir, 'tis most considerate. You are a gent."

"Well, thank you, bonnet," I said, running my fingers down its ribbons, "that was most useful. Now if you wouldn't mind—"

I heard a crow then, though it did not sound as though it came from the woods around me. I suspected that it was a Spanish crow and that the bonnet had done as I had wished.

The cawing ended abruptly.

"This place is most expansive. What do they call it, again?" said Captain Collins.

"Casa de Campo, sir. It's a fine spot. Plenty of trees for firewood—"

The speech stopped – like a length of ribbon cut too short – replaced by the crow again. Now there were more birds and as well as the squawking, there was scratching and flapping as though they were fighting over something.

"I don't know. Rodrigo just came back from Colonel Causey, so he might."

"Rodrigo," said Captain Collins, "Do you know if General Wellesley's at the Royal Palace?"

"¿Qué?"

"Oh, ah . . . ¿dónde está General Wellesley?"

Dónde está. That might prove useful to remember.

"El está en el Palacio Real."

"Yes, I thought he must be. Well, feather bed for him anyway. Though I might see if I can make my tent a little more comfortable."

"Perhaps a señorita or two would help."

I shook my head at their crassness.

Captain Collins laughed. "Perhaps later. I really fancy some of that Madeira wine and a good siesta but first I have to check on the men and report to Colonel Cau—"

Caw. Caw. Squawk. Flap. Peck.

"Enough," I said, irritated by the constant interruptions and sure that I had heard all that would be useful anyway. The bonnet went quiet. I supposed that Captain Collins had replaced his damaged hat, taking one from someone fallen in action. Perhaps a scrap of fabric or even tiny fibres of the hat remained with its previous owner. Whatever the case, if the hat still felt a sense of allegiance to the dead man, that might account for the unreliable connection. I snorted at how bizarre that sounded but it was the best reason my stretched mental faculties could come up with.

I did not even bother to listen to William Collins. He would be at the Parsonage or Rosings. It would be easy enough to leave him his marzipan. Charlotte's dislike of it would prevent her being in any danger but I would endeavour to get her out of the way at any rate. I could leave her a message, pretending it to be from Miss de Bourgh, asking her to meet her alone somewhere. Yes, that would do very well. William Collins would be the easy one in that sense, though the hardest in another. Having spent so many days under the same roof as him, the guilt of my betrayal was a swarm of bees that would not desist pestering me. I batted the unwanted feeling away as best I could and focussed on the task at hand.

Both Stephen and Frederick were to be in identifiable places in due course. The former would shortly be at fifty Bedford Square, waiting to bribe Mr Timothy Lane, and the latter, after he had seen his men and reported to his colonel, would be returning to his tent in the Casa de Campo, which I assumed to be in or near Madrid, the city they had just liberated. But which to go to first? I supposed that I had more time for the Spanish endeavour as the Captain would be drinking and resting, whereas the barrister might leave his house after his meeting with the principal officer of Bow Street. That settled it. I entered Pratt's shop and exited onto a street parallel to Bedford Square in London.

Mr Lane was due to arrive in around half an hour and it occurred to me then that I might have the fate of the criminal, John Griffiths, in my hands. If I allowed the meeting to take place, the officer would likely give in to the bribe and sway the jury to side with the accused. If I killed Stephen Collins before he should converse with Mr Lane on the matter, John Griffiths might very well hang.

It was not for any desire to satisfy Lady Catherine's wishes that I decided to allow the meeting to take place. I simply thought that if I were taking three lives, I might as well save one. I sat on a bench which afforded a view of number fifty and waited. At length, a thin, bearded man in a black coat arrived at the house and, minutes later, he emerged from it, tucking a banknote into his pocket-book.

I was at the door before I realised I had got up from the bench. The scales of justice, ornamenting the brass knocker, seemed to be a pair of eyes glaring into my soul. I looked aside from them and was glad that I did not have long to wait before a servant answered my knock.

"I have a message from Lady Catherine de Bourgh for Mr Stephen Collins," I said.

"Thank you, Simpkins," said Mr Collins, appearing from the front room. The servant bowed and left. "You come from Lady Catherine, you say?"

"Indeed," I said, holding out the box of marzipan. "This is a small thank you from her ladyship to you."

"*Molland's.* Good Lord! They make the best marzipan in the country."

"So I hear." I curtseyed. "Her ladyship bade me say that she shall await the news that will engender . . . " I squinted, hoping to look as though I were remembering a message, "infinitely more gratitude towards yourself and your family. She expects me to return to her carriage now though and won't be kept waiting." I bobbed a curtsey.

"I can imagine not. Give her my thanks and tell her that it's all taken care of. She'll know what I mean," he smirked. "All taken care of."

"Yes, sir." I descended the steps onto the street, then waited, hidden, peering through the window. He sat in an armchair, opened the box, smiled and popped the marzipan flower into his mouth.

"Well one thing's taken care of at least," I said as I made for the nearby milliner's shop. "Now for the captain."

I emerged from a world infused with grey into one decked in sunlight, my skin warming as though I had immersed myself in a bathtub. A cart rolled by, loaded with baskets of food and bottles. Hooves and wheels stirred up clouds of dust. Across the road was a park with swathes of browned grass and neat rows of trees. A thin girl was jumping up to reach something from a branch, a grey, shaggy dog, even scrawnier than herself, slumped on the ground and looking up at her.

"Good heavens – an orange!" I said as I saw what she was stretching towards. I took my knife to cut the stem then gave the girl the fruit.

"Gracias." As soon as she ripped through the tough skin, the fruit's sweetness made my mouth water. She gave me a piece before continuing to eat hungrily.

"¿Dónde está . . ." I searched my memory for the name of the place, "Casa – de – Campo?"

She pointed down the road in the direction the cart had gone.

"Gracias," I said, repeating the word she had used earlier, hoping it meant 'thank you' rather than 'orange'.

I followed the road which, at one point, became a bridge over a river. Sweat was dripping from my forehead by the time I had a sight of the camp. Countless tents were separated into blocks, each presumably indicating a particular regiment. If only I had discovered which regiment Captain Collins was in, I thought, grinding my teeth.

"I'm going to need some help," I said.

The bonnet obliged and I heard the captain talking with a group of men. I jumped as one of them barked with laughter, the sound slapping at my ears. I could hear him, not just in the bonnet but ahead of me, from beside a block of tents.

"And the blood was still spurting from his shoulder as he said, 'D—! Left my b— cigars in Cádiz'. Ha! I swear he said it just like that."

"Poor Broderick." This sounded like Captain Collins' voice now. "Well, lads, I hear Harrington's caught us some rabbits, so I'll see you for some of his famous stew later. God knows there'll be little food else today." He had his back to me but I felt sure I knew which man he was now. "Tell you what, I'll bring my Madeira. We could all do with a splash to celebrate the liberation, eh?"

I stole closer to the group and followed Captain Collins as they dispersed, one of them beckoning an underdressed Spanish woman into his tent.

274

"Disgraceful," I muttered, shaking my head. I noticed that he was not the only officer to have made the acquaintance of Spanish ladies. I passed one woman who giggled as an officer took her into his tent. Her limbs were thin and there were shadows under her eyes. When she caught sight of a morsel of bread, her features opened in a look of genuine desire. It was clear that the war had taken a heavy toll on the people of this city, so I reserved my judgement for the soldiers, rather than the women.

I followed Captain Collins and peered through a gap in the canvas after he entered his tent. He washed his face and hands in a bowl of water, dried himself, sniffed a pinch of snuff and left. I crept in. Hot air pressed against me and beads of sweat seeped from my skin. My heart galloping in my chest, I took a marzipan box from my reticule and considered where best to place it. A bottle of something stood on an upturned crate. Did he not mention bringing Madeira wine for their meal?

I toasted to Mrs Pepperstock before taking a gulp of the fortified wine. Feeling a little less jittery, I placed the marzipan beside the bottle and snuck out again just in time to see Captain Collins returning to the tent. I made haste to slip out of sight.

"Excuse me, signor. You are Lieutenant Pilchard?" said a Spaniard.

"Indeed."

My mouth fell open.

"I was sent to tell you that a quarrel has broken out between Harrington and Braddock. They say you know how to deal with them."

"D— fool, that Braddock. Yes, I'll be there directly."

"Thank you, Lieutenant."

For some moments, I could not move, then I took myself to the entrance of the tent. The man I had thought was Captain Collins but who was in fact Lieutenant Pilchard frowned at the box I had left, picked it up and opened it. As he took out the marzipan and brought it to his mouth, I burst into the tent and ran to him.

"Stop!"

He stared at me, the marzipan inches from his gaping mouth.

"Don't eat that, it's not for you."

"What the deuce are you doing here, miss. You're English!"

"No," I said, trying to imitate an accent I had heard very little of. "I have learnt well the language English."

He studied my face, no doubt noting my colourings which looked far from Mediterranean.

"I had English grandmother. They say I look like her. But please, let me take that. I left it here thinking it was the tent of Captain Collins. I think I was wrong."

"Indeed you were. But I can take this to him if you wish."

I did not trust the man to not eat it himself.

"Thank you but no. I must go myself."

"Why is that?"

I cleared my throat. "Because . . . I am a woman who has come upon the town."

"Which town is that?"

"I mean . . . I am a . . . you know." I lowered my voice. "A doxy."

"Eh?"

"A prostitute," I said.

He raised his eyebrows "*Oh*." Then he looked me up and down. "Are you sure?"

"Yes. I'm Captain Collins' new prostitute and I hear he pays much extra for sweets."

"But this is from Bath," he said, looking at the box.

"Can you just tell me which tent is his?"

He pushed back the canvas to let me out and shewed me to a nearby tent. "A young lady to see you, Captain," Pilchard said with a bow and a crooked smile. "I shall leave you to the marzipan – and her, apparently."

"What's all this?" Captain Collins got up from his pallet bed. "And who are you, may I ask?"

I had had enough of the prostitute persona, though I tried to keep up with the accent. "I'm no one. I'm just here to deliver this. It's a small token from General Wellesley. He received supplies from England, including some luxuries which he wants to share with those he favours the most."

"General Wellesley? Good Heavens! His affability and condescension are—"

"Quite. Enjoy his favour while you can."

He nodded, taking the marzipan flower out of the box. "Perhaps I'll save this for—"

"No, eat it now. If you see him he will want to know that you have appreciated his gift and then he may offer more."

He appeared to contemplate this as he stared at the confectionery. "It does look good." He bit into it, making a deep sound of pleasure.

"Eat it all," I said. He didn't need much persuading. After he swallowed it, I turned to leave.

"Odd that he sent a señorita instead of one of his men."

I shrugged.

"Well, thank you. What is your name?"

"Maria Benneto."

"Thank you, Maria."

I bobbed my head, then fled the Casa de Campo.

I waved to the girl with the dog as I went into the shop on the Calle de Segoria, moments later stepping out into the village of Hunsford.

I sighed. "One left." Bracing myself for the hardest challenge yet, in emotional terms at least, I focussed on what the outcome would be – security for the women of my family; not having to sink into poverty and despair; keeping Longbourn for ourselves, the home we love. Taking a deep breath, I steeled myself and marched on.

As the road turned, revealing the poultry yard at the side of the parsonage, I noticed Charlotte scattering feed to the birds. I ducked, concealing myself behind a hedge. She turned so that she stood side on to me. Her belly protruded much further than I was expecting. She rested her hand on it and smiled as she stroked it. She was a sun radiating joy, right there amongst the chickens. I could not be untouched by it. However, at the same time I felt ill.

That new little Collins had, in an instant, ruined everything.

If the baby was a boy, he would be heir to Longbourn after William Collins, an heir I felt bound to love and protect, even now. If Longbourn was destined for this boy, killing the father would serve no purpose. I need not have killed anyone at all in fact. Nothing had changed. My eyes welled up as I sat in the dirt, my head in my arms. Could nothing steer us from an unbearable fate?

'Who will connect themselves with such a family?'

I was barely aware of walking back into Hunsford village, of going from the milliner's shop there to ours at Meryton, or of heading back home. My thoughts were like rotating cart wheels and as unceasing as the chatter of Meryton gossips, complaining of the futility of my efforts. Yet behind those thoughts, there was a space of silence – the shock that Charlotte was with child, the fear that there might be nothing I could do to save us from losing our home, our security and our dignity.

As I reached the corner of the Camfields' rented land, nearing home once more, I contemplated going back in time to cancel the murders I had committed. I could not decide yet but it remained a possibility, making me feel both guilty and potentially innocent of those crimes in the same moment.

Just then, one of the Camfields' large sows charged towards me, grunting, having escaped the sty. Startled, I twisted to avoid a collision, overbalanced and fell. The fence that might have separated me from the filth beyond must have been rotten, for the wood gave way. My body slapped into the mud. After remaining there for some moments, I lifted my head, cold clumps of muck caked against my skin. In the cottage, Mr Camfield was laughing.

Picking up a handful of mud, I flung it at his window. His subsequent verbal assault chased after me as I marched back home. I did not care about my family's laughter as I entered the house, though I was surprised at Jane's lack of restraint.

"And I thought I was the one most prone to muddying gowns," laughed Lizzy.

"But look," said Jane, "your bonnet has remained perfectly clean. Isn't that odd?"

"It just makes her look more ridiculous," said Kitty.

No doubt, after all the anxiety of these last days, they were benefiting from a distraction like this. Once again, the sacrifice was mine to make. It mattered not how I looked, I was past caring. I did not bother to go back in time so as not to fall. What I really wanted to be changed could not be. If only I had persuaded Charlotte not to marry Mr Collins. If only Lydia had let me save her. If only society did not force women to be dependent upon men.

"Straight to the yard, if you please," said Mrs Hill, prodding my back with her fingertips. "I'll get a bucket."

I obeyed Mrs Hill, catching sight of the mud I had brought in. What an unthinkable change it would be if I were, in future, forced to clean other people's floors as Sarah and Sally did for us, if I had no money for books, no time to study, no friends left from the class I was born in. Would all forsake us if we fell so low? Would I ever see Charlotte again?

The next day bore no alleviation of my dejection. Rather, it brought a letter from Mr Collins and each sentence heightened the sting of our suffering.

He wrote that our distress *'must be of the bitterest kind, because proceeding from a cause which no time can remove'*. How well I knew that. *'The death of your daughter would have been a blessing in comparison of this,'* he remarked, putting me to mind of the similar blessings he was about to receive, when news of his brothers' demises reached him.

It should not have surprised me that Lady Lucas had been quick to inform Charlotte and her son-in-law of what had occurred with Lydia, or that Mr Collins had related the affair to Lady Catherine de Bourgh.

'*They agree with me in apprehending that this false step in one daughter, will be injurious to the fortunes of all the others,*' he wrote, '*for who, as Lady Catherine herself condescendingly says, will connect themselves with such a family?*' So the gossip would escalate in the natural way and the once perfect fruit of our reputations would rot and stink, repelling all respectable men.

I had woken that morning with the thought of going back to un-murder Mr Collins' brothers but now, after reading his letter, I decided that my decision on that matter could wait. I had been saving up plenty of stitches in any case.

At church on Sunday, while the congregation were taking their places, Lady Lucas turned around in her pew to face us.

"Is your Mama still indisposed?" she said.

"She is," said Jane. "She mostly keeps to her room."

"Then please be sure to offer her my condolences and accept them for all of you too."

"Really," Lizzy whispered to Jane, "need she speak so before so many people?"

"You are very kind," said Jane to Lady Lucas.

"Oh, I hope you realise I was referring to the shocking news about Mr Collins?" Lady Lucas added. "I did not mean to refer to . . . Well, perhaps I had better not mention what."

"What news, pray?" said Lizzy.

"Why, that he's dead. Have you not heard about it?"

"Dead?" Kitty shrieked, much to the alarm of the assembling congregation.

I leant forward. "Mr Collins is dead?"

"Not Charlotte's Mr Collins, you understand," said Lady Lucas, "but his brother, Mr Stephen Collins, the barrister."

"Good Heavens!" said Lizzy. "How did he die?"

Lady Lucas lowered her voice. "He is thought to have been murdered."

"Surely not!" exclaimed Jane.

Mrs Pepperstock, who was seated further down Lady Lucas' pew, spun around and leant over the back to face Papa. "Miss Mary couldn't have done it," she slurred. I tried to shush her but she continued, spurred on no doubt by the excess of gin in her veins. "She was at my cottage all day on Wednesday the twelfth. I can vouch for that with utmost surety!"

Her comment met with a stunned silence which came to a fortunate end with the vicar's greeting: "Let us gather and contemplate our hearts and deeds, for all have sinned and fall short of the glory of God."

I knew I had. Though I might not have done so had society allowed women the same opportunities in life as men. As the vicar preached, I wondered if Clarke's might still have a copy of *The Vindication of the Rights of Woman*. It seemed about time to give that pamphlet another try.

"Oh, my poor, poor Lydia! My poor, darling child," wailed Mama from her bed, a breakfast tray bearing a bowl of porridge, toast, bacon and plums beside her. Her having slept in so late, Mrs Hill had rightly anticipated her increased appetite.

"I can barely eat, I fret for her so. Ooh, bacon," she said, lifting the dish that kept the meat warm. "But indeed, I should not wish to cause my dear family alarm by allowing myself to waste away." In moments the bacon was gone and she had moved on to the porridge.

It was testament to Mama's blind affection for her youngest daughter that, not only had she kept to her rooms for thirteen days, to be waited upon as an invalid, but that during that time, no word of criticism or reprimand of Lydia had passed her lips.

"Fetch me some fresh tea, Mary," she said. "This pot has been left to get cold."

"Very well."

"Oh, that villain, Wickham! If Papa had found him and killed him, it would have been just what he deserved!"

"Oh, Mama," said Kitty, "do not you think all would have been well if we had all gone to have a jolly time in Brighton? If Papa had but listened to us!"

"If only he had not let Lydia go at all," I muttered as I left with the tea pot. Through the window on the small landing between two flights of stairs, I noticed Papa in the garden with Jane and Lizzy, deep in serious conversation. Unfortunately, there were no hats or bonnets amongst them with which I might hear what was said. When they returned to the house, Papa went straight to his library and Jane and Lizzy to the breakfast room. I put my ear to the door, though I could only hear snippets of their conversation.

"How strange this is!" said Lizzy. "And for this we are to be thankful . . . wretched as is his character."

Some mumbling from Jane, then: "How could he spare half ten thousand pounds?" This had me intrigued.

"Wickham has not sixpence of his own," I heard Lizzy mention, though I could have guessed as much myself. "If such goodness does not stop her misery now, she will never deserve to be happy . . ."

"We must tell Mama," said Jane.

The door opened but I leapt across the vestibule and hid myself behind the clock as they walked past. When they were in the library, asking something of Papa, I dashed upstairs again.

"Thank you, Mary," said Mama. "Do pour some would you?"

I realised then that I still had the cold teapot in my hands. "Oh, I forgot to get more tea."

"Where that head of yours is at sometimes, I could not say for all the world. What on earth could have distracted you so?"

Jane came into the room then, followed by Lizzy who had a letter clutched in her hand.

"Lord! How frightfully absent-minded you are, Mary," said Kitty, though I ignored her.

Jane sat beside Mama. "Uncle Gardiner has written," she said, glancing back at Lizzy, "and the letter contains good news."

"Good news?" said Mama. "What does he say?"

Kitty leant over Lizzy's shoulder as she read.

"He writes from Gracechurch Street, this very morning, as follows," said Lizzy.

> *My dear brother,*
>
> *At last I am able to send you some tidings of my niece. Soon after you left me on Saturday, I was fortunate enough to find out in what part of London they were. The particulars, I reserve till we meet. It is enough to know they are discovered, I have seen them both. They are not married, nor can I find there was any intention of being so; but if you are willing to perform the engagements which I have ventured to make on your side, I hope it will not be long before they are. All that is required of you is, to assure your daughter, by settlement, her equal share of the five thousand pounds, secured among your children after the decease of yourself and my sister; and, moreover, to enter into an engagement of allowing her, during your life, one hundred pounds per annum. These are conditions, which, considering everything, I had no hesitation in complying with, as far as I thought myself privileged, for you. I shall send this by express, that no time may be lost in bringing me your answer. You will easily comprehend, from these particulars, that Mr Wickham's circumstances are not so hopeless as they are generally believed to be. I am happy to say, there will be some little money, even when all his debts are discharged, to settle on my niece. If you can send me full powers to act in your name throughout the whole of this business, I will immediately give directions to Haggerston for preparing a proper settlement. We have judged it best, that my niece should be married from this house, of which I hope you will approve. She comes to us today. I shall write again as soon as anything more is determined on. Yours, etc.*
>
> *Edw. Gardiner*

A moment of quiet descended as Lizzy finished the letter, in which I could almost see the internal workings of Mama's mind. Of course, she would not be analysing the subtle inferences it contained. Wickham had nothing but debts to call his own; he would not have agreed to marry Lydia unless my uncle had paid him a great deal of money. The hundred pounds mentioned would not go far and her inheritance would only provide an annuity of fifty pounds a year after our parents' deaths. That was no incentive for Wickham. I chewed my thumbnail as I wondered how much my uncle had sacrificed for Lydia and for us all while Mama clapped her hands, her jubilation bursting forth in a fountain of high pitched vocalisations.

"My dear, dear Lydia! This is delightful indeed!— She will be married at sixteen!— My good, kind brother!— I knew he would manage everything. How I long to see her and to see dear Wickham too! But the clothes, the wedding clothes!" She prattled on about getting Papa to send money for unnecessary fineries.

"We are persuaded," said Jane, "that our uncle had pledged himself to assist Mr Wickham with money."

"Which I imagine must have been an ample sum," I said.

"Well who should do it but her own uncle?" said Mama.

I shook my head at her sentiments and her return to the subject of Lydia's clothing, as if one poor decision about muslin, cambric or silk would be the cause of utmost disaster.

At last, Mama rose from her bed and readied herself to go to Meryton and tell all who would listen about Lydia's good fortune.

"Lizzy," I whispered, catching her arm while we were both on the landing. She turned to me in surprise. "What do you think this means? For our family reputation, that is. Do you think any of you might have a chance of a decent marriage?"

She paused. "Only time will tell how much lasting damage Lydia has done to us. Jane is more optimistic than I am."

"That's in her nature I suppose," I said.

She leant her head to one side. "What do you think, Mary?"

I was surprised that she returned the question to me, seeming to value my opinion. "I think Jane is right to have hope but I agree with you. Only time will tell us who would, as Lady Catherine says, 'connect themselves with such a family'."

When Lizzy nodded, there was sadness in her eyes. Her sorrow appeared to come from so tender a place that it was not inconceivable that she truly loved Mr Darcy. The thought came to me then that, whilst Lydia was living in a way that brought shame upon us, Mr Darcy could not have married Lizzy but now the situation was perhaps even less likely to allow their union, for surely Mr Darcy could not stand to join himself to a family which included his old enemy, Mr Wickham.

I embraced Lizzy then, something I had not done for a long time. She tensed, though she did not pull away from me.

"Do not give up hope," I said. I had little of that emotion myself but it would not serve for others to feel as I did.

VOLUME III, CHAPTER XI

Mr & Mrs Wickham

"How was she today, my love?" said Uncle Gardiner.

Aunt Gardiner sighed. "I tell you, I am reaching the end of my patience with that girl and the thought of having to wait nigh on two weeks longer..."

"The banns must be read so that all seems right and proper."

"*Seems* right and proper!" My aunt gave a bitter laugh. "Indeed, it must seem so from now on which is why I am determined that she shall not leave this house until she is wed."

"Could she not walk out with you and the children in the mornings?" my uncle asked.

"My dear, in Brighton she ran from the care and safety of the Forsters' residence. I will not risk her doing the same now and I told her as much. She was desperate to go shopping and went quite red in the face as she stamped and exclaimed at how I was mistreating her. I told her how unreasonable she was being, how she was making herself look ridiculous by such behaviour. Imagine a bride acting like a hot-tempered two year old! Sometimes I wish I could take your place and let you manage the household. I would much rather have met with Haggerston and Mr Darcy today."

Mr Darcy? I wondered what he was doing there.

Kitty burst into my room then. "Why are you wearing that bonnet indoors?" she asked.

"No reason," I said. "What do you want, anyway?"

"Well that's polite! We need you to make up a second table for whist.

Mama says it's too early for you to retire when we have guests."

"I'll be there directly." I ushered her out of the room and returned to the conversation occurring at the Gardiners' house in Cheapside.

"In the end," continued my aunt, "I told Agnes she would be excused from completing her chores, if she would run errands for Lydia instead. I told my niece she had no reason to go out as Agnes would make any purchases or enquiries she required." Poor Agnes, I thought. "So, how did you get on with Haggerston and Mr Darcy?"

"Haggerston was happy with all the paperwork, as I expected. Mr Darcy would not hear of my making the contribution we'd discussed. Though I confess that was not unexpected either."

"He must truly care for Lizzy. Did he ask after her?"

"No," replied my uncle. "Again, he gave as his reason for his assistance the fact that he ought to have been less private about his affairs and less proud, then Mr Wickham's character would have been generally known and he might not have inflicted this sort of damage on any family."

"I am not convinced by that. No one would think him to blame in the least. I believe he acts not from a sense of guilt but out of love."

"Speaking of acting out of love, my love,"

"Hmm? Oh, Mr Gardiner!" My aunt giggled in a way I had never heard before.

I froze, then pulled the bonnet from my head but it got caught in my hair.

"These buttons are most fiddly," said Mr Gardiner.

"That's quite enough of that!" I said, managing to extricate the bonnet from my head at last. I then hurried downstairs to join the others for coffee and cards, hoping that no one enquired as to why I had been absent.

"Why is your face red?" asked Kitty as she handed me a cup of coffee that had gone cool. I sat in the empty chair next to Mama.

"Have you any news from Hunsford?" I asked Lady Lucas, ignoring Kitty.

Lady Lucas finished her mouthful of cake. "Indeed, yes. We had a letter from Charlotte just yesterday and one from Mr Collins the day before."

"And, pray, how is our dear cousin, Mr Collins?" asked Papa. He had a way of saying 'dear cousin' that teetered delicately on the border between politeness and sarcasm.

"Well, I believe. He writes that the de Bourghs are in good health too, though they have seen little of Miss de Bourgh. He says that Lady Catherine has been most helpful in advising Charlotte as to what they should be eating and how best to budget her housekeeping expenses."

"Attentive as ever, I see," said Lizzy, sharing a smile with Papa.

"And Mr Collins is profoundly grateful, I am sure," he added.

"Indeed. His letter was full of other examples of her Ladyship's condescension of late."

"But what does Charlotte write?" I said. "How is she?"

"She is managing the household well and her chickens are thriving." Lady Lucas and Maria shared a look. "She is in good health though complains of feeling somewhat fatigued from time to time."

"I'm not surprised in the least," I said, thinking not only of the physical tiredness she must be experiencing due to her condition but also the effort it must require to bear the company of Mr Collins and, all too often, Lady Catherine as well. Papa inclined his head towards me, offering a smile as though I were Lizzy making a witty comment. I was so unused to sensing his approval, I did not know how to respond, so I took a slice of cake and gave my attention to that. "Oh, and congratulations," I added. "It must be most pleasant to anticipate being grandparents."

The Lucases stared at me, open-mouthed.

"Mary, what are you talking of?" said Mama lightly with a laugh, then leaning towards me, she whispered urgently: "Is it true?"

"I did not know that Charlotte had written to you of it," said Lady Lucas, "or that it was to be generally made known but, yes, she and Mr Collins are expecting a blessed arrival."

Kitty swiftly hid her grimace of distaste by taking a very long sip of coffee.

Mama sighed. "It is most strange to think that their child, if a boy, may one day own Longbourn." Her gaze swept across the room as though she were taking her last glance of the place.

Sir William coughed uncomfortably.

"Now now, my dear," said Papa, not unkindly.

"Oh yes," said Mama putting on a smile, "congratulations to you all. It is the way of life, is it not? Hopes come and go but why estates are entailed away from the children who call them home, I shall never understand. Perhaps it is inappropriate to bring it up as your family shall benefit from our disadvantage. But neither you nor we control the turning of Fortune's wheel, do we?"

I was half embarrassment, half exaltation. Mama's directness was a flaw which had reflected ill on us on more than one occasion. However, my heart lightened at this instance of her speaking her mind.

The Lucases did not stay long after that.

"Perhaps it is right to state unfairness and injustice when we see them," I said, after they had left, "in the absence of the ability, as Mama put it, to turn Fortune's wheel."

"The entail is, of course, unfortunate, but do you consider it an injustice?" asked Jane.

"My thoughts, of late, have been that way inclined."

"But it's in place for practical reasons," said Lizzy, "its purpose being to prevent the estate from being divided."

"I think you'll find its purpose is rather to keep it in the hands of men and prevent female independence."

"It seems we have a revolutionary in our midst," said Papa with an amused grin. "I did not expect that of you, Mary."

"Well," said Mama, "if speaking sense makes someone a dangerous revolutionary, then by all means call in the militia!"

"Yes please," said Kitty, sounding rather too much like Lydia.

Papa glared at her.

Within the fortnight, Lydia and Mr Wickham were married. I listened to the quiet ceremony which took place in London, not out of sisterly feeling for Lydia but to make sure that all occurred as it should. I heard Mr Darcy there, speaking with my uncle before the ceremony, and wondered at his presence. Perhaps he wanted, like me, to make sure that the marriage took place, after all his efforts to bring it about. I did not know whether or not I might allow myself to hope that this indicated his feelings for Lizzy were strong enough to overcome the fact of Mr Wickham as a brother-in-law.

Shortly after they became husband and wife, the Wickhams came to stay at Longbourn. Papa had previously forbidden Mr Wickham from visiting. However, as with most of Papa's stronger feelings, his anger ebbed away. He had more appetite for laughing at others than waging war against them.

Our new brother-in-law was all fawning courtesy and seeming goodness and I could tell that Papa took pleasure in observing his talent for insincerity. He referred to each of us as 'my dear sister' at numerous times during their stay, though not one of us returned the compliment of calling him 'my dear brother'.

Lydia was Lydia still, only more so. Now that she was married, she walked about with her head held high, as though she had accomplished the one thing in life worth doing and wished to remind us by her incessant smugness that we had not. I smiled when this posture of hers caused her to tread in horse muck during a walk, though it would have been more satisfying had Lydia noticed what she had done.

"Only think of its being three months since I went away," she said, later that day when we were gathered in the drawing room. "It seems but a fortnight I declare. And yet there have been things enough happened in the time. Good gracious!"

I pursed my lips so as to prevent myself from openly asking why she was so vulgar as to be alluding to her time living with Mr Wickham before their marriage.

"When I went away, I am sure I had no more idea of being married till I came back again!" She laughed, not seeming to notice that no one else did. "Though I thought it would be very good fun if I was."

Lizzy's nostrils flared. Papa looked at her as though she were a stranger to him. Jane looked about to cry with mortification, such had been the burden of emotion she had tried for so long to suppress. Even Kitty and Mama looked uncomfortable.

I got up, my hands balled into fists, and marched up to her where she sat. "Do you not know what hell you've put us through these last weeks?" I shouted. "You brainless, frivolous, selfish cow!" With that, I punched her hard in the face.

VOLUME III, CHAPTER XII

Wedding Bells

Lydia shrieked, clutching her bleeding nose. "Mama! Mama! Look what she did!" she cried, barely coherently.

Mama and Kitty tended to Lydia at once. Jane went pale. Lizzy's mouth fell open and she looked about to laugh. Papa blinked at me as though he were seeing me for the first time.

Lydia glared at me as Mama held her. "I hate you, Mary! I *hate* you!"

It was more than worth the stitch I used removing the incident from the knowledge of anyone but myself and, as I listened to Lydia's audacious comments once more, I smiled, caressing the fist that had lodged itself, with such perfect precision, into her irritating face.

The day of the Wickhams' departure came soon, though not soon enough for my liking. Mr Wickham had gained a position in the regular army, based in Newcastle where he would have the two unenviable tasks of quelling the uprisings of mill workers and living with his wife.

Mama wept as she held Lydia in her arms. "Oh! My dear Lydia, when shall we meet again?"

"In thunder, lightning or in rain?" I muttered. No one heard my reference to Macbeth's witches but Papa who stifled a snort.

"Oh, Lord! I don't know," said Lydia. "Not these two or three years perhaps."

Thank God, I thought.

Mama pressed a handkerchief to her eyes. "Write to me very often, my dear."

"As often as I can. But you know married women have never much time for writing. My sisters may write to *me*. They will have nothing else to do."

"Farewell, my dear, dear family," said Wickham, bowing to us and kissing the hands of all the Bennet women. "I shall miss you more than I can say. As we go north, I feel as though I leave something of myself behind."

I wondered what that something might be, as they ascended to their seats. Just before the carriage pulled them out of sight, he glanced at his wife in such a way that made me think that what he had shed and discarded was his self respect – if, indeed, he had any to begin with.

"He is as fine a fellow," said Papa, "as ever I saw. He simpers and smirks and makes love to us all. I am prodigiously proud of him. I defy even Sir William Lucas himself to produce a more valuable son-in-law."

Now it was my turn to laugh.

Mr Bingley returned to Hertfordshire but a few days after the Wickhams had quitted it. Everyone said how natural it was that he should come to the country estate he was tenant of, particularly when there were plenty of birds about to shoot. However, most of Meryton wondered if he had other motivations and they did not have the benefit that I had of being able to listen to certain pertinent conversations of his.

"Good Heavens, Darcy," said he. "I hope my nervousness shall not be obvious to the Bennets."

"No doubt you shall settle into your customary ease of manner," said Mr Darcy.

"Do you expect she will be there?"

"It is most likely."

"Good Lord." Bingley exhaled loudly. "Are you sure that we should call on them today?"

"We've come this far."

Kitty peered out of the window. "There is a gentleman with him, Mama. Who can it be? La! It looks just like that man that used to be with him before. Mr what's his name. That tall, proud man."

This information brought about an alteration in Lizzy's mien. She sat stiffly, clutching her embroidery ring though she made no more stitches, lowering her gaze, keeping it fixed in the opposite direction to the window from which Kitty was watching the gentlemen's approach.

"Good gracious! Mr Darcy!" exclaimed Mama, joining Kitty, "Well, any friend of Mr Bingley's will always be welcome here to be sure; but else I must say that I hate the very sight of him. Get that bonnet off, Mary, for Heaven's sake!"

During the gentlemen's visit, Lizzy's brows drew together more than once in glances at Mr Darcy. He occupied his customary position by the window and spoke little and then only when asked a direct question. This was perhaps not surprising.

When mentioning Mr Wickham's having been helped into a position in the army, Mama said, with a frosty glance at Darcy: "Thank Heaven he has *some* friends, though perhaps not so many as he deserves."

Such rudeness was accentuated by the excessive courtesy Mama shewed to Mr Bingley, addressing all her conversation to *him* and all but lining up Papa's birds ready for him to shoot. The mortification this discrepancy occasioned in myself can have been nothing to that felt by Lizzy, whose face grew decidedly red. Mr Bingley kept shifting his gaze between Mama and his friend, as though watching an invisible game of battledore and shuttlecock and my heart chilled with the fear that Mama's rudeness to Mr Darcy would put both of them off visiting again.

I mentioned this visit in a letter to Charlotte and also detailed that of Lydia and Mr Wickham. After writing of the newlyweds, ending with my relief at the Wickhams' departure to the north, I leant back in my chair and exhaled a long breath, not having realised how tense my posture had become. I repeated my enquiries as to Charlotte's health more than once in the letter, there having been no more word of her interesting condition from any of the Lucases. '*You cannot know the vexation of having a mother who is so adept at causing her daughters embarrassment and misery'*, I wrote, returning to the topic of Mr Bingley's visit and Mama's manner. *'Why she cannot see that, despite her dislike of Mr Darcy, she would better recommend herself to his friend if she treated him with equal civility, I do not know. Perhaps common sense has a habit of skipping a generation.'*

My frustrations with Mama dissipated when its effects turned out to carry little evil. Not to be frightened off by either Mama's exaggerated civilities towards himself, nor her unveiled dislike of his friend, Mr Bingley appeared only to require the courage and opportunity, which a matter of days allowed him, to make his proposal of marriage to Jane.

The day following the commencement of the couple's engagement, Sarah, the housemaid, found me into the garden and my heart leapt when she held out a letter addressed to me, written in Charlotte's hand. She wrote inviting me to join her mother and sister in a visit to Hunsford. *'We have much to speak about'*, she wrote, *'though you shall only have to see me to understand the nature of my news'.*

This time, Mama had no objection to my going.

Watching the fields, woods and villages trundle by, I laughed to myself, thinking how much quicker it had been for me to travel to Spain. I winced at the idea that I was still a murderess, then pushed the thought out of my mind.

Charlotte's belly was larger than I thought it could possibly get and it pressed against my own when we embraced.

"How I have missed you," she said.

"And I you."

Lady Lucas and Maria hovered around her the rest of that day, fetching food she had not asked for and shawls when she was already warm and placing screens between her and the fire when she sat in the chill of a draught.

"I am so glad you are here," she said, entering my room that evening after we had both retired early. "My mother and sister mean well but their attentions are quite wearisome. Now," she said, sitting beside me on the bed, "tell me all that you have not yet told me in your letters."

I did not have permission to make Jane's engagement known but I made an exception in Charlotte's case.

"Engaged? That is wonderful news, especially after all you went through this summer."

"I confess, my optimism has risen to such a height that I dare hope for a match even greater than this."

"Lizzy and Mr Darcy? I know he had proposed to her once but, after what you told me of his history with Mr Wickham, do you think—?"

At this moment, there was a sneeze outside my door followed by a flurry of footsteps which faded down the corridor.

"I think a servant overheard us," I said. "Ah well. No matter."

Expecting Charlotte to be confined to the house, though in fact she still took walks down into the village, Lady Catherine descended upon the parsonage on the second evening after our arrival, having invited herself to dine with us.

"Lady Catherine, this is Miss Mary Bennet," said Charlotte after the great lady had established herself in the best armchair. "You of course know her elder sister, Elizabeth."

I curtseyed.

"Mr Collins relayed to me your family's misfortune regarding your younger sister and the son of the late Mr Darcy's steward," Lady Catherine said, affording me the barest of glances.

"But the unfolding of a new circumstance elevates the status of our visitor," said Mr Collins, a tremor in his voice. "Her eldest sister has become engaged to Mr Bingley of Netherfield Park and Miss Elizabeth has received an offer that is many times more worthy of note." He caught my eye as I glared at him and he shuffled back so that the sopha stood between himself and the women in the room.

"And to whom, pray, is she engaged?"

Mr Collins coughed.

"Who is the gentleman you speak of?" she reiterated.

"Your nephew, ma'am."

Lady Catherine's nostrils grew wider just as her spine elongated several inches.

"Mr Darcy," Mr Collins added.

By now her eyes had become two narrow slits.

The butler entered to announce that dinner was served and I pitied the man for the fiery blast he received from Lady Catherine's gaze.

"I find I have no appetite, Mrs Collins," she said. "I shall have my carriage sent for."

Mr Collins stared at the candelabra throughout dinner and didn't say a word. Maria was almost as quiet, her face a decided pink.

My hopes withered to a husk as I followed Lady Catherine's progress to Hertfordshire and listened to her as she confronted Lizzy. My fear was not that she might deter Lizzy from her wish to marry Mr Darcy, should the opportunity arise, but that Mr Darcy might, by a similar conversation be thus persuaded against marrying her. Lady Catherine spoke to Lizzy of the betrothal of Miss de Bourgh and Mr Darcy, arranged since their infancy. She stressed the insuperable obstacle of Lizzy's and Darcy's difference in rank. She painted a vivid picture of the disgrace of such a match and how she would be ostracised from Mr Darcy's family and friends. She did not know Lizzy. When pushed, Lizzy pushed back.

"I am no stranger to the particulars of your youngest sister's infamous elopement," said Lady Catherine. "I know it all; that the young man's marrying her was a patched-up business, at the expense of your father and uncles." I shuddered at the degree of her knowledge. "And is such a girl to be my nephew's sister? Is her husband, is the son of his late father's steward, to be his brother? Are the shades of Pemberley to be thus polluted? Unfeeling, selfish girl! Do you not consider that a connection with you must disgrace him in the eyes of everybody?"

"Lady Catherine, I have nothing further to say. You know my sentiments."

"You are then resolved to have him?"

"I have said no such thing. I am only resolved to act in that manner, which will, in my own opinion, constitute my happiness, without reference to *you*, or to any person so wholly unconnected with me."

Before many days had passed, my towering anxiety had quite collapsed. Mr Darcy visited Longbourn again with Mr Bingley and found the opportunity to walk out with Lizzy, out of earshot of others, excepting myself.

"You are too generous to trifle with me," he said. "If your feelings are still what they were last April, tell me so at once. My affections and wishes are unchanged but one word from you will silence me on this subject forever."

There was a pause.

"My sentiments," began Lizzy, "have undergone so material a change since then as to allow me to receive your present assurances with gratitude and pleasure."

For a while, all I heard was the rustling of tree branches and the steady padding of their boots on the path as they walked together.

I had not managed to hear Lady Catherine's visit to Mr Darcy; she must have removed her bonnet. However, I had been mistaken in thinking that she might persuade him against renewing his offer to Lizzy. In fact, her dissatisfaction regarding her interview with Lizzy gave him the hope he needed to lead to this happy conclusion.

Overflowing with joy, I walked out into Rosings Woods so that I could smile to my heart's content without attracting unwanted questions. I even jumped and danced about, punching the air. I walked on, as if in a dream, but knowing I would never again wake up to the prospect of future destitution. As the facts took root in my mind, I considered how well provided for we Bennet women would be when Longbourn would be taken from us. For several nights, I laughed myself to sleep at the enormity of our good fortune and it pleased me to consider that these events would never have come to pass had I not, through great striving, brought Mr Bingley into the neighbourhood, ensured the opportunities for Lizzy and Mr Darcy's courtship in Hunsford and at Pemberley, and disclosed the information that was overheard and spread via Mr Collins to Lady Catherine which led to Lizzy's and Mr Darcy's revelations to one another.

With Jane's and Lizzy's astounding prospects in mind, it occurred to me that Lydia had not ruined us after all – though it had been a very near thing! – and I need not have dispatched Stephen and Frederick Collins. I had enough reason now and still plenty of stitches to expunge my murders. However, I was having too pleasant a time in Hunsford to give the task much consideration.

VOLUME III, CHAPTER XIII
A Barouche With Death

November saw me back in Hertfordshire to witness Jane's marriage to Mr Bingley and Lizzy's to Mr Darcy, the events taking place at the same ceremony in the church at Meryton. It was an occasion of much delight for all of us, not least for Papa who remarked on his good fortune at having three daughters married whilst only having paid for one wedding. Mama cried profusely, as did Kitty, though I suspect that the latter had cried mostly at the thought of me being her main companion from now on.

My only regret at that time was that Charlotte was unable to attend the wedding, having entered into her confinement. With the use of the bonnet, I made frequent checks on her every day until, at last, her labours began.

I felt for her in her discomfort and in the pains that gripped her. I almost felt angry at the child who caused her this much suffering. When at last the midwife announced: "You have a daughter!" I collapsed onto my bed with relief.

"Let me hold her," said Charlotte, with such love in her voice that it pulled at my heart.

My family may have wondered at my absence that day and the fact that I declined joining them for dinner but I could not put away the bonnet until I was assured that Charlotte was recovering well.

"And where is the father?" asked the midwife. "Surely he will want to know that he has a healthy daughter?"

"He went to meet Lady Catherine to accompany her from Town so that she would not have to travel alone."

I rolled my eyes. How typical it was that he remained more concerned about Lady Catherine than any other person in the world. My bonnet ribbons twitched and, all at once, Charlotte's voice faded to be replaced by grinding carriage wheels and thudding hooves.

"Why are you stopping, Wilkins?" asked Mr Collins.

The servant shouted something unintelligible.

"What?"

My mind began to drift to the last piece of poisoned marzipan, safe in a travelling case in my closet. However, I was thrust back into the present by Wilkins' words.

"Highwayman, sir! Highwayman!"

"Then for God's sake, go faster – get us away from here!"

"He's in the middle of the road!"

Lady Catherine made an exasperated noise.

"Take this," said Mr Collins. "It's all I have. Now please go away, I beg you."

"Get that woman to give me her gold bwooch."

"Her gold what?"

"Bwooch! Or I'll ask my blunderbuss here to give her balls of lead."

"How dare you, ruffian!" boomed Lady Catherine. "Don't you know who I am?"

"Sounds like she alweady has balls," said the highwayman, "unlike someone else in this cawiage."

"Lady Catherine, please!" Mr Collins' voice was squeakier than I had ever heard it. "Just give the man your brooch!"

"Lady *Cathewine*?" said the highwayman, "*de Bourgh*? We meet at last."

"Do you presume to know me, vermin?"

A deep, gruff laugh vibrated through my bonnet ribbons. "I do pwesume as much. I know who you are and what you've done. I know of the woman who wuined my mother's life for the sake of family pwide. Good day, Lady Cathewine."

A resounding bang, shortly followed by a second, left me feeling dizzy and unable to hear anything else for a time.

Eventually there came the distant sound of pounding hooves which faded, presumably as the highwayman, Mr Griffiths, fled the scene.

"Lady Catherine? Mr Collins? Oh, God. They're dead. Dead! Oh my!" exclaimed poor Wilkins.

It occurred to me that, had I poisoned Mr Stephen Collins before he met with Mr Timothy Lane, John Griffiths would likely not have lived to be the means of Lady Catherine's or Mr Collins' tragic ends. Neither was it lost on me that Lady Catherine would not be dead now if she had not wished to pervert the course of justice. Her shameful treatment of her cousin could also be said to be what led to her demise. Both her unshakable family pride and my moment of compassion had therefore led to this conclusion.

I could have gone back in time to save them, just as I could have gone back to remove my own crimes. But I didn't. We had the prospect of wealth and security now – that was no problem – but I preferred not to require the charity of either of my brothers-in-law. With no male heir to inherit Longbourn after my father, it would go to us Bennet girls. I would now live with joy and independence in the home I loved and which I would always call my own.

So it was that, without the shadow of destitution looming over us, cast by the structures of a society that had served us ill, life at Longbourn resolved into a state of tranquillity, only to be disturbed by such trifles as Kitty's romantic pursuits, Papa's frequent absences visiting Pemberley and Mama's occasional fainting fit brought on by her resuscitated fears of highwaymen concealed at every turnpike.

Mrs Pepperstock, with renewed vigour and a regular supply of winnings from the gaming tables, which her frequent use of the bonnet allowed her to achieve, went into business with Mrs Clapton, combining molly house with gin emporium. It had the patronage of many of Chamberlayne's London friends and the advantage of a time traveller who could tell them when a raid might be expected.

Lady Anne de Bourgh came into her position as mistress of

Rosings with an ease that surprised most who thought they knew her. Without her mother persuading her that she was too weak to exert herself, she found that inner vitality which I had once witnessed on the cricket pitch. Whilst Lady Catherine had been known for bestowing her condescension on a select few who sought positions as vicars or governesses, thriving off the praises and gratitude she felt her due, Lady Anne, not seeking fame for her charity, became an anonymous patroness of schools and hospitals as well as local villagers in their business enterprises. However it was for the bonds of friendship, rather than the duty of charity, that she was quick to secure for Charlotte an annuity which would allow her and her daughter to live comfortably.

Charlotte bought a cottage in the village of Bower Green, not two miles from Longbourn, though she always had a room reserved for her at Rosings whenever she wished to visit. It was with tenderness of feeling that I accepted the role of godmother to her child and, at Charlotte's request, I suggested a name for her which she agreed suited her beautifully.

I enjoyed visits to Lady Anne at Rosings with Charlotte and little Harriet and to the library at Pemberley but my heart remained in Hertfordshire. With an increased sense of ownership of the Longbourn estate and concern for it after what now appeared to me as years of poor management, I focussed much of my energy into acquiring knowledge of new farming methods. After long years of Papa regarding me as an object of ridicule for my philosophising, something he might have had no reason to do had I been allowed the formal education he was privileged enough to have had, he began to shew respect for my practical suggestions regarding such things as the introduction of a seed drill or the reclamation of land through draining. In time, he allowed me the power to give orders to our land agent and, over the years, the farm produced almost double the revenue that it once had done. I was quite aware that Mama snuck banknotes into her letters to Lydia but I turned a blind eye.

Despite the zeal I had for my new endeavours, I spent more of my time at Bower Green than Longbourn, Charlotte's cottage becoming a second home to me. Charlotte and my god-daughter, Harriet, came to be as my own kin, time only serving to strengthen our affections. Before little Harriet was old enough to talk to others of what we did, we travelled together to many places, I wearing the bonnet, its ribbons tied about the wrists of my two favourite companions as we left poor Mr Pratt's shop for Paris, Venice or wherever else we took a fancy to. I believe this is what gave my god-daughter the passion for travel which threaded through her adult years.

Jane and Lizzy enjoyed the unlikely blessings of marrying rich men whom they loved and who adored them in return, whilst I took pleasure in the secret – which I shared only with Charlotte, Chamberlayne and Mrs Pepperstock – that it was my bonnet and I who had been the means of uniting them.

On my last visit to Netherfield before Jane and Mr Bingley quitted it in order to settle near Pemberley, I found occasion to be alone in the small room with the painting of Great Aunt Harriet and her companion. I smiled as my gaze fell upon the green and gold fabric worn by the unknown figure and laughed aloud at the depiction of the tricolor cockade, wondering what kind of adventures they may have had during the French Revolution. The painting's size was such that it was possible, though challenging, to carry it between my knees, under my gown. Thus it travelled to Longbourn and to my room, where it remains.

EPILOGUE

Dear Mary,

Your letter, manuscript and bequest found their way to me in Venice. Despite devouring the whole of your story – and taking much pleasure from it, I might add – I managed to make a blunder in my first use of you-know-what. I found a seller of elaborate masks and hats for carnevale which I hoped would provide me with a quick route to Meryton to see you. Intending to spend more time with you, I unpicked many bunches of flowers before entering the shop. Of course, this sent me to a time in which I had no bonnet to travel with, forcing me to come here, rather conventionally, by ship and carriage. I look forward to a novel, less tiresome method of travel, though I am in no hurry for it and am quite relieved that it shall be in your possession for a long while yet.

Upon finding you asleep, I wished not to disturb your repose and, having thought of some errands I had to do in Meryton, I went out. Upon my return, I shall repay your storytelling by regaling you of my life and adventures on the continent.

Yours ever,
Harriet

Dear Charlotte,

Just as I finished reading your daughter's note, I heard an Italian aria being played on my pianoforte and walked to my room to find her there. She beamed when she saw me and I sat beside her to play a lower part that blended well with hers. After we had congratulated ourselves on our performance, she embraced me and enquired as to my health and present state of comfort. Then she proceeded to produce objects from her basket. "Thank God!" I said when she revealed a bottle of gin. "They've stopped letting me drink now, you know." I intend to hide this in my closet and you must partake of it with me on your next visit, or else I'll bring it over to you.

She also brought me some Italian marzipan from her travels. Whilst she said it was of fine quality, it was not 'to die for' as some of our English marzipan is.

Whilst I enjoy the thought of my dear god-daughter going off on her adventures, I feel much more comfortable having her here with us. I look forward to the days ahead in which the three of us can savour the comforts of Longbourn. You must come as soon as you can, my dear. What a merry party we shall be! I can see us now, sitting in the window seat, eating, drinking, talking, laughing and sewing as the world through the window goes about its business, as candles around us are lit, the yellow-gold warmth peeking through a gap between the grey curtains into the darkening world outside.

Your Mary

ACKNOWLEDGEMENTS

Dear Reader,

Whilst it goes without saying, I shall nevertheless state that this novel would not exist without the dazzlingly brilliant and much beloved author, Jane Austen. It feels special to me that she was born and did the majority of her writing close to where I come from in Hampshire. From my first experience of her work, via the 1995 BBC adaptation of *Pride and Prejudice*, when I was eleven or so, I was hooked. It was a story that opened up a rich and fascinating world of literature for me and eventually led to the idea for this novel, the writing of which was so much fun. Cheers, Jane!

In taking the liberty of playing around with her masterpiece, I have two lines of defence. One is that I hope she would not disapprove of a little absurdity, jocularity and whimsy, as her juvenilia abounds in these qualities. Secondly, such precedents have been set by many others before me. There are too many reimaginings of and tales inspired by Jane Austen's novels for me to mention them all here but I will perform a respectful curtsey to Jo Baker's *Longbourn*, Seth Grahame-Smith's *Pride and Prejudice and Zombies*, ITV's *Lost in Austen* (2008) and the hilarious improvisation theatre group *Austentatious*. I have also found Roy and Lesley Adkins book, *Jane Austen's England*, an invaluable resource.

I want to thank my family – particularly Mum, Dad, Jemma, Jo and Jamie – and my friends for your belief in my writing and your encouragement. Though my grandparents passed on quite some time prior to my writing of this book, I want to thank them all too as they were so supportive of all our endeavours.

I give particular thanks to my sister, Jo Stanley, for her wonderful cover design and her meticulous formatting work for the paperback version. I am also most appreciative of my editor, Cressida Downing. She helped me rework a subplot so that the novel became more cohesive and her suggestion of removing certain parts led me to have some new ideas which I am so pleased made it into the book. My thanks too to Aimee Dewar who cleverly formatted my novel for eBook, something I would have had no idea how to do.

Lastly, I want to thank each reader of *Back to the Bonnet*. When you read it, the story becomes at least as much yours as mine. I hope that, rather than a Mary Bennet eye-roll, it inspires joy and a few laughs.

Yours affectionately,
Jennifer Duke

Printed in Great Britain
by Amazon